# THE SHADOW N...
## by Anne Logst...

## DAGGER'S EDGE

Jaellyn's feisty Aunt Shadow knows what a woman born of royal *and* elvan blood needs to survive when a demon comes to call—a little dagger, and a lotta luck . . .

"ENTERTAINING!"                    —*Science Fiction Chronicle*

## SHADOW

*The original!* Introducing Shadow, a master thief as elusive as her name . . .

"BRIGHT, CHEERFUL, AND CHARMING, HOTLY SPICED WITH MAGIC AND INTRIGUE!"
—SIMON R. GREEN, author of
*Robin Hood: Prince of Thieves*

## SHADOW HUNT

Shadow returns, on a quest to recover a stolen jewel—but her guide is an assassin who could take her life as easily as she takes a breath . . .

"THOROUGHLY SATISFYING!"                    —*Dragon*

## SHADOW DANCE

Shadow must lead a band of warriors into a horror-laden swamp to find the cure for the Crimson Plague—a deadly disease sweeping through the str... ...mere . . .

"ROLLICKING GOOD...                    ...ction Review

## GREENDA...

Generations b... ...ives of the Mother Forest had to ... ...in forces with humans to defeat the barba... ...who sought to destroy them . . .

*Ace Books by Anne Logston*

# Dagger's Point

## ANNE LOGSTON

ACE BOOKS, NEW YORK

*To Jeff Hicks and Alan Palcher
and everyone else who suffers from
chronic sore feet*

This book is an Ace original edition,
and has never been previously published.

DAGGER'S POINT

An Ace Book / published by arrangement with
the author

PRINTING HISTORY
Ace edition / January 1995

All rights reserved.
Copyright © 1995 by Anne Logston.
Cover art by Duane O. Myers.
This book may not be reproduced in whole or in part,
by mimeograph or any other means, without permission.
For information address: The Berkley Publishing Group,
200 Madison Avenue, New York, NY 10016.

ISBN: 0-441-00134-3

ACE®
Ace Books are published by The Berkley Publishing Group,
200 Madison Avenue, New York, NY 10016.
ACE and the "A" design are trademarks
belonging to Charter Communications, Inc.

PRINTED IN THE UNITED STATES OF AMERICA

10  9  8  7  6  5  4  3  2  1

# FOREWORD

Shadow, a skilled elvan thief, returned to the trade city of Allanmere after over three centuries' absence. She was reunited with her old friend and companion Donya, who turned out to be the only child and Heir of the city's High Lord and Lady. Shadow quickly became embroiled in the growing conflict between the city's Council of Churches and its Guild of Thieves, both of whom seemed very interested in a magical silver bracelet with the power to undo any lock, which Shadow had stolen from a young lord. Her own Guildmaster seemed to have paid the notorious assassin Blade to follow and then to kill Shadow. Shadow foiled the assassin and uncovered and stopped a plot by Bobrick, the assistant to Vikram, head of the Council of Churches, to assassinate Vikram, seize power in the Council of Churches, and discredit and destroy the Guild of Thieves to seize power in the city, in the process causing Bobrick's death and having to fight and kill her treacherous Guildmaster. Shadow reluctantly assumed the seat of Guildmistress of the Guild of Thieves.

A year later, Shadow was in the process of rebuilding the Guild of Thieves and trying to stay out of trouble with the Council of Churches. She learned, however, that a valuable magical gem, the Eye of Urex, had been stolen from the Temple of Urex, a theft so difficult that suspicion naturally fell upon Shadow herself, and Guild War once again threatened Allanmere. Shadow learned that the gem had once belonged to a powerful mage, Baloran, who had created and owned the Eye during the Black Wars, and speculated that Baloran himself had reclaimed it; Shadow also discovered a link between Baloran and the mysterious assassin Blade. Blade had once stolen a magical dagger from Baloran, only to fall under his curse, condemning her to living on the life of energy of others forever. Shadow confronted Blade and enlisted her help in recovering the Eye of Urex in exchange for Baloran's whereabouts. Blade agreed, and the two embarked on a perilous journey across the swamp north of Allanmere, the Dim Reaches, to find Baloran's keep. During the journey, an uneasy friendship grew between Shadow and Blade. Unknown to Shadow, however, her friend Donya, fearing for Shadow's life, had gathered a troop of guards to force Baloran into giving up the gem before Shadow got there. Instead, Donya was captured and magically enslaved by one of Baloran's minions, and when Shadow and Blade made their way into Baloran's keep, he captured them as well. Shadow learned that Blade was the one who had stolen the Eye of Urex, attempting to get Shadow to locate Baloran for her, and hoping that the gem might be used to buy from Baloran a release from her curse. Instead, the gem was destroyed, and Baloran revealed that it had contained the spell which would have freed Blade from her curse. With Donya and Blade's aid, Shadow escaped, killing Baloran with Blade's soul-drinking dagger and almost being killed herself in the process.

The Guild continued to thrive under Shadow's leadership, and the elvan voice in the city continued to grow. But with it grew an anti-elvan faction among the human population of the city, fearing that human influence would decline. Shadow accompanied Donya to the Planting of the Seed, an elvan spring festival, where Donya planned to consult with the elders about a poacher recently captured in the Heartwood. The poacher, who was apparently ill, was of a race no one had ever seen before, with six digits on each hand and foot and unable to speak any language anyone understood. Donya decided to take the stranger back to Allanmere for healing. Shadow, Donya, an elf name Mist, and the stranger returned to Allanmere only to find a strange disease breaking out in the city. With rest and a translation spell, the stranger, Farryn, told them that he had come from the great mountains to the north. His people's valley home was being harassed by northern barbarians who had brought a debilitating sickness among them, and Farryn had journeyed south to where some of his folk, the Kresh, had once settled in the hope of finding a cure. Donya and Shadow realized that those barbarians were the same race who has almost destroyed Allanmere in the Black Wars. Farryn himself had carried the Crimson Plague to the Heartwood, where the elves, themselves immune, had carried it to the city, where it proved fatal to humans. Shadow, Donya, Farryn, Mist, and Argent journeyed into the swamp to find ruins Shadow had seen there a year earlier, which she believed to be signs of Farryn's people. Donya spent a single night with Farryn, and later herself contracted the Crimson Plague. The adventurers found a temple Farryn's kin had left behind, but it was long abandoned. Farryn passed through a magical Gate within the temple to ask his god for aid and returned, but his god Adraon had offered Farryn either a cure for the debilitating disease or a spell to close the pass through which the barbarians came, and Farryn had chosen the spell. Shadow also passed through the Gate and was tested by the god; she battled Adraon and stole the plague cure, bringing it back through the Gate in time to cure Donya. Farryn returned to his people and Shadow, Donya, Mist, and Argent returned to the city with the plague cure, only to find that Donya's father, High Lord Sharl, had died while they were gone, and High Lady Celene immediately abdicated the throne of Allanmere to Donya. Donya asked Argent to marry her for political reasons, and he accepted.

Nearly twenty years after the Crimson Plague had come to Allanmere, the city was almost split as humans and elves struggled against each other for power, the anti-elvan faction led by Ankaras, High Priest of the Temple of Baaros. Jaellyn, Donya and Argent's oldest daughter, was to be declared Heir, which was the cause of some conflict in the city because of her strange single birth and unusual appearance and the fact that any magic in her vicinity usually went awry. Jael sneaked into the Temple of Baaros to spy on one of its rituals, accidentally warping the magic and causing another entity to be summoned instead of the god Baaros. Shortly thereafter a mysterious young lord came to Allanmere to reform the Temple of Baaros, and he immediately showed an interest in Jael. Jael learned that her magic-warping effect was due to a missing part of her soul, and later discovered that she was in fact Donya's daughter by Farryn, not Argent, and

partly of Kresh blood, and that Kresh were given their souls at
adulthood instead of being born with them. Meanwhile, Jael and
Tanis, her friend and an acolyte at the Temple of Baaros, inves-
tigated a series of gruesome murders in the city in which Ankaras might be involved. The new High Priest of the Temple of
Baaros, Urien, turned out to be a servant of the Greater Darkling
Eiloth and planned to sacrifice Jael. Jael escaped and killed
Urien, then began making plans to search for her Kresh father
and gain the missing part of her soul.

I

• Jael dodged desperately, the breath rasping in her lungs, sweat dripping into her eyes. The sword whistled past, missing her by only a fingersbreadth. Wearily she attempted to parry, but the attacker drove her to her knees. Jael forced her sword up one more time, but her opponent's heavier blade rang against it, and Jael's sword dropped from numb fingers. The greatsword flashed down relentlessly.

"Yeow!" Jael cried, both hands clasping her side, where she could feel the bruise already forming. "What're you trying to do, cut me in half?"

"I'm not, but sooner or later someone will," Donya said grimly, lowering her blunt-edged practice sword. "And if you keep thinking instead of acting, they'll do it, too."

"I'm doing everything you told me," Jael exploded. She tore the light practice helmet off her head and threw it to the hard-packed soil. "I kept moving, guard up, watched your eyes and—"

"You can't parry directly," Weapons Master Rabin told her, joining them on the practice ground. "Her sword's too heavy; the impact alone will take your sword right out of your hands, just like it did. Angle your blade more and *guide* her stroke aside, don't meet it head-on. If your blade wasn't made of such strong stuff, that stroke would've broken it right off."

"If my blade wasn't guarded, I'd have broken *hers* right off," Jael argued, folding her arms resentfully. It was bad enough to have her mother, the High Lady of Allanmere and the most formidable swordswoman Jael had ever heard of, pounding away at her on the practice ground, but two teachers at a time was *too much*.

"A fancy sword's no substitute for skill," Donya told her sternly. "Rabin's right. You usually do better than this, Jaellyn, with that sword. Stop trying to meet me straight on. Now put your helm back on and try again."

"Oh, please," Jael groaned. "I'm tired."

"And I suppose you're going to tell all your opponents that, and they're politely going to say, 'Oh, sorry, let's take a break and let you catch your breath before I kill you'?" Donya said sarcastically. "If you waste your wind early on in a fight, you've got to learn to go on without it."

"Come on, Doe, that's enough," Shadow said, making them all jump. As usual, no one had seen or heard the elvan thief approach; now she was sitting cross-legged on the practice ground wall, delicately scratching one pointed ear with her dagger's tip. "You already killed her; no need to trounce the corpse."

"I'm trying to keep her from *becoming* a corpse," Donya said flatly, scowling at Shadow for interfering.

"Well, if you'll let me borrow the corpse for a few hours, I've got a couple of maps to show her," Shadow said good-naturedly. "And Tanis is sitting up in the dining hall too scared to come out here and tell Jael he's arrived."

"Scared of what?" Donya said impatiently.

"Oh, I don't know," Shadow chuckled. "Maybe scared of a High Lady swinging a sword almost as tall as he is and wearing a scowl fit to fell a dragon, let alone a poor human apprentice thief. Come on, Jael; in the face of certain death I always find it wise to retreat and leave the purse for another day."

Jael eagerly unbuckled and tossed aside her padding, but she unguarded and wiped her sword with more care before she sheathed it. She didn't need High Lady Donya to tell her to be careful with that blade; the strange pale metal was so hard and the edge so fine that a clumsy movement could easily take her fingers off. Her mother was still scowling, but Rabin gave Jael a reassuring pat on the shoulder as she followed Shadow out of the practice field.

Ordinarily, when Shadow was back in Allanmere she preferred to stay at an inn near the center of town, convenient to the taverns and the market and only a short distance from the Thieves' Guildhouse where she still liked to visit. This time, however, the ex-Guildmistress had accepted Donya and Argent's offer of a room at the palace; impoverished as usual, the elvan thief had maintained that she'd only be in Allanmere for a few days, and what with spending most of that time with Jael, she'd rather pocket what she had time to glean from Allanmere's market than spend it on an inn. Jael had chuckled at that, knowing Aunt Shadow far too well—after one or two forays into the market or the Mercantile District, the elf would be laden with gold enough to live in luxury until she lost it again on a bad fall of the dice or spent it on wine or some fellow with a handsome face and a sad story. In the meantime, the elf's empty pockets and tales of her adventures won her a comfortable suite of rooms at the palace, all the fine food and wine she could swallow, and likely a heavy purse slipped quietly into her pack when she left.

At the moment, however, Shadow's bed, table, and press were strewn with maps—fine leather maps, rough-tanned hides, expensive parchment, and even a few clumsy bark scratch-maps. Shadow cleared the table with one sweep of her arm and rifled through the collection impatiently, looking for the particular one she wanted.

"Where did you get all these?" Jael asked curiously. "The palace archives? You must've cleaned the place out."

"Mapmakers' Guild," Shadow corrected. "Run downstairs and fetch Tanis, will you? Whatever I tell you, you'll have forgotten it in half a day."

Jael grimaced but obediently trotted through the drafty corridors and stairwells to the dining hall, where she found her friend Tanis nibbling at cheese and bread and looking thoroughly ill at ease alone in the cavernous room. He smiled with relief, however, as Jael entered the room.

"There you are," he said, running his fingers through tumbled dust-blond hair in lieu of a comb. "I thought maybe your mother was hacking you to pieces on the practice ground again."

"She was," Jael said ruefully. "Can't you smell? So where was my partner to rescue me, huh?"

"What do you expect from an ex-priest turned apprentice thief?" Tanis protested. "Do you want me to give the High Lady of Allanmere a lecture on the virtue of mercy, or maybe pick her pockets?"

"That chicken's all feathers and no meat," Jael said sourly. "You're better with a sword than I am, and you know it."

"Not anymore, not when you're using that sword," Tanis corrected, nodding at Jael's scabbard. "I'm out of practice, and you've become Baaros-blessed *good* with that thing. Once we're out of town, you're going to be giving *me* lessons, don't think you're not! But in the meantime, I thought you might like a last evening in the market before we leave. I heard somebody's got dragon roasting at the west end of the market."

"I'd love that," Jael said eagerly. The thought of roast dragon dripping with spicy sauce made her mouth water. "But before we go, Aunt Shadow's got some maps she wants us to look at."

"When did Shadow get back into town?" Tanis asked in surprise, following Jael. "Guildmaster Aubry didn't say anything, and she always visits the Guild when she's around."

"Yesterday morning," Jael told him. "She sneaked into the palace by the secret back entrance as usual. She's only passing through on her way south, but wanted to see me before we left. Besides, her purse is empty and she needs to run the market."

Tanis shook his head.

"How the former Guildmistress of the Guild of Thieves and the best thief I've ever heard of always manages to be so poor, only Baaros knows," he said. "I'm hardly out of my apprenticeship, but I've always got a few coins in my sleeve to get by on."

"Aunt Shadow would rather live like a High Lady for three nights than 'get by' for a year," Jael laughed. "And if you'll tell *her* she's the best thief you've ever heard of and flash those big blue eyes at her, she'll probably give you whatever coin she's got left. Plus teach you a few of her tricks, if you're lucky."

When they arrived in Shadow's room, however, Shadow seemed completely absorbed in the scroll she'd spread out over the table.

"Pour yourself a goblet and come look," she said.

There were a dozen partially filled jugs of wine to choose from amidst a jumble of empty jugs, bottles, and wineskins. Tanis and Jael exchanged a grin, and Tanis poured a goblet full of wine before joining Shadow at the table. Jael filled her own cup from the water pitcher.

"I knew when I went north last year that I wouldn't find anything," Shadow said, tapping a dot that marked the city of Ramant near the far north edge of the map. Beyond that point, only a jumble of mountainous peaks had been marked on the map's edge, and Shadow herself had drawn in a winding road and the suggestion of a valley village amidst the peaks. "Twenty-two years ago Jael's father, Farryn, returned to his people in the far northern mountains. He said they'd go west to find the other clans of the Kresh, from which his own clan had separated centuries earlier. What with all the trouble he said his folk had had up there in the mountains, earthquakes and rockfall and barbarians from the lands north of the mountains, I knew they'd have left not long after he returned to them. If so, they'd be long gone after two decades. So I didn't bother chasing off into the mountains; I started looking for rumors in Ramant, and I found them.

"About twenty years ago a legend sprang up," Shadow continued, drawing a gold pin from the tall coil of her black braid and idly scratching one delicately pointed ear with it. "There was talk about a mysterious band of people who would abruptly appear in an area, stay for a night or two, and just as abruptly disappear. No one had traded with them, no one had spoken with them, and if anyone saw one of them alone and approached, he'd just disappear. Like magic."

"Disappear?" Tanis repeated. "Like a mage, you mean?"

Shadow turned to glance with surprise at Jael.

"You never told him?"

"Jael told me that her true father—that Farryn—was one of these Kresh folk," Tanis told her. "That's why she can melt stone sometimes, right?"

Jael rolled her eyes. Shadow grinned sympathetically, but made no effort to explain for her.

"I'll tell you the whole thing again later," Jael sighed. "We're going to have months of evenings to talk over campfires. Can we just look at the maps now, please?"

Tanis raised his eyebrows in surprise, but turned back to the map to examine the spot where Shadow's finger still rested.

"So you didn't go north of Ramant?" he asked.

"I didn't go, no," Shadow confirmed. "Luckily or unluckily, I arrived in Ramant just in time for the first winter storms, so I had weeks to question the merchants as they came in. A few of the mountain nomads who had come to Ramant to trade were snowed in, too, and like most folk, they were willing to talk with a few mugs of ale in their belly and a few coins in their purse. They knew of the Kresh, all right, although they called them by another word in their own language—windwalkers, or something very like it—but the nomads said they'd left about twenty years before, just picked up and left, leaving behind everything they couldn't easily carry on their backs. There was some fine scavenging in their old village, and the nomads still use the houses occasionally, so the story hasn't gotten old and stale yet.

"As I said, I talked to some of these nomads. Nobody knew where the Kresh had gone, but it wasn't hard to puzzle out. North was impossible. Once there had been a pass through the mountains leading to the frozen lands, and the northern barbarians occasionally tried to fight their way through that pass and invade the southern lands—you two remember this from your histories of the Black Wars. But a huge rockfall had completely blocked the pass only a year or two before Farryn left his valley, so they couldn't have gone north—and even if they could, why would they walk right into their enemies' land? South was impossible, too, or they'd have been seen; the land's too settled here for them to pass completely through without stopping somewhere. East's the same, only worse, and before they got too far, they'd just run into the sea. So that only left west, the way Farryn said they'd go."

Jael leafed through the other maps scattered around the room.

"None of these maps show the lands very far west of Allanmere," she said.

"No; the west, after a point, has hardly been settled," Shadow told her. "There aren't many merchant trains to or from the western lands, either, and it was hard getting much news. But when spring came and I was able to move on, I found the stories I'd been looking for.

"Western folk called them 'ghost people.' Sometimes folk would see their fires, hear their songs from a distance, and in the morning they were gone as if they'd never been there, no tracks leading to the campsite or away from it. Sometimes folk even saw them traveling, mere flickers of movement like the beat of a dragonfly's wing, running so fast and so light they could dance right across a lake's surface like that same dragonfly." Shadow shook her head. "I'd give a good many Suns to have seen it my-self."

The elf sighed regretfully and turned back to the map.

"Here, here, and here," she said, tapping three points on the map. "Here's where I heard the stories. It wasn't city folk who had seen them, of course—Fortune knows the Kresh would've avoided the cities—but cities are where the stories live, in taverns and inns and brothels, and that's where I went hunting them. The Kresh traveled fast, but they were limited by the young, the old, and the sick, and they had to hunt occasionally, and when they stopped, they were seen. Now look at this."

Shadow picked up a strip of thong and laid one end of it on the spot she'd marked in the northern mountains. "Put your finger on that." She stretched the thong westward; the three cities she had indicated formed an almost straight line under the thong's length.

"Allowing a bit for the fact they were seen outside the cities, the Kresh traveled in almost a perfectly straight line," Shadow told them. "Not straight west, but west and south a bit from the mountains north of Ramant. Drawing a line along that trail, you can get a pretty good prediction of their course beyond that. I'll draw that on a traveling map for you. At some point you'll begin reaching lands that aren't mapped, and this may be the only thing you have to guide you. Fortune knows that even if they'd left tracks, two decades would have eaten the traces. Whenever you can find a city or a village, find the old folk and ask about the rumors. As long as you're on the right track, there'll be someone who saw them."

Tanis traced a fingertip along the western edge of the map.

"How far beyond this might they have gone?" he asked. "Do you have any notion where this homeland they're seeking is, or even what it's like?"

Shadow shook her head.

"Farryn told us the story of his ancestors traveling east," she said. "He said they came through a land of plains and low, rocky hills, and he mentioned mountains, I think, but I've got to tell you, stories get mightily twisted around over the course of twenty centuries, and that's how long his folk had been gone from their homeland. There's plains aplenty to the west across the Brightwater, but after a point you start getting forest instead, and I've never heard anything of rocky hills or any western mountains. If the Kresh

liked to live among the mountains here, though, it makes sense that
they'd have come from a similar land."

"Months," Tanis said slowly. "We're talking about months of
travel."

"Months of travel in bad country," Donya interrupted, stepping into the room. The High Lady had exchanged her ragged
practice leathers for one of the ornate gowns she so hated, but
had to wear for official functions. "Shadow showed me her maps
earlier. The farther west you go, the more vague the maps become and the less populated the land. The trade roads, such as
they are, will be prowled by brigands and the like. Before you
get too far, there may not be any roads at all."

"But there are a few blessings," Shadow said, shrugging.
"Languages move west with settlers and you should be able to
make yourself understood most of the time. It'd be otherwise, I
can promise you, if you went too far south. At the same time,
Donya's right. Sparsely settled country breeds desperate types.
I'd keep your noble birth a close secret, Jael, and keep your
money hidden. Use small coins when you spend. It's safer, too,
to travel with well-guarded merchant caravans as long as you
can—more comfortable, too, bet on it, and you'll eat better. For
Fortune's sake, Tanis, you don't want to tell the merchants
you're a novice thief."

"I probably could have worked that out myself," Tanis said
wryly. "But coming from a Mercantile House and serving a trade
god for so many years, I won't have much difficulty convincing
anyone that I'm the younger son of a House, gone west to make
a start for myself. The way Jael looks, she could be any elf with
the wandering itch."

Shadow gave Tanis a crooked grin at his last comment.

"Well, there aren't so many of us wandering the world as all
that," she warned. "Elves out of the Heartwood look odd compared with the eastern city elves, especially those of us with the
old wild blood showing in their faces like Jael. She looks a little
remarkable even to the other elves hereabouts."

"There's one thing," Donya said firmly, "and I'm not taking
any argument about it, Jaellyn. I've asked Shadow to ride with
the two of you for the first couple of days, just to see that you
get started safely."

Jael opened her mouth to protest, but closed it again at a warning frown from Shadow. The elf herself appeared equally irri-

tated but resigned, and Jael could well imagine that despite her love of Jael and her long and dear friendship with Donya, Shadow would far rather spend the days in an inn with plenty of wine and some handsome fellow than riding days out of her way. Jael swallowed her protest; if Donya had been able to push Shadow into this errand, she was utterly determined and there was nothing Jael could say that would change her mind.

"I wish you'd take one of those mirrors with the farspeaking spell," Donya said with a scowl. "I don't like the thought of wondering for so long where you are, what's happening to you."

Jael fought back a retort that the last thing in the world she wanted was to have to use the magical mirrors her grandmother Celene had invented to call her parents every night.

"How do you think I'm going to use one of those?" Jael asked impatiently. "The minute I touch it, I'll ruin the spell."

"If it doesn't explode in your hand," Shadow chuckled in agreement. Jael winced. She found the warping effect that she had on magic much less amusing than Shadow did.

"We could give the mirror to Tanis," Donya said. "He could use it."

"Mother, light globes explode across the room from me," Jael said, a little irritated by the High Lady's persistence in treating her like the child she appeared, but was not. "Sometimes in other rooms, as you know very well. How far away from me do you want Tanis to ride—a mile? Two?"

"All right, all right," Shadow said mildly. "Travelers have been getting by without farspeaking spells for a good many centuries, including you and me, Doe. Pull the reins in much tighter on this filly, and she's going to buck hard enough to throw you."

"You're right." Donya sighed and shrugged. "At her age I'd have said, 'Whatever you want, Mother,' and then *accidentally* dropped the mirror on the first rock I found. Jaellyn, I wasn't really eavesdropping on your plans. I just wanted to let you know that Argent would like to see you before supper. Now I'll leave you be. I'm in audience this afternoon, anyway."

"Looked like it," Shadow said sympathetically, gesturing at Donya's gown. "What is it this time, poachers in the Heartwood or squabbles between the temples?"

"Neither," Donya said wearily. "City Council meeting." She turned away without another word.

Jael was sorry she had snapped at her mother, knowing that

Donya's brusqueness was only her way of hiding her worry, but she was more than a little relieved when the High Lady left. If Donya had her way, Jael wouldn't be leaving at all; failing that, Donya would settle for making her leave-taking as difficult and miserable as possible.

"You go ahead to Argent," Shadow told Jael kindly. "I'll give Tanis the maps and tell him what I know about the lands to the west. No need wasting your time with it. You could get lost in your own bedchambers, little sapling, I'm afraid."

Jael left reluctantly, more than a little vexed by Aunt Shadow's typically blunt comment. It was unfortunately all too true, only one of the legacies of the uneasy mixture of her true father's Kresh blood and her mother's elf and human ancestry. Jael had spent almost every summer of her life with her foster father Mist in the Heartwood, trying to learn all the elvan arts, but she could still manage to get lost less than a mile from their camp, just as she could likely find something to trip over standing stock still on a bare stone floor. She was so tired of her clumsiness, her inability to remember the simplest lessons from one day to the next, of the strange missing part of her soul that warped any spell in her vicinity and left her seemingly frozen in childhood. More than anything else, however, she was tired of the bad luck that seemed to follow her like a wolf on the trail of a deer. It was worth almost anything to hope that her father's people could help her gain the missing part of her soul; certainly it was worth a couple of months of travel in new and exciting places, exploring wild and unknown lands. Mother and Shadow might moan about danger and discomfort; Jael could hardly wait to leave. Nothing could possibly be worse than living like this, caught between worlds, neither one thing or the other.

High Lord Argent was in his study, or rather *the* study; High Lady Donya, not of a scholarly bent, was far likelier to spend her time in the practice yard than poring over old books and scrolls, so Argent had turned the study attached to their rooms to his own use. Missing the herbal store which his sister Elaria now managed alone, Argent had created his own herbal workshop, where he could putter in his few free hours.

Allanmere's High Lord was as tall as his wife, but he was pale where she was sun-browned, slender where she was muscular, his features delicate where Donya's were strong, his braid silver-white where Donya's was almost as black as Shadow's.

At the moment Argent was grinding something pungent-smelling with a mortar and pestle while reading out of an ancient herbal. His sharp elvan hearing, however, was not dulled by his concentration, and he looked up, smiling, as Jael stepped through the doorway.

"Good afternoon, Jaellyn," he said warmly. "Sit down for a moment. I'm almost finished."

Jael took her usual seat on the edge of the table. She loved to watch her father work; as his herbal preparations seldom involved magic, his workshop was one place where her presence didn't invite disaster—as long as she didn't move and send fifteen bottles and vials crashing to the floor, at least.

Argent finished blending the paste in the mortar and scraped it carefully into a clay jar. He cleaned the mortar and pestle meticulously before he turned to face Jael.

"How are you faring this spring?" he asked. "Your breathing doesn't sound much better."

Jael shrugged in resignation. The fact that Argent could hear her raspy wheezing from that distance was answer enough. Argent understood, if Donya didn't, that part of the reason Jael lost her wind so quickly was because breathing was difficult in the damp springtime air. Her eyes and nose ran like the Brightwater River, too, all spring long. She'd have some relief in summer, if the weather was dry and there weren't too many flowers in bloom, but she'd be miserable again once the leaves fell and the autumn rains started.

"I have two new mixtures for you to try," Argent said. He handed her the jar he'd just filled and a flask filled with greenish liquid. "Put five drops of the potion in your goblet at suppertime and see how you feel this evening. Rub the paste on your chest tonight. It should help your breathing." He handed her another jar. "And this is for the aches and pains your mother left you with today."

"Salve to ease my pains?" Jael chuckled. "And I thought she wanted me to ache at every step, just to remind me of my lessons. At least she didn't bruise my bottom, not for want of trying."

"Your mother would rather see you bruised than dead, and so would I," Argent said kindly. "If she's a little zealous lately in that regard, it's only because she loves you and worries about you so much. Sometimes it's difficult for her to say those things with her mouth, so she tries to say them with her sword instead."

Jael sighed, again regretting her sharp remarks. It wasn't as if anything Donya had said wasn't true. Unlike Argent, however, Jael had no excess of patience to compensate for Donya's occasionally sharp-edged manner.

Argent picked up another bottle, this one half-filled with bright blue liquid of a rather syrupy consistency.

"Were you planning to take any of this with you?"

Jael hesitated, then nodded.

"Two bottles, just for emergencies," she said. "It's either the Bluebright or that elvan dreaming potion you made for me before, and that puts me to sleep for hours. I'm taking some of the Calidwyn black tea, too. It settles my stomach."

Argent nodded, sighing.

"The Bluebright does seem to temporarily relieve many of your problems—allows you to use your Kresh stone-shaping ability, keeps you from warping magic around you—but I don't like you using it," he said slowly. "I haven't been able to find out where it came from or what it's made of, and that makes me uneasy. The fact that it has an aphrodisiac effect worries me even more. At least I know the tea is harmless."

"Well, Bluebright can't be magical, or it wouldn't work on me, especially since I *want* it to work," Jael said practically. "So what's the harm?"

"A snake's venom isn't magical, but that would be small comfort after it killed you," Argent said patiently. "Potions powerful enough to affect the soul can have unforeseen effects, or they can create dependence. Do *you* trust the Bluebright, knowing who brought it?"

Jael grimaced. Like Donya, Argent had a way of driving home a point—but unlike the High Lady, he didn't need a sword to do it. She didn't like to be reminded that the Bluebright had been brought to Allanmere by a false priest planning to raise one of the Greater Darklings, or that Jael had been so won over by his charming manner that she had all but handed herself over to him as the very sacrifice needed to bring his master into the world. Where Urien might have come by the Bluebright, or from what he might have made it, were questions Jael didn't like to ask herself.

"The Bluebright couldn't have been meant just for me," Jael said after a long moment's thought. "He offered it to all of you, and I saw him use it himself. He was going to trade it in Allanmere if Mother would have let him. If the Bluebright had any strange effects, it would have drawn attention to him, and he didn't want that. And you haven't come up with anything that works any better for me."

"That's true." Argent looked at the bottle in his hand and sighed again. "I've tried several doses myself with no apparent ill effects. So has your mother. But, Jaellyn, even if the potion itself isn't magical, I have a strong suspicion it was magically made, and any magic that Urien might have used was without doubt drawing on the demonic realm. That's probably why I haven't been able to determine what it's made of; demonic magic isn't my field of knowledge, or that of any legitimate mage in this city. I'd be relieved if you would promise me that you won't use it unnecessarily."

"I promise," Jael assured him without hesitation. She wouldn't use the Bluebright unless it was necessary—but *she* would be the one to decide when it was.

"I've prepared a kit," Argent continued. "If the potion and salve I just gave you are helpful, I can easily mix more before you leave. There are other salves in the kit, for infections, for that weed rash you get sometimes, potions for fever and headache and such as that, and a little dreamweed. If you and Tanis want to get silly over a campfire, use the dreamweed, not Bluebright, please." He hesitated. "There are bandages, of course, and needle and sinew. I know Mist has fully educated you in field medicine, but I don't know what kind of training Tanis has had."

Jael chuckled.

"Tanis knows how to tend wounds, dig firepits, build a trail shelter, use a lodestone or the stars—"

"Can he hunt?" Argent asked sharply. "Can he feed you both if merchant caravans fail you and your supplies run out? Remember that many of the food plants you know here won't be available farther west."

"He's no shot with a bow," Jael admitted. "But he can set snares and lines well enough. *I* can set snares and lines, if it comes to that, and get far away before the animal's caught so I won't have to feel it die. We should be able to get by. Please, Father. You're starting to sound like Mother."

"Well, we won't be badgering you too much longer, so try to bear with us." Argent smiled and hesitated a moment. "Jaellyn, I truly hope you are successful in finding your—your father. I want you to know that."

"I never doubted it." Jael closed the distance between them in one step, let him fold her in his arms, taking comfort in his warm embrace and familiar scent as she had always done. "And I hope you know that no matter what I find, you'll always be my father, really—in every way that matters."

"I never doubted it," he said quietly, and Jael could hear the smile in his voice. "Now, listen to me for a moment, please."

Jael stepped back a little, surprised by the sudden tension in his voice.

"Your mother and I have come to a decision," Argent said, and the look in his eyes told Jael that she was speaking to the High Lord of Allanmere, not her father. "After you've left, we'll wait a few days to make sure you're safely off. Then we're going to officially announce our selection of Markus as Heir."

Jael gaped for a moment, then let out her breath in an explosive sigh of relief.

"Thank the gods," she grinned. "You waited so long, I thought you and Mother were going to stick me with it after all."

Argent chuckled.

"I thought the news would please you," he said. "But we weren't sure you would be happy that we were doing it in conjunction with your leaving, as if—"

"What, as if you were giving me up for dead?" Jael returned. In fact, that was, she realized, likely what her parents were doing. It was a fair strategic move. Her thirteen-year-old brother Markus—half-brother, really, although the citizens of Allanmere would never know that—was far more elvan in appearance and by nature than his twin sister Mera, although both twins had the same half-human blood. The elves would be pleased that the more elvan of the twins was chosen, and the remaining anti-elvan faction in Allanmere, dwindling but still vocal, would be pleased that firstborn Jael, so extremely elvan in appearance and a subject of great controversy throughout the city, had been bypassed.

"Well, nobody really knows Tanis and I are leaving," Jael said thoughtfully. "We were planning to go at dawn day after tomorrow, but we can easily sneak off a few hours earlier. That should help make it look less planned."

"That's a good suggestion," Argent agreed. "Yes, it would make things easier. I wonder that your mother didn't think of it. After all, it's exactly what she would have done herself. Well, why don't you work it out with Tanis, and see if he can stay to sup with us tonight? In fact, he may want to stay here at the palace until you're ready to leave."

"That's a good idea, too," Jael agreed, an idea forming in her own mind. Why not sneak away in truth? It would save her the obligatory final lectures and warnings, and even better, the next day's sword practice. Much as she loved Shadow, too, she resented the elf seeing them off like a pair of children on their first stroll in the forest. She already had most of her belongings packed, and the horses were ready—Donya had checked them four times. Trail food had already been packed and was waiting in the cellar storerooms. A little quiet preparation that night, and they could easily slip away before dawn.

Argent squeezed Jael's shoulder.

"Don't let your mother's worries bother you," he said. "She's thinking back to her days on the road with Shadow. She claims Shadow was forever dragging her into one scrape or another, although Shadow tells it somewhat differently. I doubt myself that you'll get into such chilling escapades as Shadow likes to tell about, and if you do, I believe you're capable of dealing with them. There's more to you than Donya knows—likely more to you than you know yourself, and I think this time and this journey is exactly what you need."

"I can hardly wait," Jael admitted.

Argent chuckled.

"I think you have a little of Shadow's wandering itch," he said gently. "I hope the open road proves as sweet a wine to you as it is to her. But, Jaellyn—" He laid both hands on her shoulders, turning her to face him. "Don't become drunk on that wine. Remember where your home and your family is, and remember that we'll be waiting and wondering every day while you're gone."

Jael smiled and let him embrace her again.

"How could I ever forget?" she said, chuckling. "The bruises alone will last for weeks. Don't worry, Father, I'll be back, safe and sound and likely with stories even Shadow can't best."

Argent smiled. "Frankly, I hope you come back to us with nothing more interesting to tell us than how bad the weather was and how sick you became of dried meat and hard bread."

"Well, I never could tell a story like Aunt Shadow anyway," Jael said wryly. "Likely there'll be nothing to tell."

*But I hope not,* she thought.

# II

● Jael found Tanis in her rooms, perusing a map. From the markings on the hide, Jael supposed that Tanis and Shadow had gleaned whatever information they could from all the other maps and transferred it to this one sheet of leather.

"Hello," Tanis said, looking up from the map. "Shadow suggested I come to supper when we get back from the market. I didn't know where else to wait for you."

Jael glanced outside her door, looking up and down the corridor. There was no one in sight. Closing the door, she sat down next to Tanis on the bed.

"Listen, how much have you got left to put together?"

"Not much," Tanis said after a moment's thought. "I don't *have* all that much anymore. Just a few things at the inn where I stay. Why?"

"Could you just bundle it together and stay here tonight? There's plenty of rooms," Jael said.

"I could," Tanis said slowly. "I meant to say goodbye to Guildmaster Aubry and do a few errands in the market, but nothing I couldn't manage this afternoon. But why?"

"Everything's ready, or nearly," Jael told him. "Why don't we slip away late tonight? That way we can avoid hearing all the last-minute warnings for the fourth time, and get away without Aunt Shadow, too."

Tanis raised his eyebrows, then grinned.

"I could easily finish packing and be back here before supper," he said. "But we'll have to carry all the gear down to the stables. And how will we get out past the guards at the gate?"

"The secret door at the back, the one I showed you," Jael said. "It'll be a little tight getting the horses through, but we can make it. We'll have to ride all the way around the city to take the south ferry across the Brightwater, but if we went the shorter way around north and west to the Docks, I'm afraid the wall guards would recognize the horses."

"What about the ferrymen?" Tanis asked. "Won't they recognize you?"

"I've got new clothes, and I'll wear my cap," Jael said. "I haven't gone across the ferry often enough for them to know me too well by face. Besides, what if they do recognize me? Unlike the guards, the ferrymen won't have any authority to stop me. Mother and Father aren't going to send guards after us to drag me back."

"Not unless they know about it beforehand," a voice interrupted, and Jael and Tanis whirled around to see Markus's and Mera's faces peering in through the now cracked-open door.

Jael ground her teeth. Sometimes the benefit of being an only child seemed worth the price of Heirship. The twins were thirteen years old now, and while Jael had finally managed to surpass even sturdy Mera at swordplay and unarmed combat, so that the two had gradually stopped ambushing her, they still delighted in spying on Jael and teasing her exhaustively about her every failing.

"Mother would be furious if you and Tanis sneaked away before you were supposed to go," Mera said saucily, tossing her black braid.

"If she knew *we* knew and kept silent about it, she'd be furious at *us*," Markus added slyly. "We wouldn't want that."

"Besides, it's dishonest," Mera said somberly. "After all the supplies Mother and Father are giving you—"

"—to just sneak away without even saying goodbye," Markus finished. "And when we tell Mother what you tried to do, she may not even let you go at all."

Jael almost laughed at the threat. Markus and Mera had been

told only that Jael was leaving for the summer, and the twins assumed, of course, that Jael was simply fostering in the Heartwood as usual. The extra supplies that Jael was taking could be
explained this year by the presence of city-bred Tanis and the
possibility that finally Mist might let Jael try to take care of herself in the forest. The twins, therefore, had little material for
blackmail this time. Their tattling might earn Jael a lengthy lecture and possibly even a guard outside her door to make sure she
didn't leave before the appointed time, but Donya had promised
Jael could go, and the High Lady's word was solid as stone. Still,
better to negotiate with the twins now than to suffer through another trouncing on the practice field tomorrow.

"Oh, don't stand in the doorway like that," Jael said crossly.
"Come in and shut the door."

The twins quickly ducked inside. They were rarely allowed
within the sanctuary of Jael's room, a boundary Jael would defend with naked blade, if necessary, and the mere fact that Jael
invited them inside meant that serious bargaining was about to
take place.

"If you two will keep your mouths shut," Jael said, "I'll tell
you a secret, something that nobody else but Mother, Father, and
Aunt Shadow know. An important secret."

"How important?" Mera asked suspiciously.

"Important to the whole city," Jael said mysteriously. "And it's
partly the reason why I'm leaving early this year." That was true,
in its own way.

"If it's really important, a really *good* secret, we'll keep
quiet," Markus promised.

"You may as well," Jael said casually. "Because if you tell
tales on me, Mother will want to know how you learned, and
when she finds out it was because you were listening at my door,
you'll be in bigger trouble than me."

The twins exchanged calculating glances. Jael's statement was
proven fact.

"All right," Mera said. "Tell us the secret."

"Sometime not long after I leave," Jael said, "Mother and Father are going to announce their choice of Heir to the city, and
it isn't me."

Markus and Mera gaped for a moment, then glanced at each
other, eyes sparkling.

"Which of us is it?" Mera asked eagerly.

"I don't know," Jael lied. "And they won't announce it until I've been gone for a bit, so the sooner I leave, the sooner you'll know. Of course, if you tell them Tanis and I were planning to sneak away, they won't let me leave at all, and as I'm firstborn, if I don't leave the city, they may think it'll cause too much trouble to proclaim one of you Heir anyway. So it's up to you."

"All right," Markus said quickly. "We won't say anything. And we'll help you carry your things down to the stable tonight, if you want."

Tanis exchanged a grin with Jael. The twins were young and annoying, but one thing they could do adequately was slip quietly through the palace—the mere fact that they'd been able to surprise Jael, with her keen hearing, was proof of that.

"Then you and I can visit the market and pick up the rest of my belongings," Tanis said. "Maybe the twins can put the rest of it together here." His blue eyes twinkled at her.

"I don't know," Jael said doubtfully. "I still need our food from the cellar, and I'll need a few other supplies, lamps and oil and the like. If Mother and Father—even any of the servants—figure out what's going on, the whole plan's off."

"Markus can stand guard at the door while I get your supplies," Mera said defensively. "If any of the servants come, Markus can warn me, and keep the servants busy long enough for me to hide until they're gone. And Markus and I can carry things out to the stables, and nobody will notice—we take food and toys into the hayloft and play hide-and-find in there anytime we like."

"I suppose we'll have to trust them," Tanis said with resignation, although his eyes still gleamed with amusement. "They seem to have this planned better than we do."

The unexpected change in Markus's and Mera's status from obstacles into allies made preparations much simpler. Jael could have summoned one of the carriages to take her and Tanis to the market, but it might be a good many months before she'd see the city again, and she was content to walk through the dusty streets with Tanis, memorizing the city's sights, sounds, and scents.

To Jael's delight, Tanis had been right—a warrior was indeed selling dragon on the west side of the market. Jael treated for thick slabs of the tough, strong-flavored meat dipped in a fiery sauce, and they walked through the market, sauce smearing their cheeks. The closing of the Temple of Baaros and a year of relative peace in the city had somewhat diminished the number of humans in the city still hostile to elves; Jael thought to herself that Markus's selection as Heir would likely quiet the rest of that faction. Meanwhile, elvan businesses were once more flourishing in the market, and Jael was glad to see some humans conspicuously avoiding those few establishments still refusing elvan patronage.

Most of the older thieves in the market had known Jael almost from infancy, and many of the newer thieves were Tanis's friends; Jael and Tanis quickly found it almost impossible to make their way through the market without being greeted, slapped on the back, or offered sweets, meat pies or other pilferage. The two were glad to finally reach the Copper Cup, where Tanis had been staying.

After gathering Tanis's extra clothes and few belongings, they considered returning to the palace by way of Rivertown's back alleys, which led into the Noble District, but eventually decided to pass through the market again. While there were no demons prowling the alleys of Rivertown anymore, it was still a dangerous place even by day, and besides, between them Jael and Tanis had just enough coin left for another helping of dragon. Once more they ate as they walked, but when Tanis noticed Jael admiring a handsome set of low black boots, the leather soft enough to accommodate the small extra toe on Jael's left foot, he guided Jael to a quiet corner behind an unused stall where she could sit.

"Just finish your dragon," he said, grinning. "I'll have the boots by the time you're done."

Jael sat down and nibbled at the meat rather dubiously. Tanis had far more confidence in his fledgling thieving skill than Jael did; from years of watching Shadow, Jael knew a successful snatch was far more difficult than it looked, and she'd have been more comfortable if Tanis did not attempt anything so risky. And sometimes Tanis's judgment was clouded by his feelings for Jael, feelings that she, with almost a child's body and a soul that was not whole, could not return, and that made her more uncomfortable still.

Jael craned her neck around the stall, but there was no sign of Tanis, and if she ventured out and he saw her, she might distract him at a critical moment. Jael was just considering making her way in a wide circle to approach the tanner from the opposite side when searing pain wrenched through her throat, closing off her breathing and sending her almost into unconsciousness. Jael gasped desperately for breath, tumbling backward off the overturned bucket she'd been using for a seat, and the remainder of her dragon rolled out of her numb fingers to drop into the dirt. A moment later the horrible choking pain faded, and Jael gulped air gratefully, pushing herself up from the ground.

A quick glance around her revealed the source of her discomfort: she was sitting only a short distance from a stall selling roast fowl, and the proprietor had just wrung the neck of a fresh bird. Jael shuddered, no longer interested in the dragon or any other food; then her stomach heaved and she barely managed to turn her head aside in time to vomit behind the abandoned stall. She shuddered, spat again and again to clear her mouth, then stood, gazing around her for Tanis. She no longer cared about the boots, but maybe Tanis could steal a cup of something to drink, since they had not so much as a copper left between them. Unfortunately, Tanis was nowhere in sight.

Jael crept away from the puddle of vomit and sat down again, shivering. It had been a long time since her uncontrolled, intermittent beast-speaking sensitivity had caught her unaware in the market, but then she always took good care to stay away from slaughterhouses, poultry pens, and the like when she left the palace. Since Jael's childhood, it had been a firm rule that no animals could be slaughtered or even kicked on palace grounds lest Jael take another of her "fits." Jael would gladly have given the last drop of her elvan blood to be rid of her miserable remnant of beast-speaking ability—often she could sense animals' sensations, especially strong pain or death, but she had no control over what she felt; she couldn't *stop* feeling those pains, nor could she truly sense the thoughts of animals, or communicate her own thoughts to them as true elvan beast-speakers could.

Tanis appeared, ginning widely as he held up the black boots. "Not a bit of trouble," he said proudly. "As neat a job as ever I've—" Then he stopped, his grin fading as he noticed Jael's pale face and shaking hands. "What's happened? Are you all right?"

"Uh-huh." Jael stood a little awkwardly, taking a deep breath to force herself to stop shaking. "Let's go back now, Tanis. Right now. All right?"

"All right." Tanis hurriedly stuffed the boots into the bundle of his clothes and slid one arm around Jael's waist, guiding her quickly through the worst of the crowd. "What happened? Did somebody hurt you?"

"Not me," Jael mumbled. "Just a chicken."

"Oh. Oh!" Tanis raised one eyebrow in realization. "Sorry, Jael. I shouldn't have left you alone there without checking around. I was just thinking about our journey, how comfortable those boots would be on your feet." He hesitated. "Jael, are you going to be all right? I mean, traveling with merchant trains, somebody whips a horse or shoots a deer for supper—"

Jael shrugged. She'd given that problem some thought herself.

"What else can I do?" she said quietly. "It'd be no better if we were on our own, with you having to hunt every meal. And if I don't go, I might be this way forever. Anyway, it doesn't happen all that often."

Tanis nodded silently. There was really no reply he could make. He quickly changed the subject, and they talked of trivial matters during their walk back to the palace.

They were cheered, however, to find how the twins had passed the time since they'd left. Jael and Tanis had hardly been out the front gates before the twins had made their way to the cellars—a somewhat risky endeavor, as preparations for supper were already underway and servants would be in and out of the cellars fetching foodstuffs and wine. However, it was as likely as not that the High Lord and Lady would spend the evening entertaining some dignitary. If that were so, the servants would be up late, and the increased risk of discovery would continue far into the evening. Markus and Mera's team strategy had proved invaluable, for whispered warnings from Markus had sent Mera scurrying behind boxes and barrels five times before filling the bags, waxed skins, and jars Jael had gathered for their supplies. In the end, Markus and Mera had not dared to attempt carrying up the bulging parcels, but hid them as best they could in one of the less-used storage rooms. By the time they had finished their task, Jael and Tanis had returned, and the four had barely time to reach the dining hall before supper.

Fortunately, even Jael's imminent departure from Allanmere had not changed the laws of politics—Donya and Argent would have doubtless preferred to spend supper giving Jael and Tanis another round of instructions and warnings, but representatives from several of the border elvan clans had appeared during afternoon audiences to present grievances about increased poaching.

Elvan hospitality customs demanded that Donya and Argent invite them to sup at the palace, but no custom forbade the elves from using the opportunity to press their arguments for more stringent punishments to be applied to poachers caught by the City Guard returning from the forest. It was a complicated issue, and the arguments kept Donya and Argent conveniently distracted.

Shadow was nowhere in sight; she hated political discussions, and likely had gone off to prowl the taverns instead. Jael was sorry she would likely not see Shadow again before she left, but in a way she was also relieved; the canny elf was so sharp-eyed that she might have noticed how unusually well behaved the twins were, fairly brimming with their secret, or seen the nervousness that Jael could not help but feel.

Jael and Tanis stuffed themselves—who knew when they'd eat like this again?—and Jael remembered to mix the potion Argent had made for her with the juice she drank instead of wine at supper. It gave her juice an odd, musky taste, but midway through supper the constant running of her eyes and nose stopped as if by magic. Now Jael almost regretted their precipitous departure; it meant she wouldn't be able to get a further supply of the wonderful potion for her journey.

Tanis had been given a room near that of the twins—Jael found it rather amusing that although she'd be spending the next months alone with Tanis, her parents had given him a room well away from Jael's—and he promised that he'd wake Markus and Mera a few hours before dawn. Jael privately wagered that they'd wake him; the twins were obviously far too excited to sleep.

Jael found that sleep similarly eluded her. She poked restlessly through the bag of clothing and other necessities that she'd packed. Suddenly they all seemed so unnecessary. How could she have a proper grand adventure when they were carrying along half the contents of the palace? How much more interesting to take only a few necessities: her strange and wonderful sword, the one her father—no, that *Farryn*—had given Donya, and Donya had given her, and of course also the wonderfully sharp Kresh dagger Aunt Shadow had given her, her Bluebright, a change of clothes, and a bedroll. Taking along so many supplies seemed almost like cheating.

On an impulse, Jael emptied her jewelry box into her lap.

They'd have to leave without the purse Donya and Argent would have given them; at least they could sell the jewelry. She poked a little disgustedly at the intricate silver jewelry, set with the odd red-purple stones, that Urien had given her. The jewels were an unpleasant reminder of the intimate suppers she'd had with him, the picnic by the streambank where she'd confided in the charming schemer, the evening at his house when she'd nearly given her body to him, the horrible ceremony at the Temple of Baaros where his Greater Darkling master had nearly consumed her soul. The jewels seemed sinister now. She'd be glad to be rid of the things. But like the rest of her jewelry, the bracelet, pendant, and earrings were expensive stuff. They'd be remarked upon by any merchant who bought them. Selling such obviously valuable jewelry might well make Jael and Tanis a target for thieves who would willingly kill them for what other treasures they might be carrying. Jael reluctantly placed her jewelry back into its box. She'd have to depend on Tanis to steal whatever coin they'd need.

She curled up in her favorite nook by the window, thinking perhaps she'd drowse for a few moments, but to her surprise she found Tanis shaking her awake, the twins peering in from the doorway.

"Are you certain you still want to do this?" Tanis asked gently. "We don't have to. We could still wait another day and leave as planned."

"And go through all those goodbyes and last-minute do's and don't's?" Jael retorted. "Grab that pack and let's go. Quick."

Markus and Mera took Tanis's and Jael's packs, carrying them out to the stables and making sure no guards were in the area while Jael and Tanis fetched the rest of the supplies from the cellar. With some difficulty, Jael and Tanis managed to wrestle the heavy sacks across the courtyard to the stables, where, to Jael's impatience, Tanis insisted on checking through everything one last time. At last the horses were loaded and ready—the two that Jael and Tanis would ride, and one pack horse—and the twins were so impatient that they nearly pushed the travelers and their mounts out of the stable.

This led to the more difficult problem—getting the horses across the moonlit grounds without the wall guard seeing them. Once again the twins proved their usefulness, Markus creeping around through the bushes near another part of the wall and rustling them to distract the guards while Mera kept watch for Tanis and Jael, motioning them from one group of trees and bushes to the next when they could progress without being observed. At last they reached the hidden door, where Markus, beaming with pride at their maneuver's success, joined them.

"You better never tell Mother and Father we helped you sneak away," Mera warned Jael.

"Even if you don't starve in the Heartwood or get eaten by a bear and never come back," Markus added practically. "If you do, we'll tell Mother and Father that you told us about the Heirship, and they'll know you've been listening to them when you weren't supposed to."

"Don't worry, I won't tell them," Jael said wryly. "Even if I somehow manage to come back alive. Now I've got to go while the guards are still at the other side, or they'll see us riding away from the wall."

"Give Mist a hug for us," Mera told her sternly.

The twins scurried back into the bushes, but Markus turned back at the last moment.

"Jaellyn, why are you taking the ferry?" he asked curiously. "The edge of the Heartwood's only a short ride straight west."

"We wanted to surprise Mist," Jael said quickly. "So we're going around to the south side of the forest instead of the west. And if we travel on this side of the Brightwater, the elves will see us coming so long before we get there that they'll have time to send a message to Mist in Inner Heart."

Markus accepted that and disappeared into the bushes with Mera. Jael and Tanis mounted their horses, Jael leading the pack horse, and they rode away from the wall as quickly as the trail, too near the marshy edge of the Dim Reaches and too seldom used to be in good condition, would allow.

Once away from the city, Tanis and Jael hurried; paying the ferry to take them across the Brightwater before dawn, before people began coming into the city from the southern farms, would be more expensive, but would lessen the chance that someone would recognize Jael.

They reached the river before dawn, although the sky was beginning to lighten slightly to the east. Perhaps because of the early hour, there were only two cloaked ferrymen waiting at the Brightwater. Jael stepped up to the nearer of the two, coins in hand, but froze as the figure turned toward her. Even in the dying moonlight, Jael's elvan vision revealed the unbelievable—that the dark-cloaked man's face was as black as if carved from onyx, even his eyes unreflective pools of darkness.

Jael froze as she stood with her hand outstretched, cursing herself for a fool. For comfort while riding, she'd stupidly buckled her sword in its scabbard to her saddle. She'd be dead before she reached it. Carefully, Jael inched her free hand toward the Kresh dagger at her hip. Likely that strange, sharp blade could kill even this impossible creature.

A black-gloved hand seized her wrist, halting its progress, and a familiar pale face peered out of the second figure's hood.

"We have no need of your coin, High Lady's daughter. But there is indeed business to be discussed between us."

Jael immediately released the hilt of her dagger, and Tanis, who had leaped from his horse with sword half-drawn, froze motionless. While it was arguably possible that Blade, the most renowned assassin in Allanmere, could be harmed by mortal steel, there was not the faintest doubt in Jael's mind that she or Tanis would be dead—or likely worse than dead—before either of their weapons was drawn. Jael could only pray to whatever gods might be listening that Blade's "business" had not been transacted with one of the citizens of Allanmere who would gladly pay well to see Jael disappear permanently.

"Bring your friend and your horses aboard the ferry," Blade said, her fathomless black eyes on Jael's, not releasing Jael's wrist. "We will speak while we cross the river."

Jael nodded to Tanis; there was nothing else she could do. Tanis slowly led the horses onto the ferry. The black-skinned man released the mooring and stood by the huge rear oar, handling the ferry with amazing ease.

As soon as the ferry launched, Blade released Jael's wrist and turned away as if unconcerned with any move to escape or attack that Jael or Tanis might make. Jael imagined she *was* unconcerned; there probably was indeed nothing Jael or Tanis could do before Blade and her silent companion could kill them both. Jael felt cautiously relieved, however; if Blade had wanted either of them dead, they would doubtless be dead by now.

"Come, Lady Jaellyn," Blade said without turning around. "You stink of fear. Have you forgotten that you owe me a certain debt, or were you in fact fleeing payment?"

A flood of relief, followed quickly by consternation, almost dizzied Jael. True, more than a year ago Shadow had taken Jael to Blade, an "expert on souls," to learn why Jael's very presence seemed to make magic go awry, why Jael's body seemed forever frozen in childhood. True, Jael had promised Blade a future favor in exchange for her help, and true, Blade had diagnosed the missing portion of Jael's soul, the legacy of her true father's Kresh blood. But even more so now than then, what could Jael offer this strange creature, now that she had not even the possibility of the power of Heirship ahead of her?

"I remember," Jael said, steadying her voice as best she could. Her fingers went unconsciously to the thin white scar on her left wrist where Blade's dagger had once drawn blood. "I promised you a favor in return for what you told me, as long as that favor didn't harm my family or friends, or break the laws of Allanmere. And I wasn't trying to dodge keeping that promise."

"Then you are wiser than rumor would have it," Blade murmured. "But no matter. Your journey is westward, is it not?"

"Yes," Jael said warily. She didn't like the fact that Blade had known she was leaving at all. How could she have heard anything of Jael's destination, much less when Jael was leaving and what road she'd take? And who was Blade's silent black-skinned companion?

"Then it is time for you to pay the debt you owe," Blade said. She turned again to face Jael with those disconcerting eyes, and Jael shivered. "It is known to me that some decades past a mage named Duranar journeyed west, taking with him a certain book, the Book of Whispering Serpents, a book speaking of demons and their binding. It is said that he died in the west and that the book passed into unknown hands. I very much desire to possess this book."

" 'West'?" Tanis repeated, speaking for the first time. "How could we ever find this book, even if the person owning it issued proclamations announcing the fact, with only 'west' to go by?"

"You have planned your own journey on little more," Blade said icily. "There will be rumors. Only a mighty mage would hold the Book of Whispering Serpents. If you should happen upon the book, fetch it back to me. If not, at least you may hear word of what has befallen it. Perhaps such knowledge will satisfy me; perhaps not. But that is the payment I demand of you, High Lady's daughter. The book is large"—Blade held her hands apart, indicating—"with a leather cover, with silver serpents entwined on the spine."

Tanis looked inclined to protest, but Jael spoke quickly.

"All right," she said. "I'll do the best I can to bring you the book, or at least bring you whatever knowledge of it I can. But only if you'll swear to me that by giving you this book I won't be bringing harm to my friends or family, or breaking the laws of Allanmere. We don't need anyone raising demons here—" She bit down before she could say "again."

Blade's eyes narrowed ominously; but, surprisingly, she gave a short laugh.

"There is likely only one other in all the lands who would ask, or accept, an oath of me, High Lady's daughter," she said wryly. "Now I see why she was bold enough to bring you to me. Very well, Lady Jaellyn, you have my word. In fact, if this book contains the information I seek, by giving it to me you may well rid Allanmere of its much-dreaded and infamous assassin. Does that satisfy you?"

"Yes, it does," Jael said, relieved, holding out her hand.

Blade ignored the proffered hand and turned away, moving to stand by the black-skinned man as the ferry approached the opposite shore of the Brightwater. She glanced back over her shoulder at Jael.

"Unless I am much mistaken, you are expected," she said.

Jael peered in the direction indicated by the pointing black-gloved finger, and her heart sank. Despite the morning river mist cloaking the shore, there was no mistaking the slight elvan figure standing beside a pony, tossing a dagger from hand to hand impatiently as the ferry landed.

"Wine, anyone?" Shadow asked brightly.

Jael stepped disgustedly from the ferry, leading her horse after her. Tanis, equally silent, coaxed the other two horses after her. For a moment, Shadow and Blade gazed at each other, expressions inscrutable. At last, the corner of Blade's mouth twitched up in the barest suggestion of a smile, and Shadow dipped her head briefly in acknowledgment. Blade turned back to her silent companion, and the ferry began its slow journey back to the north shore of the Brightwater.

"I *know* you didn't follow us, unless you can ride over water," Tanis said exasperatedly to Shadow. "How did you manage to get here before us?"

"I didn't have to ride the long way around the edge of the forest," Shadow said mildly. "I simply rode through the Noble District and took the west ferry at the Docks. Much shorter."

"I'd have bet my sword that nobody saw us leaving," Jael said, sighing. "What did you do, camp in the stables to watch the horses?"

Shadow chuckled, ignoring Jael's disgust.

"Little acorn, you're more like your mother than you know," she said. "I had my pony packed last night. Now mount your horses and we'll ride while we talk. No profit in losing good traveling time. Oh, by the way, here." She handed Jael a satchel. "From Argent. Potions and salve and strict instructions to use them if they work. If not, just throw the lot away. Also a hefty purse, which tested my honesty far too harshly. Nonetheless, I'll have you know I took not so much as a single copper—even though your premature escape cost me a comfortable night's sleep."

Jael sighed again, hanging the satchel with her other bags.

"So I suppose you all knew about this and were just chuckling behind our backs," she said sourly. Well, at least she'd *still* managed to miss the sword practice and the lectures.

"I wouldn't say that 'chuckling' described the sounds Donya made," Shadow grinned. "And to say that she was annoyed would be like saying a dragon is a tree-lizard with a bad temper. So she gave me a hefty scolding to pass on to you and all but pushed me out the door to meet you here."

"And I suppose I'm to be flayed alive when we return, for helping her," Tanis said resignedly. "Well, scold us and be done with it."

"No scolding, and no flaying," Shadow chuckled, climbing with some difficulty onto her pony and urging it forward so she was riding closely beside Jael. "Donya used this same trick—more successfully, I might add—some twenty-two years ago, and you might bring that fact to her attention if you come back and find she's been whetting the edge of her tongue. So are you bound for Westenvale now?"

Jael nodded dismally, hoping that Shadow would not insist on accompanying them farther than the first city. Surely Donya would not have taken revenge by having her friend nanny Jael and Tanis for their entire journey.

"Good." Shadow nodded briskly. "There's a good-sized mer-

chant train that left for Westenvale just yesterday morning. With
a fair pace, you should catch up to them sometime tomorrow."

"'You'?" Tanis repeated, his brows arching. "Does that mean
you aren't—"

Shadow waved a hand negligently.

"I've got better things to do than shepherd a couple of younglings for days out of my way," she grinned. "If I hurry, I can just
catch a southward-bound caravan myself. If you can't manage to
get to Westenvale alive on a well-traveled road and in the safety
of a merchant caravan, the presence of one puny elf won't make
any difference, anyway. Promise me you'll catch up with the caravan, and I'll relieve you of my unwanted presence with nary a
lecture." She spit into her hand and held it up to Jaellyn. "Bargain?"

Jael spit into her own hand and shook Shadow's hand, leaning
far down to do so.

"Bargain," she said gladly.

"One last piece of advice," Shadow said, gazing into Jael's
eyes. "Don't go to the Kresh and beg for what you need. Walk
straight up to them and demand what should be yours. If they're
all like Farryn, they're a people who respect strength. Remember
that."

Jael nodded.

"I won't forget," she said.

"Then you can follow the wagon tracks in the road, and Fortune favor you both," Shadow said, giving Jael's hand a last
squeeze. "Stay warm, stay wise, and don't waste your wine."

"Thank you, Aunt Shadow," Jael said humbly.

"Thank you," Tanis repeated. "We'll be careful."

"Be careful," Shadow agreed with a grin, "but better yet, be
lucky."

She gave them a last wave as she turned south. In a few minutes, her pony had disappeared into the morning mist. Jael
watched after her until she was out of sight, then turned back to
Tanis.

"Let's go," she said, excitement swelling in her chest until she
thought she would burst. "The road is ours."

# III

● Jael shivered and huddled deeper into her rain cloak, letting her horse follow the wagon ruts and choose its own footing. With the typical unpredictability of spring weather, a good-sized rainstorm had gathered and broke only a few hours after she and Tanis had parted from Shadow. They hadn't packed the loads on the horses with rain in mind, and the first drops had forced them under cover of a stand of trees to repack, covering the sacks with the waxed skins they had brought before they donned similarly treated cloaks. A waterproofing spell would, of course, have been more useful, but Jael blessed Tanis's tact in not pointing this fact out. It wasn't *her* fault that most magic anywhere in her vicinity went awry, the more so if she touched it or focused her attention on it, and thankfully Tanis didn't seem inclined to blame her for their present discomfort.

The road was already slick and muddy from other recent rains, and the poor footing and poorer visibility slowed their progress. The merchant caravan, with waterproofing spells, sturdy wagons, and large teams of heavy draft horses, was likely moving faster than they were. It was probably nearing sunset now, and they'd made pitifully little progress. Jael could only hope that the rain would stop soon, or, failing that, the road would become so soft that the wagons would bog down in the mud and allow Jael and Tanis to catch up.

"I'll take the lead for a while, see if I can find somewhere to camp," Tanis said, urging his horse forward to ride beside Jael. "Take the pack horse."

Jael relievedly reined her horse in, tying the pack horse's lead to her saddle. With Tanis leading them, Jael didn't need to be able to see any farther than the rump of Tanis's horse; she could draw her hood farther down over her face and pull her cold hands into her sleeves, riding in slightly greater comfort. Jael shivered inside her cloak, wishing she could stomach a little wine to warm her. Unfortunately, Bluebright was the only liquor—if she could call it that, having no idea what it was or how it was made—that did not turn her queasy, and Jael had no desire to add an upset stomach to her complaints, nor to risk the dizzy euphoria the Bluebright brought.

After a time Tanis dropped back to ride beside her again.

"There won't be any road shelters this close to the city," he said loudly, over the rain. "Let's just stop at one of these farms. They'll let us stay in the barn for a copper or two."

"All right," Jael said reluctantly. It galled her to stop still so near the city—they'd have made twice the distance in good weather—but there was no need to contract choking sickness when they'd just started on their journey, and her nose was running already. "You talk to the farmers, though. They might recognize me. I've spent too much time around the market."

"And I haven't?" Tanis asked mildly. Still, Jael's point was good; if the farmers recognized Tanis as a thief, the worst that might happen is they'd refuse the travelers shelter. If the farmers belonged to the anti-elvan faction in the city and recognized Jael, she and Tanis could be in very serious danger. Fortunately, there would not have been time for news to have reached the farms that Jael had disappeared from the palace, so none of the local farmers should be too suspicious of a couple of young wanderers caught in a spring storm.

Despite Jael's keen vision, it was Tanis who spotted the stone farmhouse through the rain. Tanis dismounted and trotted to the house while Jael led the horses to what slight shelter could be found under the thatched eaves of the barn. After a few long moments, Tanis reappeared.

"We can stay," he said. "They charged us half a Moon, probably because I look too young to know better than to pay it, but they'll give us supper and hay for the horses and lend us dry blankets if ours are wet."

Jael refrained from telling Tanis that for dry blankets and hot supper she would well have paid an entire Sun. She followed Tanis into the barn, and together they unloaded the horses. Fortunately, this was one of the ancient joined-block barns that had been built long ago; Jael was glad she wouldn't risk ruining the weatherproofing spell on one of the new block-and-daub buildings currently being built. The barn was dry and fairly clean, although last autumn's hay in the loft smelled a little musty when Jael spread their thankfully dry blankets there, and the livestock below were comfortable—no bellyache or hoof-spot to twinge through Jael's uncontrolled beast-speaking sensitivity and keep her awake all night.

While Jael made up the pallets, Tanis ventured out into the rain once more to fetch their supper. He returned with a large covered bowl of bubbling hot, rather greasy stew and a loaf of crusty, warm bread, and they fell to with more enthusiasm than they had shown at the palace the night before. As the hot stew warmed her, Jael reflected that there was some mysterious quality of hot, simple stew eaten in a barn at the beginning of a great adventure that surpassed the finest viands served in the same dining hall she'd seen almost every day of her life. Tanis, however, perusing their map, was not so cheerful.

"Even if the rain stops before dawn, the road will be awfully muddy," he said. "Unless the merchant caravan's gotten mired, there's little chance we can catch up with them tomorrow. Not unless we cut across country instead of taking the road."

"I don't know that that will save any time," Jael said, shaking her head. "It's late enough in the spring that most of the farmers have already plowed their fields, making them even muddier than the road after that rain. Besides, some of those farms have dogs or even drakes to protect them."

Tanis sighed and rolled the map.

"Then I suppose we just hope that the caravan's moving slowly enough that we can catch them. We can't bet on kind farmers every rainy night that comes."

Jael mopped her nose on her sleeve.

"It's only a few days' ride to Westenvale," she said. "If we don't meet the caravan tomorrow or the next day, it won't be worth the money we'll have to pay to join it. What if we just go on without the caravan?"

"Remember what your mother said about bandits?" Tanis said patiently. "She wasn't exaggerating. I've ridden on more trade roads than I could count, and I've seen a *lot* of bandits and their work. Robbers love these trade roads, especially a trade road between two large cities like Allanmere and Westenvale. If a merchant caravan's large enough, they won't dare attack it, just look for something smaller. Such as two young people with a lot of baggage traveling alone."

Jael grimaced. Adventure and discomfort was one thing; getting their throats slit was another.

"So we have to catch up with the caravan," she said. "At least the foul weather will keep bandits under shelter, too. Well, likely the rain will stop tonight. The weather-mages weren't predicting any long storms for the next few days. In the meantime, is there any stew left?"

"Not a drop." Tanis frowned as Jael sneezed. "You haven't caught a chill already?"

Jael shook her head.

"Just my usual spring sniffles, I hope. Plus I'm still cold, and sitting on dusty hay, too. I suppose I should use some of the potion Shadow brought from my father." She found the bottle and carefully measured the drops into her cup.

"I don't suppose that helps with any of your other—ah, problems?" Tanis asked delicately.

Jael sighed.

"I wish it did."

"Because I was thinking," Tanis said hesitantly, "that if you're cold, we could move the two pallets together. For warmth."

"Tanis," Jael said slowly, "I don't think that's really a very good—"

"Just for warmth," Tanis repeated. He smiled. "I mean it. I know better than to expect anything else."

"All right." Jael sighed again. As always, Tanis refused to speak a word of blame, but Jael felt guilty nonetheless. Jael knew that Tanis wanted her, maybe even loved her; that was one fact. They both knew that until Jael could fill the void that was the missing part of her soul, she could never quite reach adulthood, could no more desire Tanis than she could the livestock in the pens below them; that was the other fact. Those thoughts

hung unspoken between them, aching like an old wound. Jael
had thought it best to place their pallets as far apart as the loft
would allow—why torment Tanis?—but if it gave him some
comfort to have her near, maybe that was better than nothing.
And the nights *were* still cold.

They pulled the pallets together, and Jael crawled rather hesitantly between the blankets. The straw was soft and quickly
warmed, and their closeness meant that they could double and
share the covers, but Jael felt acutely uncomfortable.

"It's all right," Tanis said softly. "Come here."

Jael scooted over awkwardly against the warmth of Tanis's
body. He folded his arm around her, pillowing her head on his
shoulder. Surprisingly comfortable, and glad not to have to look
at his face as she asked, Jael dared a question that had gnawed
at her for over a year.

"Tanis, have you ever—you know, been with a woman?"

Tanis tensed a little, and Jael was almost sorry she had asked.
But Tanis was her dearest friend, and they couldn't live so
closely for months with walls between them.

"A couple of times," Tanis said rather abashedly at last.
"Women in brothels. It's only been since—uh—"

Since he'd told her how he felt about her, since he'd learned
why she couldn't return his desire, Jael laid her own arm over
his chest comfortingly.

"I'm glad," she said, grinning into the darkness. How she'd
dreaded learning that he'd been foolishly waiting for her out of
some misplaced romantic notion, as if his suffering did her any
good!

"You are?" Relief and amazement were plain in Tanis's voice.

"Of course I am," she assured him. "You're the best friend
I've ever had, besides Aunt Shadow. I don't want you to be unhappy because of me." She remembered the fire she'd felt in her
own body when she'd tasted Bluebright, how near she'd come to
giving herself to Urien, a virtual stranger. Was that what Tanis
felt? What an amazing thing, that Tanis could feel that way about
*her*, all gangly legs and elbows! "Were they beautiful, the
women?"

"Look, Jaellyn, can't we talk about something else?" Tanis
said uncomfortably. "Why don't you tell me about your fa- —uh,
Farryn again."

"It's all right, you can say he's my father," Jael told him. "It doesn't bother me that I'm a bastard. Not much, anyway. Anyway, you know the story already. Farryn appeared in the Heartwood, sick with the Crimson Plague, and the elves captured him. They'd never seen anyone like him before, so they called my mother to come look at him. She took him back to the palace."

"That was foolish, if he was sick," Tanis said wryly.

"Nobody had ever heard of the Crimson Plague at that time, and none of the elves who had been near him had gotten sick," Jael said patiently. "Nobody knew it was something that elves couldn't catch but humans could. Anyway, Farryn got better; Crimson Plague wasn't as serious to the Kresh as it was to humans, either. But by the time Mother was able to get a translation spell so she could even talk to Farryn, plague was already in the city, probably brought in by the elves, and people were starting to die. Farryn told them—"

"Who's 'them'?" Tanis interrupted.

"Mother, Father—Argent, that is; they weren't married then—Aunt Shadow, Mist, my foster father, Grandma Celene and Grandfather Sharl," Jael told him. "Farryn told them about the Kresh living up in a valley in the northern mountains, and said that his own people had caught the plague from northern barbarians who were trying to overrun the Kresh's valley—the only pass through the mountains—to come south. The Kresh had almost always defeated the barbarians before, but now that so many of them were sick, Farryn was afraid that the Kresh would be defeated. Then the barbarian army would get through the pass and head south, just like what happened during the Black Wars, only this time they'd be bringing the Crimson Plague south with them, too.

"Some of Farryn's people had once lived near Allanmere, in a place that's in the Dim Reaches now, and he'd come to ask them for help, for a cure for the plague and maybe some way of fighting off the barbarians. Aunt Shadow had been through the swamp and had seen the houses where Farryn's folk had lived, and she knew they were already dead or gone, but Farryn said there was a temple where records would have been left. So Mother decided to go with Farryn to find the temple and hopefully a cure for the plague. She took Aunt Shadow with her, because she'd been through the swamp before, and Mist because Farryn was really his prisoner by elvan law, and Argent because he was an herbalist and there was a plant that grew in the swamp

that they were using to try to cure the plague." Jael grinned.
"That's what Mother says. I think Father went because he loved
Mother and didn't want her to go without him. Anyway, they *did*
find the cure in the temple and brought it back, and Farryn went
back to his people."

"But when did you get—well, planted, as the elves would
say?" Tanis asked.

"Mother spent one night with Farryn," Jael said. "I think it
was after the battle with the giant daggertooth, although Aunt
Shadow won't say. Nothing gets Mother's blood up like a good
swordfight, though. I've seen her drag Father right out of audience after a good practice match. Get Aunt Shadow to tell you
the whole tale sometime, especially the part about making the
daggertooth into a boat. She's a much better storyteller than I
am."

"I still don't understand," Tanis complained. "Where does the
stone melting fit in, and why are you missing part of your soul?"

"I'm not certain I understand that part of it myself," Jael admitted. "According to Aunt Shadow, there were different clans of
Kresh, just like there are different elvan clans. Farryn's clan could
run like the wind, almost faster than you can see, like Aunt
Shadow said. There was another clan who could mold stone without touching it. Long ago, when those two clans lived together
near Allanmere, they intermarried, so Farryn must have carried a
little of their blood himself, and that's the part that came out in
me. The gods know *I* can't run over water. I can hardly run over
good solid ground without tripping over my own feet."

"But there are plenty of mixed-bloods in Allanmere," Tanis
said. "None of them have ever lacked part of their soul, not that
I've heard."

"Farryn told Aunt Shadow that Kresh aren't born with their
souls," Jael told him. "They're given to them in a ceremony
when they become adults, kind of like the elvan passage ceremony I tried last year. So I've never been given the Kresh part
of my soul, and it's missing."

"How can someone else give you a soul?" Tanis asked skep-
tically. "More to the point, how can someone else give you *part*
of a soul?"

Jael shrugged.

"I don't know. But unless I want to go through the rest of my
life wrecking spells and looking half-grown, I'd better find out."

Tanis was silent, but Jael could sense the unasked questions—*If* Jael and Tanis could find the Kresh, could they indeed give a Kresh soul to a half-breed Kresh? And if they could, would they? Would Farryn, if he was still alive, welcome the arrival of his mixed-blood daughter, or would she be an embarrassment to him? Thankfully Tanis asked none of these questions; Jael had no answers, and she didn't particularly want to consider the idea that even if she could find the Kresh, her whole journey might be for nothing.

But what choice did she have?

As if reading her thoughts, Tanis squeezed her shoulders comfortingly, and Jael sighed and buried her face in his shoulder. She'd been wretched for years not knowing who or what she was—walking the dagger's edge between elf and human, Aunt Shadow had once told her, took good balance and like as not left you with sore feet anyway—but learning the answer hadn't solved her problem. Now she was teetering on the dagger's point between three peoples, and every step cut to the bone.

Tanis's arm around her was warm and solid, and Jael was glad that Tanis had suggested moving the pallets together, even though she had nothing to give him but her friendship and she knew he wanted much more. Tanis snored slightly, and Jael grinned in the darkness, unaccountably comforted by the sound.

The dagger's point wasn't quite so sharp when you had a friend to hold you in the dark, even if he snored while he did it.

They awoke to the farmer's good-natured cursing in the dim near-dawn light as he fed the livestock and milked the cows, and a pail clanged at the foot of the loft ladder. Jael snuggled deeper into Tanis's side, then turned on her back abruptly before her nose could drip on his tunic. Gods, she could hardly breathe!

Hay and fur, Jael realized disgustedly. They'd been sleeping all night on hay in a livestock barn.

"They's bread, milk an' hot parridge," a gruff voice announced. "Ye younglin's eat up an' begone with ye. 'S a fine day lightin'. Hear?"

"We hear, and thank you," Tanis called down. He carefully eased his arm out from under Jael with a grin of apology. The grin turned to a grimace as Tanis felt his arm, then shook it, wincing, rubbing his hand as he stumbled to the ladder.

Jael stretched and sneezed several times, then grimaced herself. She'd been so comfortable against Tanis's side last night, but this morning her left arm, wedged between them all night, was half-numb and as stiff and prickling as Tanis's apparently was. She rifled desperately through her pack for a kerchief to mop her stuffed nose, then poured a few drops of her potion into a cup of water.

"Milk, bread, and porridge as promised," Tanis said cheerfully, setting down a tray holding a cloth-wrapped loaf, a small jug, and a deep bowl. "That half-Moon seems like a better price this morning. And the rain seems to have moved east. Fill your stomach, because if we're going to catch that caravan, we'll have to dine and sup, too, as we ride."

Jael was not at all fond of porridge, but she ate heartily, reminding herself that things could be worse—such as having to live on herbal teas and boiled greens for days on end, as she had before her elvan passage ceremony. This time Jael and Tanis packed for rain despite the clear sky, tucking everything that could be damaged by water deep into the packs and covering each bundle with waxed hides.

The rutted wagon track was sodden and slick, and Jael and Tanis rode in the grass at the side of the road rather than force the horses to flounder through the mud. The sun rose in a perfect cloudless sky, Argent's potion had wondrously cleared Jael's nose, and Jael wanted to shout with joy. Now *this* was what a journey should be—the road, the great wide world before her and the open sky above her, a wonderful horse to ride and a good friend to ride with. Who needed caravans and cities?

In his year of apprenticeship at the Guild of Thieves (and probably during his tenure as an acolyte at the Temple of Baaros, too, although Jael would never suggest such a thing), Tanis had learned a good many bawdy songs, and Jael knew as many more, so they spent most of the morning singing and laughing helplessly as they rode. By noon, however, the laughter rang a little hollow as they both grew stiff and tired of riding and the unclouded sunlight became hot and glaring instead of bright and pleasantly warming. Despite Tanis's morning advice, they were forced to stop; having packed the load for rain, Jael and Tanis now had to unpack several of the bags to reach the rations they had tucked away underneath their other supplies. Jael had chosen elvan journey cakes for the trip, and the cakes of dried ground meat, nuts, and dried fruit, held together with rich rendered fat,

were tasty, but Jael wished wistfully for fresh, cold water instead
of the tepid liquid that had sat in her skins all night and under the
sun all morning. Another mistake—they should have refilled their
waterskins from the farmer's well while they'd had the chance.
Tanis complained bitterly because all the wine had soured. He
blamed the hot morning sun, and Jael held her peace; it was far
more likely that the wine had been protected by an aging spell,
which Jael had ruined when she repacked the food that morning.

Tanis was not pleased at midafternoon, either, when Jael insisted that they stop to rest the horses.

"We're not going to catch that caravan like this," he grumbled,
uncorking another skin of wine. He sipped, grimaced, and poured
out the wine on the ground.

"I can't help it," Jael sighed. "They're hot and tired and upset.
I can't ride another step feeling that."

"By Baaros's purse, Jael, I'm hot and tired and upset, too,"
Tanis said bitterly. "And none of us are going to feel any better
if we're attacked by bandits tonight while we sleep. Including
your poor, hot, tired horses, who will be stolen and ridden and
likely treated somewhat less kindly by those bandits."

"Well, why don't you tell *them* that?" Jael said irritably.

"Why don't you?" Tanis snapped back. "You're the one who's
so concerned with how our three horses feel."

"If I had enough control of my beast-speaking ability to tell
our horses anything at all," Jael said between clenched teeth, "I
would tell them to shut up and stop griping, which is the same
thing I'd like to tell you. So shut up and stop griping."

Tanis glared at Jael, who glared back. At last Jael half-
smiled—as close to an apology as she was going to get—and
Tanis sighed and smiled back.

"Think your friends are about ready to go?" he asked.

"I think I can bribe them with a couple dried apples," Jael
said. "Know any more bawdy songs?"

"Do you know the one about the three priests, the courtesan,
and the goat?" Tanis grinned.

"You do the verses, I'll do the chorus," Jael chuckled.


Occasionally they passed farmers in their fields despite the
mud, most of them picking rocks out of the soil in preparation
for plowing or planting. Jael deemed it wise to keep a distance,
since these farmers were still close enough to Allanmere to trade

their crops in the market there, but Tanis did not hesitate to hail the men and women as they passed by, asking how long it had been since the merchant caravan had passed. When Jael and Tanis rode near another farmhouse, Tanis asked for and got permission to draw water from the farmer's well to rinse the wineskins, replenish their water supply, and water the horses. After speaking with one of the children running in the yard, Tanis relievedly reported to Jael that the caravan was no more than two or three hours ahead of them.

"But it's almost dark," Jael said doubtfully. "Even if we just keep riding until we find them, what will they think, us riding up to them in the dark?"

"They'll think we're riding front for a troop of brigands," Tanis sighed. "That's what I'd think. But they'd rather have us where they can see us than drive us away and wonder where we are and what we're doing. So they'll take our coin and watch us very narrowly all the way to Westenvale. But when we get there, if we can find another caravan soon, they can inquire of this one, and at least *they'll* know we're not highwaymen."

Cheered by the proximity of the caravan, Jael took the lead so that when the sun descended below the horizon, her elvan vision could help them avoid bad spots in the road. At last they saw the fires of the caravan ahead. Almost simultaneously, a voice boomed out of a thicket.

"Who are you?"

"My name is Caden, and my elvan friend is Acorn," Tanis said. "We're bound for Westenvale. We were hoping to join your caravan in Allanmere, but were delayed in leaving and then slowed by the storm yesterday. May we speak to the wagonmaster?"

"Leave your horses and your weapons here and I'll take you to Wagonmaster Nezed," the voice said from the thicket, but a second figure appeared from the other side of the road. A tall woman armored in leather and carrying a crossbow approached them.

"I'll hold your horses," she said.

"I'll talk to the wagonmaster, and Acorn can stay with our horses and our weapons," Tanis corrected.

This was apparently acceptable, for a man, also armed with a crossbow, emerged from the thicket and wordlessly beckoned Tanis to follow him to the cluster of wagons. The woman stayed where she was, crossbow still in her hands.

"Acorn, eh?" she said. "Sounds like one of those local elves near Allanmere. You look it, too. Is that where you're from?"

Jael nodded.

"My mother's mother was Silvertip," she said briefly. Jael knew something of the history of the Silvertip clan from Mist, who had Silvertip ancestry; she could even manage the Silvertip accent in her Olvenic if she had to.

"I'm Reda, second in the guard company," the woman said, lowering the crossbow slightly. "I've met some of the elves in Allanmere. They're honest enough folk, a jolly lot, too, not so distant and puffed up on their own wind as the ones from the elvan cities to the east. Is this your first time out from the forest?"

Jael hesitated, then nodded again.

"Caden's traveled," she said. "So I decided to come with him this time."

"Wagonmaster'll let you come," Reda said after a moment's thought. "But he'll charge you dear, unless you can do anything useful. Can you?"

"I'm good with horses," Jael said. She could break spells, too, but she was hardly going to say *that*. "I can cook."

"We've cooks aplenty," Reda told her. "And two grooms. But several of our horses are limping a bit—not exactly lame, but it's slowed us up a good bit. Groom says it's just stone bruises, but in this mud? Have a look, and if you can do anything, I'll give the wagonmaster a word to slip back some coin to you and your friend."

"I'll do that, when Caden returns," Jael said relievedly. She *did* know a fair bit about horses, mostly from the many times she'd been given stable chores as punishment, but also from a genuine interest; most horses didn't much care how clumsy Jael was or whether she made the palace mages' silver-polishing spell tarnish the goblets instead. If the horses were indeed stone-bruised, Jael's beast-speaking sensitivity (if it happened to be working at all at the moment) would tell her that quickly enough, and she could recognize a poorly shod hoof if she saw one.

Tanis returned presently, attempting to look irritated, and Jael guessed that the wagonmaster had, as Tanis predicted, charged rather more than the impoverished younglings they were pretending to be would have been glad to pay.

"We can travel with them," Tanis said when he reached Jael. "They'll feed us, and we can sleep under one of the wagons if it rains, but we're to make our own camp a little away from theirs otherwise. Which assures we don't sneak into their wagons and rob them blind at night, and makes us sentries of a sort, too, and they don't even have to pay us."

"Reda wants me to look at some of the horses," Jael told him. "If you'll pick a spot for us to sleep and see about supper, I'll go with her."

Tanis agreed, and Jael could see that he was actually as pleased with the arrangement as she was. He might feign disappointment that their camp was to be separate, but they both were relieved. Their isolation would mean less contact with the merchants and therefore less need to construct a more and more elaborate lie. Jael preferred to avoid the merchants for another reason—any of the merchants might be annoyed, or worse, suspicious, if his firestarting spell or soupstone suddenly failed when Jael walked by.

Jael was relieved to find that the horses were, on the whole, healthy and contented creatures, preoccupied with their food and well accustomed to handling. Aside from their natural weariness from the day's work and one horse's bad tooth, however, none of them were feeling any pain that Jael could sense, nor were any of the horses Reda indicated favoring a sore hoof. When Jael touched the first affected horse, however, she was surprised by the familiar tingling sensation she immediately felt. Jael's beast-speaking might be rather one-sided and unreliable, but her magic sense was usually correct. But why would there be magic on the horses? Surely the merchants would not have fetter-spelled the horses, as they were securely tethered.

"Does this caravan have a mage?" Jael asked Reda.

Reda shook her head.

"We're not carrying magical goods," she said. "Hiring a mage to accompany our caravan would drive the prices up. Why?"

Jael ran her hands slowly over the horse's body, neck, and head. The tingling sensation continued until she slid her hands down the horse's front legs to its fetlocks. Abruptly the sensation ceased under her touch as the spell was disrupted. Some variation of a fetter-spell, then. But why?

Jael checked each of the horses. All had been bespelled, although on some of the horses the warm tingling was fainter than on the others; the spell had likely been cast by an amateur mage or a very inept one. She checked each horse again, making certain that her touch had dissolved the spell.

"I'm not a real mage," Jael said, thinking fast, "but I believe your horses have been hinder-spelled. I have a little of the mage-gift, not much, but I believe I've broken the spell."

Reda narrowed her eyes warily.

"I'll have to speak to the grooms and the wagonmaster," she said. "You should've gotten permission before using magic on our horses. Go back to your camp and stay there."

Jael sighed and obeyed. Tanis had already laid out their bedrolls and built a small fire—the merchants had brought peat for fires, as there was no wood to be found on the open plains—and he shook his head when Jael told him what had happened.

"The wagonmaster's going to be furious, but not necessarily at us," he said. "The possibility that there was a hinder-spell on the horses means that either someone in the caravan now, or more likely someone back in Allanmere, wants this caravan delayed. It could be a competitor, but it's probably an organized band of highwaymen."

"Why would highwaymen want the caravan slowed down?" Jael asked him. "It's not as though the spell's enough to stop the wagons completely, and they can't travel all that fast to begin with. What's to be gained?"

"If the highwaymen are setting up an ambush, they need a certain amount of time for their henchmen in Allanmere, who know when the caravan's leaving and what it's loaded with, to ride all the way around the caravan well out of sight, reach the rest of the band, and prepare the ambush," Tanis told her. "I've heard of such plans before. Any band of highwaymen willing to dare a caravan this size and this well guarded would have to be fairly well manned and organized."

"Are you going to warn the wagonmaster?" Jael asked.

"I doubt I'll need to," Tanis said, shrugging. "Anyone who's been in this business for a few years will know how these people work. What he'll end up doing, much though it hurts him, is thanking you kindly for the warning once it's obvious tomorrow that the hinder-spell's gone. As things stand now, though, it's just as well I'd already claimed our supper, or likely we wouldn't get any. It really would have been better to ask permission first."

"I couldn't do that," Jael sighed, and after a moment, Tanis nodded his understanding, although neither wanted to voice their thoughts, as someone from the caravan might be within earshot. Of course the hinder-spell would have been broken as soon as Jael touched it, and if there had been a mage or even another magic-spotter in the caravan who later examined the horses, he would find no spell, and the wagonmaster would either assume that Jael had been lying or that she had already broken the spell. Either way would have earned Jael and Tanis the same suspicion they were already receiving. At least this way the horses' improved pace on the morrow would prove Jael's honesty.

Despite her weariness, Jael found that sleep eluded her. She felt safer with the guards and merchants nearby, but the ground was hard and uncomfortable, and she missed the soft hay of the night before, even if it had made her nose run. When she spent the summers with Mist in the Heartwood, they'd stayed in his comfortable hanging bower in a tree near Inner Heart. Even on their frequent journeys through the Heartwood they'd woven sleeping nests in willows when they could, or at least piled leaves or some such to soften their bedrolls. Here there was a lump the size of a small mountain under her hip, and the bruises from her last sword practice ached.

The small fire, too, had been good enough to cast a little light and warm the roast fowl for their supper, but the ground was cold, unlike the hay in the barn the night before. Jael squirmed uncomfortably, remembering the warmth of the shared blankets and of Tanis's arm around her the night before. She wriggled around onto her other side, scrabbled under her bedroll, and tossed the offending rock aside. Now there was a hollow where the rock had been.

Jael scrunched down a little lower in the covers, then sighed and gave up. She rolled over again.

"Tanis?"

"What?" Tanis's eyes were open, and Jael wondered whether he'd had difficulty sleeping, too.

"Can I move over there with you?" Jael asked sheepishly.

Tanis grinned back at her.

"I'd have asked if you hadn't," he admitted. "Bring your blankets and come on."

Combining their pallets gave them more cushioning from the packed earth and twice the covering over them, and the warmth of Tanis's body against hers banished the last of the spring chill.

Her cheek pillowed on his shoulder, Jael finally relaxed and slept.

Morning dawned cold and foggy, rain-heavy clouds hanging low. Jael and Tanis rode behind the caravan, cheerful despite the weather. When the first hour of riding revealed that the limping horses now stepped along at a much improved pace, Reda had ridden ahead to confer with the wagonmaster. She rode back to hand Tanis a small purse of coin.

"You can camp at our fires tonight and until we reach Westenvale," she said. "Wagonmaster Nezed says if it rains today, you can tie your horses behind his wagon and ride inside if you don't mind sitting on boxes of copper pots." She rode away before Jael or Tanis could make any reply.

"They don't exactly smother you in thanks," Jael said wryly.

"I'd rather have a dry place to sit and a comfortable camp than thanks anyway," Tanis said, chuckling. "Plus, of course, some of our coin returned."

"How much did you have to pay to begin with?" Jael asked.

"Ten Moons," Tanis admitted. "Expensive. And that was after I bargained him down from the fifteen Moons he asked. I'll wager he'd have asked no more than three or four Moons if we'd joined the caravan under less suspicious conditions."

"We paid half a Sun just to follow in their wagon ruts and camp on the ground?" Jael asked, shocked. "How much did he give you back?"

Tanis opened the pouch and looked inside.

"It looks like about five Moons' worth of coppers," he said. "Well, that's much more reasonable, although on our next caravan I hope you don't have to break hinder-spells to earn a fair price."

"I don't mind the spells," Jael said slowly, "but what about the highwaymen? Do you still think they've set up an ambush ahead of us?"

"I don't know," Tanis said, his voice lowered. He guided his horse to ride closer beside Jael. "The wagonmaster's sent some of the guards to ride ahead and look for any places where robbers could have enough cover to hide and wait for us, and I see the guards have their bows ready, too. But it's not impossible that the highwaymen could have someone inside the caravan—maybe even the person who cast the hinder-spell. So we'll stay behind the caravan, and if there's any trouble, we'll ride like there's a dragon chasing us in the other direction. Hopefully the highwaymen won't bother chasing us when they have a whole caravan to loot."

"Shouldn't we help defend the caravan?" Jael asked doubtfully.

"Jaellyn, they're not paying us to be guards," Tanis told her firmly. "And I'd be very, very happy if we never had to draw our swords from now until we get back to Allanmere. Do *you* think either of us is skilled enough to fight a band of murderous brigands?"

Jael sighed. Her mother would have gladly matched her sword against any twenty brigands, and Aunt Shadow would have slipped away unseen while pocketing the choicest valuables from caravan and robbers alike, but Jael and Tanis would run like frightened rabbits, five Moons the poorer and nothing gained.

A slow drizzle began around noon, but to Jael's irritation, Tanis insisted that they stay with their horses instead of riding in the comfort of the wagon. By the time the caravan stopped for the evening, Jael was cold, wet, stiff, sniffling, and absolutely furious. The drizzle continued, driving the merchants into their wagons for shelter. Despite the cold, if the dry spot under the proffered wagon had been wide enough, Jael would have gladly placed her bedroll far from Tanis. Tanis was in no better mood than she, and they hunched silently in their shelter mopping up stew with half-stale bread. Jael listened sourly as the merchant in the wagon over their heads made certain sounds indicating that he was not alone.

"Is the potion High Lord Argent gave you working?" Tanis asked at last.

"Not yet," Jael said shortly. She wiped her nose on her sleeve. The merchant and his doxy became more vigorous, causing the wagon to shake.

Tanis glanced upward, grimaced, and poured himself another cup of wine.

"I'm sorry you got wet and chilled," he said irritably. "But are you going to sulk about it all night?"

"That depends," Jael said sourly. "Are you going to make me sleep out in the rain, too?"

"Don't tempt me," Tanis retorted. "I'm not going to apologize again. I really thought there might be danger. I suppose I dodged when I should have parried. It's happened to you once or twice, too."

Jael had to grin at that.

"You mean once or twice in the last two days, don't you?" she said, relenting. "I suppose even a bad case of the sniffles doesn't quite pay me back for demon-scratches, does it?"

Tanis touched his tunic where it covered the five scars puckering the skin of his right shoulder.

"They ache in this weather, too," he said proudly.

Jael reached for her pack.

"You should've said something sooner," she told him. "I have a salve that's good for aches that aren't in the bone. Take off your tunic and shirt and I'll rub some of this in."

Tanis winced a little as he pulled his tunic over his head, and Jael raised her eyebrows in surprise. In the little more than a year since he had left the priesthood and become an apprentice thief, Tanis had lost his acolyte softness and developed a thief's lithe, wiry musculature. The five angry white furrows started just below the collarbone on the left side of Tanis's chest, crossed the point of his shoulder, and tapered off at his back. Jael remembered the ferocity of the demon who had given Tanis those marks, and shivered. He'd been lucky not to lose his arm—or his life.

Tanis sighed contentedly as Jael rubbed the pungent-scented salve over his shoulder, working the unguent into his skin with practiced fingers. She'd have to remember to thank Mist, who had tutored her in every aspect of trail medicine, and Shadow, who had taught Jael the art of rubbing the soreness out of muscles. At least it was a way of passing time other than lying there and listening to the merchant and his bed companion shake the wagon.

"That's wonderful," he said. "Allanmere lost a great herbalist when Argent left his shop. And you have a healer's touch. Whatever were you carrying that salve around for?"

"I suppose Father thought I'd need it for all the bruises Mother left on me in sword practice the day before we left," Jael said with a grin. "She could split a bull in half head to foot with that monster of a sword, so you can imagine what it's done to me, even a practice blade with a dulled edge and through padding."

Tanis shook his head sympathetically.

"Bad?"

Jael pulled up the side of her tunic in answer. The bottom of the huge, mottled bruise was plainly visible on her back and side.

"It looks as if you could use some of this ointment, too," Tanis said, grimacing. "You should have mentioned it before. Lie down and let me put some of this on your back. Are you sure you haven't cracked a rib?"

"It's just a few bruises," Jael said, somewhat embarrassed by his concern—it didn't speak well for High Lady Donya, did it, if she cracked her daughter's ribs in sword practice? "She mostly tries to hit me with the flat, anyway."

"On a sword that heavy, that's enough."

When Jael had stretched out on her stomach on the blankets, Tanis gently pushed up the back of her tunic, murmuring in dismay at the bruises he uncovered. The cold, wet night air on her bare back made Jael shiver, and she started when the gob of ointment touched her skin, but Tanis's hands were warm and his touch was very gentle as he smoothed the paste into her skin.

"I imagine this means it would be best to postpone *our* sword practice for a few more days," Tanis said, chuckling. "I'd never forgive myself if I added any more bruises on top of what's already there." He was silent for a moment, scooping up a little more ointment to rub into Jael's shoulders. "Of course, if I get to do this every time I beat you black and blue, the prospect gets much more tempting."

Something in his tone made Jael uneasy.

"You know," she said slowly, "maybe it's not a very good idea for you to—I mean, maybe you'd better stop."

Tanis's hands kneaded the muscles at the base of her neck, then slid caressingly down her back.

"Must I?" he asked gently.

Oh, no. Jael closed her eyes and sighed.

"Please don't," she said hesitantly. "You know this just isn't going to work."

"Won't you let me try?" he asked softly. "Just this once, can you let me try? If it's not right for you, I won't ask again. I promise."

Jael twisted her head around as far as she could to look at Tanis. His blue eyes were direct and unshadowed, his expression sincere. He was the best friend she'd ever had besides Aunt Shadow, and if she couldn't trust him, she'd picked a poor companion indeed for this journey. Gods, he wouldn't be here sleeping on the cold, hard ground if it weren't for her. And it wasn't as if she didn't *want* to be able to feel those things he wanted so much for her to feel.

"All right," Jael said at last. "But you promise—"

Tanis brushed his fingertips over her cheek.

"I promise," he said. "You know me better than to believe I'd ever do anything you didn't want."

The gentleness of his hands sliding over her back was soothing, and Jael found herself becoming drowsy. The merchant in the wagon above them was quiet now. Tanis drew the tunic up over Jael's head and lay down beside her, pulling the blankets over them both.

It was warm and safe and dark there together under the wagon, and the heat of Tanis's skin against hers and the familiarity of his scent were comforting. When Tanis bent to kiss her, Jael tried to respond as best she could. It was an awkward business; she didn't know which way to tilt her head, and the noses got in the way, but it wasn't unpleasant overall. Jael clung to Tanis as if somehow his passion could soak through his skin and into hers, but when Tanis trailed his lips down the side of her throat, one hand gently caressing Jael's small breasts, Jael burst out in helpless laughter.

"What's so funny?" Tanis murmured against the skin of her neck.

"I'm sorry," Jael giggled. "I can't help it. That tickles."

"What about this?" Tanis tongue traced a path along the line of her jaw, holding Jael close as his free hand slid down her side, slipping under the waist of her trousers. Jael held her breath as long as she could, but at last she could not longer suppress a shriek of laughter.

"Oh, for Baaros's sake," Tanis said disgustedly, releasing her. He found Jael's tunic and flung it at her, then snatched up half the blankets.

"What are you doing?" Jael asked, not laughing anymore. She clutched the tunic to her bare chest.

"Just go to sleep," Tanis snapped. He stomped off into the darkness, cursing under his breath. Jael sat there listening until she heard him settle himself under another wagon nearby.

Oh, gods. Jael pulled her tunic over her head and crawled back under the blankets, almost in tears. What should she do now? Would apologizing to Tanis help, or would it just make things worse? And why should she have to apologize? He knew it was no more Jael's fault than it was his own that she couldn't desire him.

He'd always been so understanding and patient, Jael sometimes forgot that while a pure-blooded elf of twenty-two years of age might still be a child, human males of Tanis's age would be at that stage where they did little else but dash from one brothel to the next.

Well, there was no chance of sleeping now. Jael wiped her eyes, wrapped her cloak around her shoulders, and scrambled out from under the wagon into the light rain. Tanis had tethered their horses near the wagon where they were to sleep, separate from the merchants' horses—another of Tanis's silly just-in-case-brigands-attack precautions—and they were near enough that Jael could occasionally feel their irritation with the weather and their frustration as they strained to reach the grass beyond the circle of their tethers.

Jael moved the horses' pickets to fresh spots and offered each of them some of the dried fruit from her pack in apology for their discomfort. There was nothing she could do about the rain; there weren't even any trees she could move them under for shelter.

The horses accepted the dried fruit, rubbing their heads against Jael or nibbling affectionately at her sleeve. Jael was not a true beast-speaker, and there was no real communication between her and the horses, but her sensitivity made her a desirable companion. Every horse in the palace stables had come to recognize Jael as a person associated with relief from small discomforts, one who never appeared without some tasty snack for her friends and who invariably knew just where to scratch.

Jael suddenly froze, her ears straining. Had she heard a footstep, a harsh breath that hadn't come from one of the horses? She squinted into the darkness. Surely those dark forms at the very edge of her vision, creeping silently around the edge of the camp, weren't the caravan guards.

As quietly as she could, Jael edged back to the wagon, glancing desperately around to locate Tanis. There he was, under the next wagon over. She crept to his side, clapping her hand firmly over his mouth as she shook him.

"Wmmmf!" Tanis bolted upright, tearing Jael's hand away from his mouth. "What in Baaros's name do you—"

"Shhh," Jael whispered desperately. "I think the caravan's surrounded, or nearly. Should we wake everyone?"

Tanis immediately pulled Jael under the wagon, bearing both of them flat against the ground. Even in his anger when he'd left her, he'd been wise enough to take his sword with him; now the blade was naked in his hand.

"Get your sword, and scramble our packs together if you can," he whispered so softly that even Jael barely heard him. "I'll warn the guards and the wagonmaster."

Despite her question about defending the caravan earlier, Jael would have stopped him if she could, but Tanis was gone before she could grab him. Quickly Jael snatched Tanis's blankets and scuttled back for her own, wadding them haphazardly into the best bundle she could manage, scrabbling for her sword. Gods, how could she ever get all the packs onto the horses and get them saddled in time to get away before she and Tanis were slaughtered? Jael froze in horror as she heard quiet footsteps approaching the back of the wagon, even as she saw a stealthy figure creeping closer to where her three horses were tethered.

At that moment, a cry sounded from the other side of the cluster of wagons, and Jael thought she recognized the guard who had first met them, then others. The footsteps at the rear of the wagon halted, and now Jael could see the feet and leggings of the stepper, wearing low boots and filthy leggings—no merchant or guard, then, but as Jael had feared, one of the highwaymen.

One of the feet disappeared as the bandit began to climb into the wagon. Without thinking, Jael grabbed the other foot and yanked it hard toward her; the bandit, surprised and off balance, fell hard behind the wagon. Jael could hear the merchant and his doxy bolt awake above her, and to her relief she heard the hiss of a sword being drawn from its scabbard.

Suddenly the clearing was full of running feet and flashing blades, and Jael decided she'd more than done her part in defending the caravan; now all she wanted in the world was for herself and Tanis to escape with as much of their goods as they could and with their hides still intact. She swept up two packs and her sword and ducked out from under the wagon, dashing for the horses as fast as she could.

Gods, she'd forgotten the man who had been creeping up to the horses! He was there now, reaching for one of the picket ropes with one hand, a knife in the other.

Jael tossed the packs aside; one of the first lessons she'd ever had was *never clutter your fighting ground*. Then there was no time to remember her lessons; Jael only had time to think *Thank the gods he didn't throw that knife* as the bandit drew another knife from his belt and stepped forward to meet her.

He was human, so Jael had that much of an advantage—her night vision was superior to his, and her sword gave her a greater reach despite her shorter stature. But he knew where the rest of his people were and wasn't worried about watching his back, nor did he need to be concerned about whether his companion was busy getting skewered. And even in practice, Jael had rarely fought against an opponent with two knives.

Jael grimly shut out the shouts and the clang of blades behind her; if Tanis was being killed at this moment, there was nothing she could do to help. The fact that the brigand hadn't yet thrown a knife didn't mean that he couldn't; Jael's only hope was to keep him too busy to set up for a throw.

He was fast, blindingly fast, deflecting but never actually meeting her strokes. Try as she might, Jael could find no opening past his constantly moving knives; all she could manage was to reverse their positions so that he couldn't use the firelight from the caravan to see her better. A moment later she discovered why he'd allowed the reversal as Jael narrowly missed tripping over one of the picket ropes. Now she'd have to divide her concentration to watch her footing as well.

The bandit feinted with his left knife while thrusting with his right; Jael had been expecting such a maneuver and turned his knife aside easily. In a motion so fast that Jael saw only a blur, however, his left knife flashed toward her face. There was a second blur, and the bandit cried out and stumbled backward, dropping his knife to clutch at the stump of his wrist. Jael stared dumbly down at the blood on her sword blade. Then she took a deep breath and struck deliberately, nearly severing the bandit's head as her blade slid effortlessly through the meat of his throat. The bandit dropped to his knees and then collapsed, his choked gurgling tapering to silence even as he fell.

Immediately Jael pivoted, half-expecting to find one of her opponent's compatriots ready to sink a knife into her back, but there was no one. Quickly Jael wiped her blade on the grass, then dragged the two packs over to where the horses, now agitated by the noise and the smell of blood, paced restlessly. There were still the other packs under the wagon, and the saddles, too, but Jael was no longer concerned about them. More importantly, where was Tanis?

Jael paused only long enough to pick up the dead bandit's knives—a disagreeable chore, as one was still clutched in the severed hand. But unlike her Kresh dagger, these were knives she could throw and then abandon if need be.

It was amazing to realize that only moments had passed, that guards and merchants and bandits were still fighting. Jael ducked under the wagon and nearly collided with Tanis, who was diving for the same shelter but from the other side. The left sleeve of his tunic was stained with blood, and his sword was still bloody, too.

"There you are!" he panted. "I've been looking everywhere. Can you carry most of these? The arm's not too bad, I don't think, but I can't grip well. Come on, hurry before someone sees us here."

Jael loaded her arms, praying she wouldn't need to use her sword again, and Tanis managed to tuck both saddles under his good arm. Jael had to guide Tanis through the darkness to the horses, unhappily aware of how much noise they were making, stumbling through the grass. Tanis nearly tripped over the corpse of the bandit Jael had slain.

"Keep watch while I take care of the horses," Jael told Tanis. "There's got to be a few bandits staying outside, making sure no one gets away."

Jael saddled the horses and loaded the pack horse as quickly as she could, but even as she drew the last strap tight on Tanis's saddle, she heard footsteps and hoarse breathing quickly approaching, even before Tanis gave a warning shout.

"Get on your horse," Jael said grimly, thrusting the reins into Tanis's good hand. "I'll give you a hand up."

"I'm not leaving you," Tanis began, but Jael interrupted him.

"You don't have to. I can run and jump into the saddle. Just get up, will you?"

Tanis awkwardly pulled himself into the saddle with considerable help from Jael. As soon as Jael was sure Tanis would not fall off, she slapped his horse into motion. At the same moment, a merchant stumbled out of the circle of the wagons and collapsed, a dagger protruding from his back. Two bandits followed, ignoring the fallen merchant as soon as they saw Jael.

Jael seized the reins of her horse and the pack horse and urged them to a trot. Hearing the footsteps now close behind her, she grasped the horse's mane tightly and jumped—

Jael's toe caught in a knotted clump of weeds, and the horse's mane tore free of her fingers. Jael fell heavily, the breath driven out of her lungs, but worse was the sound of two sets of running feet behind her while her horse's hoofbeats faded into the night.

Reflexively Jael rolled, and that reflex saved her life. A dagger thunked solidly into the ground where Jael had been. Jael swiftly grasped the dagger and threw it—Gods bless Aunt Shadow and her patient lessons—and heard an answering cry, although she could not tell whether it was a cry of pain or of fear at a near miss.

Almost simultaneously she rolled again, freeing her scabbard so she could draw her sword as she scrambled to her feet. The weapon leaped to her hand, familiar there like an extension of her arm. She let it guide her around, her entire body following the motion of the sword. The blade flashed in the moonlight, and Jael felt it ring against metal before she saw the bandit's sword. Her opponent's sword shivered, but held, and Jael strained her ears, listening for the second bandit.

What she heard instead was hoofbeats approaching, and Jael's heart leaped in recognition of the voice calling her name. Tanis!

Once more Jael's sword flashed as if of its own volition, and Jael followed the stroke through, the blade dancing fiery patterns in what little moonlight shone through the breaks in the clouds. The bandit's sword rang against hers again, but this time his steel was no match for the strange metal of Jael's blade and snapped off at the point of impact. Jael whirled and slashed blindly, not caring much where—or even whether—she hit, running to meet Tanis.

Tanis leaned down from the saddle, his good hand extended. Jael reached up to clasp his hand solidly, her foot making it to the stirrup this time. Carefully holding her sword clear, Jael threw her leg over the horse's rump and settled herself behind Tanis, releasing his hand to clasp her arm firmly around his waist. There was no time to sheathe her sword; Jael could only keep her seat and hold on grimly, every moment expecting to feel a dagger thunk into her back. As the seconds passed, Jael slowly realized that they were away, that there was no mounted pursuit, and she sobbed with relief into the back of Tanis's tunic.

"Can you stop?" she asked at last when she had enough breath. "I need to clean my sword and sheathe it."

"I don't want to stop," Tanis called back. "I've got to catch the other horses, and I can hardly see as it is."

"Then stop and let's switch," Jael told him. "There's plenty of light for me, and I can feel the horses ahead of us, too."

Reluctantly Tanis reined in his horse.

"Do you hear anyone coming?" he asked worriedly.

Jael listened carefully. Far behind them, she could still hear cries, and she could see a glow of fire—at least one of the wagons was burning. The fine drizzle of rain had started again.

"No," she said at last. "I think we killed all the bandits who noticed us leaving. I don't hear anyone coming. Don't bother getting down; if you scoot back, I can climb back up in front. It was hard enough getting you up here the first time."

Jael noticed uneasily that Tanis's forearm was still bleeding heavily. When she slid off the horse, she wiped and sheathed her sword, then yanked off her cloak, tunic, and shirt before Tanis's astonished eyes. Shivering, she pulled her tunic back over her head, donned her cloak, drew her dagger, and cut ruthlessly through her shirt. When she climbed back onto the horse in front of Tanis, she pulled his arm around her side and in front of her where she could cut away his sleeve. The long slash down the top of his forearm looked deep, but there was no time to stitch it now, not if they wanted to catch the horses. Jael had to settle for wrapping his forearm as tightly as she could before they continued.

The horses, confused and frightened, had bolted straight north, but as their panic faded, they had gradually turned back toward the camp and Jael. As soon as Jael could see them, she whistled, the cheerful, coaxing whistle she used to call them to the fence when she had a treat for them. The horses turned toward her with gratifying eagerness, and when Jael was close enough, she easily collected the reins.

"Don't worry, you'll get your treat," Jael laughed as the horses snuffled at her hands, "but it'll have to wait until I can get into the saddlebags. Tanis, can you ride alone? We'll make better time if we don't tire your horse out with the weight of both of us."

"I'm all right," Tanis assured her. "I haven't bled enough to weaken me. I'm depending on you to find someplace where we can find shelter."

Jael's heart fell. Find shelter? Find *safe* shelter? She'd have difficulty enough finding the road again!

"What about the bandits?" Jael asked carefully. "Do you think we should go back to the road?"

"We'd better not head straight back to the road," Tanis agreed after a moment's thought. "If the bandits come back west, they might see us. We're probably a couple miles north of the road now; let's turn straight west, and we can meet back up with the road tomorrow."

West? Gods, which way was west? Jael scanned the sky, but the moon and stars were well hidden behind the clouds. All right, they'd ridden north after the horses, and then a little east, so west must be—yes, that way. Jael pulled two lengths of rope from her saddlebag.

"I'll lead your horse and the pack horse," she offered. "If you can get a little sleep in the saddle, so much the better."

Although they were far from the road, this was open plain, not farmland, and the ground was reasonably firm and level. Despite Jael's keen night vision and the good ground, however, Jael did not press the horses beyond a comfortably slow, steady pace. The gods alone knew how far they'd have to ride in the dark before finding shelter, and the horses did not share her night vision; if one of the horses lamed itself, Jael and Tanis could be in serious trouble.

Tanis drowsed, and Jael led the horses across the wet, grassy plain that seemed to go on forever. Was she still heading west? There was no knowing. There was no tracking their trail back, either, in the tall grass. For all she could tell, they might be heading in a large circle that led right back to the bandits. At last, however, Jael sighted a line of trees and bushes, likely growing at the edge of a stream or small river. At least the foliage would provide enough shelter for them, and perhaps the bushes would be tall enough to hide the horses.

When Jael reached the trees, she found that they bordered a good-sized stream, rather swollen with the spring rains but still well below its banks. A little exploration revealed a promisingly thick clump of bushes, large enough to hide the horses and allow them to forage, and a thicket where Jael could make a passable shelter from the rain.

Tanis was delighted with the discovery, and insisted on helping Jael arrange their cloaks as a ground cloth and stretch their oiled tent hide over the bushes. As soon as the camp was arranged, however, Jael insisted on lighting one of their lanterns and tending his injury. The cut was not as deep as Jael had feared, but Tanis made so much fuss while she cleaned and carefully stitched it that Jael would have thought the wound mortal.

"Sit still," Jael said irritably when Tanis jerked his arm for the tenth time. "You didn't give the healers this much trouble when that demon almost took your arm off."

"They gave me a potion and put something on the scratches for pain, too," Tanis retorted. "Can't you make larger stitches and less of them?"

"Not unless you want a lovely big scar to show the ladies in the brothels and a crippled hand to ruin your career as a thief," Jael snapped. "I'm sorry I'm not a healer with a hundred potions in my bag for every possible ailment. You're lucky the knife wasn't poisoned, or you'd be dead now. How did you get this cut, anyway?"

Tanis was silent for a long moment, and Jael looked up to see a very sheepish expression on his face.

"What?" Jael demanded. "You didn't stop to tumble one of the merchants' whores, did you?"

"No, but—" Tanis reached into the front of his tunic and pulled out a heavy pouch. "I did grab a few of these."

"I was fighting for my life, and you stopped to cut purse strings?" Jael asked indignantly. "Who did you rob, the brigands or the merchants?"

"A bit of both," Tanis admitted, grinning embarrassedly. "I got trapped at the other end of the camp when the brigands attacked—my warning gave the guards time to wake everyone there—so I had to fight my way out of an awful tangle of robbers and merchants and guards. There were people lying on the ground dead by the time I got through to the clearing in the middle, their purses just hanging there and fairly begging me to take them, so how could I resist? But while I was taking a dead brigand's purse, one of his friends managed to creep up behind me, and I'm lucky I took his knife in my arm instead of my back." He reached into his tunic again and dropped five more purses, one at a time, on his lap.

"I can't fathom why you'd be fool enough to bother over purses," Jael said, scowling, although she was inwardly awed by the pile of money in Tanis's lap. "Mother and Father gave us plenty of money. That was nothing but greed."

"Well, I'm a thief now," Tanis said, shrugging a little uncomfortably. "Greed's part of my profession. Besides, I didn't know but we'd have to abandon some or all of our gear to get away quickly. I thought the extra money would help us replace our things in Westenvale, if we needed to." He grinned engagingly. "Besides, it's the best haul I've ever made."

Jael sighed as she knotted the last stitch and cut the sinew off cleanly with her dagger.

"Well, you paid dear for it," she said, shaking her head. "And we may yet have to spend some of that coin on a healer when we reach Westenvale if the muscle draws up." She clasped his hand. "Squeeze my fingers if you can."

Tanis complied, although he grimaced with pain as he tightened his fingers.

"Well, that's good," Jael said relievedly. "I'll have to change the bandages often in this wet weather or it'll fester, but the wound's clean enough. It'll probably heal all right. Tomorrow morning I'll pack one of those pouches with small pebbles, and you should squeeze it often while the cut heals, and bend your wrist all around, too."

Jael glanced around their small shelter and slowly tucked the needle, sinew, bandages, and salve back into her pack, not meeting Tanis's eyes.

"There's not much room here," she said slowly. "Is it all right if—"

Tanis laid his good hand over hers, and when Jael looked up, his smile was warm.

"I'm sorry I left you alone," he said humbly. "I acted like a brain-blighted idiot. I promised you I'd be patient and I wasn't, and that makes me a scoundrel as well as a fool. It was just that Baaros-cursed merchant right over our heads—"

"I know." Jael sighed and squeezed Tanis's hand. "I'm sorry, too. I shouldn't have complained about staying with the horses and being ready to leave in a hurry. You were right to be careful. I'll listen from now on." She hesitated. "You know nobody wishes more than me that—well, that things were different."

"I know." Tanis sighed, then half-smiled apologetically. "Have I abused our friendship too much, or can we still share the blankets?"

"We pretty much have to," Jael admitted. "Some of them got muddy when I had to drop them on the ground to fight."

Tanis laughed and reached out to hug Jael.

"Best apology speech I ever made," he chuckled, "and it was all unnecessary because of wet blankets. Come on, friend, and let's keep warm, and let the rain pour down all night if it likes."

IV

• Jael drew her horse to a halt, staring at the front gate of Westenvale and sighing disappointedly.

"I thought it would be larger," she said.

Tanis pulled his horse to a stop beside hers.

"What are you complaining about?" he asked her. "It's almost as large as Allanmere. It's large enough to have merchant caravans heading west from it, and some comfortable inns, so what else do you need?"

"I don't know." Jael shrugged. "It's just the first city I've ever seen besides Allanmere. I suppose I was expecting—"

"Gates of solid gold and paving stones of silver?" Tanis teased gently. "Nobles standing on the wall and flinging jewels to the crowds below?"

"All right, all right," Jael said embarrassedly. "I can't help it if you've been to dozens and dozens of cities and I've never been farther than the Heartwood. At least *I* can hit my mark with a bow."

"What good does hitting your mark do, if you can't point your bow at anything we can eat?" Tanis asked practically.

Jael sighed again and did not reply, urging her horse forward toward the gate. Tanis was a wonderful friend, but after nearly a week in his constant company, all she wanted in the world was a hot bath, a fresh meal, and a few hours without hearing the sound of Tanis's voice.

"Name and business," a bored gate guard demanded, and a wrinkled scribe sitting at a table looked up at them, her pen poised expectantly.

"My name is Caden, and my friend is Acorn," Tanis answered. "We've come from Allanmere. We're looking to join a merchant caravan heading west."

The scribe scribbled quickly on her sheet, but the guard squinted suspiciously at Jael and Tanis.

"Two younglings like you, riding alone all the way from Allanmere?" he said dubiously.

"We were with a caravan," Tanis told him. "Nezed was the wagonmaster. But they were set on by brigands, and Acorn and I got away as fast as we could. I don't know what became of the rest of them. I wish we'd have gotten away a little faster." He held up his bandaged arm. "We've been following the sunset since then, avoiding the road until we started seeing farms again."

The guard raised an eyebrow, his bored expression vanishing.

"How many brigands, and where?" he asked, gesturing to the scribe. The ancient woman handed him a rolled sheet, which, when unrolled, turned out to be a large map.

Tanis dismounted and surveyed the map.

"I'd be guessing," he said apologetically. "It was raining pretty heavily a good part of the way, and I couldn't keep good track of the road. But I'd say here." He indicated a spot on the map. "There were at least twelve or fifteen of the brigands, probably more, but I didn't get much of a look at them, either. None of them used bows, but that might have been because they attacked well after dark. Oh, and they may have had a mage working with them," he added. "The caravan's horses had been hinder-spelled, maybe back in Allanmere."

The guard nodded and rolled the map back into a neat cylinder.

"You've been a help," he admitted grudgingly. "When you're in the market, ask for Merchant Karina. She's taking a load of cheeses west, or so I hear, and you can tell her I sent you. My name's Everd. And if you're looking for an inn, the Horn of Plenty's clean and cheap, and you won't get knifed in the night." He raised a hand and lazily waved them through the gate.

The road was muddy from the recent rains and thick with dung, so Tanis mounted his horse again and rode at Jael's side.

"Are we going to stay at the Horn of Plenty?" Jael asked him. Tanis grimaced.

"I'd choose not to, but we'd likely best stay there," he said. "If Wagonmaster Nezed's people turn up here, they may be looking for us, thinking we were in league with the brigands. But if that guardsman is suspicious, too, and checks at the Horn, he'll wonder why we didn't take his recommendation. Maybe we'll be lucky and it'll be full."

To Tanis's disgust, however, the Horn of Plenty was only half-full, and the innkeeper, a cheerful ex-guardswoman with one leg missing just above the knee, lowered her price for the room to half a Moon when Tanis mentioned Everd's name.

"Supper's at sunset if you're eating here, and that's three coppers," she told them. "Two coppers stabling and food for each horse, and five for a bath with soap and towels."

Jael grimaced at the prices, but Tanis counted out the coins resignedly. The room was plain but clean, as Everd had promised, the bed linens and straw mattress fresh-smelling, and the water in the jug on a table in the room was clear and sweet. Jael sighed contentedly and flopped back on the bed, luxuriating in the softness under her.

"I think I could sleep from this moment until the same time tomorrow," Jael declared.

"Well, you'd best not," Tanis said practically. "We've got to find Merchant Karina and bargain for a place in her caravan, and we've got to buy more supplies. Besides, I want supper, don't you?"

"I'd kill for a hot meat pie and a bowl of dumplings," Jael said wistfully.

"I want to drink a whole skin of the best wine I can buy," Tanis said, sighing. He glanced sideways at Jael. "Why don't we each take some money? You can buy the supplies, and I'll find the merchant, and we can each do as we please for supper."

A moment before, Jael would have rejoiced in spending some time away from Tanis; realizing, however, that she was in a strange city trying to buy supplies for their survival, the prospect suddenly frightened her.

"Don't you think it'd be wise to stay together?" Jael asked hesitantly.

"Oh, I think it's safe enough," Tanis said, rather too quickly. "Just keep your money in your tunic and only take out a few small coins at a time. You know trail supplies as well as I do—maybe better—and you've been through the market in Allanmere hundreds of times. A market's a market, only this one won't be quite as big."

"Well, we could meet back here for supper," Jael suggested. "That still leaves part of the afternoon to run our errands."

"Well—" Tanis hesitated. "I have some errands I want to do, and I—I may not be back till late. Better just do what you like for supper." Unaccountably, he blushed.

Suddenly, seeing the blush, Jael realized why he wanted to be alone, and what sort of errand he had in mind.

"Gods, Tanis, if you want to go brothel-hopping, why didn't you just say so?" Jael said, chuckling. "I'll wager the innkeeper could direct you to a good place where you won't catch whore's-rot. And if the brothel has a healer—I hear some of the good ones do—maybe he'll look at your arm, too."

"Baaros have mercy, Jaellyn, just shut up, will you?" Tanis's face was flaming now. "I don't want to talk about it."

"All right." Jael shrugged. "I'll go to a money changer and get some small coin in exchange for some of the money Mother and Father gave us, and you can take all that money you stole and have a grand tumble with a hundred whores if that's what you want. Just find out about the caravan first, will you, and if you're going to be out all night long, leave me a message." She dug into her pack until she found the pouch Shadow had given her. She pulled out a few small gems and a handful of Suns and tucked them into her sleeve, then stuffed the rest of the pouch into a pocket inside her shirt.

Tanis watched these preparations unhappily, but without comment. At last he stood and left without another word.

Jael waited a little while before leaving, to give Tanis time to talk to the innkeeper if he wanted. After a fair interval, she found the innkeeper herself and asked for and got directions to the market. On the street, however, she found that in Westenvale, as in Allanmere, all she really needed to do was follow her nose.

It was late afternoon, and Westenvale's market was still busy. As Tanis had told her, it was a little smaller than the market in

Allanmere, but the strangeness made it seem larger. Still, as Tanis had said, a market was a market, and Allanmere's market had always been Jael's second home. Here were the same smells, the same noises, the same crowds, even the same urchins and thieves and beggars populating the spaces between stalls and carts. Among all that clutter and clamor, it was possible for Jael to almost ignore the growling belly of a dog searching for scraps in the alley or the pain of a horse as its noble rider dug spurs into its sides.

After several passersby stopped and stared, however, Jael discovered that Westenvale was, in fact, very different from Allanmere in one way. There were elves in the market, both buying and selling, although not as many as might be seen in Allanmere, but these were not the familiar elves of the Heartwood, laughing and arguing and no two alike. These were elves from the eastern elvan cities, every one of them tall, slender and pale, graceful as swans on a lake, their conversation punctuated by flowing gestures so elaborate that the elves seemed to move in a never-ceasing dance. A few of them paused to gaze at Jael with gently surprised curiosity.

Jael changed her Suns and gems at four different money changers' shops for Moons and coppers. After that the market was hers, and she roamed among the shops and stalls nibbling blissfully on a too-hot meat pie, buying some sweets here, a dried-berry tart there, all the while watching the haggling at the stalls where journey food was sold. When she had a fair idea of who sold good-quality merchandise and what she could expect to pay for it, she made her purchases. She would rather have bought the food later than make an extra trip back to the inn to stow the food, but what if they had to leave soon? Better an extra walk now than an empty belly on the road.

After Jael had deposited the sacks of supplies in her room, however, it was suppertime, and she decided reluctantly that it was easier to sup at the inn than make another trip back to the market. Besides, she wanted her bath.

Because of the poor soil and vast plains surrounding Westenvale and the whimsical drought-or-flood weather, many farmers preferred to herd livestock for meat or milk instead of depending on uncertain grain or vegetable crops. Consequently, meat was cheap and good, and even simple inns like the Horn of Plenty could serve all the rich roast spring lamb its patrons could eat for a three-copper supper. Jael stuffed herself to drowsy repletion and then ordered her bath.

Unlike Allanmere, Westenvale had no magically drilled taps to subterranean hot springs, and bathing water had to be laboriously heated in the kitchen; that, of course, was why a bath in an inn in Westenvale cost five times what it would in Allanmere. To Jael's surprise and dismay, however, the price of the bath included the services of a bathboy to scrub her back and rinse Jael's soapy body with fresh water. When Jael stepped out of the tub and thanked him, however, the bathboy hesitated.

"Will there be"—the young man's eyes swept over Jael's towel-wrapped body—"anything else?"

"Huh? Oh! Uh—no, no, thank you," Jael said hurriedly, scrabbling for her purse to press a few coppers into his hand. "Just empty the tub and take it away."

When the bathboy was gone, Jael latched the door and curled up on the bed, luxuriating in its softness and the cleanliness of her skin. Despite the noise from outside and the strange surroundings, she was soon asleep; it seemed only a few moments later, however, when she was roused by Tanis calling through the door. When Jael raised the latch, Tanis stumbled in, smelling strongly of wine, perfume, and musky incense. He mumbled something incoherent. Jael, still half-asleep herself, only caught the word "tomorrow" before Tanis sagged limply onto the bed. Jael shook her head, irritated, and pulled Tanis's boots and tunic off before she crawled back under the covers. Whatever it was, it could wait.

"Jaellyn. Wake up."

Jael bolted upright, and Tanis winced, shading his eyes from the morning sunlight.

"What is it?" Jael mumbled, trying to shake the sleep-fog from her head.

"Get dressed. We've got to go." Tanis's face was gray and his eyes were shot heavily with red, but he stepped away rather gingerly and reached for his clothes.

"Huh?" Jael rubbed her eyes. "What do you mean?"

"The caravan." Tanis peered out the window and winced again. "It leaves this morning. I've already paid for us to join it."

Jael poured herself a goblet of water, glanced into the goblet, and poured the water over her head instead of drinking it.

"Why didn't you tell me that last night?" she said annoyedly. "You could've left a message."

"I'm sorry." Tanis also poured water into a goblet, but settled for splashing his face. "In case you didn't notice last night, I was drunk. I don't even remember coming back here."

"I suppose you won't have time for your bath, then," Jael said, sighing. "And you need it worse than I did."

"Sorry. Believe me, I'd much rather lie in bed for another half-day and soak in a bath for hours more." Tanis tied the top of his pack and slung it over his shoulder. "Come on, let's get the horses loaded. There won't be another caravan traveling west for days. It's a good thing you got the food last night."

Jael was tempted to make a retort about the relative value of his and her evening's activities, but seeing Tanis's pasty face and shaking hands, she decided that a little mercy wouldn't be wasted on her friend. Instead, she quickly pulled a potion out of her kit, poured a few drops into a goblet of water, and offered it to Tanis.

"Try that," she said. "Father makes it for my rainy-season headaches, but Aunt Shadow says it's good for bad mornings, too."

Tanis gulped down the water without replying, but by the time they had carried their belongings down to the stable and loaded the horses, he was already less pale and no longer winced every time Jael spoke too loudly. Just as well, for they rode out of the inn directly into the morning going-to-market crowd, and only their height on horseback kept them from being swallowed in the press of peasants and nobles hurrying to buy and farmers and craftsmen hurrying to sell.

It would have been quicker to ride back through the city gates and around to the west side, but there was no question of trying to fight the inexorable tide of bodies pushing toward the market. They were forced to ride amidst the crush of people, carefully keeping the pack horse between them so that nobody could cut its reins or rob the packs, and Jael was already weary by the time they made their way to the west gate of the city, where the caravan was almost ready to depart. Jael was relieved to see that the train of wagons fairly bristled with well-armed guards; obviously there were more valuables on this caravan than simply cheeses!

"There you are." A tall, stout woman dressed in riding clothes, apparently Merchant Karina herself, came to greet them. "Thought you'd fallen in love with Westenvale and decided to forego traveling with me and my cheeses. Tie your horses at the back and ride with me if you like. I've cut a wheel of my best, and I'll gladly make you sick of it while I pry out everything you can tell me about every cheese seller who works the market in Allanmere."

Jael glanced at Tanis, and to her delight this time he nodded. The two quickly tied their horses behind the wagon.

"Everd says you're the ones gave warning about the bandits on the road from Allanmere," Karina continued, walking along the other wagons and nodding to the drivers. "That warning gave me time to hire a few more guards. Hopefully we'll make Gerriden with our goods and hides intact. Sparing your bottoms from the saddle's the least I can do. I've hired a fair cook, too, so we won't starve. Guess you can tell from looking that I'm one to expect a goodly meal. Well, the others look to be ready if you are, Durgan," Karina added to a tall, dark-skinned young guard standing beside the horses hitched to the lead wagon.

"Almost ready, Mistress Karina," Durgan said, smiling and half-bowing. He raised his eyebrows as he saw Jael and Tanis. "Cesanne is checking the horses for the last time. Is this lovely young lady and her friend to be a part of our company?"

"This is Caden, a merchant's son, making his way west from Allanmere," Karina said, "and Acorn, one of Allanmere's forest elves. Caden, Acorn, this is Durgan, my guard captain and wagonmaster."

"I am delighted to meet you," Durgan said, taking Jael's hand and bowing over it.

Jael almost snatched her hand away as she felt a familiar tingle at his touch. Gods, he was wearing some kind of magic—maybe something as simple as a trap-spell on his purse or a water-repellant spell on his clothing—and the gods grant she hadn't just ruined it!

Durgan released Jael's hand and turned toward the horses. "Cesanne, come and meet our new friends. Caden, Acorn, I present my sister Cesanne."

An extraordinarily beautiful woman, as dark of skin as Durgan but her hair golden as the sun, stepped out from behind the horses. She was as slender as Durgan, but not as tall, and her radiant green eyes slanted exotically like his dark brown ones.

Like Durgan, she was dressed in butter-supple riding leathers, a sword at her hip and a bow at her back.

"My lady." Before Jael could say a word, Tanis had stepped forward and bowed over Cesanne's hand. When he straightened, Cesanne smiled slowly, and her fingers lingered on his for just a moment longer than necessary. Jael sighed to herself.

"Well, then, let's be gone," Karina said with just a hint of impatience. "Gerriden's not getting any closer while we stand."

Jael quickly found that traveling by wagon also had its disadvantages. The trade road was in poor condition after winter and the recent rains, and the wagon jolted as the horses did not. Merchant Karina was cheerful and hospitable, but her incessant conversation proved as annoying as the constant bouncing of the wagon seat. Jael munched on the proffered cheese—it *was* really excellent cheese—and let Tanis and Karina talk about the market as much as they liked while she watched the countryside roll slowly by like the Brightwater River on a lazy afternoon.

This was how Aunt Shadow saw the world, sitting on a jolting wagon seat while some merchant lord droned on unendingly about how his last shipment of goods had gotten damaged on its way to market and how the price of hiring additional guards to dissuade highwaymen had driven up prices. Somehow Jael had never thought about that; she'd pictured Shadow lying on soft cushions in some handsome lord's arms at night, sipping expensive wines and nibbling sweets from the farthest cities, not sweating in the noon sun on a hard wagon seat while she bounced up and down. But then Jael had never thought much about highwaymen and cold, rainy nights, either.

Occasionally Durgan or Cesanne would drop back and ride beside Karina's wagon. Cesanne often smiled at Tanis, a slow, sweet smile, and then Tanis's conversation with Karina would falter and die. Jael chuckled to herself.

Near sunset Durgan brought his horse up beside their wagon, and Cesanne followed.

"Some of us will scout the road ahead and do a bit of hunting for our supper before the wagons frighten away the game," Durgan said. "Would you wish to join us?"

"Acorn doesn't hunt," Tanis said before Jael could answer. "But I'd be glad to join you."

"Yes, do come and hunt with us," Cesanne said, speaking for the first time. Her voice was low and silken, like honey. "There are wild deer with long horns that run these plains, fleet as the wind. It's been said that if you find such a deer with a perfect white coat and kill it, and if you eat its heart, then under the moon you can take its form and run like the wind over the tops of the grass." She reached out and took Durgan's hand, sliding her fingers caressingly over his own.

"Now, that's a horrible tale," Karina said, scowling. "Sounds like the curse of the shifters to me. Ride along, then, young Caden, if that's your wish, but don't be eating the hearts of any white deer, thank you very kindly, and changing into any uncanny thing while you ride with me!"

She stopped the wagon, and Tanis quickly ran around to the back. When he reappeared on his horse, Jael saw that he had removed the saddlebags, and she wondered whether he had loaded them on one of the other horses or thrown them in the back of Karina's wagon. Tanis had unpacked his bow also, and Jael wondered amusedly whether he would try to use it, likely to his humiliation.

Tanis gave Jael a rather abashed look, but rode off after Cesanne and Durgan. Jael sipped from her waterskin and picked up another piece of cheese from the basket Karina had laid at their feet, munching thoughtfully.

"Have you known Durgan and Cesanne long?" Jael asked at last.

Karina shook her head.

"No. They've come recently from the far west, or so Durgan says. But they were well recommended by Lord Tedrin, who brought a load of spices from Gerriden. They got his caravan through safe even though a couple of guards deserted in mid-journey, just disappeared in the night. Not a pinch of his shipment lost, and some of those spices were worth Suns for a featherweight."

"Do you think—" Jael stared after the riders. "Durgan and Cesanne, do you think they're a couple?"

"They're brother and sister, or so Durgan says, but that sort of thing isn't uncommon in the wild country." Karina shrugged. "I'd say yes but for the come-to-the-bushes-m'lad looks she's been giving Caden." Karina glanced sideways at Jael. "Is she grazing in someone else's pasture?"

Jael shook her head.

"Caden and I are good friends. That's all. If he wants to tum-

ble every female between here and the edge of the world, I wish
him a strong back. But Durgan moves like he knows how to use
that sword. I wouldn't want any trouble."

Karina had no reply to that, and to Jael's delight, they rode in
silence until they sighted the camp ahead. A fire was already
burning, and there were not one, but two spiral-horned plains
deer roasting on spits. Apparently Tanis had managed to shoot
one of them, for he strode around the fire to meet them as
proudly as if he had slain a dragon.

"Good hunting," Jael greeted him, sliding down from the
wagon seat. "Which one's yours?"

"That one." Tanis indicated the closer of the two deer, then
grinned sheepishly. "Cesanne drove it practically into my bow. If
I'd missed at that range, I don't think I could have held my head
up under the shame."

Jael was glad to see that Tanis was neither too proud of his kill
nor too smitten with Cesanne to help her set up their camp. They
did not camp under a wagon; after what had happened with the
last caravan, Jael thought it prudent to set their tent a bit apart.
Karina refused to have her cheese unloaded to clear space to
sleep in any of the wagons, but she used a cunning arrangement
whereby the waxed cloth of her tent fastened to the wagon top
and formed a lean-to against the side of the wagon, comfortably
large enough for her to lay within it the straw and feather mat-
tresses she had brought with her.

By the time the camp was finished, the roasting deer were
seared to juicy perfection. Durgan sent out the guards in short
shifts so each of them had time to eat their fill of the hot, strong-
flavored meat, roasted tubers brought from Westenvale with
Karina's cheese melted over them, and a pot of early spring
greens the cook had managed to gather while the others had set
up the camp. There was wine, too, but Jael had no desire to ruin
a good meal with the sick belly wine always gave her, so she
filled a pot with water and brewed some of the black tea she'd
brought with her.

The rich, aromatic flavor of the tea, although it had come from
Calidwyn, not Allanmere, reminded Jael of home. Mother, Father, and the twins would be at supper now, too, possibly wondering how Jael was faring.

Tanis was almost embarrassingly attentive to Cesanne over
supper, jumping up to cut her a slab of meat or fill her cup of

wine as soon as it was empty. Cesanne rewarded him with the sort of smile Jael had seen Aunt Shadow use to devastating effect on a few occasions. Jael sighed to herself, but said nothing.

Once Jael's eyes met Durgan's over the fire. Durgan glanced at Tanis and Cesanne, then back at Jael, the corners of his lips turning up slightly and his eyes twinkling as if he and Jael shared a private joke. Jael was vastly relieved; at least he wasn't roaring with anger and drawing his sword. But when supper was finished, Durgan stood and took Cesanne's hand, leading her toward their tent, which they had pitched at the far end of the camp.

Tanis, rather disgruntled, finally followed Jael back to their own tent, but there he sat and brooded rather than curling up comfortably with Jael as he usually did.

"Come on, don't be foolish," Jael said at last. "She's only toying with you, like the noblewomen flirt with the young lords. She doesn't mean anything by it."

"Oh, I know that," Tanis said rather crossly. "Look, I'm not going moon-mad over her. She'd be a grand feast of a tumble, that's all. I'm not all *that* interested in her. It's just that—well—"

"Well, what?" Jael prompted, grinning. "You can't plead a long fast, can you, after your games last night almost made us miss the caravan?"

"Oh, please," Tanis groaned. "If you hadn't given me that potion, I think I'd have cut off my own head just to be rid of the ache. Can you just imagine, bouncing around on that wagon seat all morning?"

He chuckled in spite of himself, and Jael joined in.

"Well, there's plenty more of that potion, so if you want to whore yourself sick every time we reach a town, go ahead," Jael said, chuckling. "At least that's safer than a quick night's tumble in the grass with a woman who can use sword and bow, and whose lover is the guard captain of the caravan."

"He's not her lover," Tanis protested.

"I'll wager you five Suns they are," Jael countered. "Want to creep up on their tent and listen?"

"No!" Tanis flushed. "The guards would see us before we got close enough."

"I don't have to be very close," Jael told him. "But it doesn't matter, really, if you're 'not *that* interested,' does it?"

"I suppose not," Tanis said, sighing. "Look, just leave it be, will you please?"

"All right," Jael said, relenting. "Let me look at your arm, and then we'll go to bed."

The long slash was still ugly to look at and painful when touched, but Jael pronounced it to be healing cleanly, and Tanis could move his fingers freely, although he admitted that pulling his bow had made the wound ache ferociously. Jael cleaned and dressed the wound and fetched Tanis a cup of wine, and he was quickly asleep. Jael smiled to herself as she curled up against Tanis's warmth; having such a wound cleaned and probed was enough to take any man's mind off a woman, no matter how fetchingly her breasts might bounce.

The next two days were much the same. The weather stayed fine, and the caravan made good progress. Gradually the endless rolling plains were broken by lone trees, then stands, then small woods. By the third day they were nearing the edge of a large forest. There were no more farms now, although Karina told Jael that they were no more than another three days' travel from Gerriden; Gerriden's farmers had settled farther north and west, where they did not have to clear seedlings and stumps from their land and where the river had deposited rich soil.

On the second day of the trip, Cesanne had made excuses to ride back to Karina's wagon often—she wanted another taste of that cheese, she needed to tell Karina of deep ruts in the road ahead, and perhaps those clouds meant more rain was on the way. Each time she would linger to chat with them, her remarks increasingly directed at Tanis. When she would ride away, Tanis would stare after her, and Jael would stifle a sigh.

By the third day Tanis frequently abandoned his seat on the wagon and rode with Durgan and (more importantly) Cesanne, although he excused himself from the second day's hunting trip, stating truthfully that pulling the bow overtaxed his wounded arm. Jael thought to herself that nothing but pure luck had let hm make his shot on the first hunt, and Tanis was reluctant to risk ruining the impression he'd made of himself to Cesanne as a great hunter. Still, Tanis did not go out of his way to pursue Cesanne, and Jael was grateful that he showed that much common sense. Soon they'd be in Gerriden, where Tanis could find safer tumbles than with guardswomen with swords and bows and formidable brothers.

By and large, Tanis's absence left Jael the unhappy audience for Karina's unending chatter. Jael tried to guide the conversation into channels somewhat more interesting than cheese, and found that Karina was in fact a wealth of stories garnered from trade cities east to west. To Jael's delight, Karina had heard of the Kresh, though not by that name.

"Ah, the invisible people," Karina answered Jael's query, nodding sagely. "I spoke to a man once who'd seen one, a woman filling a waterskin at a stream. He said she looked at him and vanished before his eyes, leaving no tracks behind her except two footprints in the mud of the riverbank where she'd stood. When I first heard that, I thought he'd swallowed a skinful himself, and not water, either. But a couple years later I met a warrior who'd seen one of their camps—like any camp it was, firepits and trampled grass and flat spots where they'd likely pitched tents. He showed me an arrowhead he'd found there, half hidden in the weeds. It was the oddest metal—pale and light so the arrow had to be weighted with clay rings, I'd wager, and sharp as a fishwife's tongue." She showed Jael a scar on the pad of her thumb. "Cut myself near to the bone just testing the edge. Since that time I've heard tales hereabouts. It wasn't so easy to laugh after I'd seen that arrowhead."

She had heard tales, too, of the Book of Whispering Serpents.

"Duranar the Pale passed through, aye, and bearing such a book, or so it's said," she said. "I've heard it told he rode on the back of a demon horse whose coat shone like gold and whose feet were claws instead of hooves. But he went south and disappeared into the wilderness there. None's heard from him since, not that I've been told. Some say he went south all the way to the sea, but I'd wager he met his end in a shifter's or a dragon's belly long before that, and likely his book moldered into dust."

Jael nodded agreement, but privately she disagreed. Any mage powerful enough to bind demons would come to no such ordinary end.

There was plenty of game near the forest, but the hunting trips became less frequent as Karina would not allow the guards to leave their posts. A forest offered too much cover for highwaymen. Unfortunately, as they neared the forest, the ground dipped and became quite swampy, forcing the group to camp nearer the trees than Karina would have liked. Because of the increased danger, Karina insisted that Jael and Tanis camp near the wagons so that the guards would not have to widen their perimeter.

This time Durgan included himself in the night watches but
not Cesanne, stating that as his sister had more forest experience,
on the morrow she would command the guards and would need
to be fully awake and alert. Jael imagined that Cesanne gave
Tanis a significant look when Durgan said this, and Tanis
blushed and quickly looked away. Jael thought to herself that she
probably had more forest experience than all the guards in the
caravan combined—though doubtless Cesanne had far more experience in finding private, cozy thickets—but there was no point
in saying that to these guards, who would certainly follow one of
their own rather than some half-grown elf; besides, Jael's knowledge of combat certainly did not include group command.

Jael personally found the night noises of the forest familiar
and soothing, but everyone else was nervous and sat around the
fire later than usual; at last there was only Jael, Tanis, and
Cesanne. Jael resignedly excused herself, but was surprised when
Tanis politely said good night to Cesanne and accompanied Jael
back to their tent.

When they reached the tent, however, Tanis reached into one
of the packs and pulled out one of the bottles of Bluebright.

"Have you had any of this since that night more than a year
ago?" he asked, gazing thoughtfully at the syrupy blue liquid inside the bottle. He spoke very softly so that his voice could be
heard only inside the tent.

"Uh-uh. Father doesn't like me to use it." Jael lay back on her
bedroll. "Why? Were you wanting to try it? It won't hurt you.
Mother and Father have both tried it."

"It cures you, doesn't it?" Tanis asked, tilting the bottle and
watching the liquid roll slowly. "Makes your soul whole for a
while, right?"

"Something like that." Jael shrugged. "Father says some potions can temporarily create a sort of balance inside, like the elvan dreaming potion. I don't know if it actually does anything to
my soul, or just makes my soul *think* there's nothing wrong. I
don't understand how such things work. All I know is when I
drank it, I could shape stone. Not very well, but that's just because I hadn't had practice. But at least I could do it."

"Did it cure your other problems, too?" Tanis asked her. "So
that you could use your beast-speaking, for example?"

"I don't know." Jael shrugged again. "We never had a chance
to test that. As I said, Father doesn't like me using it. After the

demon was killed, Father took all the Bluebright and kept it. He and Mother have tried it a few times, and he's tried to learn how it's made, but he's never let me have any of it back until I started packing supplies for this journey."

"When you drank it with Urien," Tanis asked slowly, looking at the Bluebright instead of Jael, "did it make you want him?"

"Gods." Jael sighed. "Tanis, is that still itching under your skin? I swear, Urien and I never did *anything*, even when I was silly drunk on Bluebright." The memory of that night made Jael flush with embarrassment; she *had* gotten pretty silly, Urien feeding her tidbits and whispering compliments while she simpered and giggled like a fool. And they "never did anything" not out of any fortitude of Jael's, but likely because Urien had no intention of risking his greater plan.

"But you could have, couldn't you?" Tanis asked deliberately. "When you drank the Bluebright, you could have if you'd wanted to. And you could want to, too, couldn't you?"

Startled by something in Tanis's voice, Jael peered at him through the darkness. His face was turned away from her, but his fingers clutched the bottle so tightly, like a shield—or a weapon.

"What are you saying?" Jael asked slowly. "Are you wanting me to take a potion to make me want you?"

"It's not the same," Tanis muttered. "It's not like a love potion or something. If all this stuff does is make you whole, and then you want me, what's wrong with that?"

Jael sat up.

"Tanis, at the risk of making you more jealous than you already are, when I drank some of that Bluebright I wanted Urien, too. For all I know the stuff *is* a love potion of some sort. Either that or—" Or she'd been an awfully easy mark, as Aunt Shadow would say. It was embarrassing to think she could be that undiscriminating, or that stupid, either.

Tanis might have followed the rest of her thought, but he kindly said nothing. He sat silently, holding the Bluebright and gazing at Jael in the darkness. At last he tucked the bottle back into the pack.

"Forget I asked," he said rather remotely. "It was a bad idea." He lay down, turning his back to Jael.

Jael flopped back on her bedroll, sighing. *Now* what should she do? What could she say? She couldn't tell Tanis the real reason she'd been reluctant to use the Bluebright. What if, even

with her soul whole, she still didn't desire Tanis? What would he
do if he learned that he'd stood by her all this time for nothing?
But, gods, was she being fair to him? Didn't he deserve to
know—and didn't she deserve to know, too?

But what if he learned she didn't want him and decided to
leave her? Much though Jael might admire Aunt Shadow, Jael
herself was no such wily traveler; she might as well turn back for
Allanmere and hope she could make it even that far alive. But at
this rate, with Tanis getting so upset, maybe he'd just leave her
anyway.

He'd promised to be patient, knowing Jael couldn't give him
any promises in return. He'd *promised*. But he could promise to
stop the sun rising, too; that didn't mean he could necessarily do
it. Gods, what harm could there be in one night's illusion, even
if it was nothing more than that, even if it dissolved like dew in
the sun's light?

Jael hesitated, looking from the pack to Tanis's back. In that
moment of hesitation, Tanis sighed, sat up again, and crawled out
of the tent without a word.

Jael sat up, too, listening. Maybe he'd just gone to use the
privy pit. Maybe—

Tanis's voice, low. The crackling of the fire. Cesanne's voice,
soft and rich. Then footsteps and laughter.

Then silence.

Jael turned over, pulling Tanis's blankets and her own over
her. All right, this wasn't quite the same as a tumble with some
whore in a brothel. But Tanis was sensible, practical—usually
more practical than Jael herself. He knew better than to let a
strange woman on the road become too important to him, even
if she was tall and well favored and so very, very *whole*. This
changed nothing.

Jael pulled her head farther under the covers and shivered.
There was, of course, nothing to worry about. But fear was a bitter taste in her mouth, like tears.


Green. Green.

Jael's spirits lifted as they moved through the forest, although
this was not the Heartwood she knew so well. Many of the animal sounds were different, and different plants lined the edge of
the trade road, different leaves arched over the wagons, but the
warm, rich spring smell of damp earth and growing plants was

the same, and the filtered afternoon sunlight trickling through the leaves made familiar emerald-stained patterns on the ground. Jael pulled the packs and saddle from her horse and rode beside the wagons, singing elvan ditties for Karina's entertainment.

Tanis had ridden ahead with Durgan and Cesanne to try to find a suitable campsite. He'd ridden with them all day. That fact, and the fact that he'd hardly said a word to Jael as they'd loaded their horses that morning, was all that marred Jael's joy at being in the forest again—any forest at all.

Jael's singing faltered as she thought of Tanis. Karina sighed. "That was lovely," she said. "Sing another."

Jael grimaced, but obediently began "New Leaves." She'd barely finished the first verse, however, when searing pain speared through her, choking off her voice. Jael reeled on her horse's back, barely clinging to the mane to keep her seat. The piercing agony continued only a moment longer, gradually fading, but it was some time before Jael was once more aware of her surroundings. She gasped for breath, realizing that the caravan had come to a halt and that Karina was standing beside her, steadying Jael on her horse and peering at her with a concerned scowl.

"Are you well, youngling?" Karina asked worriedly. "You didn't get a bellyache from my cheese, did you? Zanafar help me, I inspected every single cheese in this shipment myself. We don't have a healer in the train, but if—"

Jael rested her forehead on the back of her hands, still gripping the horse's mane tightly, and breathed in the comforting scent of the horse: dirt and hair and sweat.

"I'm all right," she said. It was true; she was well enough now. "I'm sorry I frightened you. I take these fits sometimes." She couldn't tell Karina the true reason for her "fits"; most folk had never heard of beast-speaking, and such an ability would make Jael very memorable indeed. And Karina spoke very freely to anybody who would listen.

"Well, if you choose to take another," Karina said, disgruntled, "best take it in the wagon, else you'll split your skull."

Jael managed a weak grin as the portly woman returned to her wagon and waved the other drivers to continue. Jael wiped the sweat from her forehead and sat up. Somewhere nearby Tanis and his friends had made a kill—a doe, even though it was springtime and no self-respecting hunter would take a doe in spring. And Tanis knew very well what making a kill so near Jael would do to her.

Once more the caravan found their campsite prepared, the doe roasting over the firepit. At least the carcass was fairly plump; Jael hoped that meant there'd be no starving fawns left behind. Durgan was clearing the last bit of brush from around the firepit; Tanis and Cesanne had brought buckets of water from a stream Jael could hear nearby and now were stripping the branches from saplings to use for tent poles, chatting amiably as they worked.

Jael slid down from her horse's back, but when she stepped toward the pack horse, Karina shook her head.

"Sit," Karina commanded sternly. She glanced around, then pointed to a fallen log. "There! Sit!"

Jael sat meekly.

"You!" At Karina's shout, Tanis and Cesanne both looked up, startled. "Caden, or whatever your name is. Come here."

Tanis hurried over.

"Merchant—"

"Get your horses and your gear and your friend and take care of them," Karina said implacably. "Hear me? And next time it's wise to tell a merchant that your friend takes fits. Some folk hereabouts would've thought her bespelled."

Tanis's eyes widened and he glanced at Jael, then hurried forward to take the horses.

"I'm sorry," he murmured to Jael as he passed her. "I didn't think." He selected a site for their tent near Karina's wagon and quickly arranged their small shelter, waving aside Jael's offer of help.

"Maybe you'd like some more tea," Tanis suggested awkwardly when he was finished. "I'll put the pot of water on for you."

"I'm all right," Jael said embarrassedly. "It was just—well, you know. It was only a moment or two."

"We got off the road," Tanis said apologetically. "To be honest, I didn't realize we were so close to you. I suppose I wasn't paying attention."

Jael shrugged.

"No harm to me," she said with a sigh. "I just wasn't expecting it. It wasn't usually this bad when I was younger."

Tanis held out his hand.

"Can you eat some supper, even though—"

"I'd have starved by now if I couldn't," Jael said wryly, accepting Tanis's hand and his apology at the same time.

The venison was tough but good, and chewing on the stringy meat gave Jael something to do besides watching Tanis and Cesanne; she didn't want Tanis to know that she was worried. At first Tanis was attentive to Jael, as if in atonement, but before supper was over he had once again devoted all of his attention to Cesanne. Jael excused herself as soon as she was finished eating, not surprised when Tanis remained at the fire.

It was far too early for sleep, and Jael had no desire to lie in their small tent listening to Tanis and Cesanne at the fire again, so she strolled around the perimeter of the campsite. The sounds and scents of the forest were so sweet and familiar that Jael could not resist a visit to the stream; the moon was out and there would be enough light for her to have a quick bath.

Karina's guards were reluctant to let Jael wander off to the stream by herself, but she insisted, and as the stream was no more than a few dozen paces from the camp, the guards on watch would certainly hear her if she cried out. In the end Jael had her way, although the guards made Jael take her sword and dagger, and she delightedly picked her way through the brush to the streambed, carrying her spare clothes and a jar of soft soap.

The water was cold still, but it ran over rocks and sand and so was clean and sweet. Despite the chill of the water, it was wonderful to scrub off the dirt and sweat and horse-smell of the last few days. Bathing in the cold stream in the moonlight reminded Jael poignantly of her summers in the Heartwood with Mist, and for the first time she felt something like homesickness. She pulled handfuls of wild mint from the plants growing thickly on both banks; she'd tie the sprigs into a cloth and roll them up with her soiled clothes so her packs wouldn't become smelly.

A slight rustling sound in the bushes sent Jael diving for her sword; when it proved to be only Durgan, however, who stepped into view, Jael slowly lowered the point of her blade.

"Oh, pardon me," Durgan said quickly, averting his eyes. "When Elster told me you'd left camp, I lectured him sternly for letting you go off alone. It's just not safe. I had no idea you were—well, already undressed."

"That's all right," Jael said, slowly relaxing. "I just wanted to scrub off some of the grime. You startled me, that's all."

Durgan still did not look directly at her, but he smiled.

"I've never been to Allanmere, and I don't know your people's customs," he said. "But if I stand guard while you finish your bath, would you do me the courtesy of returning the favor?"

"All right," Jael said after a moment's thought. The slightest cry would bring the other guards, after all. She almost wanted to laugh at Durgan's care in averting his eyes—what a fuss people make over seeing a little skin! "Let me rinse off and then I'll take watch."

Durgan took a perch atop a tall, mossy boulder on the bank of the stream where he'd have a clear view of the area around them. Jael sat down in the cold water to rinse the last of the soap out of her hair. She had no clean cloth left to use as a towel, but the night was a little too cool for sitting in the moonlight naked to dry, so she pulled her clothes on over her wet skin.

As soon as Durgan abandoned his perch, Jael scrambled up with some difficulty onto the high rock where Durgan had sat, her sword across her knees. In deference to human custom, Jael looked politely away, but she sneaked a glance over her shoulder when the amount of splashing indicated that Durgan probably wouldn't notice. Durgan was tall and well-muscled, with an absolutely amazing quantity of black hair curling over his skin. Jael smiled to herself, wondering if under other circumstances the very sight of such a fellow bare in the moonlight would stir her loins and make her act as silly as Tanis was acting. At the moment she could admire Durgan in the same way she might admire a sleek wolf—as one of nature's more marvelous and handsome creatures. Jael quickly turned away again before Durgan saw her looking and became embarrassed, or worse, misinterpreted her interest. Only a moment later, however, Durgan's voice startled her.

"Lady Acorn, might I beg some of the soap I see you brought?"

"Oh, of course," Jael said. She hurriedly pulled the pot back out of the bundle of her soiled clothes; no sense offending Durgan with the smell of *those*, even if his nose wasn't as keen as hers.

Durgan stepped around the rock to take the pot Jael held out. As his hand brushed hers, Jael again felt the same warm tingling she'd experienced when he'd touched her in Westenvale, and Jael was hard put to conceal her surprise. Why, whatever spell he'd had cast, it was on *him*, not his clothing! Suddenly Jael was uneasy; what spell would a man like Durgan have on him? A glamour-spell to charm ladies? He'd made no effort to court *her* attention, nor that of any of the other women in the caravan, not that Jael had seen. Some kind of a protection spell, perhaps? But why hadn't the spell been dissolved when Jael had touched him the first time? True, sometimes magic survived Jael's touch, but *twice*?

Jael thought fast, turning slightly on the rock so she could see Durgan out of the corner of her eye without appearing to gaze directly at him. Even if Durgan had some kind of magic on him, there was no reason to assume a malevolent purpose. But a spell of such a type that Jael's magic-warping effect did not break it— gods, *was* there such a spell? The best mages in Allanmere had failed to find it. That alone was cause for suspicion.

Well, simple enough to test.

"This rock's a little high," Jael said embarrassedly when Durgan had dressed. "Could you give me a hand down?"

"Of course," Durgan said, smiling. "Hand me your bundle, and then you can slide down and I'll catch you."

That made sense; rather reluctantly, Jael handed Durgan her soiled clothes and her sword, wishing she'd belted her scabbard back on before she'd spoken. Now she had no polite excuse to do so. Quickly Jael slid down the rock, Durgan's hands clasping her firmly under the ribs.

This time Jael could not keep the surprise from her face at the strength of the tingling wave that swept through her at Durgan's touch. No, this was no ordinary spell to be broken by Jael's touch; it was more as if Durgan himself *was* magical, and Jael had heard stories of magical creatures in human form—

Durgan must have seen the involuntary expression of surprise on Jael's face, for his eyes widened slightly. Jael had no more warning than that; before she could act, his right hand clamped firmly over her mouth, his left hand pinioning her right wrist and his body holding her against the rock.

"My regrets, Lady Acorn," he murmured, his voice growing hoarse and strange as he spoke. His hand seemed to flow over her mouth, covering her nose as well. "My sister was to have provided our meal, not me. But you've forced me to change the plan."

Even as Jael watched, his face was melting like the wax of a candle, re-forming into new and alien contours. Jael froze with terror. Skinshifter! Gods, she'd heard tales enough about the cursed folk who came out of the wild lands and attacked the unwary to feast on human—or elvan—flesh and blood. Even if their victim somehow survived to escape, the merest bite or scratch could carry the dreaded shifter curse. Her mother had been forced to kill her own brother when he'd become infected.

Even as these thoughts raced through Jael's mind, she was clawing with her free left hand at his fingers—now a solid band of flesh—covering her nose and mouth, but to no effect. Durgan watched her struggle with amusement in his eyes, although his nose and mouth were still re-forming, his teeth growing long and sharp in preparation for his feast.

Quickly Jael jammed her fingers into those eyes as hard as she could. Noxious black fluid spurted from the sockets, and Durgan's head rocked back; although he did not cry out—even such a strike wouldn't seriously harm a shifter—his grip over her nose and mouth loosened slightly, and he was blinded until he could form new eyes. Jael was suffocating, though; she'd had no time to draw a quick breath in preparation, and her vision was already dimming.

Desperately Jael twisted her body sideways, using the rock for leverage as she forced her knees up between them. With all her strength she thrust outward with her feet, simultaneously wrenching at Durgan's hand over her face with her own ichor-slimed fingers.

Her small weight and inferior strength were not enough for her to rip loose from Durgan's grip entirely, but she did manage to free her nose and mouth, although Durgan maintained his grip on her right wrist. Some niggling thought at the back of her mind kept Jael from crying out, but in any wise, she was too busy gasping in great sweet lungfuls of air even as her free hand scrabbled across her body for her dagger, pulling it free.

Already new eyes were forming in the black ruin of Durgan's sockets, but there was no more amusement in them. His sharptoothed mouth opened wide, his neck elongating, and his head snaked forward.

Sheer panic surged through Jael. She ripped her Kresh dagger up between them, opening Durgan's body in a diagonal line from hip to shoulder, then with all her strength thrust upward with the tip. It was an awkward angle and she had little leverage, but the amazing sharpness of the Kresh dagger did not fail her; the tip sheared upward through Durgan's chin into his skull, pinning his mouth closed. Entrails gushed out of his belly and blood trickled from the corners of his mouth, and Durgan released her, stumbling backward, but still he did not die—gods, how *did* one kill a shifter?—and his hands clawed blindly at the hilt of Jael's dagger, trying to pull it loose. He stumbled over his own dangling entrails, but even in those moments, the wound in his belly was drawing closed.

Still, Jael was free now, and she quickly found her sword, pulling the light Kresh blade free of its scabbard. Even as she armed herself, however, Durgan pulled the stained dagger free, and, still horribly silent, leaped at her with it.

The sight of her dagger in his hand suddenly struck Jael like a splash of cold water on a sweltering day, washing her fear away as if it had never been and leaving cold anger in its wake. Upstart beast, to hold a blade of her people's making as if he'd earned the right to wield it! She'd show him what a woman of Kresh blood could do with such a blade, and what no pathetic skinshifter ever could—

The silver-white blade caught the moonlight and sliced it into a thousand sparks as Jael gave her anger free rein, the sword moving on its own, pulling her around so she easily sidestepped Durgan's rush, the blade flashing downward in the moonlight to bite solidly through Durgan's spine. Durgan collapsed to the ground, his body all but severed at the waist, although his limbs still twitched and spasmed.

Jael breathed hard, fighting down her anger as she quickly pried her dagger loose from his grip. Was he dead in truth? Well, surely he could not live, or at least attack, without his head! Taking a deep breath, Jael brought the stained blade down on Durgan's neck; there was scarcely a sensation of impact as the head rolled free.

Seizing the head by the hair—no profit in taking chances with skinshifters!—Jael raced back to the camp as quietly as she could, now realizing why she'd kept her silence. If Durgan was a skinshifter, likely so was Cesanne, and if Cesanne had any warning, she'd be close enough to Tanis to attack before anyone could stop her.

When Jael stopped just outside the guard perimeter, however, there was no sign of Cesanne and Tanis by the fire where they'd been when she left. Quickly Jael thrust Durgan's head under a bush, located the nearest guard, and whistled, beckoning him to her.

"Lady Acorn!" The guard stared at her gory appearance. "Are you harmed? Captain Durgan himself went to—"

"Durgan's a skinshifter," Jael whispered urgently, waving her hand to silence the guard when he would have exclaimed. "He's dead now—I think. His head's under that bush. But where's Cesanne and—uh—Caden?"

"They only just went to get a blanket. I think they're going into the woods." The guard's eyes narrowed. "But how do I know you're telling the truth?" He nocked an arrow, drawing his bow on Jael as he spoke.

"If I'm a skinshifter, that won't do you much good," Jael said practically. "Look at that head for your proof. The rest of the body's down by the stream. We'd best burn it to be sure. But first we need to get Caden away from Cesanne before she realizes she's discovered. Hurry, won't you?"

His eyes never leaving Jael, the guard toed the head out from under the bush. He glanced down, then gasped, his bow lowering slowly. The half-formed face was barely recognizable as Durgan's, but apparently it was proof enough.

"I'll send two guards to fetch back the body for burning, and bring two more with me, if you can track your friend in the dark," the guard told her. "Give me but half a moment."

It took longer than that to convince the other guards, suppress their panic, and organize them, so long that Jael was ready to leave without them, even if that meant taking on Cesanne alone. But at last the three guards were ready, having exchanged their bows for more practical swords, and Jael easily picked up Cesanne and Tanis's trail at the edge of the camp. They'd made no effort to hide their tracks—why would they?—and Tanis's poor night vision had made him stumble several times.

They had gone farther from the camp than Jael had, however, likely to avoid any possibility that Jael or the guards might hear them at their sport, and Jael fumed at the noisy, slow pace of the human guards as they did their best to keep up with her. Gods, maybe she'd best leave them to follow—it couldn't be much farther—

Tanis's horrified scream interrupted Jael's thought, and she launched herself as fast as she could toward it; never mind the trail now, or the guards. It was only a few dozen paces more, however, before Jael found the small clearing where Tanis had spread his blanket.

Tanis was there, naked, armed with nothing but a dead branch he'd apparently snatched up, stark terror on his face. He couldn't have gotten to his sword—between him and the bundle of their clothing and weapons squatted Cesanne, or what had been Cesanne.

Gone was the lovely, exotic face and streaming hair. This was a creature from nightmare, its eyes glowing red pits, nose and mouth elongated into a muzzle filled with sharp white teeth. Its ears swept up and back like those of a bat, and the once-lithe body was now bent and gnarled, the limbs re-forming even as they watched.

The sight of the head Jael had produced had somewhat prepared the guards for what they saw, and apparently folk hereabouts were more accustomed to dealing with shifters; they did not freeze in fear as Jael had done, but attacked immediately, surrounding the creature with swords flashing. Jael was desperately glad to leave Cesanne to their attentions and turn to Tanis, who still cowered numbly on the blanket.

"She was—I mean, we were—and she just started changing," Tanis whispered, his eyes glazed. "I threw her away from me— Baaros have mercy, I don't know how I ever did—and I couldn't even scream—I couldn't scream—"

"You did scream," Jael said gently. "Good and loud and long. And you threw her a goodly distance, too, from the looks of it." She folded her arms around him, holding his head on her shoulder so he wouldn't hear Cesanne's last gurgling scream or see the guards finishing their gory work, hacking her head from her body.

Jael had forgotten the stinking slime caked on the front of her tunic. Tanis, still shaking, thrust her away, squinting at her in the moonlight.

"Baaros, you're a mess," he said, his eyes widening. "What happened? Are you all right?"

"Durgan came after me while I was bathing at the stream," Jael told him. "He's dead. I came after you as soon as—well, as soon as it was finished."

"That's how you got here so soon after she changed," Tanis murmured, his face dead white in the moonlight. "Durgan— Baaros help us, he didn't try to—"

Jael shook her head and grinned.

"I don't think he was interested in anything but dinner," she said.

"But what *were* they?" Tanis whispered.

Jael raised her eyebrows.

"That's right, you came from the east," she said. "But hadn't you ever heard stories of skinshifters?"

"I thought that was just a story," Tanis said dully. "I never supposed they were real."

"Real enough to nearly kill the both of us," Jael said, chuckling. Then she got a whiff of the stench of her own clothing and wrinkled her nose. "Fehhh. Real enough to ruin my clothes, too."

"A skinshifter," Tanis repeated, a look of new horror in his eyes. "And I laid with her—with it—" He barely turned aside in time before he vomited again and again, continuing to heave even when his stomach was long emptied.

One of the guards stepped over, as ichor-spattered as Jael herself. He gave Tanis a sympathetic glance.

"Lady Acorn, we'd best go back to camp," he said kindly. "I wouldn't like to think their kin are nearby."

"Uh-huh." Jael picked up Tanis's belongings, but Tanis was too numb to do more than wrap himself in the blanket, although Jael made him slip his boots back on. They stumbled back to the camp, Jael trying not to look at the gory and misshapen bundles the guards were carrying back.

They were greeted at the wagons by the stench of burning flesh and Karina's grim face.

"Put those on the fire," she told the guards. "Cloth and all. All your clothes as well." She turned to Jael and Tanis. "Your clothes, too, and that blanket. There's a bucket of water by the fire, and soap. Wash yourselves and your weapons and stay there in the light."

Jael was already stripping off her slimy tunic, but Tanis clung to his blanket.

"What are they doing?" he asked her, his voice low. "What's the matter?"

Jael dropped the tunic and started on her trousers.

"She didn't bite or scratch you, did she? Even a little?" she asked Tanis. "Even the smallest bite or scratch can infect you sometimes."

Tanis's eyes widened with horror, but he shook his head.

"I don't think so," he said hesitantly. "Not even when we were laying together."

"That's good." Jael examined her boots critically. "These should be all right. Don't worry, Tanis. They just want to check us for bites or scratches, and wise of them, too. Just to be safe, when we get to Gerriden we'll find a mage to examine us. It's only a day away, plenty of comfortable time for a cure even if we were infected."

Tanis shivered violently at the thought, but he followed Jael to the fire, throwing the blanket into the flames as if glad to be rid of it. Jael, Tanis, and the three guards eagerly scrubbed the last of the gore from their skins, Karina bringing fresh water for them to rinse. Even Tanis, still frightened and miserable, appeared untroubled by modesty as Karina inspected each of them, frowning over a cut on a guard's leg.

"How'd you get that, Eran?" she asked.

"I think it was Danik's sword," the woman sighed. "But I can't be certain. I'd be obliged if someone'd burn it for me."

"I'll do it." Karina laid the blade of her dagger in the fire until it glowed red, then drew the flat of the blade down the cut. Eran gritted her teeth and cursed, but she held still until the entire wound had been seared.

"When we reach town, I'll find a mage to check that," Karina told her. "As you took that cut in my service, I'll pay the cost."

The merchant turned to face Jael.

"I can thank you that those shifters are dead and the rest of us still alive, and don't think I'm not grateful," she said slowly. "But I trust you'll understand when I ask to see the color of your blood." She drew the other dagger from her belt and held it out to Jael, hilt first.

Jael took the dagger and inspected the blade. It looked clean enough. She spit on the metal and wiped the flat against her bare hip, one side and then the other, before she cut her thumb slightly, holding it up for Karina to see the red blood welling there.

Tanis reached for the knife, but Karina took it instead, seizing Tanis's hand. She scrutinized the bandage on his forearm, then cut it off, shaking her head over the wound.

"The bandage was clean, and I can see from this your blood's red enough," she said. "But I don't know as I've ever heard of anyone tumbling a skinshifter and surviving, so there's no saying whether you could be infected or not. You'll go to your tent, young Caden, and there you'll stay with a guard outside. And tomorrow you'll stay well in my sight until we reach Gerriden. Acorn, you can tent with me tonight."

Jael shook her head.

"Thank you for your concern," she said. "But I'll stay with Caden."

Karina frowned darkly.

"Are you sure? If he's infected—"

"Then we'll pay for two cures instead of one." Jael shrugged.

Karina shook her head and sighed, but said nothing more. Jael picked up Tanis's clothes and the dirty garments she'd discarded before her bath and followed Tanis back to their tent. Tanis slowly dressed, and Jael reluctantly pulled her dirty clothes back on. Until she bought more, she had nothing clean to wear.

When Tanis finished dressing, he curled up mutely under the blankets, facing away from Jael. Jael frowned and laid her hand on his shoulder. He started violently at her touch.

"Thank you for staying," he said, his voice almost inaudible. "You don't have to."

"I know. I'll stay anyway, unless you want me to leave." Jael rubbed his shoulder. "Want to talk about it?"

Tanis didn't answer, but Jael saw his head shake in the darkness.

"Do you want me to go?" Jael asked gently.

Tanis shook his head again, to Jael's relief.

"All right." Jael rummaged through her kit, hoping her father had possibly put in a sleeping potion, but there was none. Jael found her cup and stuck her head out of the tent, waving the guard over.

"Does anyone have something stronger than wine?" she asked hopefully, holding out her cup. "We won't drink out of anyone's flask, but it'd be a blessing to help Caden get some sleep."

The guard would not leave his post, but he called Eran, who had a flask of brandy. Eran poured Jael's cup full, then winked at her and swigged heartily from the flask herself.

Jael crawled back into the tent and touched Tanis's shoulder again.

"This'll take the taste out of your mouth and help you sleep," she said. "Can you drink it?"

Tanis scrubbed vigorously at his face with his sleeve before he sat up, and Jael diplomatically ignored his puffy eyes. Tanis drank the brandy without a word, gulping it down as if it were water and then coughing helplessly.

"All right now?" Jael asked softly.

"I suppose I won't know that until we reach Gerriden." Tanis wouldn't meet her eyes.

"I know. I got Durgan's blood all over me. I'm scared, too," Jael admitted, and when Tanis at last looked up, she could see the relief in his eyes.

"You are?"

"Of course I am." Jael managed a grin. "At least you're human. Can you imagine what the shifter curse might do to *me*?"

"Baaros protect us." Tanis croaked out something that was probably meant to be a laugh. "Guess we'd better find out what mage Karina's sending that guard to."

"Guess we'd better." Jael crawled under the blankets next to Tanis. "How about if we let *my* shoulder get numb for a change?"

"Thank you." Tanis's whisper was so soft that even Jael barely heard it, but Tanis let her draw his head to her shoulder. Jael felt a suspicious dampness on the shoulder of her tunic, but she ignored it, as she ignored the shaking of his shoulders under her arm until he finally fell asleep.

Sleep came harder for Jael. It had finally struck her—gods, she'd fought a *skinshifter*! The thought made her shiver. But she'd fought and won. She hadn't fallen over her own feet, she hadn't dropped her sword, she hadn't gone all stupid in the battle, she hadn't tripped over roots running to help Tanis. She'd fought against a *skinshifter* and she'd *won*. She and Tanis, maybe every person in the caravan, were alive because of it. And tonight Tanis needed *her* to hold *him*.

This was how her mother felt after battle—scared and shaken, maybe, but proud and *right*. This was how a warrior felt—a *winning* warrior, Jael reminded herself sternly, as she realized the loser might well not feel anything at all. Just as she'd come close, much too close, to feeling nothing at all. Suddenly her pride vanished, and she felt very small and alone in the darkness. Then Tanis snored softly, and Jael was somehow comforted.

Not alone. And frightened or not, perhaps not so small, either, after all.

V

• "That's it," Tanis said glumly, dropping the pitifully small purse on the bed between them. "We're in trouble."

Jael peered into the pouch and stirred the coins with her finger, hoping against hope that a few Moons might peep out from under the small pile of coppers.

"Isn't there *anywhere* we can change a Sun or one of the gems without someone getting suspicious?" she asked with a sigh.

Tanis sighed, too.

"There's no money changer in a town as small as Willow Bend," he said. "The innkeeper gave me a look when I paid with a Sun for our room, and that was our last Sun, too. Now we're down to the jewels. There's certainly no place we could sell a gem here. And even though there's nothing much to steal, if the rumor gets about that one of us might be a thief, we'll likely be thrown out of the inn, too."

Jael shook her head dismally. They'd been stranded in tiny Willow Bend for six days already, and according to the innkeeper, they'd just missed the only caravan that traded supplies west, taking a chain of rafts slightly south and west to Tilwich. It'd be at least half a moon cycle, likely more, before the rafts returned, and even then it would be some time before they departed again.

Jael and Tanis had been taken aback when the merchant train they'd been traveling with arrived in the tiny village that appeared to be little more than a small cluster of huts. There were no shops; the villagers gathered and bought their wares directly from the wagons. There'd been no possibility of buying more journey food; it was late spring, and most of the villagers had long since eaten the dried meat and fruit they'd put up for the winter before.

Even if there'd been supplies aplenty to be bought, Jael and Tanis had few coin left. The towns had become so small as they'd moved west that there were no opportunities to sell gems or change Suns to fill their purses. Jael realized unhappily that they should have changed the rest of their gems to silver and copper nearly a month ago in Gerriden, but the gems were lighter and easier to conceal in their clothing, and carrying all that coin would have meant suspiciously heavy and bulky purses.

Jael had thought that while they were passing through the woods, they could gather and sell those leaves, roots, barks, and seeds commonly used by mages. The woods were seemingly unharvested, and Jael had been delighted to not only replenish her stock of medicinal herbs, but to gather such rare plants that she'd been certain they could line their purses well on her harvest. After leaving Gerriden, however, Jael had been unable to find a single mage to whom she could sell her wares. Tanis had queried an innkeeper about this seeming anomaly and was told that the farther west one went, the more poorly magic worked.

"Duranar the Pale once passed this way," the innkeeper had said, "and he was one of the greatest mages to walk the land. But magic turns sour here in the wild lands, and he went south."

So Jael had earned no coin at all, and her carefully harvested treasures had been wasted.

Nor had Tanis been able to replenish their hoard of small coin by thieving. His arm had healed nicely, and the mage they'd consulted in Gerriden had drawn a little of their blood, chanted over it, and pronounced them both free of the shifter curse—Jael had professed such nervousness that she'd had to leave the room before he cast the spell—but Tanis had been so shaken by his encounter with a skinshifter that his thieving had suffered terribly. He'd taken only one poor purse in Gerriden's market and was

nearly caught doing that; after that he'd stopped even trying. He
stayed well away from the brothels, too.

Jael had hoped the situation would improve in Manan, the
only city marked on Shadow's map to the west of Gerriden, but
Manan had proved to be much smaller than Jael had hoped,
hardly more than an overgrown village. The one money changer
in the city had seemed so shifty and sly that Jael and Tanis had
thought it unwise to show him any large coin or gems.

As they moved westward, the towns became smaller and
smaller and poorer and poorer, and the roads became narrower
and rougher and wilder, and the merchant caravans became more
and more suspicious of a young merchant and an elf wanting to
travel west into savage country. Wagon trains went heavily
guarded, and even then one caravan fought off two bands of
highwaymen in the four days Jael and Tanis traveled with them.
Jael and Tanis were informed they were fortunate to even find an
inn in Willow Bend; there was one there only because a number
of northern trappers brought their pelts down the Willow River
by raft to trade, and because of the bad stretch of river just south
of Willow Bend, they often stopped at the village to rest before
proceeding south to Tilwich.

Their only good fortune had been in the wealth of legends that
survived in the west. Many of the older villagers had heard
of—or seen themselves—Shadow's "ghost folk" some two decades before. Sometimes memories were vague and stories often
conflicted, but Tanis carefully noted each location on their map,
and Jael was relieved to see that the course of the Kresh remained a relatively straight line. She and Tanis were still on
course, if they could only manage to continue westward. There
were stories aplenty, too, about Duranar the Pale and the Book of
Whispering Serpents, and it seemed universally believed that
Duranar had gone south toward the coast—far out of the way of
Jael and Tanis's course.

More worrisome to Jael was Tanis's wary withdrawal since his
horrible encounter with Cesanne. She'd been amused at first
when he'd shunned Gerriden's brothels—small wonder, after
all—but now, nearly a moon cycle later, at supper tonight he'd
utterly ignored the rosy-cheeked and buxom innkeeper's daughter, Illse, who'd brought their meal, even though the girl had
flirted outrageously with Tanis and had bent so low while plac-
ing his bowl of stew before him that her ample bosom had nearly

tumbled forth into Tanis's face. Tanis had looked, all right—
gods, even *Jael* had looked—but he'd only blushed furiously and
devoted his attention to his meal.

"Choices," Tanis said slowly. "We can hope the innkeeper will
take a gem and not talk too much about it and try to stay here
until the cargo rafts come back and are ready to leave for Tilwich
again."

Jael shook her head.

"We'd likely be murdered in our beds first," she said glumly.

"We can go west on our own."

"And get murdered on the road instead of in our beds," Jael
said. "Or starve to death instead, since we can't buy supplies, or
stop to hunt all our food and make no progress west."

"We go back east until we can replenish our supplies and our
money and come back when the cargo rafts are ready to leave,
or stock ourselves well enough to go on by ourselves overland."

"We can't be sure when the rafts will be back," Jael said patiently. "And we'd have to go far back east, maybe as far as
Gerriden, to change the gems and stock ourselves well enough to
go on our own."

"We hire guards to escort us to the next village, whatever that
is," Tanis said with a sigh. "After the Willow River, we're off the
map."

"We'd have to pay the guards in gems, and then we'd *still* be
murdered in our beds," Jael retorted. "Besides, I don't think there
*are* any guards for hire in a town this small. If there were, they'd
have gone downriver with the cargo rafts."

"Then there's only one choice." Tanis shrugged. "We spend
the rest of our coin to pay a trapper to take us downstream to
Tilwich. It's not on our map, but since all the trappers say they
trade there, it must be large enough that we can get some money
one way or another and buy supplies. Supposedly it's only a day
or so by river, so the coppers we have left should be enough to
pay for the trip."

"I don't know," Jael said doubtfully. "I don't like to go south
out of our way. How will we get back?"

"Ride along the river, or pay a trapper to ferry us back up,"
Tanis told her. "If the land's clear enough, we can simply strike
out west overland from Tilwich. According to the innkeeper, it's
mostly hills and scrub around Tilwich, although the forest gets
thick south and west of there."

Jael was silent, thinking. Could they buy a raft and try to ride the river to Tilwich by themselves? Well, yes, *if* they had enough money to pay for a raft, having no idea of how to build a proper one themselves, and *if* they had enough knowledge of the river and of river travel and exactly where Tilwich was. Tanis was right; it really was the only choice.

"All right," she said. "Are there any trappers in town now?"

"Just those three who took the room upstairs," Tanis said gloomily, jerking his thumb upward. "Letha and Bergin and Nilde. But I heard Letha at supper tonight saying they'd be leaving tomorrow morning for Tilwich."

Jael grimaced. Letha was a coarse, unkempt woman whose over-loud conversation was liberally seasoned with oaths. Bergin was an even coarser and larger fellow whose grimy black hair formed a ragged curtain through which he peered rather vapidly. Nilde was a smaller, quieter woman; unremarkable in appearance and demeanor, there was still something about her that Jael did not altogether trust. The three made so much clamor in their room at night that they might be having a jolly-tumble or slaughtering each other for all Jael and Tanis could discern.

"All right," Jael said again with a sigh. "If those three are all there are, then I suppose we'd better talk to Letha."

Listening, Jael and Tanis could easily locate the three trappers in the public room downstairs. Letha and Bergin were laughing raucously at some jest, but they stopped when Jael and Tanis approached their table. Nilde only gazed at them warily.

"We understand you're bound for Tilwich," Tanis said hesitantly. "We'd like to hire passage downriver with you."

Letha leaned back in her chair and swallowed a gulp of ale.

"Well, we're indeed bound for Tilwich," she said sarcastically. "What else is there in this mule-humping wilderness? Passage for the two of you, eh?" She eyed Tanis and Jael critically. "Well, you don't look too heavy. No more'n five-six bags, though."

"What about our horses?" Jael protested.

Bergin guffawed, and Letha waved him to silence.

"No room for horses, youngling," she said mildly. "And you can't ferry horses down rough river on an open raft anyway. Better sell 'em. You can buy horses aplenty in Tilwich." She turned to Tanis. "But I haven't heard no offer. This may be the ass-end of the world, but nobody rides my raft for nothing."

"Wait, now," Jael insisted. "Our horses—"

"We'll pay twenty coppers," Tanis told Letha. "Surely that should be enough for two extra passengers on a trip you're making anyway, and downstream as well."

Again Jael started to argue—they had only thirty coppers—but she was silenced by a warning look from Tanis.

Letha chuckled.

"Twenty coppers? I wouldn't let you *look* at my raft for that hereabouts. Four Moons, and not a copper less."

"Two Moons," Tanis countered.

"Three, or find your own way to Tilwich," Letha said, shrugging. "We've a full load of pelts and no need for your coin if we don't want to take it."

"All right," Tanis said reluctantly. "Three Moons. But only one now, and two on arrival in Tilwich."

Letha shrugged again.

"Good enough. We can scarce spend it on the river. But I'll see the coin before we leave. We'll not be cheated, boy. And be at the river and ready at dawn, or we go without you."

"We'll be there," Tanis promised, then dragged Jael away quickly before she could protest further.

"Just stop there," Jael said hotly when Tanis pulled her out the door of the inn. "What gives you the right to say we'd sell our horses without even asking me first, and to promise money we haven't even got?"

"Jael, look," Tanis said in answer, gesturing at the Willow River.

Jael crossed her arms over her chest stubbornly, but she looked. The light was dimming, but the Willow River looked much as it had every day since Tanis and she had arrived in Willow Bend—wide, calm in the deep parts, but white foam showing where rocks lay beneath the fast-moving water.

"So?" Jael demanded. "There's no real ferry, true, but the man who owns that large raft would take us across."

"Right, so we get to the other side," Tanis said patiently. "You and me and our horses, and no supplies. We could likely make it to the next town, or the one after that, or the one after that, but what are we going to spend to buy food when we get there? Either we go south to Tilwich or we decide that we're going to hunt and forage our own food from here until—well, until we get wherever we're going. We're going to lose the villages soon

enough, but I'd much rather have a good store of dried meat
and such when we do. We have no way to know what kind of
land we're going to cross. What if it's desert? We need supplies,
and there's nowhere to get them but Tilwich, and there's no way
we can boat horses to Tilwich on that river."

Jael stared at the broad expanse of the Willow River, hating it.
Tanis was right and she knew it; that didn't make the thought of
selling the horses any less bitter. They were almost *friends*. But
even if they could ride the horses all the way south to Tilwich,
there was no guarantee they could get the horses across the river
once they got that far. Unless there was a road approaching
Tilwich from the east, there would likely be no ferry. Merchants
boated their goods south from Willow Bend to Tilwich, or north
from the southern cities.

Jael had one last argument to make, however.

"How do we know there'll be horses to buy in Tilwich?" she
said. "Or are you planning for us to *walk* west of there?"

"Letha said we could buy horses aplenty," Tanis told her.
"Someone in the area must be raising them, or maybe merchants
can get horses to Tilwich on those big boats north from the coast.
But you can be sure I'll check Letha's word against a few other
people before I'd sell our horses. It may be nobody here would
buy them anyway."

Well, there was that. Jael nodded and sighed.

"All right," she said reluctantly. "But I'm going back to our
room. I just can't watch while you—you know."

"It's all right." Tanis patted her on the shoulder. "I promise I
won't sell them to anyone who won't treat them well."

Tanis's words were small reassurance as Jael trudged gloomily
back to their room and curled herself into the smallest possible
ball on the bed. Maybe this was why Aunt Shadow never kept a
horse of her own—so she'd never come to a place where she'd
have to sell it, or, worse, where the horse might be killed by wild
animals or stolen by brigands. But, then, Aunt Shadow only traveled from city to city, never into the wild country where she'd
have to carry quantities of supplies.

Jael grimly turned her thoughts away from the horses and back
to Tanis, remembering how he'd blushed and turned away from
the ample charms of the innkeeper's daughter Illse. That worried
Jael considerably; it had more than a little of the look of a child
thrown from a horse and afraid to climb back on. Well, Jael

could hardly push him into a brothel by force, could she? Especially in a town so small that there was none. Maybe in Tilwich, though—

Jael's thoughts were interrupted by Tanis opening the door and stepping inside, a broad grin on his face and their two saddles in his arms. Pulling one hand out from under the saddles, he dropped two clinking pouches onto the bed before laying the saddles on the floor.

"I sold the horses," he said. "For a good price, too—fifteen Suns for the three, all paid in silver. But better yet, you'll call me a liar when you hear who I sold them to."

"Who?" Jael asked dully. She didn't really want to know.

"Dron, the merchant we came here with," Tanis told her. "He'd been hoping to put his pots on the rafts to Tilwich, so now he's got to wait for them to come back. He said the horses are good enough to take all the way back to Gerriden to sell. He promised he'd be choosy when he sold them."

That cheered Jael somewhat. The short, chatty copper merchant had admired the horses several times, his hands sure and gentle when he'd stroked them or unerringly found the itchy places behind their ears.

"He said Letha's right and there are good horses to be bought in Tilwich," Tanis continued. "And they always have trail supplies in stock for the trappers. The inn's always full up, though; that's why so many of the trappers stop here before going on down the river to trade."

"I hope you didn't do all that bargaining in the public room," Jael said worriedly.

"Oh, no, I talked to Dron alone in the stables," Tanis assured her. "And I gave Letha her Moon and showed her two more, but nobody's seen the rest. So it looks like we continue west from here, money in our pockets. How about a mug of ale to celebrate?"

"It'll just make me sick," Jael said with a sigh. "But why don't you see if Illse will drink with you?"

Tanis grimaced.

"She's probably tumbled every flea-ridden trapper who's come through here," he said. "I think the only reason she flirts with me is that I've still got all my teeth and hair. So why don't you buy a mug of cider and at least drink that with me?"

Jael took a deep breath, then reached into her pack and drew out the bottle of Bluebright.

"Better yet," she said slowly, "we could both stay here and have some of this instead."

Tanis drew in his breath sharply. Slowly, he sat down next to Jael on the bed.

"I thought—" He hesitated. "I thought you didn't want to do that."

"It wasn't really that I didn't *want* to," Jael said, shrugging uncomfortably. "It was just—well, it's just that now I *do*. All right?" It was hard to explain; Tanis probably would never understand how knowing that he himself was afraid made Jael feel a little less so. "Besides, this might be the last real bed we sleep in for a while."

Tanis laid his hand over hers on the bottle, and Jael was surprised to feel his fingers shaking just a little. There was nothing but concern in his eyes, however, when she glanced up.

"If you're sure it's what you want," he said gently.

Jael forced a grin and pulled the stopper out of the bottle. Thankfully, her own hands weren't shaking.

"I'm going to have some," she said. "If you don't want to, that's all right."

Tanis was silent a moment longer, staring at her. Then he dug in his pack and drew out his cup, grinning.

"You pour," he said.

Jael looked at the cup and laughed.

"That much would probably kill us," she said. "All it takes is a drop or two. Urien put it on lumps of sugar."

"Well, we don't have any." Tanis reached for the Bluebright. "I'll take just a taste."

Jael watched as he put the bottle to his lips and took a tiny sip, his eyes widening as he handed the bottle back to her.

"By Baaros," he muttered. "That's quite a sensation."

Jael took a deep breath, then sipped from the bottle herself. The sudden burst of heat inside her mouth, quickly followed by a delicious fresh coolness, was as delightful as she remembered. She carefully placed the stopper back in the bottle and tucked it back into the pack. When she turned back to Tanis, however, he had lain back on the bed, his eyes half closed.

"How odd," he murmured. "I feel like I'm drifting on water."

A warm wave of relaxation washed through Jael's limbs, and she lay down beside him, propping her head up on one hand.

"Is that good?" she asked.

"Mmmm. Yes." Tanis rolled over to face her. He raised one hand lazily to comb his fingers through Jael's shoulder-length curls. "Do you know your hair is just the color of new bronze, and your eyes, too. It's lovely. But do you know what I've always liked best?"

"What?" Jael couldn't imagine Tanis finding anything about her lovely. She was as knobby and gangly as a half-grown fawn and just about as graceful.

"Your hands." Tanis took Jael's hand and held it up, tracing it with his fingertips. "You don't have the hands of a noblewoman or a warrior or even a thief. You have hands like a mage—hands that look like they'll make something marvelous happen." His voice became wistful. "I wish you *could* run like the wind over water. You were made to do something special, something magical."

Tanis's words made a tiny glow of pride in Jael's heart, and she smiled.

"All right," she said. "I'll do something marvelous and magical just for you. Watch." She reached for the purses Tanis had set aside and drew a copper out of the pouch.

Cupping the copper in her palm, Jael stared at it a little dubiously. It'd been more than a year since she'd tried this, and even then she hadn't been sure what she was doing. How did she even start? Maybe . . .

The copper felt solid and comfortable in her hand, and deep within it Jael felt a memory of fire burning deep in the earth, fire that melted rock, that turned copper into spattering liquid formless as water, flowing smoothly between her fingers—

"Woops!" Jael laughed, catching the dripping copper in her other hand, her concentration broken. The copper coalesced into a formless blob. "Well, I meant to make a *T*, for Tanis. But it is *something*, isn't it, something marvelous?"

Tanis touched the blob hesitantly, as if afraid it might burn him, then picked it up, gazing at it wonderingly.

"It certainly is, marvelous and magical," he agreed. Then he turned to gaze at Jael warmly, dropping the piece of copper to clasp her fingers. "And so are you."

Jael let Tanis pull her lips down to his, relief eclipsing even the wonderful warm desire that his words, his touch, brought. Yes, she wanted him, very much indeed, and she was glad to want him, glad to be *able* to want him. But even better was the ability to want *Tanis*, her wonderful friend who couldn't shoot an arrow straight and who complained too much and sulked when he didn't get what he wanted. And it was she, Jaellyn the Unlucky, all clumsy elbows and knees and elvan ears and Kresh eyes, who wanted him. And maybe this sudden bright warmth in her heart was love, and maybe it wasn't, but it was *real*, a part of herself, not something that flowed from a bottle. And maybe when the Bluebright wore off, she wouldn't feel these feelings again for a while, but that was only because they were hiding in a place inside herself where she couldn't reach, waiting for Jael to find them again. And one day, please, gods, one day she would never need Bluebright to find those feelings again.

Tanis pulled away from her, and Jael knew a moment of fear—whatever was the matter? To her relief, however, he only grinned sheepishly and stumbled rather clumsily to the door, setting the heavy wooden latch in place. He sat down on the edge of the bed and pulled off one boot, then the other, pulling off Jael's boots as well. He stared blankly at her feet.

"Did you know," he said slowly, "that you have six toes on your left foot?"

"Uh-huh." Jael laughed. "And you knew it, too. I showed you once before."

"You did? You did," Tanis admitted after a moment's thought. He gazed at Jael with sudden seriousness. "Jaellyn, I feel so strange. Am I going to remember this tomorrow?"

"Uh-huh." Jael nodded. "So you'd best not do anything you'd rather forget."

"Better yet," he said softly, "I'd best do something worth remembering."

Jael had a fair secondhand knowledge of coupling; the elves in the Heartwood were not much concerned with privacy or modesty, and when Jael had fostered with Mist she imagined she'd seen probably all there was to see. It had always looked like a rather awkward business to her—how did they ever know where to put their elbows to get them out of the way, or which way to tilt their heads so their noses didn't collide when they kissed? And didn't all that long hair fall in each other's faces, or get painfully pinned underneath someone's shoulder? Still, despite all the bother, they seemed to enjoy it immensely; certainly they spent a goodly amount of time doing it, and Jael *didn't* believe all that was just practice in the hope of finally getting it right.

Jael had been prepared, therefore, for the awkwardness, for Tanis's Bluebright-fogged clumsiness and her own fumbling inexperience. She wasn't too unprepared, either, for the pleasure Tanis's lips or fingers could find in the most surprising places—in the tender bend of her elbow or under her ear, behind her knee or at the nape of her neck. She *was* a little surprised by the hairiness of Tanis's skin against hers, but she had scarcely time to notice before Tanis found another of those wonderful places to touch.

Even better than the pleasure, though, and utterly surprising to Jael, was the wonderful feelings of *all there* and *not-alone*, the marvelous knowledge that for this one brief time, every part of Jaellyn was there in that bed, all working properly. And Tanis was there with her and *wanting* to be there with her, and they were hardly two separate people anymore, joining their bodies together as closely as they could, as if the warmth between them could melt them together as Jael had melted the copper.

At last, lying comfortably tangled together (except that Jael had nowhere to put her left arm, and Tanis's damp hair was tickling her nose), the sweat cooling on their skin in the darkness, Tanis sleepily stroked Jael's cheek.

"Was it worth remembering?" he asked drowsily.

"Uh-huh." Jael grinned in the darkness. "I wonder how long the Bluebright will last."

Tanis chuckled, too.

"If I were a real friend, I'd warn you to use caution with that stuff," he murmured. "But that's asking more of my sense of duty than I can reasonably expect of myself."

"And more caution than I've ever had a right to claim," Jael said, yawning. "Gods, why didn't we do this sooner?"

"You're asking me?" Tanis shook his head. "Go to sleep, Jaellyn."

"Well, I would, only—"

"Only what?"

Jael giggled.

"You're lying on my hair."

"Jael, wake up."

"Uhhhh." Jael's nose was icy cold. She rolled over and burrowed deeper into the covers, but Tanis shook her shoulder insistently.

"Come on, Jael." Warm arms slipped around her, and Tanis's bare chest was hairy against her back. Then Jael remembered foggily why her back and Tanis's chest were bare, and she rolled over in his arms to look at him.

Tanis smiled, his eyes as bleary as Jael's, and kissed her chastely on the forehead.

"We'd better get dressed or Letha will leave without us."

Jael sighed, but she sat up, shivering in the predawn cold. Tanis jumped out of bed and hurriedly pulled on his clothes, his teeth chattering. He picked up Jael's clothes and tossed them to her so she could dress under the covers.

Jael dressed as quickly as she could, then left the warm comfort of the blankets to help Tanis bundle their bags together. It was unseasonably cold; Jael could see her breath steaming thickly in the air. It took three trips to carry all the bags down to the river's edge, but Jael and Tanis had no way to distinguish Letha's raft from the half-dozen drawn up on the sand and tied to stakes deeply anchored farther up the bank. They laid their bags on the bank and sat down, shivering in the cold mist.

"Where are they?" Jael demanded irritably. Dawn was lightening the sky.

"I don't know. We'll just have to wait." Tanis put his arm around Jael and huddled closer.

The sun was well over the horizon when Letha, Bergin, and Nilde shambled down to the riverbank, carrying heavy bundles of pelts. Ignoring Jael and Tanis, they loaded one of the rafts and pushed it down to the water. At last, Letha turned and scowled at them.

"Well, are you coming or not?" she demanded. "No servants here to carry them bags."

Jael and Tanis hurriedly scooped up the bags, and Letha and her compatriots waited impatiently, arms crossed, while they loaded their belongings as best they could. Almost before the last bag was in place, Bergin was pushing the raft into the water; Jael lost her footing, as usual, and sprawled over Tanis and their bags.

The river was rougher than it had looked, and the raft was less well made than *it* looked. Water sloshed up between the logs, and now Jael saw the reason for the small raised platform built near the center of the raft; likely sometimes it doubled as a floor for a sort of shelter, but now it provided a dry base for Letha's pelts. Tanis once started to move their packs to this platform, but Nilde, speaking from the first time, told Tanis sharply to stay away from their pelts. Jael and Tanis had to make do by wrapping their bags in the waxed cloaks so that their few remaining supplies would not be totally soaked. They themselves had no such protection against the water that slopped over the sides or sprayed abruptly into their faces.

Jael quickly found that her few paltry excursions by small boat had in no way prepared her for the Willow River. Except during the spring floods, the Brightwater was slow, deep, and placid near Allanmere. The Willow River flowed fast and often rough and shallow—she couldn't imagine how the large boats came up from the coast to Tilwich, unless the river improved dramatically farther south—and now Jael could appreciate Letha, Bergin, and Nilde's expertise in carefully guiding the raft through the swirling currents, between foam-covered rocks that Jael could not even see until they were upon them. So intent were the three upon their difficult task that Jael and Tanis had no notion of offering their help; they simply sat as quietly as they could near the center of the raft, clinging together and to the logs when the wooden platform lurched under them.

Jael's stomach lurched with the raft. She'd never traveled long by water before, and the placid expanse of the Brightwater and sparkling small streams in the Heartwood had never made her head spin and her guts roil as the Willow River did. Three times she lurched to the side of the raft to vomit, Tanis holding her securely so she should not tumble in if the raft jolted. After that she had nothing left to vomit and could only heave dryly until she was exhausted. Tanis looked none too pleasured by the ride, either, although he had traveled by river before and his stomach was not so affected. Letha, Bergin, and Nilde ignored them for the most part—the river demanded their full concentration almost every moment—although they directed a few contemptuous chuckles in Jael's direction when she was ill.

They stopped the raft at noon to sup, and although they offered Tanis and Jael none of their food, Letha was almost friendly, spinning tales of the wilderness and the trappers who roamed it. She did not ridicule Jael, either, when Jael took a potion from her kit to ease her stomach. Even so, when Tanis of-

fered her some of the dried meat they had left, Jael quickly
waved it away.

"No rain of late just here," Bergin said sagely, nodding his
head at the river. "That's why she's so low and fast and in such
a temper."

"Times we'd travel on through the night, letting the river carry
us and watching in shifts," Letha said. "Too many rocks showing
their backs now, though, and no hope of dodging 'em all in the
dark. We'll put up on the banks come sundown and camp."

After supper, Jael was glad enough she had not eaten. The
river became even rougher and faster, and this time Letha was
glad to have Tanis lend his strength at the heavy oar with which
Bergin steered the raft, although she had no other pole for Jael
to assist herself and Nilde at the sides of the raft where they
pushed away from rocks, and in any event Jael was so sick-
bellied she'd have been of little enough use. Water splashed so
freely over the raft that everyone was quickly drenched, and Jael
feared that their bags might be washed into the river. After Jael
herself was nearly flung into the water more than once, she
quickly bundled together those items most likely to be ruined by
the water—her herbal kit, including the bottles of Bluebright, 
and what little journey food they had left. Satisfied that Letha, 
Bergin, and Nilde were well occupied with steering the raft, Jael 
quickly stuffed the small packet in under the pelts, and as an afterthought shoved her precious sword and dagger under the pelts 
as well, lest they be knocked loose and lost if Jael fell into the 
river. She almost stored the pouch of gems in her tunic with the 
rest, but on reflection that was foolish—if Letha and her friends 
discovered the small parcels, they might be angered; if they 
found the gems, however, there might well be worse trouble. Jael 
was glad, too, that Tanis had the silver safe in his tunic. That, at 
least, would not get washed into the river unless Tanis did, and 
Tanis appeared fit enough, despite the rough water, to keep his 
feet under him.

They stopped a little before sunset, Letha saying that beyond
that point the river became more treacherous, although to Jael's
inexperienced eye the water had appeared to deepen and grow
calmer not long before. The bank was too steep to draw up the
raft, but Bergin tied it securely to the protruding roots of a tree
growing out over the river. To Jael's surprise, Letha did not unload the pelts. Unfortunately, this meant that Jael had no chance

to reclaim her small bundle; the trappers cast a suspicious eye
when Jael or Tanis even wandered too close to the platform. Jael
had to be content with carrying their other baggage ashore and
hoping that on the morrow the trappers would again be busy
enough that Jael could reclaim the rest of their belongings before
they reached Tilwich.

Nilde disappeared briefly into the forest, bow in hand, and returned only a short time later with five rabbits. These she
skinned and gutted and stuffed with herbs Jael did not recognize,
wrapped the hares well in leaves and then covered them in mud,
and placed them directly into the fire. Some time later, Nilde removed the rabbits from the fire and cracked off the mud, then almost as an afterthought pushed two of the rabbits toward Tanis
and Jael. The meat was succulent and tender, the unfamiliar
herbs lending it a strange but savory flavor. The trappers were
tired but cheerful over dinner, Letha stating that they'd gotten
farther than she'd expected.

"With an early start, we'll land in Tilwich by midmorning,"
she said, swigging from her skin of ale. "Then you can buy new
horses, and with the Moons you're paying us, we can fill our
skins with the finest wines boated north all the way from
Zaravelle."

She offered Jael and Tanis the aleskin. Jael refused politely,
and was not surprised when Tanis also declined. Letha, with her
half-rotten teeth and foul breath, was not the sort of person with
whom most people would gladly share a bottle.

After dinner, Bergin produced a treat—small sweet cakes prepared by the cook at the inn in Willow Bend—and offered them
to everyone, but Jael had no stomach for the sweets. She'd
thought the meal would make her feel better, but now she began
to question the wisdom in eating as her stomach began to churn
once more.

"You don't look so good, youngling," Letha said, peering at
her through the flames. "Sure you won't have a sip of ale? Very
settling."

Jael shook her head, wondering if the potion she'd taken
earlier might help—if she could get it from the raft, of course.
Her belly was starting to cramp painfully, so severely that the
pain almost doubled her over. She glanced over at Tanis. He was
pale, swaying dizzily. As their eyes met, realization passed between them, and Tanis's hand dropped to his sword.

"Go on, youngling, draw it," Bergin chuckled. "If you can."

Tanis staggered to his feet, swaying weakly as he dragged his sword from its scabbard. Jael tried to stand, but her cramped belly constricted sharply and she fell to her side, groaning. Helplessly she scrabbled at her belt, suddenly realizing that her sword and dagger were still on the raft.

Tanis had his sword out now, but the point wavered unsteadily, the hilt only loosely clasped in his shaking hand. Bergin stood, stretched indolently, and sauntered toward Tanis. It took only the slightest shove to crumple Tanis to the ground, and a single kick sent the sword sliding away.

Letha strolled over to Jael's side and rolled her over with one booted foot, chuckling contemptuously.

"Little fool's not even armed," she said. "Bergin, you watch them while Nilde and I check the packs first, give the drug a little longer to work. The boy's unconscious, but the girl's still moving. Nilde, you said this stuff would work on elves, didn't you?" Nilde grunted her agreement.

Jael was too overcome by her pain to watch Letha and Nilde, but she could hear them rifling through the packs, tossing the contents aside after they'd been pawed through, and she heard the irritated cursing as Letha found nothing of value.

"I know they must've gotten some good coin from selling the horses," Bergin said. "Search them."

Jael struggled, but only feebly, as Letha's grimy fingers pawed through her clothes. Before Letha could search far, Bergin covered the silver in Tanis's tunic, and Jael hoped that Letha would be distracted. To Jael's dismay, Letha was not too distracted to finish her search, and she eagerly seized the small pouch hidden in the waistband of Jael's tunic.

"Ha! What's this?" Letha exclaimed, carrying the pouch over into the light of the fire. "Nilde, let me use your small dagger. The cord's knotted well."

There was a fumbling sound, then three sharp gasps as the gems were revealed.

"It's a blessed fortune!" Bergin shouted joyfully. "Just look at those jewels!"

"Take your hand away!" Letha said sharply.

"Now, don't you take that tone," Bergin warned. "I'm due a share of those jewels and I mean to have them."

"And I," Nilde said coldly. "You'd not have them without my drug."

"Pah, two puny younglings, one not even armed?" Letha scoffed. Then her voice sharpened. "Back away, Bergin! I'll not tell you twice!"

"And I'll not say again that I mean to share in those gems!" Bergin roared. "Divide them now, or I'll have them altogether!"

"Not while I live," Nilde hissed.

Jael heard a few more exclamations, angry and incoherent, behind her, scuffling and then shouting, then the clang of blades. Desperately she forced herself to her knees, retching weakly, alarmed to see blood staining the bile that spattered the ground in front of her. But there was no time—while the trappers were distracted—

Haltingly Jael crawled to Tanis, her sounds muffled by the now-ferocious argument going on somewhere behind her. Tanis lay where he'd fallen, stubbornly fighting unconsciousness although his eyes were only half-open and he was shaking so hard he could scarcely push himself up from the ground.

"The raft," he muttered when his eyes finally focused on Jael. "It's our only chance. Can you make it?"

"If you can," Jael gasped, retching again. A scream sounded somewhere behind them, and Jael thought that meant that the fight might soon be over. Arms around each other to lend what support they could, Jael and Tanis stumbled toward the river as quickly as Tanis's shaking legs and Jael's half-squatting posture would allow. Tanis fumbled with the knot tying the raft to the tree roots, but Jael shook her head, pushing him toward the raft.

"My knife's there, under the pelts," she said, splashing through the shallow water to half-fall onto the wet logs. That brought a fresh bout of retching, and it was Tanis who crawled to the platform and found Jael's dagger.

Lying only half-conscious on the raft, Jael saw Tanis crawl painfully toward the rope, but before he reached the edge of the raft, the cramps seized her painfully once again, dragging her down into blessed darkness.

# VI

● When Jael opened her eyes, she
found herself lying naked on a
pile of rather musty-smelling
pelts, more pelts thrown over her as a makeshift cover. It was
hard to judge the time by the angle of sunlight on the bobbing,
turning raft, but Jael estimated it was still fairly early in the
morning. Her head throbbed ferociously and her belly ached as
if she'd been run through, but she was warm enough and, thank
the gods, alive. She started to sit up, then groaned as dizziness
made her fall back.

Tanis, clad only in his trousers, immediately appeared at her
side, holding his dripping but clean shirt.

"We don't have a cup," he said regretfully, "but I'll squeeze
some of this water into your mouth. Don't try to talk until
you've drunk some. You've retched your throat raw, I think."

Even nodding sent fiery pain stabbing through Jael's head, so
she lay still and let Tanis soak the shirt in the river again and
again until Jael could drink no more. The cold, clean water
steadied her enough that she was able to scrabble through the
pelts to find the kit she'd hidden and swallow a little of the potion her father had given her for her stomach. A few minutes
later she could sit, if unsteadily.

"How long have you been awake?" she rasped, her voice a painful croak.

"Only since dawn," Tanis said, sitting down beside her. "Letha lied; the river's been calm as the Brightwater at midsummer, or we'd have broken up on the rocks during the night. You'd vomited all over yourself, and you were chilled through, too, so I rinsed your clothes in the river and laid them on the logs to dry." His brow furrowed. "You had me pretty frightened. I didn't know how to use the herbs and such in your bag, but I was about to chance it when you woke up. Whatever Nilde put in our food, all it did was make me sleep, but it half-killed you."

Jael chuckled, then winced at the pain in her throat.

"She said her drug worked on elves. But I'm not as elvan as I look, either."

Tanis was silent for a long time, staring out at the river, and Jael finally spoke again.

"We've passed Tilwich, haven't we?"

"I imagine so." Tanis's voice was carefully neutral. "I've been watching since I woke, and there's been no sign of a town, or even docks or other rafts or boats. I think we must've passed it in the night. Baaros alone knows how far south we've gone."

Jael was also silent. The river had widened and apparently deepened, too, and although the water was calm, the current remained steady and fast enough.

"There's not much chance of getting back upriver, is there?" she asked at last.

Tanis sighed and shook his head.

"Even if we were strong enough to pole a raft this size upriver—and we're not, that's certain—the water's too deep now. I'm sure the trappers never went south of Tilwich on their rafts for just that reason. We might be able to steer the raft to the west bank and try to walk back up the river, but we've got only a very little food, these pelts, your knife and sword, and some herbs and such." Tanis forced a cheerful grin. "I think we'd fare better staying with the river until we come to another town or even a city. On a river this size, there's bound to be some, since Tilwich gets its trade goods from the south."

He didn't say what Jael knew they both must be thinking—that they'd already been carried probably leagues out of their way south, and even if they could make it back to Tilwich, they'd only likely encounter Letha, Bergin and Nilde—or whichever of that threesome had survived their quarrel—and possibly many of their trapper friends.

"South sounds good," Jael said, also forcing a cheerful tone, although her heart was leaden. "At least the nights won't be so cold. And you're likely right, it can't be that far south to some kind of town or village."

Tanis half-grinned and patted Jael's hand. He snatched a few pelts from the pile and spread them over the logs. On the top pelt he laid his copper Guild token, his gold and ruby temple-service ring with the emblem of Baaros, and, to Jael's amazement, five Moons.

"I tucked them in my boot with my ring when I sold the horses," he said rather sheepishly. "A habit I picked up from my thieving apprenticeship. It's an old trick; I wonder that Bergin didn't find them."

"Well, it's a good habit," Jael said approvingly. "I wish I'd done it."

"There's this, too," Tanis said, indicating the brass buckle on his belt. "But unless we need it, I'll keep it on, thank you."

Jael laid her sword and dagger on the pelts, then slipped the thick gold rings, each set with three green gems, from her ears and laid them on the fur, too.

"I suppose Letha got too interested in the pouch to bother with those," she said. "It's a good thing, too." Emptying the sack she'd hidden under the pelts, Jael slowly laid out their few contents—her herbs, potions and salves, bandages and wound dressings, the small pouch of dried meat and journey cakes, and the two bottles of Bluebright.

"That's all I have, except my clothes," she said, sighing. It seemed a pitifully small hoard.

"Well, it's not as hopeless as all that," Tanis told her. "We have the five Moons. My ring and your earrings should fetch some money, and the pelts we could trade anywhere, even the smallest village. At least Letha and her friends left us something in trade, although it's not a bargain I'd boast of." He chuckled. "And the pelts are a little smelly, too."

"Whenever we stop, I'll rub them with sweet herbs. It's an old elvan trick." Jael shook her head. "We don't even have our map. But I suppose it doesn't matter now, does it?"

"Well, we were leaving the mapped territory anyway," Tanis

said cheerfully. "We'll make a new map when we learn where we are."

Jael stared out at the river, considering.

"Fresh water we've got aplenty," she said. "But no shelter and not much food, and no weapons but my sword and dagger—nothing much to hunt with, I mean."

"Unfortunately I'm no bowyer," Tanis said regretfully. "And by the time we made a bow and found something to tip the arrows, we'd likely starve. Baaros, what I'd trade for a handful of fishhooks."

"Hooks!" Relief surged through Jael. "You don't have to trade. Look." She pulled the small pouch of needles and sinew from her kit of herbs. "We can bend the needles into hooks and cut barbs into them with my dagger. We can bait them with some of our dried meat."

Jael was still too weak and sick to be of much use, but Tanis quickly put this plan into action, forming three hooks which he proclaimed strong enough for fishing. Threads from Tanis's shirt were carefully unraveled and then laboriously braided into strong line. Jael and Tanis briefly tried the hooks, but stopped to plan as soon as they caught their first fish. There was no way to cook the fish on the raft, and Tanis and Jael were not quite hungry enough to eat them raw. The fish would quickly spoil on the raft in the sunlight, however, so it was quickly decided that as soon as Tanis had caught a good number of fish, both to eat and to smoke, they'd land the raft to camp for the night, even if it was well before sunset.

"We should try to hunt and smoke some meat, too, as we'll have the extra time today," Tanis said hesitantly. "I can set snares when we camp. I'll go as far as away as I can, but—"

"I know." Jael grinned ruefully. "Even when you killed the fish, I felt it, but there's no help for it, is there? I guess I'd rather feel you kill something than have you wander too far away and maybe get killed yourself. I wish there was something I could do."

"There is, and plenty, when we land the raft," Tanis told her. "You can try to make some kind of shelter when we stop, and see if you can get a fire started to cook the fish. Maybe you can find flint, though I don't know if we can strike sparks on that metal of your dagger. Once we've landed, maybe you can set lines for eel. And if you can forage anything to eat, too, that would help. Meantime, though, you'd best rest and save your strength."

They dined on some of their journey food, preferring to cut up any tiny fish they caught for bait. By early afternoon, however, Tanis had caught nearly a dozen large fish, and the sun had grown so hot that Jael gladly agreed that it was time to find a suitable spot to land. Unlike Letha, Jael would not be content with tying the raft to tree roots with their short length of rope, and besides, she wanted to locate flint. At last they spotted a rocky bank, and with both Jael and Tanis using all their strength, they were able to draw the raft a little way up on the rocks where it could be securely tied to a boulder.

To Jael's joy, willows lined the riverbank, and she quickly found one large enough to support a good-sized woven-switch bower for herself and Tanis. With the pelts for their bedding, they'd sleep in greater comfort than they'd likely enjoyed since they'd left Allanmere. She found a piece of flint, too, on the shore and was delighted to find that it would spark against her dagger.

By the time Tanis returned from setting his snares, Jael had the shelter prepared. Rocks and mud made a small drying oven where the fish could smoke over green wood overnight, and she'd set eel lines baited with fish heads in the river. By that time, she was too exhausted to make the lean-to she planned for the raft; it would simply have to wait until tomorrow.

It was then Tanis's turn to watch the fire and the fish while Jael explored the woods near the camp; however exhausted she might be, she couldn't stomach the thought of nothing but plain fish for supper. There was no fruit or nuts to be had this early in the year, of course, but there were tender young greens to pluck and roots to dig. To Jael's utter embarrassment, she had to call out to Tanis and follow the sound of his voice back to camp, although she wasn't more than five hundred paces away.

There was no pot to cook the greens and roots in, but Tanis solved the dilemma by wrapping two fresh-caught and cleaned eels, together with the greens and tubers, in clean rushes and then in mud and laying them in the fire as Nilde had done the rabbits. Jael was not particularly fond of eel, but baked with the fresh herbs, it was tasty, and certainly better than what little dried meat they had left.

When they finished eating, Tanis checked his snares and

brought back three large water rodents of a type Jael had never seen before, although she recognized the pelt as one she'd seen among Letha's furs. Tanis carefully cleaned the pelts while Jael cut the meat into neat strips for drying.

When Tanis saw Jael's hanging bower, however, he gave it a rather dubious glance.

"Sling beds are one thing," he said. "Sleeping three man-heights above the ground is another. What's the matter with a lean-to?"

"I'll make a lean-to for the raft tomorrow. But what if it rains tonight and the river rises?" Jael said practically. "We'd be flooded out with the bank so low here. Besides, trust me, we'll sleep safer and more comfortable up there. I've done it a hundred times at least."

Tanis said nothing further, but he made Jael climb up first, and then she had to help him climb out onto the limb and through the opening into the fur-lined bower. Once he was settled, however, he admitted that the nest was cozy and comfortable.

"I wish I'd fostered in the Heartwood with you last summer," he said with a sigh, nestling into the furs. "But I'd hardly begun my Guild apprenticeship, and besides, I—well, I like the city. But there's no denying you've learned some useful skills."

Jael laughed and rolled over beside Tanis, propping her chin on his chest.

"Probably nobody but you or Aunt Shadow would ever say that," she said. "In the forest, Mist thinks—oh, he'd never say so—I'm all but useless. I can't hunt, I get lost, I sniffle and wheeze all the time. And in the city, Mother thinks my swordsmanship and my unarmed combat are pitiful and weak, I'm too clumsy to be a thief, and I can't be a scholar if I can't remember what I've just studied."

"Well, your swordsmanship and your unarmed combat were good enough to best a few highwaymen and a skinshifter," Tanis said, folding his arms around her. "We haven't gotten lost, and you don't sniffle and wheeze when you remember to take the potion High Lord Argent gave you. As for scholarship, I couldn't have woven this shelter or built that little oven or found the plants you brought back, and *you're* the one who taught me how to set snares and catch fish, so I guess you learned the important things well enough. And as for thieving, it's just as well you *can't* do it, else you'd have no use for me at all."

"I could always use someone to gut fish and steer a raft," Jael teased. "Carry bags, such as that."

"Maybe I can think of something better." Tanis reached for the sack he'd brought up with him and pulled out one of the bottles of Bluebright, raising his eyebrows inquiringly.

Jael took the bottle, then hesitated.

"You know, we've come a good distance out of our way," she said slowly. "It may be even a longer journey before we find my father's people than we'd expected. We really shouldn't waste it. I can't get any more. Besides," she added, sighing, "I just don't feel very good still."

Tanis sighed, too, but he nodded.

"You're right," he said. "I guess I wouldn't expect amorous inclinations from the greatest courtesan in Allanmere if she'd been mostly poisoned the night before." He was silent for a moment. "Listen. It's starting to rain a little, I think."

Jael grinned; she'd already heard the falling drops, even with the gentle murmur of the river almost under them.

"Do you think the raft's safe, and our food smoking in that little oven?" Tanis asked after a moment's thought.

"If they're not, there's nothing we could do to make them more safe," Jael said, shrugging. "The raft's up on the rocks as far as we could pull it, and it's tied. There was nowhere higher to build the oven, either."

That was true enough; there was nothing to do but snuggle deeper into the furs and hope that the river would not rise far. Jael was still weak from the drug the night before and bone-tired from her exertions; she did not worry overmuch, but was asleep almost as soon as she laid her head on Tanis's shoulder. Occasionally she would half-wake, listen to the gentle patter of raindrops on the leaves of their shelter, and drift back into slumber.

In the morning the air was fresh and sweet, the sun was shining in a nearly clear sky, and the river had risen just enough that the raft would be easy to push from the rocks. There were four eels on Jael's lines, and the fish and meat in the oven were well smoked. Jael wrapped the eels in rushes to cook while she and Tanis finished preparing the lean-to for the raft.

Tanis helped Jael cut sturdy poles and strip them of branches, and together they wove tight mats of rushes to form a fairly weatherproof shelter. At least the pelts would not be spoiled by rain, and Jael and Tanis would have some relief from the sun while they traveled. When the eels were finished cooking, Jael knocked her oven apart and carried the rocks to the raft, where, with a little new mud, she built a sort of bowl under the roof of the shelter in which they could build a small fire to cook any fish they caught. Tanis cut more rushes and took some of the willow switches from their bower, from which they could weave a basket to hold their catch.

This time, as they once again trusted their fate to the Willow River, Jael's heart was lighter. Yes, they were far off their path and being carried farther away all the time, but they'd make the best of it. After surviving highwaymen, trappers, and skinshifters, of what consequence was a few more leagues on their journey?

The river was flowing a little faster, likely because of the rain, but the water was deep enough that there were no rocks to worry about, and the river was so wide that the occasional fallen and half-submerged tree was easy to avoid. By midday Jael had developed a fair knack of using the large steering oar to guide the raft, and they took it in turns, one steering while the other fished or cleaned and cooked the catch, carefully saving the heads and entrails for bait. They told tales to pass the time, Tanis reminiscing about the cities he'd visited, and Jael repeating the elvan legends she'd heard in the Heartwood or spinning outrageous yarns she'd been told in her childhood by Shadow and her friends at the Guild of Thieves.

As afternoon turned to evening, however, and the sun touched the horizon, forcing them to find another bank where they could stop for the night, Jael and Tanis became silent. There'd been no sign of any settlement along the river, not even another boat.

This time Jael and Tanis merely tied the raft securely and stayed on it. There were no willows here, and why build another shelter when there was one on the raft already? Jael found a few potherbs and tubers to supplement the fish they'd caught, but tonight the food, well spiced with worry, had no savor.

They ate silently. Jael thought sourly that where there were no choices, there could be no conversation. They'd wagered there'd be some settlement near Tilwich, and they'd lost that wager. There might be nothing closer than several days' journey down the river, and now it was too late to turn back; even if they could find Tilwich by traveling on foot up the river, perhaps constructing a travois to carry the pelts, their only trade commodity, it would be a long and dangerous journey. Jael had no illusions that either she or Tanis was fit for extended rough travel through the wilderness on foot. A sword, even Jael's sword, was not much of a weapon if they were attacked by a pack of wolves. There was simply nothing to do but stay with the river until they *did* find a settlement large enough that they could trade what they had, and where Tanis might be able to steal a little money, too.

At least, Jael reflected, they could stay clean; there was the river to wash their clothes and the sun to dry them, and Jael easily found roots that lathered in water when well pounded. When the sun grew too hot, Jael or Tanis would simply strip and slide into the river, holding securely to the rope. There was always fresh water to drink, and plenty of fish and eels to eat.

It was, in fact, five more days before they began to see signs of settlement. Jael was the first to spot a small boat tied to the bank, and a well-trod path winding into the forest—doubtless someone's home. She was so excited that she almost made Tanis stop the raft then and there; Tanis pointed out practically, however, that where there was one boat and house, there'd be more, and there was no need to risk a wary settler turning his bow or his dog on them as soon as they set foot on his land.

Tanis was soon proven correct; more boats appeared, some tied only to stakes or trees, but others lashed firmly to well-built small docks. At last Jael spotted a young boy fishing from the bank, and Tanis was quick to steer the raft toward him, calling out to ask what city lay ahead. The boy listened puzzledly, then called back something in a language Jael did not recognize. Tanis knew several other languages, and he tried a few of them, but the raft was drifting onward even as he spoke, and finally he was forced to resort to gestures before the boy nodded his comprehension, pointed downriver, and said, "Zaravelle," spreading his hands far apart to indicate a large city.

"Zaravelle," Jael repeated, her heart sinking. "That's all the way to the south coast, Tanis!"

"I know." Tanis put his arm around Jael's shoulder, hugging her comfortingly. "But it's a large city, as large as Allanmere. We can buy horses there, and supplies, and sleep in an inn again. Besides, just think—I've never seen the sea, have you?"

That cheered Jael a bit; she'd always dreamed of seeing the great salty sea Shadow told such stories of. And Tanis could probably take a purse or two at the market, enough to see them supplied again. Well, they'd simply make the best of the situation, just as they had before now. And a hot bath and something besides fish to eat *would* be nice.

It was midafternoon when they reached the docks of Zaravelle. When Tanis tied the raft to one of the docks, however, and Jael handed up to him their bundle of furs and sack of supplies, a young man in what appeared to be a guard uniform hurried over, addressing them in the same language the boy had used. Tanis shook his head and again tried every language he knew, and Jael tried Olvenic as well, but without success. At last the guard succeeded in conveying through gestures that there was a fee to be paid for leaving a raft or boat tied to the docks. Pulling a handful of coins from his purse, the guard held up two coppers and pointed to Jael and Tanis, holding his hand out sternly. Jael and Tanis glanced at each other and grinned, and Jael pulled out her dagger and slashed through the raft's rope in one stroke. The guard's eyebrows shot up as he watched the raft float away downriver to the sea, but he made no protest, only shrugging as Jael and Tanis shouldered their bundles and walked into Zaravelle.

Jael had hoped to smell the sea, but her nose was immediately assaulted by the city odors she knew so well—sweat and mud and leather and dung, cooking food and incense and burning wood and urine and—

Jael sneezed resoundingly.

"We'll find an inn first," Tanis told her. "Maybe the innkeeper can direct us to someone who might buy these pelts. It's a good thing you thought of those herbs, or they'd smell musty and I'd get less for them. We'll wait about selling my ring and your earrings, though. Maybe we won't have to sell them at all."

"You ought to find out if there's a Guild of Thieves in Zaravelle," Jael said slowly. "If we're going to be here several days, you should get permission to work the market, and the Guild would be a good place for you to find out a bit about the city—any odd laws we ought to know, maybe recommendations of merchants to trade with or to avoid. If you can find anyone you can talk to, that is."

"I'll find someone," Tanis reassured her. "Thieves, like merchants, tend to see a lot of leagues under their bootsoles. With a token from the Guild of Allanmere, I should be able to get at least temporary permission to work here." He shrugged apologetically. "But I'll need some of the money. There'll probably be a fee."

Jael quickly tired of carrying the heavy bundle of pelts, but it took them some time to locate an inn that appeared clean but cheap. Bargaining for their room and supper was difficult, as the innkeeper could not understand a word they said, nor they him, but at last Tanis settled on half a Moon per night including supper, two Moons paid in advance, and Jael was able to deposit her bundle of pelts in their room. Tanis, however, kept his bundle, saying he'd try to trade the pelts while looking for the Guild of Thieves.

"I could go with you," Jael suggested. "I spent a lot of time at the Guild in Allanmere."

"It's not the same," Tanis said, shaking his head. "These aren't the people you knew. These are strangers, some of them vicious people, and you're not a Guild member. It's better if you don't come."

Jael sighed, but Tanis was right. She'd been at least fairly competent and useful in the wilderness, but here in the city there was nothing for her to do but stay out of trouble, it seemed. Tanis took two Moons with him to pay any guild fees; that left Jael with one lone Moon in her pocket and a city full of people she could neither speak to nor understand.

When Tanis was gone, Jael found her way to the market, having nothing better to occupy her time. Zaravelle's market was rather different from the one in Allanmere; as most of its trade goods were brought in on large ships, either from Tilwich to the north or along the seacoast, there were more large shops and permanent stalls, and fewer movable wagons and carts. There was no Compact here to limit the cutting of timber, and Zaravelle had not been built on a handy foundation of ready stone, so most of the buildings were wood. Too, Zaravelle had no farming community as did Allanmere, but rather a prodigious fishing industry; consequently preservation-spelled tubs of fish of all shapes, sizes, and colors replaced the quantities of fruit and vegetables Jael was accustomed to seeing. There were many wares Jael did not recognize, and ordinarily she'd have been an eager browser among the stalls, but the Moon in her pocket was all she had, and supper was the only meal she was guaranteed, so she reluctantly turned away from the fascinating goods. Besides, Jaellyn the Cursed wandering too close to the preservation-spelled fish might mean a smelly disaster for Zaravelle's fishmongers.

To Jael's delight, however, she stumbled upon a treasure—a spice shop being tended by three harassed-looking elves. These were not Allanmere's varied forest folk, but eastern elves, uniformly human-tall and fair but not pale; Jael, however, was uninclined to be choosy. The elves, too, smiled delightedly when they saw Jael approaching.

"Welcome, kinswoman!" the nearest, a slender fellow with sunburnt skin, called in Olvenic. He left the other two elves, a shorter man and a willowy woman, to deal with the customers haggling at the scales.

Jael stepped into the shop. Immediately the mixed fragrance of dozens of spices—sweet, spicy, fragrant, pungent—drowned out the other smells of the market. Jael breathed in the wonderful aroma, recalling with a pang the familiar scent of Argent's workshop at home.

"It's good to hear a voice I understand," Jael admitted. Eastern elves did not clasp hands or embrace on meeting as the elves in the Heartwood did; the golden-haired elf barely brushed Jael's fingertips in greeting, although his smile was warm and friendly.

"Well met, kinswoman," he said. "I'm Barend, and my companions are Serji and Roa."

"I'm J- Acorn," Jael said, inwardly scolding herself. These weren't her friends in the Heartwood; these were strange elves, and Jael could not afford to trust them too quickly. "I just arrived in Zaravelle this afternoon."

"This afternoon?" Barend raised his eyebrows. "But no ships have arrived, either from the eastern coast or on the river."

"My companion and I rafted down from Willow Bend," Jael explained. "We missed the boat from Tilwich."

"I hear the river north of Tilwich is terrible," Barend said sympathetically. "It must have been quite a journey, only the two of you."

"Well, it wasn't only the two of us," Jael said after a moment's hesitation. It couldn't hurt to tell Barend the story here, after all, and if Letha or either of her companions ever came to Zaravelle, Jael wouldn't mind if a nasty reputation had preceded them. "We hired three trappers to take us to Tilwich, but they drugged Caden and me and robbed us of almost everything we owned. While they were busy fighting over our money, though, Caden and I managed to escape on their raft."

"How terrible!" Barend exclaimed. "But you must sup with us and tell us your story. We'll close the shop and cook your supper."

To Jael's embarrassment, they did just that, shooing the patrons from the shop and locking the doors. The elves lived in a comfortable set of rooms behind the shop, scrupulously clean and beautifully decorated, but a bit small and close for Jael's comfort. Roa ducked out the back door and returned shortly with a basket of pincer-claws, but it was Barend who reigned at the small brazier, chatting cheerfully even while he cracked shells, ground spices in a mortar and pestle, or wielded his cleaver so rapidly that Jael was certain at least one finger must join the contents of the pan. At last he scooped great mounds of spicy pincer-claw meat, quick-fried vegetables, and buttered boiled grain onto four plates. There being no dining table, they sat down on the rug and ate there.

While they ate, Jael gave Roa, Serji, and Barend a somewhat pared-down account of what had happened since she and Tanis had left Allanmere, omitting any reference to the reason for their journey. The three elves listened raptly, their eyes wide, until Jael had finished.

"How terrible," Roa murmured at last. "I pray to the Bright One that you've exhausted the misfortune that's ridden with you on your journey."

"Perhaps you've been cursed," Serji suggested. "There's a powerful mage in the city, and I've heard it told he's especially adept at raising curses."

"I'm more interested in finding a reputable furrier," Jael said, grinning to herself. She couldn't tell Serji just how impossible it was that anyone could have cast a curse on her. "We've got some pelts to sell."

"For that you'll want Lezlas at the south market," Barend told her. "He trades fairly."

Jael chatted with the elves a bit longer, but realized at last that it must be well past nightfall. It didn't grieve her that she'd likely missed supper at the inn, but Tanis might be worried by her late return. Reluctantly, she took leave of her new friends and made her way back to the inn, proud that she only lost her way three times. As she expected, supper was long past, but Tanis was in their room, brooding darkly over a mug. Unlike the elves, when Tanis saw her his scowl merely deepened.

"Where have you been?" he demanded. "I've been waiting here for ages."

"I met some elves in the marketplace," Jael said. "They shared their supper with me, and told me about a good furrier, and—"

"You never told me you were going to be gone," Tanis said irritably.

"Well, you didn't tell me you'd be back here for supper," Jael said, a little irritated herself by his tone. "You left so late, and you were going to trade the furs and find the Guild, too, that I thought you wouldn't be back anytime soon. And you didn't tell me I was confined to our room like a prisoner, either."

"You could have left me a message if you were going to be gone so long," Tanis grumbled.

"If I'd known I was going to be gone so long, I would have, if I could have made the innkeeper understand me," Jael retorted. "Listen, Tanis, do you want to sit here and argue, or do you want to tell me what happened? Did you sell the furs? Did you find the Guild?"

"Yes, and yes," Tanis said at last. "I had to buy a full membership in the Guild. The Guildmaster doesn't grant temporary permission unless the thief won't be in town longer than three days. So I had to go back out and sell the furs so I'd have the four Moons to pay for my membership. *Then* I had to go back and pay for the membership and get my token." Tanis held up a narrow brass band that he'd slid over one finger like a ring. "Four Moons for *that*, and it's not even copper."

"What does it matter what it's made of?" Jael asked practically. "What matters is how much you steal, isn't it? But tell me about the furs."

"I tried three furriers in the market," Tanis said wearily, "but I still got only three Suns for the whole bundle. I'm no judge of some of these western furs, but I would have thought I'd get twice that, even as hard as it was to bargain."

"Were any of the furriers named Lezlas?" Jael asked. "At the south end of the market?"

"No, they were all near the north, where the Guild Hall was," Tanis told her. "Why?"

"Because the elves I met recommended a furrier," she said,

shrugging. "It might not hurt to show him the rest of the furs tomorrow and see if you can get a better price."

"Why don't you just do it, since you know so much?" Tanis
asked sourly.

"Because you're much better at bargaining than I am, and you
know more languages than I do," Jael said patiently. "And because this furrier might remember that just about the time this
odd-looking elf showed up at his shop, all his preservation spells
and waterproofing spells disappeared from all his best stock. And
because you need to look over the market anyway."

"And what are you going to be doing?" Tanis asked slowly.
"Chatting with your new friends?"

"Actually, I thought I'd look at horses," Jael told him. "I
know we can't buy yet, but a least I can find out which dealers
are honest and have good stock."

Tanis was silent for a few moments, then quietly pulled a
rolled sheet out of his pack.

"I bought a new map," he said. He unrolled the sheet and
pointed to a spot marked on it. "There's Zaravelle."

Jael stared at the map, her heart sinking. The Willow River
had carried them not only south, but east. In fact, they were not
far west of where the Brightwater emptied into the sea. So many
days of traveling, so much danger, and she had made hardly any
progress at all westward; in fact, all she'd managed was to end
up leagues and leagues out of her way south.

Jael didn't realize she was crying until a fat drop splattered on
the hide, smearing the line representing the Willow River. Another tear fell, causing Zaravelle to bleed into the sea, before Jael
could turn her head away. Then Tanis's arms were warm and
strong around her and his tunic was rough and damp under her
cheek.

Tanis let Jael cry herself dry, holding her quietly until she had
calmed somewhat. Then he remained silent a few moments
longer, letting Jael think about what they were both thinking.

"We could go back to Allanmere," he said quietly. "Get more
money, new horses, and start again. With what we'll make from
the furs, we might have enough for ship's passage east along the
coast and then up the Brightwater."

The thought almost brought new tears. The waste of time and
trouble and the danger to their lives was bad enough, but how
could Jael crawl back to Allanmere and tell her mother that

they'd been robbed blind by three dirty trappers and had rafted leagues in the wrong direction? It had been hard enough to leave in the first place; would Donya let her leave again, knowing Jael had nearly been killed three times, once by skinshifters, her mother's worst fear?

Worst of all was that if Jael returned to Allanmere, to safe stone walls and the familiar faces of people who loved her, would she have the courage to start again, knowing what she had to face, knowing she was chasing legends across an unknown land? She was terribly afraid she would not—that she'd find some perfectly good reason why her journey should wait until the next spring, and then next spring she'd find another equally good reason. And three decades from now she'd still be making the light globes explode in the dining hall during supper.

"I can't go back," Jael said into Tanis's shoulder. "I just can't. Not like this."

Tanis sighed, but he only held Jael even closer and bent to kiss her tumbled hair.

"Baaros help me," he said, "I don't think I could either."

Jael glanced up, wiping her nose on her sleeve.

"Really?" she asked, sniffling.

"Really." He grinned. "When have I ever had this much fun?"

That made Jael laugh, and then everything was all right again. Jael wiped her eyes and her nose, then honked loudly in her handkerchief. That set them off again, and it was some time before Jael could fumble through her kit for Argent's potion. Her fingers closed on the bottle of Bluebright instead, and she gazed at it for a long moment before she loosened the stopper.

"What about a drink to celebrate?" she asked.

Tanis reached for the bottle, then hesitated.

"You said you didn't want to waste it," he said slowly.

Jael shrugged.

"Just this once can't hurt," she said. "For that matter, Serji said—"

"Who's Serji?" Tanis interrupted.

"One of the elves I met today. Anyway, he said there was a great mage in town. Maybe he could divine how the Bluebright's made, so maybe we could get more."

"Just this once, then," Tanis said, smiling. He raised the bottle and sipped.

"To daring," he said.

"To daring," Jael repeated softly, taking a tiny sip of the potent liquid.

This time it wasn't quite so awkward; Jael had a better practical idea of how things were supposed to work, and Tanis's arm was almost completely healed, so they didn't have to worry about his accidentally reopening the wound. Still, as Tanis's breathing slowed and Jael laid her head on his shoulder, shivering a little as their sweat dried in the cool night air, Jael wondered privately if they'd *quite* gotten it right yet.

"Tanis," she said at last, very softly, "am I doing this right?"

Tanis chuckled softly.

"Of course you are," he said. "Why?"

"When you've been with—uh, well, when other people do that," Jael said hesitantly, "do they half fall off the bed, or do their elbows and knees keep getting caught between the bed and the wall? I mean, doesn't that mean I'm doing something wrong?"

Tanis laughed outright this time.

"No, Jaellyn," he said tenderly. "It doesn't mean you're doing something wrong."

"It doesn't?"

"No." Tanis pulled her closer. "It just means the bed's too narrow. It's not your fault."

Reassurance was a wonderful, slow joy growing in Jael's heart—that for once, in fact, it wasn't her fault. And maybe, Jael realized, the highwaymen and the skinshifters and the trappers and the river weren't her fault either, that maybe Jaellyn the Cursed wasn't responsible for every bit of misfortune that crossed their trail. The idea was almost unthinkable.

"Promise?" Jael asked in a small voice.

"I promise." Tanis rolled over to face her and grinned. "And next time we'll pull the mattress onto the floor and I'll prove it."

Jael wanted to caution him that she couldn't keep using the Bluebright every time Tanis wanted a tumble. They had only a small amount of Bluebright with them, and there might be no way to get more. In addition, Jael remembered Argent's caution about using such a drug. It wouldn't do to form a dependency.

She said none of this. There was no reason to spoil Tanis's happiness with unpleasant facts that he likely had already thought of. For now it was enough that, thanks to the Bluebright, she could still take a sensuous pleasure in his holding her, could feel mildly excited again by his hand gently stroking her lower back. Soon enough it would fade, and then Tanis would simply be her dear friend again, his touch only comforting, the smell of his sweat mildly annoying rather than heady and arousing. Soon enough it would all be gone; better not to bring too many truths into their bed to ruin this moment.

In the morning they walked together to the market. Tanis gave Jael most of the money, and he took the remainder of the pelts. At the outskirts of the market they parted; Jael would look at horses and see which merchants sold journey food and supplies, and Tanis would sell the pelts and see if he could expand their tiny hoard of cash. They'd meet again at midday, and Jael would take him to meet Barend, Roa, and Serji. In the meantime, both Jael and Tanis would try to learn when the next boat would be going up the Willow River to Tilwich, so they could attempt to buy passage.

The first priority for Jael, however, was new clothing for herself and for Tanis, and she was quite prepared to spend some of their little money for it. Fortunately, due to the extensive trade with local trappers, leather was very cheap, and as fiber plants were grown widely not far to the east, woven cloth was inexpensive as well. Also because of the trapper trade, a good number of merchants sold dried meat, fruits and vegetables, and journey cakes to travelers. Resupplying, too, would be cheap.

Horses were another matter. There might be folk breeding horses in Tilwich, but there appeared to be none in Zaravelle, and all the horses for sale had been shipped in either from Tilwich or from the eastern coastal cities, an expensive process that forced up the prices. The horses were so expensive, in fact, that Jael reluctantly decided it might be better to wait and purchase their mounts in Tilwich rather than pay the exorbitant prices, plus, of course, whatever fees the trading boat might charge to carry the horses upriver.

The horses, however, gave Jael an unexpected opportunity to earn money. She'd been looking at a set of mountain ponies in one corral when she'd felt the familiar warm tingling inside that told her magic was in use nearby. Jael quickly turned away and focused her attention elsewhere, only to find the pony merchant eyeing her so dourly that Jael was fairly forced to ask him what was the matter. She'd likely buy from this merchant if she and

Tanis decided to buy after all, as he seemed to be the only horse merchant in the city who spoke Olvenic.

"I see you don't like my ponies either. I haven't sold a pony out of this string," the merchant complained. "They're good beasts, sturdy and steady, and they can go for a long time on poor feed, but they can't hold a gait. It's wretched. I'd swear I checked each of the miserable beasts myself when I bought them."

Jael remembered the spell that had been cast on Karina's horses. It wouldn't be unthinkable that one horse dealer might hire such a spell cast on a rival's stock to ruin the merchant's reputation and drive him out of the market.

"My folk are good with animals, and we have a little magic as well," Jael said cautiously. "If I can solve your problem with these ponies, what would you pay me?"

The merchant's face brightened.

"You think they're bespelled, eh? I had the same thought—I was ready to go to Rhadaman to lift any enchantment, though it'd cost me dear. If you can show me that my ponies are once more fit to sell, I'll pay you a Moon for each pony."

Jael was so stunned by the amount of this offer—there were thirty ponies—that it never occurred to her to haggle over the price. She checked each pony, running her hands over them until the tingling subsided. The merchant put each pony through its paces, delighted with the results of Jael's treatment, and quickly handed over the money. As Jael left, however, she realized wryly that thirty Moons—only the equivalent of six Suns—was far, far less than any mage would have charged for exactly the same service. Well, Tanis had likely been well bested in his sale of the pelts; Jael, who was no merchant at all, was certainly entitled to one poor bargain, especially when she'd had to expend so little effort in exchange for the Moons weighting her sleeve. It was satisfying, too, to turn what had always seemed nothing but a curse to her benefit.

When Tanis met Jael at midday, he, too, looked considerably cheered; in fact, he was positively beaming under the grime he always rubbed over his face before thieving.

"You'll never guess—" Tanis began.

"You wouldn't believe—" Jael said at the same time, and they both burst out laughing.

"You first," Tanis said when he caught his breath, but waited until he and Jael had bought a few meat pies and found a quiet alley where they could eat and talk.

Jael told Tanis the result of her morning shopping, and showed him the new clothing she'd bought and the thirty Moons she'd earned. Tanis was duly impressed by the silver, although he agreed with Jael that she probably could have gotten more, and they chuckled a bit wondering which of the other horse dealers in the market had likely cast the spell, and how that dealer would react when the ponies began selling well again.

"Well, I can't boast thirty Moons for a few moments of petting ponies," Tanis said, "and to be truthful, I'm out of practice stealing, so I kept to the easiest marks. But I took over a hundred coppers, sixteen Moons, and two Suns. And these," he added, tossing a small packet to Jael. "I thought you might like them."

The packet turned out to contain tiny molded cakes of sap-sugar. Flattered that Tanis had remembered her sweet tooth, Jael insisted on sharing the sweets as Tanis finished his account.

"The trading boat to Tilwich will leave in five days, and they want two Moons each for passage," Tanis told her, "but they say they won't have any space for horses. I saw the boat, and they're right. So I agree with you that we'd be wise to buy our horses in Tilwich." Tanis stopped there, but his eyes were twinkling so merrily that Jael knew he still had something more to tell her.

"Come on, Tanis, and tell me whatever secret's burning the tip of your tongue," Jael coaxed. "It must be good news, from the way your eyes are smiling."

"It's good news, all right," Tanis said, grinning. "I've found that book for you, the Book of Whispering Serpents."

"You're joking!" Jael exclaimed. "Really? Here?"

" 'Here?' " Tanis mimicked. "Where else could it have been? Remember, Karina said Duranar had taken the book south, and if he got anywhere at all with it, it would be here. Karina thought he might have gotten all the way south to the sea, and he did. When you mentioned there was a powerful mage in the city, I thought I'd do a bit of asking around. The mage isn't Duranar, but his son, Rhadaman, and Duranar passed the Book of Whispering Serpents on to him. From what I heard, though, he doesn't seem to be using it, since he's not known for demonic magic. He's renowned for his healing magic and breaking curses and the like."

Jael sighed.

"That's too bad."

"Too bad?" Tanis asked surprisedly. "Why?"

Jael shrugged.

"Rhadaman isn't going to just hand the book over nicely as a gift," she said. "Even if he wanted to sell it, which he probably doesn't, we could never come up with enough money to pay for it. Which means we'll have to steal the book, and I'd feel a lot better about it if this Rhadaman didn't sound like such a nice person."

"Whoa," Tanis said quickly. "Now, wait, here. I'm barely out of my apprenticeship, and Baaros knows Guildmaster Aubry says most merchants have a natural talent for thievery, but I don't think there's a lamb's chance in a dragon's gullet that I could steal a book like that from an adept mage. Guildmaster Aubry wouldn't touch a job like that. Even *Shadow* probably wouldn't."

"Well, what do you suggest?" Jael asked patiently. "Do you suggest we go back to Allanmere and tell Blade, 'Oh, sorry, we were right there in the city with the book we promised you, but we knew we couldn't get it, so we didn't try'?"

Tanis grimaced.

"She said you could just find it, didn't she?" he asked. "If she wants it that badly, Baaros knows she's got a better chance of getting at it than we do. She said you could just bring her back the knowledge of what happened to it."

"She also said it might be enough for her, and then again, she said it might not," Jael reminded him. "Want to take a chance on her good mood if she doesn't like what we tell her?"

Jael did not say it, but another thought had occurred to her. Blade had more than implied that this book might be the end of her career as an assassin in Allanmere. If Jael could rid Allanmere of its most notorious assassin, then she'd have done something truly marvelous—miraculous, even. And even if Jael never received credit for this wonderful deed, Jael herself would know it.

"I don't think Blade *has* good moods," Tanis said in answer to her question. He grimaced. "But she won't get the book if we try to steal it and get killed, either. And I tell you, there's no chance I'm good enough to rob a mage."

"If he's that good, most of his protections will be magical," Jael argued. "And breaking magical spells is my specialty, isn't it?"

Tanis was silent for a moment.

"All right," he said at last. "Maybe we can agree on this. We'll visit this Rhadaman on some pretext—maybe to see if he can divine how to make more of your Bluebright, as you suggested. While we're there, maybe we can find out where he hides the book and what kind of protections he has. Then again, maybe we won't learn a thing, or maybe we'll find out that his protections are too strong for us to even try. If that's the case, you can go back and tell Blade truthfully that you'd heard that this Rhadaman had the book, but you couldn't find any way to get it. And if we think we *can* get to the book, then at least we can make an informed plan of how to steal it, and before we try, we can get everything ready to go so we can leave town quickly. Agreed?"

"All right," Jael agreed at last. What Tanis said was only reasonable. Even Blade would admit that knowledge of the book's whereabouts was better than nothing, and nothing was what she'd get if Jael and Tanis were both killed before they could tell her where the book was.

"Meantime, I got seven Suns for the second bundle of furs," Tanis told her. "I wish I'd known about this Lezlas before I sold the other stuff. So we've got a total of around twenty Suns' worth of coin. It's probably enough to buy horses and a good quantity of supplies, but not much more."

"That hardly matters," Jael said. "Once we leave Tilwich, we probably won't run into any other towns large enough to buy supplies anyway."

Tanis laughed.

"Jaellyn, what about coming back? We'll have to go back through all those villages and towns and cities again. Even if there isn't so much as a farm for days in any direction, there's no reason to be stranded penniless in the vast unexplored wilderness, is there? Not when another few days in the market might solve the problem. Beside, we've already paid for our room for four nights, and the boat for Tilwich won't leave for four more days."

Four days! This morning the idea of being stranded in Zaravelle for four more days would have been almost intolerable; now, however, four days seemed far too short. Jael wasn't a thief, but she'd spent enough time around her friends in the Guild to realize that less than four days to plan a theft from an adept mage was a pitifully short time. And Tanis would have to spend a good part of that time in the market, too, trying to fill their purse. Unless Jael could find another horse dealer with a fetter-spell problem, she'd be all but useless.

After they finished their dinner, Jael took Tanis to Barend, Serji, and Roa's shop and introduced him to her new friends. To her surprise, the three elves seemed very much taken aback to see that Jael's friend and companion was a human. Of course, the eastern elves were very aloof, Tanis had once told her, compared to the merry folk of the Heartwood, and there was no intermarrying of the races as in Allanmere. To these elves, Jael had fallen in their esteem to the level of someone with very questionable personal habits.

Nonetheless, years of living among humans had obviously rendered these elves somewhat more cosmopolitan than most, and when they had recovered from their surprise, Barend, Serji, and Roa were gracious and polite, if not as openly friendly as they'd been with Jael at first.

Tanis thanked them for their recommendation of the furrier Lezlas.

"I wish I'd waited before I sold the first bundle of our furs," he said wryly. "But Jael told me you also knew a good mage here in town. Mind, I'm not saying we've had a curse of bad fortune cast on us, but what harm could there be in making sure?"

"Rhadaman is the mage, son of Duranar," Roa told him. "He has a house at the west edge of town, on West Gate Road, and a small shop built beside it. Be warned, though, that his prices are high, as he's the only adept mage in Zaravelle. There are a few minimally skilled amateurs of questionable repute, but only Rhadaman is worthy of recommendation."

After a pleasant hour chatting with the elves, Tanis returned to the market, and after a moment's hesitation, Jael decided to go back and purchase the supplies she'd selected. Whether or not they got the book, they would need the supplies, and it would be likely cheaper to buy here than in Tilwich.

There might be few mages in Zaravelle, but there was no lack of thieves; Jael found it interesting just to find a good vantage point on the roof of a shop and watch them work. Some operated in pairs or teams, one or more jostling or otherwise distracting the mark while another took the purse. Others worked alone, relying on wits, quick fingers, and a delicate touch. Still others blindly cut purse strings and ran, using quick feet and dense crowds to dodge their indignant pursuers. Jael became fascinated by the various approaches, criticizing each while admitting to herself that even the rankest apprentice cutpurse could do what she could not.

To Jael's delight, she eventually spotted Tanis, and then winced—he was following his mark, an elderly nobleman clad in hideously bright colors and gaudy jewelry, much too closely, and the nobleman himself was so eye-catching as to endanger any would-be thief who might be noticed nearby. If there were any of the City Guard nearby, they'd take Tanis into some alleyway and thrash him soundly just on suspicion.

At that moment, however, Tanis turned away from his mark. Jael watched puzzledly, wondering what in the world Tanis was doing. Then her eyes widened in realization as a nearby perfume vendor reached for his purse and cried out in amazed anger. All eyes had been on the elderly nobleman, of course, and Tanis had used that distraction to his advantage. Aubry'd been right; although Tanis had spent most of his life as an acolyte to the Temple of Baaros, he had been born to a merchant house, and merchants seemingly *were* born thieves.

There still being a good three hours before dusk, Jael wandered to the west side of the city to see if she could find Rhadaman's house and shop. She had, in fact, no trouble at all; the other houses on West Gate Road were all simple, if spacious, residences, and Rhadaman's was the only shop on the street. Jael did not want to enter the shop this soon, and without Tanis, lest Rhadaman recognize her later—she was, of course, very memorable indeed in appearance—but when she'd lingered outside for over an hour without seeing the legendary mage himself, Jael could no longer resist the temptation to have just a peek. She waited until she was certain there were several customers inside, then slipped quietly through the open doorway.

The shop reminded Jael immediately of the herbal shop that Argent's sister Elaria ran. Flasks, jars, vials, and bottles lined shelves that crossed the room, and these containers were filled with unusual and, for Jael, unidentifiable substances labeled neatly in Zaravelli. Jael breathed in the pungent fragrances until her nose ran freely, then followed a small group of buyers to the weighing counter. Gods, the place was fairly overflowing with magic; she'd have to leave as quickly as she could. Still, she wanted to have a look at Rhadaman.

Rhadaman was there, if the tall, pale, emaciated man in mage's robes was indeed Rhadaman. Despite his cadaverous appearance, the mage was quietly cheerful, speaking kindly to his customers, appearing to know each one by name and apparently conversant with the problems that brought them to his shop. Jael leaned against the far end of the counter, careful not to brush against his delicate scales, while the mage mixed a potion for a young woman's cough. To Jael's surprise and admiration, Rhadaman did not sell her the potion and send her home; although Rhadaman spoke in Zaravelli and Jael could not understand a word, it was obvious that he was showing her how many drops to mix in a goblet of wine, mixing a goblet and having her drink it, and instructing her to wait in the shop long enough to be sure that the potion was efficacious. He showed the same concern for the elderly man who had come for a salve for his aching hands, applying the salve to the gnarled joints himself and waiting until the old man's delighted smile showed that the salve relieved the pain. Only once did Rhadaman glance in Jael's direction, but although he raised his eyebrows briefly in mild curiosity, he quickly returned his attention to his other customers.

Jael's attention was also abruptly distracted, although not by anyone in the shop. Behind the weighing counter were several shelves of books, and one of them, a large volume bound in leather, had two silver serpents climbing the spine, just as Blade had described. Surely that had to be the Book of Whispering Serpents, even though it was stacked among the other books with no more ceremony than an ordinary herbal.

The more Jael saw, however, the less she liked the necessity of stealing a precious volume of magic from this man. If he was using the Book of Whispering Serpents himself, he was using it for a kindly purpose. This city needed Rhadaman and his magic, and who was Jael to take away a book he might well need in his work?

Still, what was she to do? She'd given her word to Blade, and the favor Blade had asked of her was honestly owed and no more than a fair price for the vital answers she had once given Jael. True, Jael could go home and tell Blade that she'd been unable to take the book, but then Blade would more than likely come here to get it herself, and Blade's talent was not thievery, but murder. Jael didn't want to be responsible, however indirectly, for this mage's death, especially the horrible death Blade usually dealt anyone who crossed her. Jael didn't long consider the possibility of lying and saying she'd heard nothing of the book, either. Aunt Shadow was the only person Jael had ever heard of who'd escaped Blade's attack; no one had ever tried to deceive or cheat Blade and lived. No, they'd just have to find a way to get the book. Even if the theft diminished Rhadaman's power, such an injury was still better than death.

Her decision made, Jael took a final critical look around the shop and returned to the market to look for Tanis. She quickly located him enjoying a mug of ale in the shade of a wagon full of woven baskets, and when he saw Jael, he waved her over to join him.

"It's been a good day in the market," he told her. "So good, in fact, that I shouldn't take anything tomorrow, or I may annoy some of the local Guild members. Wait till you see what I got early this afternoon."

"You mean the perfumer?" Jael asked, grinning at the look of astonishment on Tanis's face.

"How did you know about that?" Tanis demanded.

"I saw you take it," Jael said, chuckling. "Well, I didn't see you *take* it, but I saw *when* you took it. Don't worry, though; if anybody else saw you around, they'd have thought you were after that noble, the one in the ugly jewelry."

Tanis grimaced.

"I thought I'd really come up with a wonderful strategy," he grumbled. "Most of the time back in Allanmere I worked with a partner. I'm not used to working alone."

"Well, it was a good strategy, even if I saw it," Jael reassured him. "I only saw it because I noticed you and was watching what you did. But I'll help you, if you like. I'm no thief, but I don't have to be one to jostle people or knock things over on them. I'm good at doing that, anyway."

Tanis raised his eyebrows in thought, then sighed and shook his head.

"Better not," he said. "Baaros knows it's tempting, and I could use the help, but there are so few elves here, and none looking like you, that you're fully memorable. People would start noticing that someone got robbed every time that odd-looking, clumsy elf was in the area, and then we'd be in trouble."

"Well, I haven't earned any more money," Jael sighed. "I

didn't stumble across anybody else who needed spells broken. But I did get a look at Rhadaman's shop, and he may even keep the book there. It was sitting on a shelf behind the counter when I was in the shop."

"You went into his shop?" Tanis said, scowling. "Jaellyn, that was a foolish thing to do. He'll remember you being there. Now when I go to have a look at the place, I'll have to go alone so he won't recognize you and figure out what we're doing."

"I really don't think he even noticed me," Jael argued. "And the book wasn't locked up or anything. If we could get him out of the room for a moment, we could just grab the book with no trouble."

"And what if he's got it return-spelled?" Tanis asked.

"That's what I'm there for," Jael said patiently. "The book isn't magical itself, so it should be safe for me to touch it, and if there's a return spell on it, that should break the spell."

"Hmmm." Tanis raised his eyebrows, then smiled thoughtfully. "Jaellyn, how far do you have to be from a spell to break it?"

"It's not so much distance," Jael said after a moment's thought. "Remember, I shattered all those light globes at the Temple of Baaros and I wasn't in the room, just looking at them through a scrying ball. If I can see something to concentrate on, that usually works. But it's not as sure as touching it. Why? If Rhadaman has wards on the shop or the book, I won't be able to see them, and I'd have to be pretty close to sense that magic in particular. That shop's fairly humming with magic."

"No, no," Tanis said quickly. "I just may have thought of a way for you to help me with a job after all, and without any danger of people noticing your presence. Let me think about it for a few moments."

"All right," Jael said eagerly. She'd occasionally gone with Aunt Shadow on some job or another just to watch—and *that* had stopped when Donya had found out about it—but she'd never been allowed to actually help.

"Your mother already thinks I'm corrupting you," Shadow had said when Jael begged for the hundredth time. "She'd flay me with a dull knife if she ever thought I was turning the Heir toward a career in thievery."

But Jael wasn't the Heir anymore, and if she wanted to help Tanis with his thievery, she could do it if she liked—she could even *become* a thief if she liked, if she weren't so clumsy and unlucky. Suddenly the heady sense of freedom seemed positively overwhelming, and impulsively Jael turned and hugged Tanis, almost making him spill his ale.

"What's that for?" Tanis asked surprisedly.

"I don't know," Jael said, laughing. "For being here. For being you. Because I'm happy. Now tell me how I can help you."

"Well, for a start you can hug me like that again when I'm expecting it," Tanis told her, grinning. "But for the rest, come and look."

Tanis led her to the north side of the market and pointed wordlessly to one of the stalls. Jael glanced in the direction indicated, but hurriedly turned away when she realized the vendor sold nothing but light globes of various shapes and sizes, some plain, others cradled in ornate holders.

"You shouldn't have brought me over here," Jael muttered to Tanis even as she focused her attention *hard* on the bolts of cloth being sold at the booth nearest her. "What would have happened if—"

"I know," Tanis said. "But look over there, the booth right beside it."

Cautiously Jael looked. Next to the light-globe seller was another booth, this one selling fine leatherwork. What Tanis wanted her to see, however, was not the finely crafted vests, scabbards, and saddlery on display at the booth, but the *three* heavy purses hanging from the vendor's belt.

"He's had a good day's sales," Tanis murmured. "I watched him earlier, hoping for a chance to get close enough, but he's smart—stays well back behind those tables and guards his wares like a dragon guards its hoard. But if I could be right there when there was a really spectacular distraction—"

"Like a whole stall of light globes exploding," Jael said, understanding.

"—then in the confusion I could likely get the purses with no one the wiser," Tanis finished, nodding. "I've seen at least three other thieves working this area, and they're always close by. If there *was* a good distraction, they'd use it to lighten the marks closest to them, and that would draw attention away from me, too, even if the leather merchant raises an outcry afterward. I think I could get away completely unseen by ducking under the tables, then cutting around the basketweaver's stall while everyone else was still panicking. When I was a good enough distance away, I could change into the new clothes you bought for me, scrub my face and put on my cap, and nobody would recognize me even if they saw me there. And you wouldn't have to run, especially if you'd been quietly buying something a goodly distance away from the area. Just to be safest, you could linger in the market a little while longer—buy some of the supplies, maybe, that we'll need—and I'd meet you back at the inn."

Jael thought the plan through and found it sound enough.

"All right," she said slowly. "It's a good plan. But after we're in place, I'm going to wait until there aren't many people right in front of the light-globe booth. He's got the sides and back of the booth draped with cloth to keep the sunlight out so people can see the globes work, but the front's open, and I don't want people hurt by flying glass. Besides, it'll work more to your advantage if the crowd's around the leather booth instead."

"All right," Tanis said, nodding. "But in that case, we'll need a signal so I'll know when to move near the stall; otherwise I'll start looking suspicious standing around a booth selling expensive wars, and me so poor and grimy. When you're ready, scratch your left ear, all right, and then count ten before you try."

This was sensible. Tanis carefully slipped Jael the purses hidden in his tunic so the coins wouldn't jingle, and Jael gave him the bundle of his new clothing. As Tanis worked his way leisurely toward the leather vendor, Jael wandered among the nearby stalls, glancing very briefly at the light-globe booth now and then. When she was satisfied that the crowd near the light globes was as thin as it was likely to get, she stopped at a nearby booth selling fried pastries and ordered three *fresh* pastries, if you please—it was a horrible bother to try to convey her wishes through gestures—tossed her coin on the table, then casually reached up to scratch her ear.

Jael counted slowly, then turned to stare directly at the light globes, concentrating on them with all her might. Almost immediately she felt the familiar tingling under her breastbone signaling the presence of magic, and she focused on that tingling, luxuriating in it, wanting more—

Suddenly one of the globes flared bright, then exploded with a loud BANG. Another followed, and another, spraying fragments of glass. A chip of glass stung Jael's cheek, and she did not have to feign fear as she screamed and dropped to the ground. A bystander shrieked and jumped backward, upsetting the pastry vendor's table. Hot oil splashed everywhere and a new volley of panicked screams split the air. A few searing droplets of oil spattered Jael's hand and arm, and several shoppers kicked her in their panic, but Jael only scuttled under the fallen table, her hands pressed protectively over her face as explosion followed explosion at the globe booth. At last there were no further explosions, and Jael dared to glance out between her fingers.

Thankfully, nobody seemed much hurt by the flying glass; everyone in front of the light-globe stall had had the sense to go to ground at the first explosion, many finding cover under tables or behind counters or stacks of goods. As a few bolder people dared to stand again, however, there was considerable confusion. Some bystanders stayed to hurl invectives at the unhappy light-globe vendor, but most simply wanted to leave the area as quickly as they could. Tanis had been right, however; it was quickly discovered that several purses had gone missing during the chaos, including those of the leather merchant.

Jael quickly brushed herself off and offered the luckless pastry vendor a hand up from the ground, even helping him to right his table.

"I won't ask for my coppers back, even though you can see I'm burned by your oil," Jael said sternly, "but I'm going to stand right here and wait while you heat fresh oil and cook my pastries, do you understand?"

The poor pastry vendor understood not a word that Jael said, but her peremptory tone and gestures were unmistakable, and he hurriedly heated the oil, giving Jael an extra pastry by way of an apology.

The sun was setting, and Jael had no desire to try to find her way back to the inn again after dark, so she put off buying supplies for the next day and hurried back to the inn. Tanis was waiting for her in a quiet corner of the public room, a bowl of stew and a tankard of ale in front of him, looking mightily pleased with himself. Jael waited, however, until the innkeeper had brought her her own supper before she asked Tanis if all had went as planned.

"Couldn't have been better," Tanis assured her, keeping his voice low. "I'd wager every copper I've ever had that nobody noticed me before or after, and certainly not while glass was flying everywhere. I'll show you something when we get back to our room."

Jael ate her stew, but found she had little appetite for it. Truth to tell, she was beginning to feel vaguely guilty about her part in

Tanis's theft. True, nobody apparently had been much hurt, not even the light-globe vendor, but someone *could* have been. And the vendor's entire stock of light globes had been destroyed. The only mage of any note in the city was Rhadaman, so the unfortunate vendor would likely have to ship in a new stock from the east.

Later, in their room, however, Tanis waved aside Jael's concern.

"If he has to ship all his globes in from the east, he'd have shipped in plenty more than the two dozen or so you saw in his stall," Tanis told her. "Go back and look tomorrow, and I'll wager he's brought out more from storage. Besides, I've never seen a law against looking hard at light globes. You never even touched them, and it's not as though you cast a spell— completely the opposite, really."

"I don't know," Jael said glumly. "Somehow I don't think Aunt Shadow would approve."

"You're right," Tanis said, nodding. "Shadow wouldn't have exploded the light globes. She'd have robbed the leather crafter, the light-globe seller, the merchants at the next four booths, and every rich noble in the crowd, too, but she wouldn't have broken the light globes. But I'm not Shadow, and we poor fumbling humans have to do what we can to make a living as a thief. Now do you want to see what I got, or do you really want to sit there and whip yourself raw for helping me get it?"

Jael sighed, but relented, and Tanis proudly pulled not three, but five purses from his sleeve.

"I got the leather merchant's purses without any trouble at all," Tanis told her, "so I grabbed two more on my way out through the crowd. I saw at least four other Guild members taking advantage of the ruckus, too. I haven't counted the coin yet—wanted you to touch the pouches first, just in case there might be trap-spells on them. That merchant was so careful, I wouldn't be surprised."

Jael obediently held each of the pouches, felt no tingle of magic, and told Tanis so. They eagerly opened the purses and dumped the coins on the bed between them, gasping at the quantity of Suns mingling with the coppers and Moons.

"Well, that's it," Tanis said, shaking his head. "I'm not stealing so much as another copper while we're here. I don't know how much the other thieves got, but all this money stolen at once is going to make the merchants very, very careful for a while.

Anyway, we won't need any more than this, so there's no need to be greedy."

"What about the book?" Jael asked doubtfully. "We still have to steal that. Or at least try to steal it."

"We'll get the book," Tanis said confidently. "Tomorrow I'll go to the shop and see what I can learn. We'll do the actual pickup the night before the boat leaves for Tilwich. By the time the mage opens his shop, we'll already be gone."

The casual tone of Tanis's voice worried Jael. Rhadaman was obviously a very powerful mage, and powerful mages were not careless people. Rhadaman wouldn't have a book as dangerous and valuable as the Book of Whispering Serpents sitting openly in his shop unless he believed it was safe there. And the book wouldn't still be there in his shop after all these years unless it actually *was* safe there.

Tanis suggested a taste of Bluebright to celebrate their first joint theft, but Jael declined. She gave Tanis the excuse that it might be unwise to take another does so soon after the last, and that was true enough. In her heart, however, Jael still wondered if their theft was in fact an accomplishment that should be celebrated. It somehow didn't feel like something to be proud of.

Tanis was too pleased with his day's thefts to be annoyed by Jael's refusal, and when he curled up beside her, he was quickly asleep. For Jael, however, sleep came less easily, and when she finally dozed off, she dreamed uneasily. The green of the forest closed around her, but it was not the sweet and welcoming forest she'd known. Now the press of leaves, of trees, of innumerable living things around her began to suffocate her, their very living presence an assault. Suddenly the green chaos faded and she sank deep into stone, into welcome silence and darkness lit only by a poignant memory of fire that burned at the heart of the world. That fire flowed through her veins as it had once flowed through the rock, filling her with strength and power, binding her into wholeness—

Jael jolted awake, almost tumbling out of the bed. Tanis sleepily murmured an apology and pulled back the arm that had dropped across her face. Jael sighed with regret for her lost dream, but there was no calling it back. She rolled over and pillowed her head on Tanis's shoulder, following him down into quiet, ordinary dreams of familiar places, familiar people. But even in her comfortingly ordinary dreams, a small part of her longed for stone, and fire.

VII

● "It's simple," Tanis repeated. "It
could hardly be easier." Jael
frowned at the diagram Tanis
had drawn on the square of leather.

"You're sure he doesn't take it into the house?" Jael asked
doubtfully. "Why would he leave such a valuable book just sitting openly on a shelf in his shop all the time?"

"Well, he does," Tanis said, shrugging. "I took the vial of
Bluebright in as near sunset as I could, to be certain I was the
last customer in the shop. When he closed the shop after me, I
was able to look in the window. He went right through the connecting door between the shop and the house, and I heard the
lock click. He didn't set any protections, not that I saw or heard,
and the book was still on the shelf."

"When did he say you should come back?" Jael asked.

"Tomorrow afternoon." Tanis rolled the piece of hide and
slipped it into the sleeve of his tunic. "He said he couldn't promise that all the ingredients would be available in Zaravelle, but he
thought at least he could get a formula for me, and I could have
it mixed elsewhere."

"How much does he want?" Jael asked him. "I mean, we
don't want to spend all our money, even though I'd dearly love

to know what Bluebright's made of, and to be able to get more if I need it."

"I talked him down to only two Suns for the formula," Tanis said with a grin. "Since he's never seen Bluebright before, if he can mix and sell the stuff, he should be able to make a good profit. If he actually can mix up a batch for us, though, he'll charge based on the cost of the ingredients."

"That's fair." Jael sighed. "Tanis, this feels all wrong."

"Oh, Jaellyn," Tanis protested. "You were the one who argued that we *had* to get this book, remember? I tried to talk you out of it, didn't I? Why is your conscience bothering you so much now?"

"I don't know." Jael shrugged. "I just can't imagine any mage leaving a book that precious unprotected in a shop in a city as full of thieves as Zaravelle. None of the mages I know would."

"But Rhadaman's different," Tanis said patiently. "There are no other real mages in Zaravelle, remember? There probably weren't any when Duranar came here, either. So Rhadaman's not used to dealing with people who know much about magical books. Everyone here in the city is dependent on his magic, so why would anyone steal his books? No one would know how to use them; probably no one would even know they were valuable, and who would they sell such a book to, anyway? So Rhadaman's never had a need to take such precautions."

"Yes, but it's a book about *demons*," Jael argued. "A book about summoning and binding demons. Magic just doesn't get much more potent than that. If he's not using that magic—and apparently he's not—then he knows it shouldn't be used. He knows how dangerous that book is."

"If he's not using it, and he knows it shouldn't be used, then why hasn't he destroyed it?" Tanis countered.

"I don't know." Jael shook her head. "Maybe he kept it in case he'd someday need it. Maybe Duranar told him to keep it."

"Well, either the book isn't as valuable as you think, or Rhadaman doesn't *know* how valuable it is," Tanis said exasperatedly, "or he's blasted careless. Or there are *two* books of magic of the same size, with the same silver serpents on the spine. Whatever the reason, have you decided now that it's worth risking Blade's anger?"

Jael shivered. That was one argument she couldn't refute. No, there was nothing to do but try. Even if they were caught, Jael doubted that the mage could—or would—do anything more terrible to them than what Blade could do.

"All right," Jael said quietly. "What should we do?"

"Tomorrow I'll go back just before sunset again and get the formula," Tanis told her. "This time go with me, and stay outside the door so Rhadaman won't see you. When he closes the shop, you'll be close enough to sense if any additional magical protections go up, and we can look again through the window to make sure he didn't just forget to take the book with him today. You can get another peek at the inside of the shop, too, while he's busy with me. Tomorrow night we'll make the final plan, and we'll make the grab the night after. If you sense some kind of spell activating when he closes the shop, then we'll know we have more to deal with than just a lock. In any event, I'll let you touch everything first, just in case there's some kind of ward or trap-spell set."

"All right," Jael said reluctantly. There was no argument she could make. Despite Tanis's seeming overconfidence, he was being reasonably cautious.

Unlike the night before, tonight Tanis was annoyed when Jael again declined to take any Bluebright, and her excuse, that they had no way to be certain Rhadaman would be able to replenish their supply, sounded thin even to her. She reassured Tanis that if they were able to get a further supply of Bluebright from Rhadaman, she could afford to be less miserly with the potent stuff, and that was true enough. Jael thought to herself, however, that knowing what ingredients formed the mysterious liquid and what effects the Bluebright might have on her would be far more reassuring than even an endless supply.

Tanis was still sulking when they went to bed, but he was not too angry to let Jael curl up beside him, her head on his shoulder and his arm around her. His heart was beating rather more rapidly than usual, and Jael could well imagine why he was annoyed with her refusal. Gods, desire was an unhandy sort of thing that turned people's lives as awry as her incomplete soul did hers, and seemed to cause every bit as many disasters. Maybe she wasn't entirely unfortunate after all. How did people like Aunt Shadow, who always seemed to be looking for her next tumble, ever manage to get anything done?

Jael grimaced.

*That sounds like the elf whose arrow missed the stag, and who told his clan the beast would've been thin and tough anyway,* she thought. *Aunt Shadow would say that if you don't enjoy today, what's the use in tomorrow? Mother would disagree, but Mother's always worried or angry, and Aunt Shadow's always laughing. No wonder Tanis is annoyed. I worry as much as the High Lady of Allanmere, and he certainly isn't as patient as Father—as Argent.*

*But sometimes it's hard to laugh with the dagger's point stabbing through my feet.*

Tanis's anger, Jael reflected, was like a summer rain in the Heartwood—quick to blow up, but equally quick to sail away on the wind. Almost as soon as they'd awakened, Tanis had apologized sheepishly for his anger the night before.

"I don't know what's the matter with me," he said humbly, squeezing Jael's hands. "It's just harder than I thought it would be, being around you all the time and remembering the two times we've really been together. I don't know. Maybe we shouldn't have used the Bluebright at all, but I can't be sorry we did."

"I'm not sorry we did, either," Jael admitted. "I'm just sorry it bothers you." She hesitated. "You know, there's plenty of brothels in Zaravelle, and we have enough money."

Tanis's face turned crimson, and he looked away.

"I couldn't do that," he said quickly. "Not now that we've— well, it just wouldn't feel right. I can't explain it."

"Oh." Jael sighed, but in a strange way she was almost glad. Immediately guilt drowned the happiness—what right did she have to become possessive of Tanis when she couldn't promise him anything but continued frustration?

"Anyway, let's not talk about it now," Tanis said hurriedly. "We'll go to the market and buy the rest of our supplies, and then there's nothing to do but enjoy the city until sunset."

Jael was relieved to abandon the uncomfortable subject, and she eagerly walked with Tanis to the market. It was wonderful to have all the money they needed again. Tanis had set aside money for horses, for passage to Tilwich, and a good purse against future needs, but that still left plenty to spend for supplies, with enough left for luxuries they hadn't enjoyed in a long time— sweets for Jael, wine for Tanis, another set of clothing for each. Near midday, Tanis suggested that they separate for a short time, and Jael eagerly agreed. She'd kept back enough money for a

handsome set of daggers she'd seen the day before, and hoped to
surprise Tanis with them to replace the ones he'd lost to Letha
and her companions. Fortunately the daggers hadn't been sold,
and they were of as fine quality as they'd looked before.

When they met at midday for dinner, Tanis had apparently had
the same idea as Jael, for he had two gifts for her—a pair of
wonderfully soft leather gloves that almost perfectly matched the
black boots he'd stolen for her in Allanmere, and a set of silver
combs set with red stones for her hair.

"The gloves I commissioned my first day in the market,"
Tanis admitted. "I'm glad they fit so well. There was a girl at the
Guild whose hands looked about the size of yours, so I had the
gloves fitted from her. But you'd better not wear the combs in
the city. I know I said I wouldn't steal anything more, but when
I saw them at the jeweler's stall, I just thought they'd look pretty
against your hair."

"I bought you something, too," Jael said, handing him the
daggers and matching sheaths. "I wish I'd had enough for a
sword."

Tanis grinned delightedly as he examined the daggers, tossing
them experimentally and testing the edges.

"They're wonderful," he said warmly, setting the daggers
aside and hugging Jael in thanks. "And just the size and weight
I use, too. And I'm glad you didn't get the sword, because I
bought one the first day, and it's nearly finished."

"But how did you have enough money to—" Jael gasped.
"Tanis, you didn't sell your ring, your temple ring?"

Tanis grinned sheepishly and shrugged.

"The ring won't keep us safe if we meet more highwaymen,"
he said. "And it's a fine sword. This southern steel is wonderful
stuff. But enough of that. Let's see if we can find something
other than fish for dinner, shall we?"

They bought pork pies and took them to a quiet corner at the
docks of Zaravelle, where, from a safe distance, they could watch
the latest fishing boat being unloaded while they ate. Like in
Allanmere, the area around Zaravelle's docks was no place to
wander at night, but during the day it was a wonderful place to sit
and watch the ships arrive or depart, or simply stare out at the
amazing endlessness of the sea. The coast was rocky hereabouts,
none of the sand that Shadow had described, but Jael and Tanis
wandered up the coast a bit and managed to scramble down to the

water, letting the spray dampen their hair and faces and wondering at the bitter-salt taste of the water. Jael excitedly pointed out crinkle-shells anchored to the rocks of a nearby jetty, far too deep in the water to harvest; then nothing would do but that they hurry back to the city and buy a bucket of the steamed seafood and eat it on the docks, speculating about the strange creatures living in the salty depths.

Jael tried to ignore the inexorable progress of the sun across the sky, unwilling for the marvelous day to end. As sunset approached, however, Tanis reluctantly suggested that they wash the salt and juices from their hands and make their way to Rhadaman's shop, and Jael equally reluctantly agreed.

It was only a short journey from the docks to the western side of the city, and soon they were standing outside Rhadaman's shop. Tanis peeped briefly through the window and waited until the only customer in the shop had left.

"Give me a few moments before you look in the window," Tanis told her. "I don't want Rhadaman to look up and see you outside. I'll speak loudly before I leave, and you can nip out of sight. All I need you to do is see if you can feel any protections going up when he closes the shop."

"All right," Jael said tersely. "But I can feel magic right now, even out here."

"Well, it's a mage's shop," Tanis said practically. "Think about something else. Think about the Book of Whispering Serpents and how we're going to get it."

That was unneeded advice; Jael could, in fact, think of little else at this point. She was terribly frightened. This was no theft for a thief barely out of apprenticeship and a girl who couldn't do *anything* very well. This was a job for a master thief, at least. But what could they do but try?

Long moments passed, and Jael dared a brief peek in the window. To her amazement, neither Rhadaman nor Tanis was anywhere in sight, but the connecting door between the shop and the house was ajar. Fear loomed sudden and large, and Jael's heart seemed to flutter in her chest. Cautiously she leaned in the door, trying to find Tanis's familiar scent among the bewildering chaos of pungent aromas.

Abruptly the connecting door opened wide, and Rhadaman and Tanis stepped back through. Tanis's shoulders were slumped, and he wore an expression of disgusted resignation. Rhadaman's hand was on Tanis's shoulder, and the mage was looking directly at Jael.

"Come in, Lady Jaellyn, and don't be afraid," Rhadaman told her, speaking in Olvenic. "And please close the door behind you."

For a moment time seemed to stretch out into stillness, and Jael could hear the thunder of her heart in her ears, feel with exquisite detail the wood of the door. She took a deep breath and forced her hand to release the door as she stepped into the shop. The sound of the door closing was loud in the sudden silence, as solid and final as the death of hope.

"Please, let's talk in my house," Rhadaman said kindly. "I'd rather you didn't linger here amongst my spells."

Tanis grimaced but said nothing. There was nothing to say. Jael quietly followed Rhadaman and Tanis through the door and into a comfortably furnished sitting room.

Rhadaman locked the shop door behind them and gestured to Tanis and Jael to sit down. Jael sat down beside Tanis, scooting as close as she could, and Tanis took her hand. Pulling a bell cord in the corner, Rhadaman opened the opposite door and spoke briefly with someone—a servant, perhaps—then turned back to them and sat down himself.

"Please don't be frightened," Rhadaman repeated. "I mean no harm to either of you, nor have I revealed to anyone your presence in Zaravelle."

"Someone else must know," Tanis said sullenly, "or how would you have found out?"

"As best I know," Rhadaman said gently, "I am the only mage in Zaravelle capable of casting a farspeaking spell for the purpose of communicating with mages in other far cities, such as Allanmere. News has already reached Zaravelle by way of trade ships down the Brightwater that Allanmere's Heir vanished from the city a few weeks ago, forcing the High Lord and Lady to choose a new heir. I hope for your sakes that no one else in the city has the knowledge to connect the disappearance of—your pardon, lady—Jaellyn the Cursed from Allanmere with the explosion of numerous light globes in the market. And certainly no one but myself would know that the calibrating spell on my scales failed when a very unusual-looking lass brushed against them two days ago. There have been rumors about you among the mages of Allanmere, Lady Jaellyn, for many years, and I've had the opportunity to hear many of those rumors."

Jael and Tanis exchanged glances, but Jael stubbornly said nothing. Tanis squeezed her fingers reassuringly, but she could feel his hand trembling.

"I'm not surprised you came to Zaravelle," Rhadaman continued, "only that it took you so long to come here. A ship down the Brightwater and across the coast would have had you here weeks ago. But it's really none of my concern."

He was interrupted by a gentle tap at the door. Rhadaman accepted a tray laden with tea, wine, and pastries and laid it on the table between them.

"Please, refresh yourselves," Rhadaman encouraged them. "No drugs or potions, I assure you." He frowned slightly when neither of them reached for the tray, then shrugged and poured himself a goblet of wine and nibbled at a pastry.

"I haven't yet notified the High Lord and Lady of Allanmere that their daughter was here in Zaravelle," Rhadaman said after a moment's silence. "I did speak with a mage I know in Allanmere, and she informed me that a new Heir had been chosen a surprisingly short time after you'd disappeared, and the High Lord and Lady had seemingly made no serious effort to find you. That makes me wonder if your 'disappearance' wasn't permitted, or even encouraged."

"I chose to go," Jael said boldly. "Nobody shipped me out of Allanmere to get me out of the way for Markus. But that's none of your concern, either. If what you're wondering is whether my parents would pay you a ransom for my safe return, yes, they will. So you may as well tell us what you want."

Rhadaman stared at her blankly for a moment, then smiled slowly, shaking his head.

"My dear child—"

"I'm not a child!" Jael snapped.

Rhadaman inclined his head in acknowledgment.

"Of course, you're not," he said. "Forgive me. Lady Jaellyn, I have no intention of holding you against your will, nor of harming you in any way. But you came to my shop for a reason, and I very much doubt that reason was this potion your friend brought—although it is an unusual mixture, I admit—or you'd have simply brought it yourself when you first entered my shop. Since a goodly number of thefts coincided with the explosion of the light globes in the market, and since your friend is wearing a token of the Guild of Thieves—"

Tanis glanced down at his hand and flushed, belatedly covering the token with his other hand.

"—I assume there's something else you want," Rhadaman finished smoothly. "Something you weren't prepared to buy or ask for openly, and something the two of you must have realized you were taking a very great risk to steal. Perhaps if you are willing to speak honestly with me, some arrangement can be reached."

Jael glanced at Tanis. Almost imperceptibly, Tanis shook his head, and Jael said nothing.

"No? Very well." Rhadaman sighed and pulled a scroll from his pocket, holding it out. "Your formula, then. I regret I don't have all of the necessary ingredients to prepare this mixture for you. You needn't pay me the two Suns we agreed upon, young Caden, or whatever your name is; I'm pleased to be of service. My servant will conduct you to the door, and you can be about your business, whatever it is. I'll warn you, though, that my belongings—both in my shop and in my home—will be very thoroughly protected. I'll keep my peace about your presence in the city so long as you make no attempt to violate those protections. Here, take your formula." He dropped it on the table.

The scroll vanished almost instantly into Tanis's sleeve, and Jael was halfway to the door before she realized Tanis had yanked her up from her seat. She caught at the doorframe, however, bringing Tanis to an abrupt halt.

"Wait," she said.

Rhadaman glanced at her, politely curious. Tanis scowled and pulled at her wrist.

"You can't trust that mage," he scowled. "Let's get out of here while we can."

Jael hesitated a moment longer, then decided.

"I'll talk to you," she told Rhadaman. "But not here. Somewhere else. The public room of an inn, or a tavern, maybe."

"Very well," Rhadaman said, unperturbed. "But for your sake, I suggest you choose a location where we can at least expect to talk without half the city hearing your business. Mine, of course, is no secret."

This made sense, and rather sullenly, Tanis suggested the Brimming Mug, a rather expensive establishment only a few moments' walk away. Rhadaman insisted on buying supper for them all, and they were seated in a quiet corner booth that gave them some privacy, but where Jael was reassured that the other patrons would see anything unusual occurring.

"We weren't intending to come here," Jael said, choosing her words carefully. "We were actually going west from Allanmere, wanting to see the unexplored country past the Willow River. But in Willow Bend we paid some trappers to take us on their raft down to Tilwich, and they drugged and robbed us. We got away with their raft, but we drifted past Tilwich—"

"—and there's nothing but wilderness between Tilwich and Zaravelle," Rhadaman said, nodding. "And that explains the thefts, of course; you'd require money for horses and supplies. Or passage back to Allanmere, perhaps?"

Jael took a deep breath; she'd considered the possibility more than once in the last hour.

"No," she said. "Horses and supplies to go north again, and then west."

Rhadaman nodded again.

"No less than what I'd expect of the daughter of the renowned High Lord and Lady of Allanmere," he said. "But money you already have, and the formula for your mixture, if that's important to you, and I certainly have no horses or supplies for travelers. What brought you to my shop?"

Jael exchanged troubled glances with Tanis again, but it was too late for reticence.

"The Book of Whispering Serpents," Tanis said at last.

Rhadaman's brows drew down and he sat back in his chair, gazing doubtfully at Jael and Tanis.

"I can sense some magic in you, of an odd sort," Rhadaman said slowly, pointing to Jael, "but neither of you is a mage, and that is a deadly dangerous book. What do you want with it?"

Jael nibbled on a roll while she considered her answer. She'd given her word to Blade that she'd get the book if she could, but she'd also once sworn she would never tell anyone of her dealings with the assassin.

"I owe someone very powerful a favor," Jael said carefully, "and that person wants the book. I swore I'd get it if I could."

"And what will this person do with the book?" Rhadaman asked pointedly.

"I don't know," Jael admitted. "But she swore—well, I can't tell you what she swore. But I believe she won't do any harm

with it. And I think if I give it to her, something good might
come of it."

Rhadaman was silent for a long moment, sipping his wine
consideringly.

"This person you speak of is in Allanmere?" he asked at last.

Jael nodded.

"I believe you would not aid in bringing harm to your home,
even to pay a debt," Rhadaman said, gazing into Jael's eyes.
"Very well, Lady Jaellyn, I'll bargain with you for the Book of
Whispering Serpents, trusting that you have been honest with me
in what you've said."

"What do you want for it?" Tanis asked warily. "We don't
have much money to spare."

Rhadaman smiled.

"I wouldn't want you to have to steal any more," he said. "No,
we'll find something else. Where did you say you were bound,
west of Tilwich?"

"No, Tilwich was just to get supplies," Jael said before Tanis
could stop her. "West of Willow Bend."

"Hmmm." Rhadaman offered her a seed cake. "Have another.
Do you have a map of your planned path?"

Tanis shook his head.

"Not here in my pocket," he said warily. "Besides, we
couldn't find any maps of the land west of the Willow River."

"There are none," Rhadaman said. "Certainly none here in
Zaravelle. But I've spoken to trappers who work west of Willow
Bend, some of whom are willing to gather herbs and the like for
me, and I've heard a few things you may find it profitable to
know. After the Willow River is more forest for three leagues
west. Here." He pulled a roll of blank parchment, a pen, and ink
from some mysterious recess in his robe. Dipping the pen neatly
into the ink, he scribbled a seemingly random series of lines and
curves that gradually coalesced into a sort of map.

"Here is Willow Bend, and the Willow River," Rhadaman
said, indicating the marks on the map. "The forest continues
west as I've said, and there are a very few tiny towns, trappers'
huts and the like. The forest breaks here, and here is a small area
of plains and low stone hills riddled with caves. South of those
foothills is said to be another forest, called the Singing Forest.
The trappers avoid that forest, say it's cursed. But look at these
hills. Dragons nest in these foothills."

Jael shivered. Dragons, and they'd been traveling blindly directly toward them. Perhaps the stroke of ill fortune that had sent them so far out of their way had not been such a curse after all.

"None of the trappers who gather plants for me will go near those hills," Rhadaman said. "Dragons are sometimes slain in the area north of the Brightwater—north of Allanmere, that is—but they don't nest there, and they're never seen at all here in the south. I've had great difficulty obtaining fresh dragon eggshells, a vital ingredient in certain powerful healing potions."

"No surprise," Tanis said wryly. "Nobody would be foolish enough to go near a dragon nesting ground."

"No one who didn't have to pass that way regardless," Rhadaman agreed. "No one who might agree to fetch a fresh bit of eggshell in exchange for the Book of Whispering Serpents." He fell silent.

Jael looked at the map and scowled.

"You said the Singing Forest is south of the foothills," she said slowly. "What's north?"

"Mountains," Rhadaman said simply. "They're believed to be impassable by everyone I've spoken to. And no one knows how far south the Singing Forest extends, because it's avoided so completely. Those who have ventured into it have never returned."

Jael frowned at the map. The Kresh could have passed the foothills easily. Dragons couldn't kill what they couldn't see or catch. There was no such advantage for herself or Tanis.

"I've learned enough from the trappers that I could create a Gate to take you near the foothills," Rhadaman told them. "That would take days from your journey. Dragons have poor vision at night; perhaps you might choose to approach the nest then. There may well be no dragons there now; it's late enough in the spring that this year's hatchlings may have already flown, and they may have moved back to the mountains. I think it's likely, though, that a few nests are still occupied. You might prefer to make the attempt during the day, when the mother dragons are hunting food for their young."

Rhadaman shrugged.

"Or you may decide my price is too high and choose not to do it at all. Nevertheless, I'll Gate you north and west as I've said, whether you decide to get the eggshell for me or not. I'll give the two of you translation spells, as well, in case you should find yourself in a difficult situation such as this again. That much I'll do as a courtesy to my mage friends in Allanmere, who would expect me to do all I could to help you."

"What's to stop us from saying yes, we'll do it, and then just keeping the book?" Tanis challenged.

Jael winced. There was no chance, of course, that a mage of Rhadaman's experience would simply give them the book and trust that they'd bring the eggshell back . . . someday. But she'd hoped that the mage would secure their promise with some kind of magical spell or binding—a geas, perhaps, which Jael could then break. She had no desire to cheat the mage, but she could just as easily come back to the nests on their journey back to Allanmere, when the nests would be long abandoned, and then have the eggshell sent down the Brightwater to Rhadaman. Maybe the eggshell wouldn't be as fresh as Rhadaman would like, but that was better than Jael and Tanis facing down an angry dragon themselves.

Rhadaman only smiled at Tanis's angry words.

"I'll give you a box for the eggshell," he said. "When you place the eggshell in the box, it will be replaced by the Book of Whispering Serpents."

"And we're to trust *you* to give us the book?" Tanis asked derisively.

Rhadaman shrugged again.

"There's no mage in Zaravelle who could verify the exchange spell when I cast it on the box," he said apologetically. "But I'd be doing myself no good by cheating the daughter of the High Lord and Lady of Allanmere."

Unless, of course, he wanted her dead, and the eggshell was only an excuse. Almost immediately, however, Jael rejected that idea. There was little enough reason for anyone to kill her now, not after Markus had been declared Heir. Besides, if Rhadaman had wanted her dead, there were certainly far less elaborate ways of doing it, and he'd certainly had the opportunity when she was inside his house.

"All right," Tanis said suddenly, before Jael could answer. "It's a bargain."

Jael stared at Tanis in amazement, but Rhadaman only smiled.

"I'm glad," he said. "When will you be ready to leave? I believe I can open the Gate as soon as sunset tomorrow."

"We can be ready by then," Tanis told him. "We still have to buy horses and the rest of our supplies. Where do you want to do the Gate?"

Rhadaman sighed.

"I have a large workroom at the back of my shop," he said. "I'll have to clear it and work there, and tomorrow you can come around to the back door. People will wonder if they see strangers leading horses into my house."

He made as if to rise, but Jael said, "Wait!"

Rhadaman raised his eyebrows, but sat back down, saying nothing.

"The formula for that liquid," Jael said hesitantly. "Can you tell what that stuff actually is, what it does? Is it dangerous?"

"Most of the ingredients are highly intoxicating and possibly somewhat aphrodisiac, but harmless enough," Rhadaman said, sitting back. "Two of the ingredients, however, are very powerful. One is powdered poison sacs of silverspines, which, as I said before, is rarely available here, although I understand it's common enough in the north. I've never made an effort to procure it, as it's used primarily in slow poisons. In and of itself, however, it isn't terribly dangerous in very small doses."

Jael grimaced. Rhadaman's tone was hardly reassuring.

"The other ingredient is distilled juice of dragonberries, so called because eating the berries produces a fiery burning sensation in the stomach," Rhadaman told them. "The berries aren't poisonous, but are used in magical potions and rituals to produce powerful visions. I use it with great caution because of its soul-affecting properties. It's mentioned extensively in the Book of Whispering Serpents, if that interests you. In short, your liquor, if you wish to call it that, is a very potent mixture. I would hardly dare to guess at what the eventual effects of much-repeated usage over a long period might be."

Jael and Tanis exchanged troubled glances, and this time, when Rhadaman rose, they voiced no objections. They had no appetite for the remainder of their supper now, however, and merely returned to the inn.

As they walked back, however, Jael finally asked Tanis the question that had been burning in her mind.

"I thought you didn't want to deal with Rhadaman at all," she said. "Why did you agree so quickly to get this piece of eggshell for him, even though you thought he might cheat us?"

Now Tanis grinned.

"You haven't thought, Jaellyn," he said. "It doesn't *matter* if he cheats us, does it? We've tried, done the best we can do, haven't we?"

"Oh!" Jael hadn't thought of that. It was true, though; they'd bargained for the book, and if the mage promised it to them, Gated them leagues to the north and west, and then cheated them, Blade could hardly blame Jael for that, could she? And if Rhadaman cheated them, Jael would feel a little easier in her conscience about telling Blade the whereabouts of the book and the likely consequences of that telling.

"But how are we going to get the eggshell?" Jael asked Tanis.

"Well, I had an idea for that," Tanis said hesitantly. "But you may not want to do it now."

"What's that?" Jael asked.

"I thought we could have a look around the hills and find out which nests were still being used," Tanis said slowly. "Then I thought you could use the Bluebright and make your own entrance through the rock. That way we could make our way to an empty nest without going anywhere near the dragons themselves. We could wait until dark to leave; as Rhadaman said, dragons are day creatures."

"That's a good idea," Jael said, nodding. "You know, Tanis, I can't ask Rhadaman to cast a sleep spell on me before I go through the Gate, or he'd have to go through with us to lift it, and he'd hardly be sending us after his eggshell if he was willing to go there himself. I'm going to have to take some of the Bluebright anyway before we go through the Gate, and hope that'll keep me from fouling up the Gate spell. We can test it going to Rhadaman's house through the market tomorrow. Besides, there's the box with the exchange spell and the translation spells he promised, too. If I don't use the Bluebright, you'll have to keep them far away from me, and even that may not be enough."

Tanis shook his head.

"Now I don't much like the thought of you using that stuff," he said unhappily. "Not after what he told us about it."

"He warned us about using it often and for a long time," Jael reminded him, although Rhadaman's words had also troubled her deeply. "Since we left Allanmere we've only used it twice. That's hardly frequent. I haven't felt any strange effects afterward. It's no different, really, then the warning my father gave me," Jael added optimistically, "that he didn't want me to be careless with something we really knew very little about. So we won't be careless."

She paused.

"But, you know, that means we shouldn't use it for—well, are you certain you don't want to find a brothel while we're here in town?" she asked slowly.

"No. No brothels." Tanis's smile was resigned, but his voice was firm. "Besides, we have too much to do tomorrow, and I don't want to waste our money, either, not when we have to buy the more expensive horses here."

"Yes, but we'll save the passage up the Willow River to Tilwich, and the food we'd eat between Tilwich and the foothills," Jael reminded him.

"And a good thing, too," Tanis agreed. "We still don't know how much farther we may have to travel west of the foothills. If we manage to get that far at all."

"We'll do it," Jael said adamantly. "It's not like we're setting out to *kill* a dragon by ourselves, only steal from one—or better yet, steal from an empty nest. Dragons are clever, but they're not as clever as we are, and I'd much rather try to trick one of them than a mage of Rhadaman's power."

"Well, there's that," Tanis admitted. He grinned and put his arm around Jael's waist, squeezing her warmly. "And it takes days—maybe weeks—from our journey. That alone is worth something."

At the inn, they spent the extra coins for baths, washing their clothes as well. It might be some time before they'd have hot water again. They curled up comfortably together in the bed, but Jael was too worried to sleep; judging from Tanis's breathing, he, too, was lying awake, although they did not speak. The night seemed endless, but Jael dozed only fitfully, and when the first light of dawn could be seen through the shutters, they rose, still without a word.

Before they did anything else, Jael wanted to test whether the Bluebright could keep her from ruining Rhadaman's Gate, and although Tanis would have preferred to take the chance—he didn't like the idea of Jael using the Bluebright twice in one day—he reluctantly agreed. They searched the market for a likely test and found that Tanis was right—the hapless light-globe vendor had indeed restocked his stall, although his few customers appeared wary of buying.

Jael took a tiny sip of Bluebright from the bottle stashed in her tunic, barely wetting her tongue-tip, and waited a few moments to be sure it had taken effect. This time she planned to take no chances on destroying the merchant's entire stock; Tanis, grumbling, bought a light globe and carried it into an alley where they had a least a little privacy and where passersby would not be harmed. To Jael's delight, however, stare and concentrate as she might, the globe remained intact. Even when she boldly held it in both hands, the globe was unharmed, although Jael could still feel the tingling awareness of the magic. Unfortunately, the Bluebright would eventually wear off, and then the light globe would become a danger, so they simply left it there in the alley, Tanis still grumbling about the two Moons wasted.

Tanis claimed his new sword, and Jael knew enough about swords to be impressed with the workmanship and the quality of the southern steel, as Tanis had said. Jael was glad to see he'd chosen a plain leather-wrapped hilt and a scabbard bare of any ornamentation; as Tanis had told her, they'd have to pass through cities again on their return, and it would be best not to tempt other thieves with expensive-looking gear.

They bought a few meat pies to munch while they walked from horse merchant to horse merchant. At last, to Jael's surprise, Tanis bought four study northern ponies from the very merchant Jael had helped the first day she was in the market. After a little thought, however, Jael appreciated Tanis's wisdom. The merchant, upon spying Jael, rambled on enthusiastically for some time about how effectively Jael's treatment of his ponies had solved his problem, and gave Tanis a nice price on the ponies once he realized that Tanis was her companion. The ponies were calm and sturdy, better suited to the rough and rocky terrain if they had to journey through mountains, and they could live on rougher forage and less grain than the horses. An additional benefit, as Tanis told Jael later, was that the ponies were excellent beasts but by no means attractive or expensive-looking, and therefore less likely to be stolen.

"They're good-tempered creatures," Tanis said approvingly as he and Jael led the ponies back through the confusion of the market to the inn, where they could be loaded. "But they'd have to be, to be boated to Zaravelle and then sold in this noise and scramble. Their hooves are tough and their teeth are good, too. We'd have paid less in Tilwich, no doubt, but I'm satisfied. With four ponies, we can load them more lightly, and that's to the good when there aren't any more roads."

Jael said nothing, but she felt a pang of regret when she thought of their three beautiful horses. Still, the ponies were more practical for this part of their journey, and Jael admitted to herself that she'd far rather have sold their horses than take them into rough country where rock and harsh living might harm them.

Tanis, in turn, was puzzled when Jael stopped at the elves' herbal shop to purchase a pot of rather pungent-smelling liniment. Jael did not explain, only tucked the pot into their bags.

The inn's stable boy helped them load their packs onto the ponies. It was still a goodly time till sunset, but Jael didn't mind; she wanted a last look at the marvelous, wide sea before they left, and Tanis eagerly agreed. They found an unused dock and tied the ponies to a post, sitting and staring out at the seemingly endless expanse of water, dangling their feet down.

"I wonder if anybody's ever taken a ship and just sailed off in one direction or another," Jael mused. "Not along the coast, just straight out to see what's there."

"That would be foolish," Tanis said, shrugging. "Ships are expensive, and so are the crews to sail them. You don't just take one and light out in a direction as we're doing, not knowing what's at the end. How would you know how much food to take, or what trade goods you might want even if you found someone to trade with?"

"I'd go anyway," Jael said wistfully. "Just to see what's there. Just to go someplace where nobody's ever been."

Tanis laughed.

"I believe you would," he said ruefully. "And, by Baaros, I believe you'd find a way to make me want to go with you, too."

"But you like this better, don't you?" Jael asked, turning to look at him. "Strange cities with busy markets, people selling things we've never seen and speaking languages we don't understand."

Tanis grinned and shrugged.

"From a Mercantile House to a Mercantile Temple to the Guild of Thieves," he said. "We all want the same things, more or less, and those things come with cities and people. But I've enjoyed traveling, too, when we have food to eat and aren't being rained on or in danger of our lives every moment. Still, even the uncomfortable parts, they're things we won't forget. They're the makings of stories, you know, to tell Markus and Mera when you get back—Jael's adventures in the great, wide, unknown world."

"Adventures," Jael repeated, savoring the word. "That's true, although I'd never thought of it—we're making stories, stories that people may tell in the market or in taverns in Allanmere, like the story of Mother and the daggertooth."

"Well, now we're in the makings of another story," Tanis said, laughing. "The story of how Tanis and Jaellyn tried to rob a mage and ended up robbing a dragon instead. And hopefully this story ends happily, or nobody may ever hear it to tell it in the taverns. Come along, Jaellyn Dragon-Robber, and let's find out how this story ends."

The sun was sinking toward the ocean, and Rhadaman was waiting at the back door to his shop when they arrived.

"I thought you'd be here sooner," he said, rather impatiently. "Hurry, please. I don't want to keep this Gate open too long considering where the other end is. Magic tends to twist about in that part of the world."

Judging from the shelves and tables in the large workroom, Jael suspected that the room had once been as full and perhaps as cluttered as Grandma Celene's workshop in the palace in Allanmere, but everything had been carried out and the tables pushed back to make room for Rhadaman to work. Magical symbols and lit candles and lamps nearly covered the floor except for a small bare place near the door, and Jael, Tanis, and the ponies were crowded into that tiny space while Rhadaman finished his casting.

Hastily Jael pulled out the bottle of Bluebright and took another ginger sip of the potent liquid. This time the accompanying burst of heat and coolness was more immediate and much stronger, and Jael remembered again what Rhadaman had said about frequent and repeated usage. Well, there was nothing to be done, and she'd have to take another dose yet, more than likely, to deal with the dragons.

Despite the dizzy euphoria the Bluebright brought, Jael was vitally interested in Rhadaman's ritual. She'd passed through Gates before—almost every year since she was very young, to foster in the Heartwood every summer—but she'd never seen one actually cast. To her disappointment, however, Rhadaman apparently had the spell already prepared, for after only a few words and gestures, the sparkling expanse of the Gate shimmered into life on one wall of the workroom.

"It's ready," Rhadaman said. His hollow-cheeked face was pale and drawn, and exhausted shadows pooled under his eyes. And no wonder, Jael thought—she'd never heard of a mage casting a Gate alone. Rhadaman must indeed be as powerful as his reputation hinted.

"Take this box," he said. It was an ordinary wooden box, quite plain, but the interior was lined with the softest wool. The box tingled powerfully against her hands as Jael held it. "Place the eggshell in the box and close the lid, then turn this clasp until it catches. When you open the box again, the book will replace the shell."

Jael touched the clasp, but carefully did not turn it. Tanis gave her a warning glance and took the box, tucking it into one of the bags.

"How large a piece of eggshell do you need?" Tanis asked.

Rhadaman indicated a small space between his hands.

"The size isn't as important as the age," he said. "I need a fresh piece, not one of last year's hatching. Dragon eggshell loses its potency quickly." He handed Jael a smaller sack. "Your translation spells are inside. Now hurry, please. I must close the Gate before it begins to warp."

Jael and Tanis exchanged glances again, Jael nodding slightly. They were distracted by the uneasy whuffling of the ponies.

"I'll blindfold them before we go through," Tanis said quickly, pulling out squares of cloth to tie over the animals' eyes. "They're not accustomed to magic."

Rhadaman extended his hand, and after a moment's hesitation, Jael took it.

"Farewell, Lady Jaellyn," Rhadaman said gently. "I wish you well."

"The next time you speak with the mage in Allanmere," Jael said hesitantly, "would you ask him to give a message to the High Lord and Lady that you heard somewhere, somehow, that their daughter is safe and well?"

Rhadaman smiled.

"Of course, Lady Jaellyn," he said.

Jael took the reins of her pony and the lead rope of one of the pack ponies from Tanis, then walked boldly to the Gate. She could feel a fierce tingling sweep through her, but she did not hesitate, stepping quickly through the shimmering curtain of light.

There was no sense of transition; Jael stepped from the smooth-polished wood of Rhadaman's floor onto rough, rocky ground, stumbling a little. The pungent smells of the workroom were instantly replaced by other, unfamiliar aromas—fresh wind free of city odors, dust, the faint disagreeable scent of something dead and decaying. Overlaying these, however, the wind brought another odor—the musky, metallic, unmistakable scent of dragon.

Jael glanced behind her, glad to see Tanis and his ponies step from the flickering light that marked this side of the Gate. Even as Tanis stepped away from the Gate, the curtain of light shimmered and disappeared. Reassured, Jael swept her gaze across the land around her.

They stood at the edge of a forest, but this was not the well-defined break from luxuriant foliage to rich pastureland that marked the edge of the Heartwood. This was sickly, scrawny growth, a few twisted saplings and yellowed bushes straggling out into dry and brittle grass in scanty patches over parched, dusty earth, the dust itself leached pale and lifeless.

Before them, far too close for Jael's peace of mind, stretched low, jagged hills of mottled stone, clumps of tumbled boulders, and dry gullies. Even from here, Jael could see shadowed crannies that appeared to be the entrances to caves, some of them smoking darkly. The hills must be honeycombed with caves.

By the smoke and the smell alone Jael would have immediately guessed these hills to be the residence of dragons, although she'd never seen a live dragon and certainly never one of their nesting grounds. There was, however, ample evidence indicating the tenants of these rocky caverns. Cracked and gnawed bones were scattered over the barren earth, sometimes in piles near the cave entrances. Some of the bones were old and dry; others had shreds of decaying flesh or fur still clinging to them. Also scattered over the dry rock were old, shed dragon scales, claws and teeth, and malodorous pyramids of droppings, some as high as Jael was tall.

"Phew, what a stench," Tanis muttered, holding his nose.

Jael shook her head.

"It's a good thing we're downwind, or they'd smell us," she said. "We'd better get back into the trees."

Because of the sickly foliage, they had to retreat a good distance into the forest, but Jael did not stop until they were far enough away that she was certain the dragons would neither see nor hear them. Donya had spoken time and time again of the creatures' piercing eyesight and keen hearing.

"That mage shouldn't have Gated us so close," Tanis grumbled, peering through the leaves. "We could've been eaten before we even knew where we were."

Jael shook her head.

"He had no real maps to work by," she said. "And we've already heard that magic doesn't work reliably in these parts." She pulled out the pot of liniment she'd bought in the market. "Here, rub some of this on your skin. It'll disguise your scent."

"So *that's* what it's for!" Tanis exclaimed. He scooped out a handful of the ointment and sniffed at it, blinking rapidly as his eyes watered. "Phew. Well, at least it smells better than the dragons and their droppings. Hadn't we better leave the horses here?"

"Uh-uh." Jael squinted out at the stone hills. To the north she could barely make out the ominous heights of the mountains Rhadaman had spoken of, and to the south she could see a richer-looking growth of forest. That was the Singing Forest, then, that they'd been warned about. "I can't see past the hills, but we're going to have to go west, exactly opposite of where we are now. We'd better work our way around to the south."

"I thought we were supposed to avoid that forest," Tanis protested.

"I know, but we can't take the ponies right up to the nests, or the dragons will smell them, liniment or not," Jael said thoughtfully, "and we need somewhere to tie them or they'll run off. If the wind changes and the dragons somehow smell us or the ponies, we may have to get away quickly, and I don't want to risk us being chased all the way back east."

Tanis squinted at the Singing Forest to the south.

"I don't like it," he said slowly, "but I don't suppose there's any harm if we stay on the fringes, don't actually go into the woods too deeply."

"That's what I thought," Jael said, nodding. "And if we have to, we can stay in the edge of the growth all the way around the hills to the west, if there's no other cover."

"But shouldn't we approach the hills from this side?" Tanis asked. "Since we're downwind, I mean."

"Can't." Jael pointed to the hills. "Too many of the caves face this way. We need to approach from a blind side, and we'll need to retreat the same way."

Tanis reluctantly agreed, and they began working their way around to the south under cover of the trees. The ponies were skittish, frightened by the scent of the dragons, but they were, as Tanis had observed, good-tempered beasts and did not attempt to bolt.

It was amazingly apparent where the Singing Forest began. The straggly, sickly appearance of the trees was immediately replaced by thick, luxuriant green growth, the soil becoming rich and dark and fairly bursting with life.

"It's beautiful," Tanis murmured. "But why do they call it the Singing Forest? And what makes it so dangerous?"

"I don't know." Strain her ears as she might, Jael could hear nothing but the normal forest sounds—wind whispering, limbs creaking, the occasional rustle of undergrowth as some animal passed—and the only song she heard was that of the birds. Still, there was something that warned Jael away. Perhaps it was the very richness of the soil or the too-green verdure, but something told Jael that this was the lair, perhaps, of some very formidable predator, one that would be more than happy to make Tanis and Jael its prey. Tanis shivered and drew a little closer to Jael, and Jael knew he felt it too, that sense of warning.

Fortunately they did not have to go upwind of the hills. Most of the cave openings appeared to face north or west, and there was a good approach from the south. Jael would have much preferred to find a hill with no smoking entrances and be certain that no nests they found would be inhabited, but that would be taking the risk that there were no fresh nests, so they reluctantly chose a southern hill with only one smoking opening, but several other openings with piles of fresh-looking bones outside. Jael and Tanis tied the ponies with some grain to keep them quiet and then belted on their swords, Jael taking another small sip of the Bluebright before slipping it back into the sack.

"Are you sure this is going to work?" Tanis said, giving Jael a steadying arm. "You're getting a little wobbly on your feet."

"I'll be all right." Truthfully, Jael felt wonderful, strong and whole, and she was utterly enjoying the sensation of Tanis's arm around her. She was not too wobbly, however, to appreciate the danger they were in, and she checked once more to be certain the liniment was covering their scent before they crept quietly to the south side of the hill Jael had chosen.

Jael laid her hand on warm, rough rock, then almost pulled her hand away again. The rock was only a thin skin over fire—was that because of a dragon inside the hill? No, this was like Allanmere, where hot springs bubbled up out of the earth. She could feel the hollowness of the hill, the caves winding through it. No wonder the dragons chose to nest there; the protected caves, the heat from the springs to warm the eggs, a continual supply of fresh water, and yet so near the mountains where the adult dragons preferred to live—it was a perfect location.

"Not here," Jael murmured, feeling the skin of the rock thinnest a few feet away. Yes, there'd be tunnels under that thin layer of rock. She pointed to the spot. "There."

Tanis grimaced but followed her, his hand lingering on his sword hilt. He glanced nervously around.

"Hurry," he said. "It's getting dark. There might be dragons coming back from feeding, and there's still enough light for them to see us here."

Jael ran her hands caressingly over the stone. It seemed to give way fluidly under her touch, and she parted it as easily as a curtain. The stone flowed out from under her hands, rippling aside to form an opening large enough for them to pass through, although Tanis had to stoop a little to step in. Through the opening was the cave Jael had tunnelled in to meet. Hot, moist air billowed out of the opening, steaming in the night air, carrying the metallic scent of dragon.

Jael hesitated, but Tanis, more frightened of remaining visible, pushed her impatiently inside, not lighting the lantern until they were away from the opening. The light flickered off puddles on the stone floor of the cave. It was silent except for the incessant dripping of water and the faint, distant bubbling of a spring somewhere not too far away. Passages wandered away in every direction.

"How will we find our way back?" Tanis murmured.

"It's simple, so simple," Jael muttered, her eyes widening in surprise. She could feel her way through the maze of passageways as easily as if she held a map in her hand. She pointed down one of the passages. "There's an abandoned nest that way. I can feel it. I think it's fresh."

"Wait!" Tanis protested helplessly as Jael dragged him down

the passageway. "What if the Bluebright wears off? We could be lost in here!"

"Then I'll take more," Jael said recklessly, her feet for once sure and quick as she pulled Tanis through the passage. Oh, this was power, this was wholeness. It seemed she could feel every crease of the stone, that her vision could stretch over the world, flowing like blood through veins of stone, making her one with the mountains, with the very molten heart of the world. Oh, gods, she wanted this to be forever, to never end.

They panted in the hot, moist air, and Jael felt her chest begin to rasp, but who could think about that when the very stone under her feet pulsed with life, welcomed her as warmly as a lover?

Something rolled under Jael's foot and she fell, slamming painfully to her knees. Stone might welcome her, but it still bruised and cut her flesh, and Jael grimaced, annoyed by the distraction. She glanced around to see what had tripped her, then bit back a gasp as her fingers found a bare white skull, apparently human. There were other bones nearby, some gnawed and split, some blackened as if they had been charred by dragon fire.

"Look!" Tanis said in a hushed voice.

They'd found an old nest. Dragons did not weave a nest of foliage as birds did, but mounded sand and gravel into piles and buried their eggs there until the hatchlings crawled out. The bowl-shaped "nest" was apparently merely a convenient depression to hold the hatchlings' food and keep the clumsy young dragons from wandering away. When the hatchlings were old enough to scatter the lip of sand and gravel and crawl away, they trampled down the rim of the nest; this much was obvious from the condition of this nest.

There were eggshells scattered about, but they were old and yellowed. Jael touched one curiously and it crumbled into sand.

"Jaellyn, look!" Tanis was holding the lantern up. Tanis moved to stand beside him and gasped, gazing down into the nest. Bones were tumbled there, and skulls. Scattered among the bones were armor, whole and broken swords, axes, daggers, and here and there the glint of gold.

Jael was as stunned as Tanis. They glanced at each other wide-eyes; then they were on their knees, sifting wonderingly through the debris. Tanis picked up gold coins, some of them ancient, and stuffed them quickly into his sleeves. Jael picked up a broken sword, wondering at its antiquity. Then another glint of metal caught her eye, and she snatched up a grime-crusted dagger. She quickly wiped off the grime, then gasped in amazement, for the near-white metal of the blade was exactly like that of the dagger and sword she wore.

"Tanis, look!" she said, handing him the dagger.

Tanis examined the dagger, nodding.

"They did pass by here, then," he said quietly. "Only some of them never made it past." He held up the dagger. "I'll keep this, if you don't mind." He picked up a molten lump of metal. "But what's this? It looks almost the same color."

"I don't know." Some kind of a pendant, obviously, as there was a length of chain still attached. Sifting through the pile of bones, she found another; then she uncovered a suit of what must have been some kind of chain mail, although it was now rent and partially charred. The tiny links of silver metal were so fine that they slipped through Jael's fingers as smoothly as silk.

Jael reached for another piece of the fine chain mail, and her fingertips brushed something hard—and a shock of some strange energy surged through her. Jael gasped and seized whatever it was that she'd touched, and Tanis turned quickly toward her.

"What is it?"

"I don't know." This was a pendant, perhaps like the lumps of fused metal Tanis had picked up earlier, but this one was intact. Made of the same white metal as the dagger, it depicted a stylized eye that Jael recognized immediately. She'd seen this symbol once before on a scrap of ancient leather, which the mysterious elf Chyrie had left for her when she'd undergone the elvan passage ceremony more than a year ago. Aunt Shadow had told Jael that it was a symbol of the Kresh, and that Farryn had worn it on a pendant that held his soul.

There was magic in this pendant, great magic the likes of which Jael had never felt before. This magic, however, did not tingle through her body; it swept through her soul like a tornado, tearing away everything in its path. Jael gasped, but her hands were already lowering the pendant over her head. She did not move, but she could feel herself straightening somehow, as if she suddenly grew taller, stronger, but from within.

"Are you keeping that?" Tanis asked curiously. "Look, here's more of that mail, too. But we'd better try to get that eggshell and get out of here before the Bluebright wears off."

"It won't wear off."

"Huh?" Tanis squinted at Jael through the darkness. "What are you talking about?"

"Never mind." Jael wasn't certain herself, but even as she spoke she knew it for truth. "Look, keep the mail, as much of it as you can find, and any other Kresh blades, even if they're broken or melted."

"What good are all the bits?" Tanis asked, but he was scrabbling up the pieces, stuffing them into the sack he'd brought. "The gold's worth more."

"Not out here." Jael bolted upright as a scratching sound caught her attention. "What's that?"

"I didn't hear anything."

"We'd better find that eggshell and get out of here," Jael said reluctantly. "I heard something moving around. There's no guessing what lives in here besides dragons." She could not find in herself, however, the slightest trace of fear. If there was something dangerous living in these caves, it would find Jaellyn more than a match for it, and that was that.

Beyond the nest was a winding tunnel that likely led outside, but Jael did not pause to explore it, drawing Tanis after her deeper into the hill. They passed another abandoned nest, but it, too, was too old, and they did not stop to explore it.

A strong scent of decayed meat wafted down from one tunnel, and Jael speculated that any kill fresh enough to smell like that meant a recent nest, but she also heard movement from that tunnel, so they passed it by. After several more tries, they at last found an empty nest where the eggshells were still fresh and white. Tanis selected the largest piece he could find that would fit inside the box—an entire eggshell would have been almost as long as Tanis was tall—and closed the box, turning the catch. Jael felt a sudden surge in the magic of the box, and told Tanis as much; when he opened the box again, the eggshell was gone, and the Book of Whispering Serpents lay inside on the cushioning folds of material. Jael would have opened the book, but Tanis took it, stuffing it quickly into the sack.

"Look at the book later," he said irritably. "For now, let's get out of here."

Jael felt an inexplicable burst of anger, and she was amazed to realize that her hand had gone to the hilt of her sword. Gods, had she actually almost drawn on *Tanis*?

"Are you sure you know the way back?" he asked, unaware of her anger.

"Of course," Jael said impatiently. What kind of fool couldn't find his way back through such a direct route as they'd taken? Why, they'd hardly turned half a dozen times.

Jael led the way so quickly that Tanis panted in his efforts to keep up, but she did not slow. The heady euphoria of the Bluebright was long gone now, but she was full of another drug—the drug of power, of wholeness, of strength. Her sword almost called to her, and she wanted to draw it, wanted to feel it light and alive in her hand.

Abruptly she stopped. The tunnel they needed to take was ahead of them, but she heard movement in the darkness there—strong, deliberate movement.

"I hear it, too," Tanis whispered. "What is it?"

"I don't know," Jael whispered back. "It's large, whatever it is. A hatchling, I think."

"But what's it doing away from its nest?" Tanis asked worriedly.

"Maybe when they're old enough, they prowl the caves," Jael said, shrugging. "I don't know anything about dragon hatchlings. Who does? But I can smell it now, and it smells like dragon."

"What can we do?" Tanis whispered.

"If we can get a little farther," Jael said, "we'll reach the side tunnel where we found the first nest. It should be well after dark now, so we can get away."

As if in answer, another scratching sound came from somewhere to one side, down one of the passages they hadn't explored. Other sounds came from somewhere behind them.

"They're everywhere," Tanis said tensely.

"They must've scented us," Jael said calmly. "I thought we wouldn't smell like prey through this liniment, but some of our own scent must've come through. Come on, this way." She led Tanis down a side passage.

"Where does this go?"

Jael paused, feeling the stone around her.

"Out the west side of the hill," she said. "We can work our way back south once we're outside."

Suddenly the scent of dragon filled her nose, hot and musky and metallic, and Jael's sword was in her hand before she realized she'd drawn it, before the bulk of the hatchling nearly filled the tunnel ahead of them, appearing as if by magic. Tanis gasped and drew his sword also, but Jael had already stepped forward, her sword raised and moving in hypnotic flashes of reflected lantern light.

Jael heard the hiss of Tanis's sword being drawn from its scabbard, but that fact was as irrelevant as the light that glinted off her sword and the dragon's scales. For once in her life Jael was calm and sure. She'd kill this dragon, and if not, it would kill her, but she'd die with a whole soul, strong and brave as a warrior should be.

The dragon roared its challenge, and Jael struck; fortunately the large passage that allowed the hatchling to maneuver also gave Jael room for her strokes, so long as she kept her pattern tight.

The hatchling roared angrily and struck with one foreclaw, but its attack was slow and clumsy. Jael wondered almost idly if it had ever dealt with live prey before, much less prey able to defend itself and even to attack.

Yes, she'd kill this dragon, slice it to slivers and gorge herself on its bloody flesh to feed her ravening hunger—

Startled, Jael faltered, falling back a step. Fortunately Tanis stepped forward, keeping the hatchling engaged while Jael recovered.

Where had that come from? Jael wasn't hungry; they'd eaten only a couple of hours earlier. And fond as she was of dragon, she certainly wasn't interested in raw, bloody meat. What had—

*Hunger. Fury. Confusion.*

All of Jael's cool self-possession faded, and she almost staggered as alien emotions, frightening in their raw intensity, surged through her. For a moment she fought merely to hold her sword, wanting to fling the strange metal away from her, leap at the hatchling and attack with tooth and nail alone, like a—

—a beast?

Jael fought down a surge of panic. How could she fight a dragon hatchling in its own lair, feeling its own feelings? Gods, could she even wound it without feeling its pain?

"Can you find any safe passage?" Tanis shouted, dodging a forepaw tipped with razor-sharp claws.

Jael's head spun. Retreat? Was this cowardly churl suggesting she *retreat* before this puny reptile? *Hunger. Anger.* Why, she could dice this overgrown lizard into pieces small enough to *tear, rend the soft flesh, crunch rich marrow from the bones.*

Gods, where could she flee from her own mind?

Here, only two places: into death, or into stone.

Jael stumbled backward into the wall of the passageway, trusting Tanis to keep the hatchling busy for a moment longer. She laid both hands flat against the wet stone, concentrating, and the hatchling roared its surprise as the stone under its feet softened, enveloping the three paws still resting there. Tanis immediately took in what was happening and danced back to dodge the reaching forepaw and to avoid being sucked in himself.

"I think that'll hold it," Tanis panted, watching the hatchling rage. "But we'd better get away from here before the noise draws others."

Now that she had a moment to concentrate, she could shut out the furious raw drives of the hatchling—gods, if only she'd been able to do this years ago!—and reach again for stone, feel the intricate net of crisscrossing passageways through the hill. Dimly she could sense other hatchlings, but her consciousness of stone was much stronger, more immediate, and she couldn't place where the young dragons were.

"The second passageway on the left as we go back," Jael panted. "Hurry!"

Tanis didn't waste his breath on a reply, but followed Jael, picking up the lantern he'd placed on the ground. They trotted along as quickly as the slippery and uneven footing would allow, but they could hear the enraged roar of the hatchling behind them—and, worse, a louder roar that likely signified an even more enraged mother trying to reach her offspring in a passage too small to accommodate her larger bulk.

"This way." Jael started to pull Tanis into the passageway, then stopped. Ahead she heard a distinct scrabbling sound, and the scent of dragon was plain in the steamy air. "Not this way."

"Well, where, then?" Tanis panted, a note of panic creeping into his voice.

Desperately Jael felt the stone again, and there she found an answer.

"Up," she said.

"Up?" Tanis looked up at the solid ceiling. "Where?"

Jael dug her fingers into stone. It melted obligingly before her touch, forming cup-shaped depressions deep enough to make good footholds.

"I'll go first," she said. "Then hand me the lantern, then you."

"Go where?" Tanis asked helplessly, but he was boosting Jael up from behind.

Jael reached the top of her makeshift ladder and laid her hand against the stone of the ceiling, feeling the thin skin separating her from the upper caverns. This was more complicated—making the stone flow aside without letting it drop down on herself or Tanis—and she had to work slowly, every moment aware of the scrabbling noises growing louder from the side tunnel. At last the opening was wide enough to climb through to the tunnel above, and she scrambled up—gods, no time to form a ridge to brace against—then reached down for the lantern. Tanis handed it up, but he was already scrambling up the footholds Jael had made.

"Hurry!" he said. "It's coming!"

A roar confirmed his fears, and Jael quickly set the lantern aside, grasping both of Tanis's wrists and bracing her feet firmly. Tanis trusted her grip, giving her his entire weight as his feet shoved desperately upward, and then he was rolling away from the opening even as a razor-tipped claw sliced through the air where he had just been. Jael rolled away also, just in time, for the hatchling thrust a forepaw actually up and into the opening. Without thinking, Jael drew her dagger and slashed blindly, and the hatchling screamed as the severed paw flew free of the spouting limb.

Now Jael could hear other hatchlings gathering below, the pungent scent of dragon almost burning in her nose, even over the metallic stench of dragon's blood from the severed limb. She kicked the repulsive remnant down through the opening and crawled over to join Tanis. He helped her to her feet and took the lantern.

"Better lead the way," he told her. "If the stone between the upper passages and the lower ones is as thin in other spots as it was there, we might fall through."

His warning was a good one. Jael hugged the wall, maintaining a constant light touch on the stone, and several times she had to warn Tanis away from solid-looking spots on the floor where in actuality the mud covered only the thinnest layer of stone. Several times she considered making a new opening to the lower level of caves, but each time she began, she immediately sensed dragons below, and wondered if they weren't somehow tracking Jael and Tanis even through the stone dividing the levels.

At last Jael stopped, shaking her head.

"Wait," she said. "This isn't working. I thought we could get past the nests or the hatchlings, but they're following us. Either that, or there're more dragons and hatchlings in this hill than we thought."

"So what can we do?" Tanis asked slowly. "Is there a way out from up here?"

Jael shook her head again.

"I'll have to make one," she said. "This is the best spot I can feel anywhere nearby, and it's still pretty thick. It's going to take some work."

Tanis squinted at her through the darkness.

"The Bluebright hasn't worn off yet?"

"It's not the Bluebright anymore." Jael grinned, touching the pendant. "It's this. It's not going away. I came looking for a cure, and I found it."

"It isn't going to do you much good if you end up in a dragon's belly," Tanis said practically. "Can you get us out of here before every dragon in the place gets stirred up?"

"I'll try," Jael said, focusing on the stone. It was terribly thick, and opening it would be complicated—she could sense weak places she'd have to work her way around, or else the weight of stone over the opening would give way on top of them. It was a frightening prospect, and Jael was painfully reminded that although she had the power to mold stone to her will, she had little experience using that power.

Grimly Jael set her hands and mind against the stone. She sank deep into stone, parting layer by layer. Twice she had to stop and reroute her efforts as stresses changed, weakening the walls she made. Once she leaped backward as the ceiling of her tunnel cracked and crumbled. By the time she smelled the fresh night air, it seemed that the entire night had passed, although Jael doubted it had been more than an hour since she'd begun. Trembling with the effort, she cautiously widened the opening, then peered outside.

"Is it all right?" Tanis murmured. "Where are we?"

"East side of the hill, high up," Jael answered, grimacing. "We'll have to climb down, and quietly, too."

"By Baaros's purse, I think I could *fly* down to be out of here," Tanis breathed relievedly. "Go on, hurry."

Jael was no less pleased than Tanis to be out of the cave, although the sensation of stone surrounding her had been almost comforting. She squeezed out through the opening she'd made, taking another look around before she accepted the lantern and helped Tanis out.

They had come out of a solid vertical rock face high on the east side of the hill, as Jael had indicated. Because of the numerous caves on that side of the hill, Jael and Tanis quickly decided it would be safer to work their way to the south side of the hill and then descend, rather than risking rocks falling or other noise near the cave entrances. The south face, as well, sloped more gradually and would be easier climbing in the darkness; Tanis, of course, needed the lantern to see his footing despite the moonlight, and they had the sack containing the Book of Whispering Serpents and the other items they'd picked up inside the cave.

Only partway down the slope, however, Jael heard roaring from the east face of the hill. Jael and Tanis exchanged glances, then silently redoubled their efforts, proceeding at an almost reckless pace. They were nearly to the bottom when the roar came again, this time from overhead. Sunlight or not, these dragons were angry or hungry enough to fly!

Jael drew her sword, but she was already running. Tanis, burdened with his own sword, the sack over his shoulder, and the lantern, was able to keep up only because of his longer legs. Suddenly it seemed much farther from the hill to the trees than it had been when they were traveling in the opposite direction.

The stink of sulfur suddenly filled the air, and before conscious thought could form in Jael's mind, she was leaping sideways with all her might, knocking Tanis off his feet so they both flew some distance before landing awkwardly. Even before they both slammed into the dirt, fire seared through the darkness, charring the earth where they had been.

Tanis took the fall better than Jael did, rolling and coming up ready, not even shattering the lantern, while Jael not only had to regain her footing but pick her sword back up as well; the dragon, however, was far too large and heavy to stop or turn so quickly and overshot them. But there was a second dragon in the air now, approaching from the north.

"Split and meet at the ponies!" Tanis shouted, dropping the

lantern and darting off to the right. Jael did not waste breath on a reply, but turned left into the first thin growth of trees. They'd have to be well into the forest before they'd be safe; the dragons could simply plow through the thin growth, although burning through the thicker forest would be slower.

To Jael's surprise, the simple trick worked; as soon as she felt safe in stopping to regain her breath, she realized there was no sign that any dragon had even tried to follow her. Of course—the dragons, who hunted by day because of their poor night vision, would have been following the bobbing lantern, and once Tanis dropped the lantern, the two small figures would be difficult to track, especially in the forest. But how would Tanis find his way to the ponies without the lantern? He couldn't see in the dark, either.

Jael cut straight west through the woods, listening. Tanis was not hard to locate as he crashed through the undergrowth as clumsily as a newborn fawn. They'd both long since sweated and rubbed off the coating of liniment, and Jael could smell his sweat and his fear—surely the dragons could, too.

Even as Jael hurried through the forest, she marveled at how quietly and easily she ran, not tripping over fallen branches or smacking into tree trunks, her mind clear and her senses sharp. It suddenly occurred to her why Tanis had suggested separating—it was to protect *her*. He knew she could see in the faint moonlight trickling through the trees and would quickly make it to safety while the dragons tracked his own clumsy noise.

There was Tanis ahead, cowering behind a tree and clutching his side as he panted heavily. He neither saw nor heard Jael approaching over his own harsh breathing, and he jumped when Jael touched his shoulder.

"It's all right," Jael murmured. "It's just me. Are you hurt?"

Tanis shook his head.

"Just can't—get my breath," he gasped.

"Put your arm around me," Jael said, sliding her sword and his back into their scabbards and looping his arm over her shoulders. "You ran past the ponies. We'll have to keep moving. I can hear the dragons flying over, and if they can spot exactly where we are, their fire can reach us."

She half-expected Tanis to make some ridiculous suggestion about leaving him behind so she could get away faster, but thankfully Tanis either loved life too much to suggest such a thing or was intelligent enough to realize that Jael would never

obey. It was, as Jael had said, only a short distance to the place
where the ponies were tied. The animals were frightened by the
smell and sound of dragons overhead, dancing nervously and
pulling at their ropes, the whites of their eyes showing.

Jael helped Tanis onto one of the ponies, but she didn't bother
with the knots on the lead ropes, cutting through the ropes with
a single slash of her dagger. With all four lead ropes in her hand,
Jael trotted through the trees as quickly as she could, staying as
near the edge of the forest as she dared.

A dragon roared overhead, and briefly the sky was lit by
flame. Jael swore and moved a little deeper into the Singing Forest with the ponies. There was nothing for it—they were going
to have to find somewhere to shelter and wait for the dragons to
calm down again and go back to their nests. But the tenacity of
a dragon on the track of its prey was legendary.

"They're just flying over the trees, pacing us," Tanis called.
"We're going to have to go in deeper, where the trees are taller.
Right now we're just circling the edge of their territory. Maybe
if we head into the forest, directly away, they won't be willing
to leave their young so far behind."

Jael paused, listening for the dragons. Yes, they were still overhead, at least two of them and maybe more, forming wide circles.
Any moment they'd be flaming the trees. Jael was wary of the
curse of the Singing Forest—the legends about skinshifters had
been true enough, hadn't they?—but whatever mysterious danger
the Singing Forest *might* hide, Jael was all too certain about the
threat posed by the very solid presence of the dragons overhead.
Tanis was right; going deeper into the forest was the only option.

Jael turned southwest—remarkable how easily she could tell
which way to go without becoming confused—and headed directly into the forest. As the growth of trees became thicker, the
trees shot up taller, competing for the sunlight. Gradually, the
sounds of the circling dragons faded. Jael hoped that meant that
Tanis was right, that the dragons simply didn't want to leave
their hatchlings too far behind, and not that the dragons would
rather give up their prey—even prey that threatened their
hatchlings—than risk the danger of the Singing Forest.

As they hurried deeper into the forest, the faint moonlight was
slowly choked out by the thick growth overhead. The familiar
night sounds, however, reassured Jael; if the birds and tree frogs
and insects found the Singing Forest a suitable place to live,

maybe it wouldn't be too inimical to a pair of innocent passersby who wanted nothing more than to be gone from the entire area.

Jael saw several convenient spots where they might make a camp, but did not stop until she had neither heard nor smelled dragons for some time. At last she tied the ponies at a thick cluster of bushes, and Tanis helped her drag the bedrolls into the undergrowth. There was no thought of a fire or even of supper; the two crawled shaking into one bedroll and heaped all the covers over them, clinging together in the darkness.

At last Tanis spoke.

"Are you all right?" he asked quietly. "I mean, are you really all right now? For good?"

Jael took a deep breath and slowly felt her shaking subside.

"I'm all right," she said. Below the forest floor she could feel the bones of the earth, good strong stone, and the feeling comforted her. She knew there were myriad animal minds all around her, some of them killing or being killed at this very moment, but she could shut them out effortlessly. "I'm really all right, at last."

"How's that possible? Because of this?" Tanis touched the pendant hanging around Jael's neck.

As Tanis touched the metal of the pendant, Jael gasped as a sort of shock ran through her—not precisely a physical shock, but a profound sense that Tanis had somehow touched *Jael*, touched her very essence.

Tanis had snatched his hand away as soon as Jael gasped, and now he raised himself up on one elbow, squinting at her worriedly through the darkness.

"Are you certain you're all right?" he asked. "Did I do something—"

Jael shuddered pleasurably, then moved closer to Tanis.

"Uh-huh," she breathed. "I think so."

She rolled over so that Tanis was under her; before he could speak, however, she covered his lips with hers, her fingers tearing at the lacing of his tunic so fiercely that the fabric ripped. Tanis was frozen with surprise for a moment; then he helped her, pulling her tunic and shirt over her head. His hands slid eagerly over her skin, but he hesitated.

"Are you sure you're all right?" he murmured. "This isn't like you."

"I'm all right," Jael assured him, bending over to brush her lips over his. "Let me show you just how all right I am."

# VIII

- "It's up to you," Tanis said, his hands gently kneading the muscles of her shoulders. "I mean, if you want to go on—"

"I don't see why we should." Jael stretched lazily under Tanis's hands. "I'm curious, sure, about Farryn and his people, but there's no need to go hunting legends just to satisfy my curiosity. I'm well now, so there's no reason to go any farther into unmapped territory. Besides, we're almost straight west of Willow Bend, so we can just go back straight east out of the Singing Forest, and we've got enough supplies to make it to the larger cities. Don't you agree?"

"There's nothing short of Baaros's halls of gold that I want more than to get back to Allanmere with both of us alive and safe," Tanis said ruefully. "But we've come this far."

"I know. It does feel a little like quitting," Jael admitted. It felt, in fact, a great deal like quitting. There was an almost unbearable longing in her to continue onward, maybe forever, to find the remote, lonely places where she was certain her people—*Farryn's* people—lived. *But that's selfish,* she told herself again and again. Every day, every hour in this unmapped wilderness was a greater risk of her life and Tanis's. There was the book, too, that she had to return to Blade before it somehow

176

got damaged or destroyed. Lastly, Jael felt a certain amount of
eagerness to show her family and friends her new wholeness and
skills, begin the delightful process of learning just who and what
this new Jaellyn really was, preferably with Tanis's help. After
more than two decades, she'd earned that pleasure.

"No, we'd best start back," Jael said firmly. "Maybe someday
we'll come back and look—with a whole caravan of our own,
though, I think!"

"Now, *that's* a thought," Tanis laughed. "We'll bring our own
cots and cushions—"

"And wine for you," Jael grinned. "In leakproof casks with
aging spells!"

"And soupstones," Tanis said blissfully. "Tents with rain-
shedding spells."

"And wards to keep out highwaymen and beasts," Jael said
firmly. "But in the meantime, it's a long road back to
Allanmere."

Tanis sighed, but nodded. He gave Jael's shoulders a last rub,
then bent to kiss the back of her neck.

"I almost don't want to leave," he admitted.

Jael rolled over, her eyes twinkling mischievously.

"No matter," she said. "It's a good many nights before we
reach Allanmere."

"If they're all like last night," Tanis smiled, "I may not make
it back to Allanmere alive."

"Complain, complain," Jael sighed. "First he moans day and
night that he can't have me, and then when he can, he complains
about *that*."

"Oh, I'm not complaining," Tanis said quickly, his grin widening. "Although if you want to be picky about it, there's some
question in my mind about who had whom last night."

Jael felt her cheeks warm. Tanis had been right last night; the
way she'd acted *hadn't* been much like her. It was almost embarrassing, how—well, how *hungry* and demanding she'd been.

"Well, people do tend to gorge a bit, their first meal after a
long fast," Jael said sheepishly. "And even with the couple of
times with the Bluebright, that was really the first time I was all
there, all myself, so to speak. So for me it *was* a rather long
fast."

"Too bad." Tanis gave Jael a hand up from the ground. "I

hope that doesn't mean that you have to go without for another twenty-two years before you tear my clothes again."

Jael flushed again.

"If you don't stop talking about it, I'm going to do it now," she said defiantly, "and then it'll just be that much longer before we get back to Allanmere. Come on, help me load the ponies."

Tanis chuckled and made a point of hesitating thoughtfully, but he helped Jael bundle the bedrolls together and tie them onto the ponies. They were both ravenously hungry—they'd had nothing to eat since their midday dinner on the docks at Zaravelle the day before—but both agreed it would be safer to eat some of their preserved supplies in the saddle than linger in the Singing Forest for the time it would take to hunt or cook something for breakfast. Besides, Tanis speculated, it could well be the act of hunting or killing, or perhaps the lighting of the fire, that caused the trappers to disappear there.

They headed confidently east, toward the morning sun—or what morning sun they could see through the dense foliage. The forest was drowsy and quiet, its scents and sounds familiar and comforting. Because of the dense canopy of the trees, the undergrowth was thinner than in the Heartwood, and the ponies tripped along easily.

They stopped at midday at a pleasant streamside clearing. They dined on journey food, and Jael and Tanis eagerly took advantage of the clear stream to rinse their clothes and wash from their skin the mud and sweat of the previous night's adventure, but Tanis hesitated to refill their water bottle from the stream.

"We should be long out of the Singing Forest by now," he said slowly. "I mean, we were near the eastern edge of it, and we've been traveling east for hours. But I haven't seen any change in the plants or anything."

"I know." Jael shook her head. "Maybe there was only such a visible difference there near the hills where the dragons lived because the dragons poisoned the soil. But surely we're far from the Singing Forest by now. Still, it's not as if we're short of water. Why don't you wait and we'll refill the bottle tonight, and just to be certain, we'll angle a little to the north. Remember, Rhadaman said the Singing Forest extended west and south."

"I'm glad you don't think I'm acting like an idiot," Tanis confessed, putting the empty water bottle away as they mounted their ponies. "It's just—I don't know. I just don't feel quite at ease. I don't know why. The country here feels odd."

"The country here *is* odd," Jael agreed. "Dragons nest here, and Karina and Rhadaman both said that magic gets twisted around here, and more so the farther west you go. All kinds of strange legends come out of the west. It's one reason why settlement west hasn't progressed any faster than it has—it's just too dangerous. So I don't think taking a few simple precautions is 'acting like an idiot.' "

They turned the ponies in a more northerly direction and rode onward. Gentle breezes ruffled the leaves and carried the scent of flowers and warm earth. Birds fluttered past occasionally, and Jael saw the occasional squirrel watching them from the branches. Once or twice they saw deer watching them unafraid from the thickets, but Tanis made no move to draw his bow. They had dried meat aplenty, and it would be foolish to shoot a deer only to waste most of the fresh meat. Besides, it seemed almost sacrilegious to spoil the peace of the forest with death.

They rode on as if in a dream, not speaking. There was no need to speak; it was far more pleasant to listen to the birdsong and smell the sweet scent of flowers and fresh green growing things. The gentle sound of buzzing bees and the warm breeze were almost hypnotic.

Toward sunset, however, Jael's uneasiness increased. *Something* was wrong. Something was definitely wrong. But what was it?

Finally Tanis reined his pony to a stop.

"Jaellyn," he said slowly, "doesn't that jumble of rocks look familiar?"

Jael frowned darkly at the rocks. They *did* look familiar. Had they passed a jumble like that just before they stopped at midday?

"We can't be riding in a circle," Jael protested. "We've both been watching the sun, and we haven't crossed our own trail."

"I think we should stop here," Tanis said. "We should make camp. Then I can take a bearing from the stars to check our direction."

"This must just look like rocks we passed earlier," Jael argued. "I think we should press a little farther while we still have some sunlight. It gets dark awfully fast in these thick woods."

Tanis shrugged and reluctantly agreed. They rode only a short distance, however, before he reined in again, and the two stared, dismayed, at the small stream where they'd stopped for lunch. The clump of flowering rushes and the mossy boulder where Jael had laid her clothes were unmistakable.

Jael slowly slid from her pony and walked to the streamside. The sand of the bank was utterly unmarked by their tracks, although Jael knew she'd crossed that patch of sand at least four or five times, and Tanis as often. The bed of moss where Jael had pried up a handful of the rich green to scrub herself with was unmarred.

"It's the same place," Tanis said quietly, joining her at the streamside. "I'd wager every copper I've ever owned or ever will."

"But there's no sign anybody's ever been here," Jael said, just as quietly. "How could that be? I can't feel any magic, none at all. It couldn't be an illusion spell. And *nobody* can move the sun."

"Well, now we *have* to stop," Tanis said practically. "We're losing the light."

"I don't like it," Jael said worriedly. "Whatever's got us all turned around like this, if that's what's happened—it could be dangerous to stay here, don't you think?"

"If we're wandering in circles in daylight, what's going to happen in the dark?" Tanis said sensibly. "Still, we'd probably be wise to take watches tonight. And just in case it *is* some kind of magic, maybe some kind you can't feel, we'd be wiser not to eat or drink anything but what we brought with us. It'd be safer, too, if we leave most of our supplies on the ponies."

Jael agreed, but when they made their camp beside the stream, she pointed out practically that they'd have to build a fire, or Tanis would have no light on his watch. Accordingly, they carefully dug a firepit and lined it with rocks from the stream. Jael picked up deadfall, laid a small fire, and lit it with a certain joyful defiance. Let whatever covered their tracks and led them around in a circle bring those branches back if it could!

Jael volunteered for the first watch; since Tanis was already disadvantaged by his poor night vision, he should not have to contend with his fatigue as well.

Now Jael was certain that something was indeed wrong; the previously friendly forest seemed alien, quietly menacing instead of peaceful. She questioned each seemingly familiar sound. Was that indeed the cheeping of the tree frogs and crickets, or merely some deception designed to lull the visitors into lassitude? Were the small, flickering lights she saw indeed merely fireflies, or were they something far more sinister, merely aping a familiar form?

Gods, had the dragons indeed ceased their pursuit not because they lost interest in their quarry, but because they feared that in the Singing Forest, they themselves might become the prey?

Jael shivered and huddled close to the fire despite the unusual warmth of the night. She drew her sword and laid it ready by her side, and drew her dagger, too, reassured by the glint of the blade in the firelight. She knew Tanis would have his sword handy, too, even while he slept.

Jael shivered again, but this time not with fear, thinking of Tanis in the tent, his sword beside him. How would he react if a hand slid under his shirt in the darkness while he slept, surprising him awake? Would he seize his sword and attack, or would he sense the identity of the one touching him and seize her instead? Either possibility seemed equally exciting.

Jael slid her hands up her arms, touching the bruise on her shoulder where Tanis had sunk his teeth into her skin the night before. His nails had dug into her hips, too, leaving crescent-shaped cuts. Jael sucked her breath in sharply, pleasurably, gooseflesh stippling her skin at the memory. Maybe Tanis wouldn't mind if she woke him. Maybe she didn't care if he *did* mind. Maybe—

Jael froze at some faint sound, something out of place— perhaps the cracking of a stick under too much weight, perhaps a rustling that seemed a little too furtive. She picked up her sword, her ears straining, her eyes striving to pierce the darkness. Here, however, the fire was her enemy; its brighter light dwarfed the faint moonlight so that her eyes could not adjust, and the darkness outside the firelit circle was nearly impenetrable.

The ponies stirred uneasily, and suddenly Jael felt their fear, their instinctive sense that something was wrong. Tentatively she reached out through the darkness, clumsily, searching for other animal minds, perhaps eyes that could see for her in the darkness.

What she sensed brought Jael instantly to her feet, backing slowly toward the tent where Tanis lay sleeping. It was simply this: nothing. There were no animal minds that she could feel in any direction—no bats or owls or drowsy squirrels, no deer in the bushes, no rabbits in their dens. There was only an emptiness that fairly shouted its menace, and a faint sense of something she could not quite grasp, a mind too complex or alien or elusive for her untrained beast-speaking ability.

The ponies were pulling at their ropes now, dancing nervously. Jael did not turn her eyes from the darkness outside the circle of fire, but she kicked blindly at Tanis's foot.

"Tanis!" she murmured. "There's something—"

"I know." Tanis was almost immediately beside her, wide awake and with his sword in his hand. "Something woke me—the ponies, I think. What's out there?"

"I don't know." Jael moved slightly to the side so that her back was to Tanis's. "Stay near the fire so you can see. Can you hold a torch and your sword, too?"

"What do you think?" Tanis asked, already reaching for the end of one of the burning branches in the fire. He raised the burning end high, sweeping it in a semicircle.

The wind shifted subtly, and suddenly a scent flooded Jael's nostrils, rank and musky, a scent that Jael found horribly familiar. There was no time for Jael to shout a warning before the first skinshifter attacked, but from the sudden tensing of Tanis's muscles against her back, she knew he recognized the scent as well.

There was no sense of transition. One moment the carefully cleared earth around the fire was empty but for Jael and Tanis; in the next moment it was filled with creatures that attacked silently and with demonic swiftness.

After the encounters with Durgan and Cesanne, Jael had thought herself prepared for the disgusting, unformed appearance of skinshifters, but in this she was mistaken. Compared to these nightmare beings, Durgan and Cesanne at their most horrible had been a delight to look upon. These creatures had wandered so far from their humanity that Jael wondered uneasily if they had retained any memory of their prior lives. Although they wore only tattered, filthy shreds of clothing, it was impossible to distinguish male from female, or to even speculate whether any of them had been human, elvan, or perhaps even Kresh. There was now a sort of obscene uniformity about them in the melting and re-forming limbs or features, in the misshapen eyes or fanged mouths that might erupt anywhere on the ever-shifting surface of their bod-

ies, in the grayish, claylike skin that rippled with fur or scales or
feathers in turn.

But there was no opportunity to ponder these monstrosities,
for they were attacking, still as horribly soundless as before;
somehow the very silence was more terrible than any cry they
might make out of those malformed mouths. Clawed hands
formed, only to dissolve into hooked tentacles that nonetheless
reached eagerly toward their prey.

There was no time for fear, either. Jael lunged to meet the attack, Tanis forgotten, a glorious strength welling up from some
hidden place in her soul. She screamed, a glad, fierce battle cry,
and her sword flashed eagerly forward, shearing through amor-
phous flesh. Foul-smelling ichor spouted, and one of the shifters
roared with pain and fury, but Jael was already moving, flowing
like water, like molten stone through the veins of the earth, unconsciously dodging a clawing talon, then pivoting to slash at
her attacker. This time the cry was choked off abruptly, and Jael
saw a head roll into the fire.

Instinctively Jael leaped to the side, turning to slash again as
a shifter landed where she had just been. The shifter's hand—if
it could be called such—closed around Jael's arm, but fell away
as Jael's sword bit deep into its midsection, cleaving it nearly in
two. To her surprise, she found her dagger in her other hand, and
realized amazedly that she'd made that strike with her sword
one-handed. Eyes sparkled in the moonlight; she slashed at the
eyes with her dagger and saw them disappear behind spurting
ichor. Shifters howled as Jael's sword sliced effortlessly through
melting flesh, clearing a comfortable space around her.

Suddenly there was another scream, and Jael realized that that
scream had come from no shifter. Abruptly she froze, remembering Tanis. Gods, she'd forgotten him entirely!

And now there were a least three skinshifters between her and
Tanis. No time for fear now, or caution. Jael moved instinctively,
relying on that wonderful *rightness* of the sword in her hand, the
swift strength that seemed to move her without thought.
Skinshifters roared and screamed, and Jael dodged the claw that
whistled by a fingerswidth from her face. Then Tanis was there
in front of her, fallen to one knee, and the smell of his blood was
hot and coppery in Jael's nose—*How badly is he hurt?*—but then
he was up again, wielding his sword with a kind of desperate

fury. Claws dug into Jael's thigh, but her back was guarded again, and her sword bit into shifter flesh with new energy.

Gradually the skinshifters fell back beyond the firelit circle as the number of fallen shifters—and shifter limbs—on the ground increased. Jael did not lower her guard; she couldn't even be certain that the shifters lying motionless on the ground were actually dead, and she knew the others were only regrouping for a new assault. With so many of them there, they could simply outwait Jael and Tanis.

"Jaellyn—" Tanis's voice was weak. "I can't keep going much longer."

For a moment, Jael felt a flash of contempt—what a pitiful weakling!—but immediately was horrified at herself. She thrust her dagger into its sheath and turned to wrap her arm around Tanis's waist; the right side of his tunic was sodden with blood, and more welled under her hand. His right hand only barely clasped his sword, but his left still firmly waved the burning branch.

"I think we can outrun them on the ponies," she said, forcing out each word. Somehow it was almost unbearably galling to retreat. "Leave whatever's not packed."

By the time she reached the ponies, having to stop twice to fend off shifter attacks, Tanis was stumbling badly and seemed only half-conscious. There was nothing else for it; Jael quickly tied the ponies together on long leads and mounted the pony behind him, holding him up. The animals were pitifully eager to be gone, and Jael didn't have to urge them to their greatest speed; in fact, she had to hold them back so that she could be certain they wouldn't break a leg on the uneven ground. For a few tense moments she could hear the skinshifters behind them, frighteningly fast and seemingly unhindered by the darkness. Gradually, however, the sounds of pursuit faded, although Jael had no doubt that the uncanny creatures were tracking them through the forest.

Now Jael faced a horrible dilemma. She had no idea how serious Tanis's injury was, and he was barely conscious. If she stopped to treat his wounds, however, the skinshifters might well catch up with them. And she was riding blind in an enchanted and hostile wood, with no idea of her direction; for all she knew, she might well be riding ever deeper into the Singing Forest.

Jael reached out desperately with her clumsy beast-speaking

ability. Now that she was away from the skinshifters, she could feel animal minds, yes—and under them, the faint sense of some larger consciousness. Gods, was the Singing Forest itself alive, some kind of gigantic hungry thing? She fumbled through the animal minds around her, wincing as she felt her clumsy touch frightening, maybe even hurting them, but at last she found what she sought—an owl hunting at what was unmistakably the edge of the forest.

Surely the owl couldn't be too far away if she sensed it so clearly. She clung to the fierce mind as if it were a beacon and rode desperately toward it, now completely supporting Tanis as he slumped unconscious in the saddle. It seemed that they rode forever in the darkness, Jael's fear for Tanis a greater weight than his body slumped in her arms.

As she rode, she concentrated wholly on the owl, and well that she did—it seemed as if the moonlight was now coming from the east, now from the west, the wind alternating confusingly as well. Branches seemed to reach down from the trees to rake at her, and twice Jael smelled the rank aroma of skinshifters on the crazily changing breeze, although none appeared to menace them.

The horses slowed as fatigue outweighed their fear, but Jael urged them on. When they again faltered, Jael grimly did what she'd never believed she'd be capable of—she deliberately conjured the image of the skinshifters in her own mind and projected it to the ponies, who surged forward in renewed terror. By the time Jael was certain that the trees ahead were indeed thinning, the horses were stumbling and exhausted, barely able to walk. At last Jael almost wept with relief to see open sky ahead, moonlight silvering the tall grass of a wide plain.

Still Jael would not let the ponies stop until they were clear of the last saplings. At last she reined her pony in and slid off its back, then eased Tanis carefully down from the saddle. He stirred, moaning a little as Jael lowered him to the ground. Jael was alarmed at the quantity of blood soaking his tunic and shirt, although she was relieved that there appeared to be no new flow of blood from the wound.

Carefully, Jael eased the cloth of Tanis's tunic and shirt up, her eyes widening as she saw the fearsome wound that had almost bared his ribs—and worse, the plain marks of skinshifter teeth in the flesh. The blood there was still fresh, but Jael was reassured

that there was only a slow, sluggish seeping that a tight wrapping
would easily control. She quickly rummaged through their packs
for her kit of herbs and salves, glad to occupy her mind with
other matters, even for a moment.

When she turned around, Tanis's eyes were open and he was
struggling to sit up.

"Jaellyn?" he gasped.

Jael rushed to his side, pushing him back to the ground.

"It's all right, we're safe," she assured him. "Lie still and let
me clean your side."

Tanis lay back, watching Jael as she pawed through the kit,
squinting at pots in the moonlight.

"Hadn't you better light a fire?" Tanis asked hesitantly. "I
mean, don't you need to burn—" He gestured mutely at his side.

Jael didn't meet his eyes.

"It's not too bad," she said. "A good firm dressing and you
should be fine, but I doubt you're going to be using your sword
arm for a while. Still, you'll—"

"Don't you need to burn it?" Tanis repeated. His voice was
shaking now, and his hand seized Jael's wrist.

Jael clasped Tanis's hand, reluctantly meeting his eyes.

"Tanis, it's too late to burn it," she said quietly. "It's been over
an hour since you were bitten. I've got some scratches, too."

Tanis said nothing, but he was shaking as Jael cleaned and
dressed the cruel wound and, almost as an afterthought, the
scratches on her thigh as well.

"Our bedrolls and the tents, I left them behind," Jael said quietly. "But there's our cloaks still. Tomorrow at dawn we'll start
back for Willow Bend as soon as I figure out how far north or
south of it we are. It can't be far to the river from here."

"But Willow Bend has no mages," Tanis said slowly. "And we
don't even know how far away it is from here. Wherever we
are."

"In Willow Bend we can find out whether there are mages in
Tilwich," Jael said firmly. "We've got time, Tanis, up to maybe
a week, and we'll ride fast and hard. We'll make it. Besides,
there's no certainty that either of us is infected."

Tanis touched the bandages at his side.

"If this doesn't make it certain that I'm infected," he said
slowly, "what would?"

"Several days or a mage's diagnosis," Jael said gently. "Tanis, you'll be fine. We both will. Now you need to rest."

Tanis squeezed her hand tightly, his own hand still shaking.

"I don't think I'm going to be able to sleep," he admitted. "And you haven't slept at all. Why don't you sleep and I'll keep watch for a while?"

Jael smiled to herself. She'd learned enough about healing to know that after a fight so fierce and a wound so serious, Tanis would be asleep very, very soon.

"All right," she said. "Let me get out the cloaks and put my salves away, and then I'll get some sleep and let you take the watch. In the meantime, just lie still."

Jael laid out the cloaks, helping Tanis wrap himself warmly in one of them, and then took her time packing her herbs and dressings away, setting out the pain potion Argent had given her. Tanis would need it tomorrow. By the time she was done, Tanis was sleeping so soundly that he did not rouse even when Jael wrapped the second cloak around him.

Too sleepy to dare sit down, Jael gazed around her. Behind them was the dark, endless bulk of the Singing Forest, but ahead stretched a great, rolling plain seemingly as endless, although she saw a darker line to the west that might indicate mountains. Tall grass was silvered in the moonlight, and gentle breezes made ripples that looked like the waves Jael had seen on the southern sea.

Jael gazed out at the plain, and although she remained silent, some part of her sighed. That deeply hidden part of her relaxed utterly and stretched pleasurably, the way she stretched sometimes in the morning as she came slowly, sweetly awake in her own bed. Every muscle in Jael's body slowly relaxed. As inexplicably as she'd felt threatened in the forest, so she now felt safe, even welcomed. It didn't have the feeling of home, but— but something like it, perhaps.

Jael shook her head, fighting down the instinctive comfort that might lead to dangerous lack of vigilance. They were in a strange land far from home and possibly infected from the shifter sickness, and as far as Jael knew, there was nothing preventing those shifters from coming out of the Singing Forest onto this plain that felt so safe and wonderful. Jael couldn't afford to feel protected here.

She brushed the ponies thoughtfully, enjoying their pleasure as she coaxed the snarls and tangles from their coats. *They* were calm and unafraid here, grazing on the thick grass, the skinshifters forgotten.

Sighing, Jael sat down next to Tanis and waited for dawn.


"Jaellyn?"

Jael groaned and opened her eyes, every muscle screaming as she moved. Gods, she'd fallen asleep, and now she was thoroughly chilled, wet with dew, and cramped from sitting.

Tanis was half-sitting, his hand clasping his bandaged side.

"What?" Jael said irritably. "I know, we were going to leave at dawn. I'm sorry I fell asleep."

"No, that's not it." Tanis's face was blank with despair. "Look at the sun."

Jael looked. The sun was still low and dark orange; they weren't *that* late. The sun looked just the same as it looked every morning, rising over the forest.

Oh, gods—*rising over the forest.*

"We've come all the way out the west side of the Singing Forest," Tanis said. "Wherever that is. Now we'll have to go all the way north around it—and back through the dragon hills, too—to get to Willow Bend. And there's probably not enough time."

Jael shook her head unhappily, her fingers involuntarily touching the scratches on her thigh.

"We'll start north," she said flatly. "There's nothing else to do. Can you ride?"

Tanis struggled up to a sitting position, his face pale.

"Uh-huh," he said. "For a while. But you'd best tie me on, just to be safe."

"Right." Jael helped Tanis onto his pony, loading a few bags on behind him for support, and tied him securely in place. She placed the flask with the pain potion in his hand. "Take small sips of this if you need it. I'll just lead your pony."

"Jaellyn"—Tanis seized her hand, looking into her eyes—"If I'm infected, if I start to turn skinshifter—"

"You won't," Jael said quickly. "We don't even know that you're infected."

"Jaellyn, listen to me," Tanis said urgently. "We all heard the rumors in town, that High Lady Donya's brother became infected with the shifter curse and she had to kill him. That's true, isn't it?"

"You don't know anything about it," Jael snapped, although

she knew it was no secret in Allanmere. Jael herself had heard the entire story, plainly and without embellishment, from Argent when she was old enough to understand that this was yet another subject she was not to broach to the High Lady of Allanmere. Donya's twin brother Danyel had become infected with the shifter curse when Donya had consented to take him on a journey into the unexplored west, forcing Donya to kill him. Jael knew, too, that that memory haunted the High Lady when Jael had planned her westward journey, and that her mother would not have been nearly so worried—or worrisome—had Jael picked another direction in which to travel.

In retrospect, the High Lady's concern had been more than warranted, and it stung Jael to admit that.

"Jaellyn." Tanis held her hand. "You have to promise me that you'll kill me—and burn me—if I go shifter. Promise."

"I promise." Jael folded her hand over his and forced a grin. "But it'd better not come to that, because then who'd see to me if *I'm* infected? Now, let's get going and find a mage to make sure this conversation stays completely speculative."

"I can't argue with that," Tanis said ruefully. "Let's see how fast these ponies can travel."

Jael was heartened to find that the ponies, while they were not built for speed, were strong and sturdy and could maintain a steady, distance-eating lope for a long time. Even as they rode, however, Jael felt her hopes dwindling. The vast green sea of the Singing Forest continued beside them unbroken and with no visible end to the north, and when Jael probed the beast-minds around her, she could find none to tell her how far it might be to the northern edge of the forest; either the animals near the northern edge were too far away for Jael's inexperienced range, or the animals' minds were too unsophisticated to uncover the particular information she wanted. She said nothing of this to Tanis, however, and continued ruthlessly northward, wringing her mind to focus on whatever beast-minds she could reach.

"Jaellyn!" Tanis's voice, heavy with pain and breathless with fear, broke through Jael's concentration, and Jael forced herself back into her mind and body with some effort. Gods, her head ached miserably, her muscles were screaming from their tense clenching, and the sun was near its zenith.

"What?" Jael said, shaking her head to clear it. The motion sent spears of new pain through her temples.

"Look to the west," Tanis said urgently. "There's something coming."

Jael squinted westward. Sure enough, there was something approaching—several somethings, in fact—very rapidly through the tall grass. Some kind of large herd animals? Very large indeed, if Jael's perception of their distance and size was correct, although it was hard to judge against the featureless grass. Something about them—yes! It wasn't herd animals at all; it was riders.

"They're people," Jael told Tanis, reining in her pony. The other ponies stopped, too, and Jael could feel their relief. "People on horses."

"People, this far west?" Tanis asked doubtfully. "Should we wait? Arm ourselves? Hide? Run?"

Jael touched her bow but did not take it from its case.

"We'll wait," she said. "Whoever they are, maybe they can help us. Where are those translation spells Rhadaman gave us?"

Tanis pulled the small sack out of his saddlebag and peered into it.

"Two copper bracelets," he said. "But, Jaellyn, how can we trust these people?"

"How can we not?" Jael asked practically. "You can't fight, and the ponies are too tired and heavily loaded to outrun anything faster than a snail right now."

"What if they want to rob us?" Tanis persisted.

"If they've got a mage who can cure the shifter sickness," Jael said simply, "they can have everything we own."

There was, of course, no argument Tanis could make to that, and he urged his pony slightly forward so he could sit beside Jael and watch the riders approaching. He did not draw his sword—he couldn't have used it in any event—but he checked the draw of the dagger in his left boot. Jael glanced at him, then slid from the saddle to stand beside him; if it came to fighting, she'd do better on her feet.

As the moving figures approached, however, Jael realized with dawning amazement that they were not riders at all—nor were they human, nor Kresh, nor elves, nor shifters, nor any type of creature Jael had ever seen or imagined in her life.

From the waist up they seemed relatively human, although their large, broad-shouldered frames were covered with a sleek pelt of hair or fur the color of dried grass. Their faces, too, were covered with shorter fur except for a narrow margin of bare skin around their eyes, noses, and mouths, and catlike ears pricked up at the top of their heads. Shaggy, wavy manes of hair, the same color as that on their bodies, cascaded over their shoulders and flowed down their backs. Their strong hands clutched spears and bows. They wore no clothing, the females as bare-breasted as the males, although they wore a good quantity of heavy gold jewelry and strings of horn and bone beads.

Below the waist, however, any resemblance to humanity disappeared completely. Now Jael realized why she'd mistaken the creatures for riders. The creatures' waists flowed smoothly to a sturdy, horizontal torso rather like that of a huge cat, covered with a fur the same color as that on the upper body, but thicker and shaggier. The forelegs and paws were catlike, too, as best Jael could see, though the hindquarters more resembled those of a horse but ended in broad, shaggy-fetlocked cloven hooves. Shaggy horselike tails dangled down from their rumps.

"Baaros preserve us," Tanis whispered. "What are they?"

"I don't know," Jael said slowly. "But they're carrying weapons, and they're not shifters—at least no kind of shifters I've ever heard of. Give me one of those translation spells."

Tanis obeyed, sliding the second bracelet onto his own wrist. Jael was reassured to feel the familiar warm tingle of magic when she touched her own bracelet. After their experience in the Singing Forest, she'd begun to fear that she'd lost her magic-spotting talent.

They waited while the strange-looking creatures approached, Jael watching intently for the first sign of one of them leveling a spear or drawing a bow, but the creatures did neither of these things. The creatures stopped a short distance away, gazing from Jael to Tanis with open amazement.

Finally the foremost creature, a male, stepped forward, and Jael found herself looking into silver catlike eyes more than a head above her. The male hesitated, glancing perplexedly from the pendant around Jael's neck to her sword, then back again. At last he extended one hand. Jael was surprised to see that his large hand had six long fingers rather than five.

Equally hesitant, Jael reached out, expecting to take his hand; as soon as she extended her own hand, however, she found her forearm clasped firmly by the huge hand. Jael clasped his forearm in return as best she could, although her fingers could not reach around the muscular limb.

"I am Wirax, leader of the Second Hunt of the grass hunters," he said. His voice was low and melodious. "Who are you and what is your clan?"

"I'm—" Jael hesitated again. "I'm Jaellyn, and my friend is Tanis. I've come seeking my people and my clan."

"What is your clan?" Wirax repeated slowly. "You are one of the mountain folk, are you not? You wear their symbol." He indicated Jael's pendant.

"My father may be one of the—the mountain folk," Jael said. "I've never met him or his people. I know only what my mother has told me of him. Can you help me find him?"

"How can you not know your people and your clan?" Wirax asked as if he had not heard Jael's last statement. "You speak our tongue. You wear their sign and have their scent." He released her arm, then grasped her wrist, holding her hand up. "But not the same. You have not the look of the mountain folk."

Jael started to explain, then shook her head.

"I'll be happy to tell you everything I know," she said. "But my friend is hurt and needs help, and we were both injured by skinshifters." She braced herself as she made that last admission, fearing that these people, like humans, would react with typical fear or hostility, fleeing or driving them away, if not attacking.

Wirax, however, only nodded.

"We will take you to our camp, and our healer will tend your friend," he said. "You can answer our questions then."

He glanced at Tanis, then at the ponies.

"Your friend is weak and your riding beasts are weary," he said. "My sister Vani and I will carry you. We carry the mountain folk sometimes on hunts to the dragon mountains. My folk will lead your riding beasts and follow."

Tanis looked alarmed at this suggestion, but Jael gave him a warning glance; it wouldn't do to anger these people. Tanis reluctantly let her help him down from the pony, and when they turned, a tall female was there. Wirax helped Tanis onto the female's back, and the female—Vani, apparently—took some of the rope from the saddle, passing it around Tanis's back and tying it around her own waist.

"Don't try to hold on, young one," Vani said, reaching behind her to pat Tanis's leg. "Your arm won't hold, and our camp is a good hour's run."

Jael squinted doubtfully at the broad expanse of Wirax's back. She was an accomplished rider, but Wirax was certainly wearing no saddle and his back, not at all like a horse's, was a good bit taller than she was used to.

Wirax, seeming to understand her dilemma, extended his hand with a smile. This time Jael gladly clasped arms with him, and with Wirax supporting her weight, Jael was able to scramble awkwardly onto his back. The fur was unexpectedly soft and thick.

"I feel the strength in your legs," Wirax said. "Do you need a rope?"

"I think I'll be all right," Jael said. She awkwardly wrapped her arms around his waist.

"Not like that." Wirax took her hands and showed her how to hold on, her arms passing under his armpits and bending up to clasp his shoulders. "Thus, or you'll bounce about. Hold fast, then, young one."

Jael gave a last backward look to be sure some of Wirax's companions were indeed bringing the ponies. Then she had to devote all her attention to holding on as Wirax launched himself forward.

Despite the rough beginning, Wirax soon fell into a smooth, rather rolling gallop of unbelievable swiftness. Jael felt the powerful muscles ripple under her legs, and his shoulders were strong and solid under her hands, his pelt soft. His scent was strong and fresh, and Jael suddenly felt her body warm to it, the smell and the feel of him. Jael shivered and held on tight, breathing in his scent as his hair blew back into her face.

The plain rolled past with amazing speed. The grass was green from the frequent spring rains, but Jael could well imagine that in summer, when there was less water, the grass would dry to just the color of Wirax's fur. If the plains hunters folded their legs and lay in ambush in the grass, their eyes would just top the tall grass, and they'd be all but impossible to see.

Far to the west she could see more clearly the mountains she'd glimpsed the night before. They were closer than she'd thought, but were veiled by a thick mist and Jael could not determine how tall they might be. She'd never seen such mountains in her life, and ordinarily the misty heights might appear grim and forbid-

ding, but something in those mountains made Jael's heart soar
with joy. As clearly and instinctively as she'd felt at peace and
welcomed when she'd set foot on the grassy plain, now she felt
a pleasurable twinge of something very like recognition looking
on those mountains, a feeling like that of homecoming.

And wasn't she in fact coming home, in a sense, after all?

Ahead of them she saw a dark spot surrounded by what appeared to be huge mushrooms. As they approached, however,
Jael realized that the dark spot was a camp of some sort, and the
mushrooms were large hide tents. More of the grass hunters, as
Wirax had called them, were coming from the camp to greet
them, including some smaller ones that Jael decided must be
children despite the perfectly functional bows and spears
clutched in their hands. Soon Jael and Wirax were surrounded by
a staring throng.

Jael looked around for Vani, and was alarmed to find her nowhere in sight. Wirax seemed to sense her alarm.

"Vani ran ahead," he said. "Your companion lost his wakening
some time ago, and she is a faster runner than I, so she took him
ahead to Vedara, the healer. You can climb down now, Jaellyn."

Jael felt something very much like regret as she slid off
Wirax's muscular back. She'd never ridden a horse so swift.

"There will be time enough for you to meet my clan," Wirax
said, raising his voice so the statement included his people as
well as Jael. "For now I will take you to Vedara and your
friend."

Jael looked back the way they'd come. There was a moving
blob on the horizon, probably the others with the ponies. Reassured, Jael nonetheless stayed close to Wirax's side as he led her
into the circle of tents. She was rather embarrassed to note that
Wirax had to slow his pace significantly to let Jael keep up with
him.

As they walked through the camp, Jael was reminded of the
temporary villages made by some of the more nomadic of the elvan clans. The tents were huge structures formed of stitched-
together hides and mounted on solid frameworks of poles. Round
holes had been cut at the top of the tents, cunningly covered by
small upside-down V-shaped "tents" to keep out the rain and let
smoke escape. The tents were bare of ornamentation on the top
and sides, but patterns of brightly dyed beads had been stitched
around the hanging flaps that served as doors.

Inside the circle of tents was a smaller circle, and then another. At the center of the circle of tents was a cluster of six large firepits, and over each of these a large carcass of some sort of hooved quadruped was roasting.

Everywhere she looked, Jael saw more of the amazing creatures and again she was struck by the reminders of an elvan village. Here, too, the inhabitants were going about their everyday duties—caring for their young, mending or making weapons, weaving baskets, scraping or stitching hides, preparing food, or simply lounging about talking. Jael was comforted by the casual appearance of the camp and the mild curiosity with which the inhabitants looked at her.

Wirax led her to one of the interior tents, and Jael saw that Vani was already waiting outside the door flap, her legs comfortably folded under her. Wirax held aside the flap.

"You may enter," Wirax told Jael. "Vedara will tend your wound."

Jael took a deep breath and stepped forward; the flap was cut high for Wirax's people, so there was no need to duck her head. The transition from the bright sunlight to the darker interior of the tent blinded Jael for a moment, and she had to stand blinking for several seconds before her eyes adapted.

The interior of the tent was lit by animal-fat lamps, judging from the smell, and a good many of them. The floor was comfortably strewn with furs except for the small firepit at the center, where a low coal fire burned. At one side of the tent a cup-shaped depression had been dug into the earth, and this was thickly filled with furs, apparently a bed of sorts. Everywhere were small pouches and pots smelling of herbs, potions, and ointments, perfuming the tent with their powerful aromas.

Tanis was lying on a sort of low table built of stacked blocks of sod and covered with hides. Tending him was a creature that made Jael hesitate near the door flap, almost afraid to move forward.

In general form it was similar to the other grass hunters, but its pelt was not the uniform light tan color Jael had seen; rather, it was mottled in shades of black and dark brown with occasional patches of glistening white. Unlike the other grass hunters she'd seen, Vedara's hindquarters were like the forelegs, ending in clawed paws. The ears at the top of Vedara's head, too, were longer, swept up and back and tufted in white fur at the tips.

Most amazing, though, were the *four* arms that sprang from Vedara's shoulders, one set below the other, all working busily on Tanis.

The long ears swiveled in Jael's direction, shortly followed by the face, and again Jael almost gasped. Vedara's face, neither distinguishably male nor female, was built in planes so angular and exotic that Jael was uncomfortably reminded of Durgan and Cesanne. The eyes were slit-pupiled like Wirax's, but they were a rich, tawny gold rather than silver. Jael thought she'd never seen a more exotic-looking—or beautiful—being in her life. It wore more gold jewelry than any of the others Jael had seen, including a marvelous bracelet in the shape of a dragon coiled around one wrist.

"Come, and welcome, Jaellyn of the Four Peoples," Vedara said, his—her?—voice as mellow and sweet as wind through elvan pipes. "He has asked for you. Quickly; he almost sleeps."

Jael couldn't bring herself to speak, but crossed the fur-covered floor and knelt on the other side of Tanis, taking his hand. Tanis's eyes were only half-open, but he seemed to recognize her, squeezing her fingers weakly.

"It's not as serious as that," Vedara told her, and Jael swiped impatiently at the tears on her cheeks. "Some blood has been lost, but most of his sickness is only pain and fear and weariness. He woke a little and showed me the potion you gave him for pain. I gave him another, a stronger one. He will sleep, likely until morning."

"Thank you." Jael had to force herself to speak, and her voice was barely louder than a whisper. "Can you tell if he's infected with the shifter sickness? Can you cure him?"

"He carries the taint of the Unformed Ones, yes," Vedara said, nodding. "But the taint is young and weak. I can slow its progress, but I have not the power of an Enlightened One to reverse that change. Come here and look."

Jael crept timidly around the table, Vedara moving aside to make room. The raw wound in Tanis's side had closed noticeably and the bleeding had stopped, but the skin around the wound was an unhealthy grayish color.

"The dressing you used was a good one," Vedara told her. "There's no infection but for the taint in his blood, and that I have slowed, as I said. There's no immediate danger for him. Now I will see your own wound."

Jael stood, flushing despite herself. Now that she was closer to the strange creature, she realized that despite its delicately featured face, it was certainly male; first, it had no breasts, and second, Vedara's fresh, musky scent affected her even more potently than Wirax's had. Healer or not, Jael was embarrassed as she pushed her trousers down over her hips, glad that her tunic hung low enough to cover her. She sat down as Vedara indicated, trying not to tremble as the healer's long fingers slid the tunic up her thigh to uncover the scratches there.

What Jael saw made her forget her sudden desire. The claw marks on her skin were puffy and inflamed, the skin around them starting to show the same gray color as Tanis's wound.

Vedara, however, appeared untroubled by either the inflammation or the obvious signs of the shifter sickness. His long fingers probed the wounds very gently, and he smiled, patting Jael's shoulder reassuringly.

"You tended your friend with more care than yourself," he chuckled. "But the Unformed Ones are dirty and their claws often carry disease—nothing that cannot be treated, of course. The Four Peoples are more susceptible to such infections than we, and to the blood taint of the Unformed Ones. Lie down, and I'll clean and dress these."

Jael obeyed, once again miserably self-conscious, alternating between arousal and humiliation. The infection of the scratches bore poor testimony to her skill in field medicine, and the fact that both she and Tanis had become tainted with the shifter curse bore equally poor testimony to her skill as a warrior.

Vedara, apparently oblivious to the effect of his scent on his patient, gently cleaned the scratches with a liquid that burned like fire for a moment, then dressed them with an ointment that was as cool and soothing as the liquid had been burning and painful. He padded the scratches with a sort of soft moss, then bandaged her thigh firmly with a wide band of soft leather.

"Your friend will not have the use of his arm for some days." Vedara said, smoothing a last wrinkle from the leather. The touch of his fingers on her thigh made Jael shiver. "But you should have no difficulty. Once your Enlightened Ones have cleansed the taint from your blood, you can both be healed completely."

"I don't know any—any Enlightened Ones," Jael stammered, wishing he would take his hand away so she could put her trousers back on.

"So Vani said." Vedara smiled again. "You don't know your clan, and your blood is not as theirs—at least to look at you. But we will help you find your kinfolk."

"Thank you," Jael whispered. She sat up and hurriedly reached for her trousers. Vedara stopped her, however, taking her hands in two of his own, his other two hands cupping her face.

"I smell your heat," he murmured. "The scent of your kind acts as potently upon us as ours does upon you. Perhaps at one time in the dim past we were all one folk. But my folk and yours are not made for mating one with the other."

"I know." Jael's face was flaming now, and she wished miserably she could just sink into the earth beneath her. "I didn't mean—"

"Shhhh." Vedara traced Jael's lips with one fingertip. "Your desire honors me. The beauty of your inner self shines like the sun. I envy your mate." He glanced over at Tanis.

"Tanis? But we're—" Jael stopped, confused. Just friends? Not anymore, not for some time. And more shame to her for almost forgetting him entirely in her lust for this strange creature, when she'd spent long nights wondering how anybody could be so foolish as to let the heat of their loins cloud their heads!

"You're right," Jael said abashedly. "And thank you."

"You are most welcome, my bright one," Vedara said fondly. "Now come outside and let my people speak to you and touch you and wonder at you and feed you, and let Wirax ask you far too many questions, and then you, too, can rest."

Jael scrambled into her torn pants and let Vedara lead her back out of the tent. Although it was only midafternoon and the sun was still high, the grass hunters had prepared a feast for her and laid it out on low sod tables similar to the one in Vedara's room. Some of the meat was still roasting, but the rest had been cut into joints and laid on the tables. Jael had not expected fruits of any kind—it was still spring, after all—but she was surprised that there were no succulent spring greens on the table, as she'd seen a good many of them growing on the plain. There was meat, flat rounds of bread, bowls of what looked like baked mushrooms, and a bowl of what appeared to be some kind of blood pudding, but that was all.

Well, she'd never cared much for greens anyway.

Following Vedara's and Wirax's example, Jael seated herself a little awkwardly on the ground at the low tables. She quickly saw the reason for their particular type of construction—when the grass hunters folded their legs under them, the sod tables placed the food at a comfortable height for the hunters' long torsos. Jael quickly found that the only way she could easily reach the food was to kneel upright. It would certainly be far too embarrassing to have to ask Wirax for cushions to sit on—not that she'd seen any cushions in Vedara's tent anyway.

Jael quickly found that the deceptively simple food was as delicious and cunningly prepared as anything she'd ever tasted. The gamy meats were roasted to a turn and strongly flavored with seasonings Jael did not recognize. The bread was soft and nutty, perhaps made of some kind of starchy tuber. The mushrooms added just the perfect earthy flavor. To Jael's surprise, there was nothing to drink with the meal but water, but the water had been flavored with some wild herb, fresh and tangy.

Jael ate hugely, thinking guiltily of Tanis as she enjoyed the fresh, juicy meat and soft bread. Despite the seemingly festive occasion, the grass hunters were a casual people and there was little ceremony to the meal; hunters came, ate, and left as they pleased. To Jael's surprise, despite the obviously friendly manner each of the grass hunters showed, except for Wirax, Vedara, and Vani, they gave Jael a wide berth. The youngsters, just like young elves, ran wild, snatching at food and running between the adults, occasionally pausing to stare wide-eyed at Jael.

Wirax let Jael eat her fill before he spoke.

"You said you've never known your clan," he said. "Yet you've come near to where the mountain folk live. How is that so?"

"My mother remembered a few hints about her—my father," Jael said. "She knew his folk had once lived to the north of Allanmere, our home, but that his people were going to move west. After that I followed legends. Even though my father's people had passed twenty years ago, people remembered them. They called them ghost people, windwalkers. I followed the stories, and that path led me—in a roundabout way—here."

"Windwalkers," Wirax said, nodding. "You are of the Wind Dancing Clan, then."

"Then why did you bring the riding beasts?" Vani asked. "You would have come faster without them."

"Vani," Vedara said chidingly. "Her companion is not of that kind."

"That's part of it," Jael agreed. "I didn't want to come alone. But I don't know that I'm a—Wind Dancer?—either. I can't run like the wind. I can melt stone sometimes."

Vani and Wirax exchanged surprised glances, but Vedara nodded sagely.

"We remember the ones who came from the east," Vedara said. "The spirits in the grass whispered to me of their arrival, and I sent a message to the Four Peoples, who came to the foot of the mountains—all of them, even the old and the young. There was great celebration among the Four Peoples at their arrival, and they feasted with us for many days. I heard it said by the Enlightened Ones that although those people were of Wind Dancing Clan, there had been Stone Brothers born among them from time to time. But tell me your father's name again."

"His name was—is Farryn," Jael said. "I suppose he would be with this Wind Dancing Clan. Do you know them?"

"We trade with the mountain folk," Vani said. "They come to us several times a year to barter their metal goods and baked clay pots for our pelts and herbs and woven baskets."

"Several times a year?" Jael asked, dismayed. "But do you know where they live?"

Wirax pointed to the mountains.

"We meet them at the foot of the mountains, at the caves where we pass our winters," he said. "There's a road of sorts, but we have never taken it. The plain is our place and we have never left it."

"You don't know how far it might be to their home?" Jael asked worriedly. "Tanis and I aren't equipped for the mountains."

Wirax shook his head.

"We've never seen their home," he said. "But we sometimes communicate by messenger birds. I will send such a message to the Wind Dancing Clan, if you like, and they can meet you at the foot of the mountain, if you wish to wait."

"But we have no way to know how long it might take for them to get here," Vedara reminded him. "And Tanis and Jaellyn require the treatment of an Enlightened One."

"Why don't you have any—uh—Enlightened Ones of your own?" Jael asked curiously. "I mean, since your land borders the forest where the skinshifters live anyway."

Vedara settled back comfortably.

"There's a great magic in the heart of the mountains," he said. "We believe the heart of the world is there, and that the Four Peoples are the guardian of that heart. But just as your blood flows outward from your heart, so, too, does the magic of the world's heart flow outward into the land here. That magic changes all it touches. Our folk were shaped by that magic, and to this day, some of us are shaped to hold a greater portion of that magic within us." He raised his four hands in illustration. "The Unformed, too, are shaped by that same magic, but by magic gone awry, as magic often does. The power in the land here is so strong that it changes all it touches, and for that reason, only the simplest of magic can be used safely. Only the Enlightened Ones, who are accustomed to wielding the power of the world's heart, can use it safely."

Jael frowned but said nothing. What Vedara had told her was a pretty legend, but it left many things unexplained—where the skinshifters had come from originally and why others could be infected with their curse, why mages far to the east could work powerful spells when they were so far separated from the magic of the "world's heart," or where and how the humans and elves, both of whom had come from the east and were only now slowly moving west, had originated. But then, Jael realized, one could walk into any five temples in Allanmere and hear five completely different stories of how the world began, none of which explained everything satisfactorily, and the elves were certainly no better. Maybe what Vedara said was true—for these people, in this place.

"I'd be grateful if you would send the messenger bird," Jael told Wirax, "but I think Vedara is right. Tanis and I had best start into the mountains and hope we'll be met. If Tanis can travel, that is." She looked at Vedara.

"I will give him potions to strengthen him and salves to slow the progress of the sickness in you both," Vedara said, nodding, "and we will give you warm furs to wear. But your friend must sleep another day, and you should rest as well."

Rest. What a wonderful word. It seemed like a year since she'd left the inn in Zaravelle, the last time she'd truly slept. Although it was still light, Jael felt she could sleep right where she sat on the ground.

"You can rest in my tent with your friend Tanis," Vedara said, observing Jael's yawn. "Come, you can tell Wirax your story tomorrow."

Wirax appeared disappointed, but Jael was too tired to care. She thanked Wirax and Vani kindly for the dinner, but gladly stumbled after Vedara to his tent. After making certain that Tanis was sleeping soundly, Vedara lifted him easily and carried him to the pit bed, settling him comfortably into the furs. Jael started to join Tanis, but Vedara laid a hand on her arm, picking up a clay cup from the ground and handing it to her.

"Drink this," he said. "It will deepen your sleep and speed your healing."

Jael took the cup and swallowed the contents quickly. There was no need to hesitate and possibly offend Vedara by her distrust; she and Tanis could hardly be more vulnerable than they were already, and if these folk meant them any harm, there was little enough Jael could do to stop them, asleep or awake. At least this way she wouldn't lie awake smelling Vedara's scent and thinking about—well, thinking. The potion was thick and sweet but not disagreeable. She raised her eyes and met Vedara's knowing gaze, and she flushed, wondering if he could somehow hear her thoughts.

"There are more furs beside the sleeping pit," Vedara said kindly, taking the cup. "I'll build the fire higher for your comfort. If you or Tanis wake in any discomfort, I'll be here."

"We don't need to take your bed," Jael protested. "We're used to sleeping on the ground."

"I would be a poor healer indeed if I put my patients on the hard ground and slept on soft furs myself," Vedara chuckled. "Now rest well, dream true, and heal." He turned to leave.

"Vedara?" Jael asked hesitantly. "How did Wirax happen to find us there at the edge of the forest? You sent him, didn't you?"

Vedara turned and smiled slowly, his eyes twinkling.

"I sent him," he agreed.

"But how did you know we'd be there?" Jael asked.

"The forest told the wind, and the wind told the grass, and the grass told me," Vedara told her. "In my dreams the grass spirits whispered your name."

There were times when Jael would have chuckled at this, but at the moment she was far too tired. She crawled quietly into the pit beside Tanis. The mound of furs was as soft and comfortable as it had looked. Tanis murmured sleepily, and Jael curled up against his uninjured side, pulling a few furs over them both. The pungent fragrance of Vedara's herbal preparations was comfortingly familiar, and the softness of flawlessly tanned furs against her cheek was familiar, too. Jael sighed as her will made one final, feeble effort not to trust these people and relax completely, then surrendered.

Sometime during the night she half-woke. The tent was dark and quiet, the fire glowing dimly, and Jael was far, far too warm. She kicked off the furs covering her, then for good measure struggled out of her tunic as well. Suddenly there were hands helping her, and Vedara's long fingers were cool against her cheek.

"You are fevered, bright one," he murmured. "Do your people use willow bark for fevers?"

Jael nodded sleepily. She heard what Vedara was saying, but his voice seemed meaningless, far away and faint. Vedara's fingers were gone, and she was still too hot, so she wriggled out of her trousers as well. Then she was freezing cold, and she shivered under the furs, squeezing as close to Tanis as she could. Vedara was beside her again, his arms supporting her, and she swallowed the contents of the cup he held to her lips, not caring that the liquid was horribly bitter.

"I'm c-c-c-cold," Jael murmured, her teeth chattering.

"No, you are very, very warm indeed," Vedara said gently. "Drink this, too, and then I'll give you water, and you'll sleep again."

The second potion was more palatable, but the wonderful cold water he gave her seemed like the best thing she'd ever tasted, even though it made her colder than ever. She drank until Vedara gently pried the waterskin from her shaking fingers.

"Enough," Vedara said firmly. "Sleep now."

To Jael's dim surprise, Vedara curled up beside her on the furs so that Jael was between Tanis and him, pulling Jael back comfortably against his chest and cradling her with all four arms. The warmth was delicious, and Jael slowly stopped shivering, letting the potion pull her back down into sleep.

Jael woke slowly, still blurred by the potion. The tent was dark and still, but Jael could see a little daylight shining in through the smoke hole and around the door flap. She was covered snugly with a huge pile of furs, but neither Tanis nor Vedara was anywhere to be seen. She must have slept deeply indeed, for she felt wonderfully rested, and someone, probably Vedara, had washed the sweat and grime from her skin. Jael blushed at the thought; just as well she hadn't woken.

Jael shook her head dully and pushed the furs off her, glancing around for her clothes. They were nowhere to be seen either, but her packs and Tanis's had been laid neatly by the door. Jael stumbled over and pulled out her spare clothes, dressed lethargically, and peered out through the door flap.

Tanis was seated at one of the low tables, Wirax and Vedara beside him. Tanis was still rather pale, and his right arm was strapped against his body, but he was stuffing his mouth with a gusto that Jael found reassuring. He smiled when he saw Jael, waving her to join him, his hand still clutching a meaty joint.

"Good morning, sleepy!" he called. "A little longer and I would have said 'good afternoon' instead. Come and eat!"

That was an appealing suggestion indeed, and Jael readily joined them. She found to her relief that Tanis had already told Wirax most of the details of their journey; it was reassuring somehow that Tanis found these people trustworthy as well. Jael was content to let Tanis finish the tale; that way she was free to concentrate on the food. Despite her illness of the night before, or perhaps because of it, she was ravenously hungry. The grass hunters were duly impressed by the story of Jael and Tanis's adventures in the dragons' nests, and nodded sagely when Tanis spoke of the strange enchantment of the Singing Forest; the grass hunters avoided the forest completely, believing it a place of twisted magic.

"We dispatched messenger birds to Wind Dancing Clan last night," Wirax told her. "But I wouldn't suggest you wait for their reply. There are frequent storms in the mountains, and their messenger birds are often delayed or don't arrive at all. There's still the plain to cross before the mountains, and unless you would chance waiting for them to come meet you at the foot of the mountains, best you begin your journey while the good weather holds and while—" He hesitated.

"While we're still well enough to travel," Jael finished. "I understand."

"I would send some of my people with you, or go myself," Wirax said, frowning. "But the mountain folk are sensitive of

their boundaries. We would not wish to offend them by tres-
passing on their land without their permission. They are a fierce
people and easily angered."

"That's all right." Jael stifled a sigh. She had no idea how a
member of this strange race might greet his half-breed bastard
offspring, or how his kinfolk might deal with her. It would have
been much more comforting to have some of Wirax's apparently
friendly folk with her.

Still, Jael could guess that Wirax had another reason he didn't
want to send any of his people with her: Not knowing how long
the journey might take, he wouldn't want to risk any of his own
people in case Jael or Tanis succumbed to the skinshifter curse.
Jael wondered if perhaps that consideration, rather than the
weather alone, didn't prompt Wirax's suggestion that Jael and
Tanis leave quickly. Jael could hardly blame them; any human
village without a mage to cure shifter sickness would immediately drive the infected away, or more likely kill them.

Wirax, however, did his best to make Jael and Tanis feel welcome. He introduced what seemed to be scores of his people to
them in a whirl of names and faces that Jael immediately forgot,
but she noticed again that the adults kept a distance between
themselves and Jael or Tanis. The pack's young showed no such
wariness but thronged around them joyfully, occasionally slyly
extending the shafts of their spears for Jael or Tanis to trip over,
poking them or pulling their hair, or suddenly hanging on their
arms. Their mischief reminded Jael poignantly of Markus and
Mera, and she surprised everyone—including herself—by joining
in their play as much as her sore thigh would allow.

From what Wirax told them, the grass hunters were a nomadic
race, following the herds of plainsbeasts across the grasslands.
During the summer they divided themselves into six Hunts, each
with its own range, but the Hunts gathered again to winter in
caves at the edge of the mountains, although any Hunt might use
the caves at any time of the year when they came to trade with
the Kresh. The grass plain itself was almost triangular in shape,
wide at the north, but tapering to a blunt point at the south where
the Singing Forest almost met the mountains. The Second Hunt
was camped near this southern tip now, preparing to follow the
herds north to their summer grazing land.

When the grass hunters had enough fine pelts and herbs to
trade, they would send messenger birds to the Kresh—whom the

hunters called the mountain folk or the Four Peoples—and send a trading party to the foot of the mountain road. Usually the Kresh would have already arrived with their trade goods, exquisitely crafted metal arrowheads and spearheads and the gold jewelry the grass hunters favored, plus more utilitarian fired clay pots. When one of the grass hunters was ill enough to need the attention of one of the Kresh's Enlightened Ones, or when the Enlightened Ones needed special herbs, a similar meeting would be arranged.

"Sometimes their hunters will come down from the mountains," Vedara said. "They ask permission to cross the northern part of our lands to hunt the dragons who live in the northern mountains. They hunt the dragons in the mountains, or we stake out plainsbeasts to lure the dragons down to the plain and we hunt them together. We help them bear the meat back across the plains, and then there's a great celebration and feast, their hunters and ours. But there are few other meetings between us. They walk a far different road than we, and seldom do those roads cross." He glanced sideways at Jael and his eyes twinkled. "Perhaps that is as well."

Jael quickly looked away, but she realized then that the other grass hunters had not avoided her out of fear of catching the shifter curse; it was out of courtesy, an awareness of the effect their scent had on Jael, and vice versa. Otherwise they'd surely have kept their children, who were too young to be affected by Jael and Tanis's scent, away from them as well.

Wirax showed them where he had tied the ponies to graze. The grass hunters had a few domesticated plainsbeasts, used to pull the carts and wagons that carried the tents and supplies and to transport trade goods to the foot of the mountains. These creatures were very different from the plainsbeasts Jael had seen occasionally in the east; these were much larger—almost the size of a horse—and with thick, branching antlers instead of the two spiraling horns she was familiar with.

Vani joined them, returning Jael's and Tanis's clothing, which had been cleaned and dried in the sun.

"We took the measure from your clothing and are making warm outer garments from our thickest furs," Vani said almost shyly. "We've never made such garments before, but they'll be ready when you leave."

"Tomorrow at dawn?" Tanis guessed.

Wirax nodded.

"Your riding beasts will run faster and longer if you're not on them," he said. "Some of my Hunt will carry you and your supplies. I'd take you there myself, but my Hunt can't spare both its leader and its healer."

"Its healer? But—" Jael glanced confusedly at Vedara.

"Both of you are far from well," Vedara said gently. "It's best that I go with you and continue to tend you. Besides, the hunters who escort you will be more comfortable if I continue to watch your condition."

"And if you should meet any of the other Hunts," Wirax said practically, "Vedara speaks as my voice. Not that it's likely that any of the Hunts will have come to the mountains to trade yet, not after the recent rains. But—forgive me—your appearance is strange enough that another Hunt might not recognize you as friends."

Jael grinned wryly. It was certainly not the first time someone had found her strange-looking, but it amused her to think that in this country, Tanis's appearance was as unusual as her own.

There was another huge feast that evening, but the casual manner in which it was enjoyed made Jael realize that the gigantic dinner of the day before had been no special celebration; it was very simply the manner in which the grass hunters ate every day. The amount of meat they consumed, supplemented only by a little bread and very few vegetables, was awesome, and Jael immediately understood why they had to separate into Hunts for the warmer months, each Hunt stocking up its own share of dried meat for the winter and pelts to trade. Otherwise even huge herds of plainsbeasts would soon be hunted into nothingness.

It disturbed Jael, however, to see how eagerly the grass hunters were turning their finest pelts and hides into warm mountain clothing and a tent for Jael and Tanis, or how much of their own smoked and potted meat was being set aside to replace the dried meat Jael and Tanis brought.

"His people may have many virtues, such as that woven fiber you wear," Vedara said surreptitiously to Jael, gesturing at Tanis, "but they know nothing of preserving meat. The stuff you showed me might be fit for soup if we season it well—and if we're very, very hungry."

That evening after supper, as they sat in Vedara's tent, Jael pulled out the broken pieces of Kresh armor and blades she'd brought out of the dragon's nest. Cupping some of the smaller pieces in her hand, she concentrated on them. To her surprise, although she'd never tried to work with a metal this hard before, the strange white metal responded exquisitely, almost as if eager to assume any form she chose. She melted the bits into a single large lump, then formed similar nuggets from the other broken bits and pieces. She considered the nuggets, wishing she had the knowledge and skill to form blades for swords or daggers, but she did not. One thing she did know, however, was how to tip arrows, and after a few attempts she was able to produce a very passable arrowhead, sharp and true. She looked at the tips on Vedara's spears, but reluctantly acknowledged that her newborn skill simply wasn't up to the larger tips; they'd obviously been filled in some way to give the spear tip sufficient weight.

Tanis watched these proceedings with great interest, encouraging Jael when she made the occasional blunder. He was duly impressed with the finished arrowheads, once again marveling at the amazingly sharp edge the white metal would hold.

"I thought I'd give these to Wirax," Jael said when she was finished. "In exchange for all the furs and the meat. They've been awfully kind to a couple of shifter-infected strangers."

"I'm sure they had reasons." Tanis glanced away.

"Why do you say that?" Jael asked puzzledly. "Is it so strange? Most clans of elves in the Heartwood would do the same."

"For other elves," Tanis said pointedly.

Jael grimaced, but she could not dispute what Tanis said. There were still clans in the Heartwood who, upon finding humans poaching in the Inner Zone of the forest, would kill the humans immediately.

"Well, our coin's no good to them," Jael said practically. "If they had any other motive, they must've wanted the Kresh's gratitude and goodwill."

"Or yours," Tanis muttered.

"I *am* grateful, and you should be, too," Jael said, wondering what in the world Tanis was getting at. "Tanis, what's the matter? It's not as if they've asked, even hinted, for anything in return."

"I just thought—" Tanis hesitated. "I think maybe I'll try the new tent tonight. It's a different type than our old one, and I pitched it after dinner. I think I'll sleep there tonight."

Jael raised her eyebrows.

"That's a pretty foolish idea," she said. "We've only got one more night to sleep comfortably on soft furs with a fire in the tent. Why waste it? Besides, Vedara wants to stay with us."

"I think he wants to stay with *you*," Tanis said softly.

"Oh, gods, Tanis, where did you get that notion?" Jael protested, glad that the dim light concealed her sudden flush.

Tanis still would not meet her eyes.

"From listening to you talk to him last night," he said.

Jael's cheeks burned, and she fought to keep her voice even. "We thought you were asleep."

"Apparently so." Tanis sighed. "I must've been, mostly. I thought I'd dreamed what I heard, until I woke up and there you were in his arms, naked."

"Oh, Tanis," Jael protested. "That wasn't anything. I woke up in the middle of the night and I had a fever and—"

"Look, you don't have to explain." Tanis poked at the fire. "I've got no right getting possessive, as you told me once before. And it's not as if I've been exactly celibate myself, ever since we left Allanmere."

"Tanis, you've got it all wrong," Jael sighed. "Just *look* at them. I couldn't do anything with Vedara, no matter how he or I might want to, and we both know it, and if you'd been awake enough to listen to the whole conversation, you'd know it, too. It's just a strange thing with his scent and mine, that's all."

"His scent?" Finally Tanis looked at her, wrinkling his nose. "He smells like an animal. They all do. They're clean, but it's not that nice of a smell."

Jael was vastly surprised by his answer. Like animals? She'd smelled a good many animals in the Heartwood, and none of them had had the delightful aroma of Vedara's people. She knew Tanis's sense of smell was less acute than hers, and if there was anything offensive in Vedara's aroma, surely it would have affected Jael even more strongly than it did Tanis. Perhaps it was only because Vedara and Wirax were males; sometimes males of a species had a special scent to attract females of that species, and vice versa.

"What about Vani?" Jael asked. "Does she smell bad to you, too?"

"They all smell alike to me," Tanis said, shrugging.

"What about me?" Jael asked. "How do I smell?"

Tanis sniffed, then shrugged.

"Right now, like that strong herb they flavored the meat with, and a little like smoke from the fire," he said. "Why?"

"Because Vedara said his people found the scent of the Kresh attractive, and the other way around," Jael said. "I can't smell my own scent. Nobody can. But that doesn't matter. The point is that you're still the only man, human or otherwise, I've ever tumbled. Anyway," she added practically, "who'd lie with someone infected with the shifter curse?"

Tanis grinned abashedly.

"I did."

"Well, not everyone's that foolish." Jael chuckled and put her arm around Tanis's shoulders. "And soon we'll be in the mountains and there won't *be* anyone else for me to tumble, and who'll you be jealous of then? The birds? The rocks?"

"All right, all right," Tanis said embarrassedly. "It's my arm that's not working right now, thank you, not my common sense."

"You certainly fooled me, then," Jael said mildly. "Now let's forget this and go to bed. As I said, it's our last night in a soft bed, and I want to get some rest."

"I'm tired, too," Tanis admitted. As Jael stood, however, he grabbed her hand. "I'm sorry I got jealous. I told myself all day long I was going to be fair about it, let you be with him if that's what you wanted. You've certainly been understanding with me all this time. But as I thought about it, it just made me angrier and angrier. It wouldn't have bothered me so much if I could do anything myself, I mean—"

"I know." Jael squeezed his hand. "But maybe it's just as well. Your wound was bad, and I was rather sick last night. Let's give ourselves a few days."

Tanis sighed, but he nodded, extending his good hand to help Jael to her feet. He followed her to the sleeping pit and sighed again, this time contentedly, as Jael curled up with him, laying her head on his shoulder.

"You've been worrying, too, haven't you?" Tanis said quietly in the darkness. "About meeting your father, I mean."

"Uh-huh." Jael sighed. "Some of the elvan clans don't like half-bloods, and I don't think the Kresh have ever even *had* any. What if I'm nothing but an embarrassment?"

Tanis was silent for a moment.

"Wirax has never made it sound like that," he said at last. "He speaks as if you finding your clan's just—well, expected, I suppose. He made it sound as if he was certain they'd welcome you."

"I wish I were that certain," Jael said softly. She touched the pendant around her neck. "You know, when I found this, I thought I'd just rather go back to Allanmere. I'm curious about Farryn, sure, and his people—my people, too, in a way—but I've never really fit in anywhere, in the city or with the elves, either. I started thinking, what if I couldn't fit in here either? That'd be hard enough to take. But even worse, what if I *did* fit in here? What if all of a sudden here I was, everything working right, everyone making me welcome? Gods, that'd be an awful choice, staying here among strangers where I fit in, or going home to my friends and family where I don't."

Tanis's muscles tensed under her cheek, but it was a long time before he spoke.

"You never talked about that," he said, very softly. "About staying once you got here. I think that's what I've been most afraid of all along."

"I never thought about it, really, before I found the soul keeper," Jael admitted. "But as soon as I saw the plains and the mountains, it was as if I recognized them, like I was coming home. But how can it *be* home without my friends and my family?" She sighed and shook her head. "Anyway, I can't stay even if I wanted to. I've got to take the book back to Blade, and I couldn't just leave my family like that."

Tanis sighed, too, but with relief.

"Besides," he said, "now that you've got your beast-speaking under control and don't break every spell in the vicinity, and now that there won't be any more controversy about you being named Heir, maybe you'll fit in better in the city, and with the elves, too."

"That's true," Jael agreed. "I can't wait to see Mother's face the first time I pick up a light globe at the supper table." She hesitated. "I still wish we didn't have to go on. It seems easier to just go home where I know I'm loved than to take a chance."

Tanis stroked her hair.

"Your family and your friends who love you, you've earned that love," he said gently. "If a complete stranger doesn't accept you as easily as you'd like, that's their failure, not yours."

"That's easy for you to say," Jael protested. "You don't have to worry about being rejected by your own race—or one of them, at least."

"No, all I have to worry about is the shifter curse or freezing in some Baaros-forsaken mountains half a world away from home," Tanis said cheerfully. "Much better."

Jael chuckled.

"You're right," she said. "I suppose there are more important things for me to worry about."

Tanis kissed her hair, and they lay silently for a moment. Finally Tanis chuckled.

"The two of us sleeping chastely together," he said. "Somehow it seems rather familiar."

"Well, famine to feast to famine again," Jael agreed. "But never worry; before long I'll be tearing your clothes again."

"With that promise," Tanis said with great satisfaction, "I can wait."

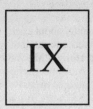

IX

● "By all the gods," Jael said
softly, staring. Tanis gave a low
whistle but said nothing.

Even from the narrow south tip of the plains, it had taken
them two days to reach the foot of the mountains, and those
mountains were taller than Jael would ever have believed possible, their heights vanishing into mist. The rock walls were steep
and jagged, bare of vegetation except for a few patches of lichen
and a little brush in the lower reaches. The mountain road, if it
could rightly be called such, seemed a mere goat path winding
upward between boulders and sheer rock faces. Jael was glad
now that they'd brought the sturdy ponies instead of horses; she
had doubts enough that *they* could manage the poor trail.

The grass hunters' caves were impressive structures, the entrances small and narrow but the caves beyond expansive, level,
and dry, and interconnected via a maze of passageways. Vani explained that the Kresh had made the caves sometime in the dim
past, perhaps for their own use, perhaps in some trade agreement
with the grass hunters' ancestors. Vani herself thought that perhaps the Kresh had used the caves as a sort of winter home, living on the edge of the plain where the weather was less harsh
and game more readily available.

Vani and Vedara showed Jael and Tanis the chambers they

213

used as storerooms. Except for personal jewelry, favorite weapons, and a few household items, all Hunts of the grass hunters shared property communally. When one of the Hunts traded with the Kresh for metal goods or pottery, they took what they needed and left the rest in the storerooms. When other Hunts came to trade, they would first check the storerooms for surpluses before determining their own trading needs.

As they'd arrived at the caves in midafternoon, Vani, Vedara, and the other hunters decided they'd start back for home. Since the ponies were already exhausted, however, Jael and Tanis would spend the night in the caves and start up the mountains the next morning. Vedara told them they were welcome to use the furs and supplies stored in the caves, and reminded them sternly to wear their warm clothing on the morrow. They should have plenty of furs and supplies even for the worst weather and several days' travel, although Vedara was certain the Kresh couldn't possibly live more than a few days' journey into the mountains and surely they had already sent a party to meet the travelers.

"And you must be certain to use the salves I gave you every day without fail," Vedara cautioned them. "Without the salve, the taint in your blood will spread more quickly. Food, sleep, and warmth are important, too, for disease spreads rapidly in a weakened body."

Jael pulled out the piece of leather in which she'd wrapped the arrowheads she had made, handing the bundle to Vani.

"I made these from metal I found in the dragon's nest," Jael said. "It's not much in return for all your help, but it's all I could think of."

Vani unwrapped the leather, then smiled delightedly.

"This is fine work," she said. "Many plainsbeasts will fall to these arrows." Then she frowned. "But I fear the few pelts and meat we gave you are a poor trade for these."

"You gave us a lot more than meat and pelts," Tanis corrected. "And I swear by Baaros's purse I couldn't ask for a better bargain."

Jael quickly slipped the earrings from her ears and handed them to Vedara. For a moment she felt a pang of loss, remembering Solly of the Thieves' Guild who had been so kind to her as a child, and who had died a horrible death at the hands of a demon.

"I want to give you these, because they mean something special to me," Jael told him. "They belonged to a friend of mine who was killed. I'd like you to have them."

Vedara smiled, touching the green stones with something like reverence. He removed the earrings from his ears and donned Jael's earrings instead.

"Then you must have this," Vedara said, removing his dragon bracelet and sliding it onto Jael's wrist. "A fitting trophy for your adventures."

Vedara's wrist was so much larger than Jael's that the bracelet was far too loose; Jael hurriedly slid it up her arm, where it fit comfortably between her elbow and her shoulder.

"Have the Wind Dancing Clan send a messenger bird, if you return this way," Vedara told her. "I would be pleased to see you again."

"This is pretty much the only way back," Jael chuckled. "But I hope we won't be quite as much trouble then."

Vedara only smiled, clasping Jael's face in two of his hands and kissing her forehead gently.

"Bright as the sun," he murmured, then turned away.

Tanis wrapped his good arm around Jael's waist, watching the grass hunters leave.

"Well, it's just us again," Tanis said, sighing, but Jael fancied she could hear some relief in his voice. "Just you, me, and the mountains."

"Oh, please, no mountains till tomorrow," Jael said wryly, rubbing her bottom. "Other than one short and panicky ride through the Singing Forest, I haven't ridden any distance since we got to Willow Bend, and I haven't ridden any distance without a saddle for—well, I don't even know how long. And I wasn't roped on like you. I won't be able to walk tomorrow."

"You won't have to walk tomorrow," Tanis said practically. "You can ride the ponies."

"Even worse, Jael said, sighing, then grinned. "Besides, look at the condition of that trail and tell me again that I won't have to walk. The ponies will be doing well just to keep their footing without our weight, too."

"All the more reason for us to rest comfortably and not worry about it tonight," Tanis said lightly. "Now, since I've only got one arm to use, and that's the wrong arm, why don't you take a pony while there's still daylight and see if you can get us some fresh meat for supper, and I'll unload the other ponies, lay a fire, and borrow a few furs from their storerooms to soften our bedding."

Jael had no desire whatsoever to do any more riding, and she doubted she could actually bring herself to kill anything, but there seemed to be no harm in trying; besides, this would be Jael's first opportunity for a little time alone in some days, and likely her last for a goodly while more.

Jael found her solitary ride over the grassy plain wonderful, refreshing to her spirit. As far as she could see around her was nothing but grass and the towering, mist-shrouded height of the mountains. The only sounds were those of the wind and the birds and insects of the plain. The only smells were those of the grass and flowers of the plains and the sweaty scent of her pony.

Ah, gods, this was what she'd wanted, this wonderful solitude with the world stretching out all around her. Even from atop her pony she could feel the stone roots of the mountains winding through the soil under her. The wind combed invisible fingers through her hair and carried a thousand subtle messages to her nose.

Drawing her bow, Jael urged the pony into the wind to follow one of those scents—no need for reins now when she could simply speak directly to the pony's thoughts to convey what she wanted. Searching with her mind, she felt the spark of life at the end of the scent trail, and followed the beacon to its source, a large hopping plant-eater Jael had never seen except cooking over the grass hunters' fires. She urged the pony to greater speed, but stopped it when the animal broke cover so she could shoot. Effortlessly she shut down her beast-speaking sensitivity as she loosed her arrow.

When the arrow hit home, however, and the strange creature fell dead, Jael stayed where she was, surprised and confused. Even now that she had some conscious control over her beast-speaking, she'd expected to feel at least a pang of sorts at the creature's death. None of the elvan beast-speakers she'd met hunted, ever; in retrospect, she couldn't imagine why she'd even tried. Even a fully controlled beast-speaker who could close out all the residual mental clamor of the animal minds in the area avoided the hunt completely, and Jael had always assumed that perhaps in the intensity of the hunt, the intimacy of the kill could still penetrate a beast-speaker's defenses. But Jael had felt nothing but a kind of savage joy, together with a sense of near regret that her prey had been nothing but a grass rodent. Was it because of her mixed blood?

Jael retrieved her kill, slinging it over the saddle in front of her. She glanced back toward the mountains, but hesitated, reluctant to return to the caves. Right now, at this moment, she was completely free, unencumbered by other presences. Why, she could start into the mountains right now, just herself and the pony. When she needed shelter, she could make a cave in the stone of the mountains. When she needed food, she could track game with her thoughts as she'd just done. She could travel much faster, and in glorious solitude, without the puny human whom she'd only have to nurse and coddle, who would hold her back—

Jael froze in the saddle, horrified at her own thoughts. What in the world had come over her? Tanis was her friend and lover. He certainly hadn't been *holding her back* the many times he'd fought by her side, protected and tended her, even saved her life. And what made Tanis "puny"? He was at least as skilled with a sword as she, and he'd done his share and more of the providing on their journey. And if he did indeed require nursing and coddling, well, he'd taken his wound helping to defend their lives, hadn't he? Jael had no illusions that if the position were reversed, he'd carry Jael through the mountains on his back, if necessary.

Resolutely Jael urged the pony back toward the caves, only to stop again. The sun was setting behind the mountains, and for the first time she could see the outline of their full glorious height. The rays of the setting sun colored the mists gold around the craggy peaks, and Jael watched, awed, as the drifting mist deepened to orange, then red, then purple. The sudden vision was like music resonating through her body, pulling her toward the mountains as inexorably as a hooked fish is drawn to shore.

*Mine,* Jael thought suddenly, every drop of blood in her veins, every particle of her bones answering that resonance that echoed through her very soul. *The mountains belong to me. And I belong to them.*

Again Jael shook her head and urged the pony toward the caves, but for the first time a deeper doubt had settled into her. Before the dragon's nest she'd been seeking her wholeness, her very self, and after that there'd been no time to question who or what, indeed, that self was. When she'd felt the gap in her soul healed, there had seemed to be no reason to go on—and, as she'd

told Tanis, more than a few reasons not to. Now that she and
Tanis were continuing on, perforce, to meet the Kresh, her own
kinfolk, Jael wondered if in truth she was seeking more than a
cure for the shifter curse, or to satisfy a natural curiosity. There
were more answers, it seemed, to be found, and Jael wondered
uneasily if these strange thoughts and feeling she experienced
were only the beginning of her self yet evolving, a Jael more a
stranger to herself than ever. Was she seeking a cure, or a key to
herself, or—

Or a home?

"I worry too much," Jael said aloud, her voice startling in the
silence. "That's what Aunt Shadow would say. I'm thinking awfully far ahead for a person infected with the shifter curse."

By the time Jael made her way back to the caves, Tanis had
a cheery fire burning. He gave Jael a curious look when she
showed him her kill, but asked no questions, helping her clean
and skin the rodent, and they jointed the animal so it would cook
more quickly.

Jael had enjoyed the open space of the plain, but she found the
cave, the sensation of stone surrounding her, even more comforting. The only problem was that over the years, the caves had become thoroughly impregnated with the scent of the grass hunters,
a scent that Jael found very distracting. Nevertheless, the feeling
of security lightened her mood considerably, and she and Tanis
laughed and joked while they ate, looking at some of the adventures of the earlier part of their journey in a more humorous light
now that they'd come so far.

At last their laughter quieted, and Jael met Tanis's eyes over
the fire.

"How's your side feeling?" Jael asked softly.

"Not too bad." Tanis's eyes twinkled. "How tired are you?"
Jael grinned.

"Not too tired."

Tanis raised one eyebrow.

"I suppose the smell in here makes a difference, eh?"

"Maybe." Jael shrugged. "You'd rather go outside in the
cold?"

Tanis rolled his eyes upward as if considering, then sighed and
shook his head.

"Just let me get my tunic safely out of the way, will you?"

• • •

In the morning they donned their warm furs. The garments were a little large, but that was good, as it permitted Jael and Tanis to wear extra clothing underneath if they later required it. They led the ponies into the mountains, as the trail was far too steep and crumbling to ride. The trail climbed at such a sharp angle that Jael and Tanis started to wonder if they wouldn't be forced to take the ponies back to the plain and abandon them after all, but by noon the trail leveled and widened somewhat. Sometimes the trail ran between rock outcroppings, but more often it was worn out of the side of the mountain, falling away at one side or the other, often steeply.

By midafternoon they were riding again, which was just as well, for the air had grown steadily colder and thinner since they began. The ponies did not seem troubled, but Tanis, already weak and tired by the morning's exertions, was so affected that Jael wondered uneasily whether he could walk if the trail became too difficult again. She herself felt wonderful, exhilarated, her chest and nose clear for once without potions. She could feel the power Vedara had spoken of, what he called the heart of the world, thrumming through the rock like a heartbeat indeed. Gods, she could spend years roaming through these mountains, exploring from the tip of the highest peak to the deepest root.

Tanis did not share her enthusiasm. He hunched miserably on his pony, silent unless Jael spoke to him, shivering even in the heavy furs. Jael wondered uneasily whether the shifter curse was spreading more quickly through his body because of his weakness.

Jael was relieved to find caves, their perfectly round mouths showing that they had been shaped by the Kresh, at regular intervals. In fact, Jael was surprised at the frequency of these shelters until she remembered that Wirax had said nothing of the Kresh using pack animals, and of course not all of them were Wind Dancers who could run so swiftly—even if the Wind Dancers could attain such speeds laden with trade goods on the treacherous mountain road. Traders would likely travel, therefore, at a normal walking speed or slower, and thus would require trail shelters at more frequent intervals. At any rate, Jael had no difficulty locating such a shelter near sunset.

The cave mouth was open and unconcealed, but Jael was surprised to see that whoever had shaped the cave had curved the passageway sharply just after the entrance, then back again, to baffle any wind that might blow into the cave. The passageway itself was so narrow that Jael had to unload the ponies before she could squeeze them inside. After the passageway, however, the cave opened into a small but comfortable dome-shaped room. There were no supplies left for travelers, no wood or peat or even coal, although a firepit had been shaped in the floor. A large rock lay in the middle of the firepit, but it was ordinary granite.

"I suppose they're used to the cold and don't need fires," Tanis said, his teeth chattering, as he followed Jael's glance at the firepit.

"They need fires, unless they eat their meat raw," Jael replied, scowling. Surely the Kresh didn't carry coal on their backs every trip they made? "At least we're out of the wind. I'll get the ponies to lie down on either side of us. That'll keep us warm enough."

Despite her words, Jael was bitterly disappointed. It would have been impossible for them to pack any quantity of firewood—even if there'd been any on the grassy plains—or coal into the mountains on their ponies. But Tanis needed warmth, and she herself would pay dearly for hot tea.

She filled the ponies' feed bags and settled Tanis in as comfortably as she could, then over Tanis's protests she ventured back outside in search of something she could burn. Fortunately she was so sensitive to the resonance of the stone of the mountains that she could clearly feel where roots dug into the rocky face, and her sword cut easily through the tough, scrubby pine saplings she found in a few sheltered nooks. The wood was still green and there was pitifully little of it, but it would burn long enough to heat the cave slightly and warm water for tea, and to mull some wine for Tanis.

Despite his protests at Jael venturing out into the mountains alone, Tanis was glad enough for the small blaze that Jael kindled from the scrubby pine. Jael was gratified that the resinous wood burned easily, even green, and the wonderful smell of the crackling fire, its cheerful light, and the hot tea Jael brewed warmed them more than its heat.

After they ate, Jael tended Tanis's side, liberally smearing the wound with the ointment Vedara had given her. She could see plainly, however, that the gray discoloration had spread across Tanis's back like an ugly rash. Jael, however, said nothing of

this, merely reapplying the dressing and assuring Tanis that despite the strenuous climb, his wound had not reopened.

"What about your leg?" Tanis demanded, and Jael, who had
hoped to wait until Tanis was asleep to tend her own wound,
could do nothing but unwrap the dressing around her thigh.

Tanis gasped, and Jael's stomach lurched when she saw how
far the gray had crept down her leg and up, too, over her hip.
She remembered what Vedara had said about the Kresh being
"more susceptible to such infection." If the shifter disease had
spread this far even with Vedara's treatment and his ointment,
how long could Jael last before the shifter curse consumed her?

Jael's hands were shaking so badly that it was Tanis who
slathered the ointment over her leg and tied the dressings in
place. Jael pulled her trousers up quickly, eager to hide the
tainted flesh from view. Tanis put his good arm around her, and
this time Jael felt none of the wonderful inner strength she'd
come to rely on—she leaned her head against his shoulder and
wept, shuddering, into his tunic until there were no more tears to
shed. They huddled together between the ponies, saying nothing,
while the small fire, like hope, burned down to ashes.

In the morning they found it had grown much colder outside,
and dark clouds warned of bad weather to come. Jael and Tanis
put on both sets of clothes under the fur outer garments, and the
thick layers kept out the biting wind, but their thin gloves and
boots, while perfectly adequate for late spring in the lowlands,
were no match for the piercing mountain winds. Jael found again
that Tanis was far more affected than she, but after a few hours
Jael, too, was slowly worn down by the freezing wind. Worse,
the trail was growing difficult once more, and the dropoff at the
side of the trail had become almost a precipice.

Sometime near midday an icy rain began to fall, and the trail
grew so slick and treacherous that Jael and Tanis stopped in one
of the frequent caves to thaw their numb fingers and toes and decide what to do.

"We'll have to stop," Tanis said, shivering and breathing on
his fingers to warm them. "If the trail gets any more icy, we'll
fall right off the side of the mountain."

"We can't stop," Jael argued. "We don't know how much farther it might be."

"How much farther *could* it be?" Tanis asked despairingly.

"We've been riding, so we've come at least twice the distance the Kresh would make in a day if they were walking, even on this road, at least since yesterday afternoon. How far into the mountains can these people live?"

"If they only trade with Wirax's people a few times a year, as far into the mountains as they like," Jael returned. "And since they *are* walking, it could take them days—even weeks—to reach us. We've got to cover as much of that distance as we can."

"We'll be covering a lot of the mountainside with our blood if we keep on in this rain," Tanis said grimly.

"Tanis—" Jael hesitated. "Remember the promise you asked me to make at the edge of the Singing Forest, that if you turned shifter—"

Tanis looked away. "I remember."

"If you turn shifter," Jael said slowly, deliberately, "there's no way for me to burn—anything—here. And I'm infected, too, worse than you."

Tanis turned back to her, a troubled expression in his eyes. He nodded.

"All right, then," he said. "We'll keep going. As long as we can, anyway."

"The cold and the air don't bother me as much as they do you," Jael said. "As long as the ponies are roped together, I think you can keep riding. You'll stay warmer that way, too."

"I can walk if you can," Tanis protested.

"Now, that's ridiculous," Jael said patiently. "You should stay warm and conserve your strength while you can. If I get too tired or too cold, you'll have to lead the ponies, and if you wear yourself out with me, then what are we going to do?"

"Freeze, I suppose," Tanis sighed. "All right. I ride. For now," he added sternly.

"For now," Jael agreed.

As they continued up the treacherous path, however, Jael quickly realized that Tanis would never be able to take her place. The trail was climbing again, the sleety rain had increased, and the air had thinned further, but more importantly, only Jael's constant silent reassurance and coaxing kept the ponies calm and cooperative on the slick trail. The effort of concentrating on both the risky footing and the ponies' fear kept her mind focused away from the cold, but Jael had not anticipated how draining the dual effort and the constant cold could be. Several times one of the ponies would slip and nearly fall; then Jael would have to stop the ponies and silently comfort the trembling animal.

The hill crested, and now they were descending on a trail that wound back and forth across the mountain's almost sheer face; Jael was dismayed to find that traveling downhill was actually more difficult than climbing the slick trail. By midafternoon she was leaning on her pony as much as she was leading it. The world narrowed to the strength of the pony beside her and the patch of ice-slick trail in front of her, and their pace slowed until Jael could measure their progress in inches instead of feet.

Suddenly the ponies stopped, and Jael looked up in surprise to see Tanis standing in front of her, holding the lead pony's reins firmly.

"Stop," he said. "Look down the trail. I thought I saw something moving."

Jael was so cold and drained that it was an effort just to raise her head, but looking down the mountainside at the loops of trail below them, she could indeed see vague, indistinct forms moving there.

"You're right," Jael panted. "There's someone coming. Or something. I can't tell."

Her eyes met Tanis's, and she could tell that he was thinking, as she was, about the conversation they'd had on the second night in Vedara's tent. Would the Kresh welcome and help them, or might they not see this half-blood stranger and her companion as intruders, even enemies?

"We'll wait here, then," Tanis said softly, laying his hand on her shoulder. Jael nodded, fumbling under her sleeve to make sure the bracelet with the translation spell was in place; her wrist was too numb to feel the tingling awareness of the magic.

*No time to go anywhere else for a cure for the shifter curse,* Jael thought with surprising calmness. *If they won't accept me, at least they'll kill us and burn us, if only for their own safety. At least there's that. We won't turn shifter.*

She realized that her numb hands were shaking; she clenched them together hard, wincing as hot tingles ran up her cold fingers. Her heart was beating so hard she thought it might burst. She realized belatedly that she had no idea what message Wirax or Vedara had sent to the Kresh.

The figures were closer on the trail below them, and in a lull in the rain Jael could see them more clearly, and although she could make out no details, she could count more than a dozen fur-clad figures. Some were dragging travois, although Jael could not discern whether they were empty or loaded.

*For us?* Jael wondered. *To carry us back for help, or to carry our bodies back for burning?*

The figures stopped on the trail below, and Jael thought she could see one of them pointing upward, perhaps at her. Instinctively Jael started to draw back out of sight, but she steeled herself—*Why prolong it?*—and raised one hand in acknowledgment. Then she blinked. Were there suddenly fewer figures down there?

Tanis's fingers dug into her shoulder, and he made a choked, unintelligible sound. Jael spun—too quickly, her vision blurred dizzily—and almost stumbled over the edge of the trail before another hand clamped firmly on her upper arm, steadying her.

Jael stared down at the six-fingered hand clasping her arm, then forced her head up to meet the gaze of piercing, strange bronze eyes that were amazingly familiar—but then, why shouldn't they be familiar? Jael realized, the sudden recognition causing her heart to skip a beat. She'd seen those same polished-bronze eyes, that very particular slant of cheekbones, in mirrors or reflected in still water all her life.

"Jaellyn," the figure said, as if tasting the word for the first time. The voice was harsh and rough, perhaps with the cold.

"Father," Jael said, and fainted.

X

● Jael dragged herself up out of
sleep as a mortally wounded
beast might drag itself from a
battle. Gods, she had to be alive; nobody could feel this awful
and be dead. Every muscle in her body ached and her head
throbbed sickly. Despite her lurching stomach, Jael forced her
eyes open.

"You're awake," Tanis said relievedly, smiling down at her.
"I've been awfully worried. It's been almost two days."

"I'm all right," Jael croaked. "I think." She forced herself up
on one elbow to look around, although the effort made her head
reel.

She lay on furs, but under the furs was stone. She was clothed
in a clean tunic and trousers, but they were not hers. She and
Tanis were alone in a dome-shaped shelter about the size of
Vedara's tent, but this shelter was of solid stone—apparently one
piece, for Jael could see no block edges. The only light came
from fat lamps and a small firepit at the center of the area; there
was a door, but it was covered with a leather flap. Her belongings and Tanis's were nowhere in sight; even their swords and
daggers had been taken, although the bracelets containing the
translation spells had been left on their wrists. There were no fur-
nishings in the area other than another heap of furs, apparently

225

Tanis's bed, but Jael realized immediately that the shelter was not without ornamentation—the entire inner stone surface of the structure was deeply engraved with reliefs that might be pictures, runes, or simply ornamental patterns. Jael felt an immediate urge to run her fingers over the carvings.

Tanis handed Jael a cup, and Jael realized she was terribly thirsty; she gulped, then almost spat in amazement as she realized the cup had been filled with plain, cold water, although the water was delightfully clear and sweet.

"What's happened?" Jael asked when she'd finished the water. The cold liquid refreshed her somewhat, but she still felt weak and sick and oddly empty. Adding to her discomfort was the impatience of the ponies somewhere nearby, far from content with the hard floor of their stalls—

Oh, gods! Jael bolted upright, oblivious to the wave of dizziness the motion caused, and groped in dismay at her throat. The pendant was gone.

"Their healer took it," Tanis said quietly. "When they took off your furs and saw it, there was a lot of argument. They'd already given me some kind of sleeping potion, so I didn't understand much of it. I think some of them didn't want us brought here at all. When they saw you wearing the pendant, though, everyone seemed to get rather angry. That's about the time I faded out, though. When I woke up, we were here alone. There are guards outside the door, too."

"Guards?" Jael shook her head and sat up. She'd anticipated possible hostility, but not this; she had supposed they'd either be welcomed or rejected outright, not taken in and then imprisoned.

Tanis nodded.

"A couple of them. I tried to go outside when I woke up. They stopped me. But I've looked at your leg, and the gray's gone. I'd like you to check my side, since I can't see myself, but I think we were cured."

"Well, that's something." Jael touched her thigh. The wound was certainly less sore.

"I'll show you something else." Tanis gestured toward the firepit. "Look at that."

Jael had to raise her self up a bit higher to see into the firepit, but she gasped when she finally succeeded. There was no fire in the firepit, only a single large rock glowing white hot. Tanis helped Jael slide closer to the firepit, and there she could feel the heat radiating outward from the stone, although she could see nothing heating the rock.

"It's been like that since I've been awake," Tanis told her. "It must be magic."

Jael shook her head, feeling none of the tingling she associated with magic.

"Not magic," she said. "Not any kind I can feel, anyway." Then she realized that she was feeling no tingling not only from the glowing rock, but from her bracelet. She shook her head and slid it from her wrist, tossing it away with a grimace.

"Ruined," she said. "Better keep yours away from me or I'll spoil it, too."

"Jael!" Tanis's voice was quiet, but Jael turned immediately to see where he was pointing—the door flap, which was raising.

Instinctively Jael dropped her hand to reach for her sword, scowling as she realized that it was gone. It took her a moment to recognize the figure in the doorway; then she clenched her shaking hands and forced herself to her feet despite her dizzy weakness. She was not going to meet her father on her knees.

Farryn approached her slowly, apparently as much at a loss for words as she. They circled each other cautiously, Jael getting her first good look at the man who had given her life.

Farryn was tall, but not quite as tall as her mother, and slender and wiry in build. His skin was darkly tanned, but his piercing eyes and braided hair were the same bright bronze shade as Jael's own, and the exotic tilt of his finely sculpted features was very like Jael's. He wore no jewelry except a pendant exactly resembling the one Jael had formerly worn, but he wore a sword at his hip as well as two daggers.

"Jaellyn," Farryn said at last, rather hesitantly, and once again Jael was struck by the harshness of his voice. This time, however, she could see its apparent cause—a white scar, likely an old battle wound, crossing the front of his throat.

"Father," Jael said, just as hesitantly, wincing inwardly. Gods, all she needed to do was faint again to make the ridiculous scene complete! She'd anticipated that Farryn would either welcome her enthusiastically or reject her outright, but she'd never thought of such an awkward, embarrassing meeting. She fought back the instinct to embrace him, elvan style; somehow he didn't seem like the embracing kind.

"You look—fit," Farryn said at last, giving Jael another head-to-toe scrutiny. Jael started, amazed that she could understand his words without the translation spell; then she realized he was speaking Allanmere's tongue. "Is your health improved?"

Jael touched her thigh, but felt too shy to pull down her trousers to look.

"I think so," she said, miserably aware how stiff and formal her voice sounded. "I still feel a little weak and dizzy."

Farryn nodded.

"That is to be expected," he said. "You are like us, slow in recovering from such infections." He glanced at Tanis. "Your companion healed more quickly."

Jael flushed, suddenly aware that they'd both been ignoring Tanis completely.

"This is Tanis, the truest friend I could ever have," Jael said, reaching for Tanis's hand—the hand *without* the bracelet. "He came all the way from Allanmere with me. Tanis, this is Farryn, my father."

Farryn nodded gravely to Tanis.

"Your loyalty and courage in bringing Jaellyn so far safely do you honor," he said. "Have you been made comfortable?"

Tanis squeezed Jael's hand.

"We've been made to feel like prisoners, since you ask," he said pointedly. "A poor welcome after coming so far."

"You are not prisoners." Farryn met Tanis's gaze directly, his own gaze troubled. "What you were was strangers afflicted with a dangerous disease."

"And now?" Tanis challenged.

"What you are now has not been decided," Farryn said evenly. "No one has ever come to us uninvited, and no one has ever been invited."

"Didn't you come here uninvited?" Jael asked pointedly. "You and all your people."

Farryn nodded.

"That is true," he admitted. "And that was a difficult time for my folk and those who accepted us here. We were years learning to be one people again. So you must be a little patient with a folk as slow to change as the stone they build upon."

Stone. Jael glanced at the pendant around Farryn's neck and fought off the urge to reach for the one that no longer hung on her own chest. She pointed to Farryn's pendant.

"I had one of those," she said. "It made me—whole. Why was it taken away from me?"

Farryn's brows drew down, and he glanced at Tanis, then turned back to Jael.

"There are matters we must discuss," he said. "But I cannot discuss them in front of one not of our kind. Walk with me, and my mate Lidaya will take your friend—Tanis—to our home and give him food, and we will join him there later."

Mate. A small surge of resentment flared, then died in Jael's heart. Why shouldn't Farryn have a mate, other children? It had been twenty years and more since he'd spent a single night with her mother. Donya had taken a husband only a few days later, albeit of political necessity; certainly there was no reason that Farryn should have pined away lonely on the other side of the world!

Still, she didn't like the idea of leaving Tanis. Tanis, however, squeezed her hand again and then released it.

"I'll be fine," he said comfortingly. "And it's right that you should talk to your—to Farryn alone. Besides, this way I can have my dinner without waiting for you." He grinned.

Farryn held out his six-fingered hand, his eyes on Jael's. Jael hesitated, then took his hand. She could not tell which hand, hers or his, was shaking.

Farryn led her to the door flap and raised the leather sheet. Tanis had said there were guards outside, but there were none now, only a leather-clad woman with a stony expression on her face. She scrutinized Jael rather coldly.

"Jaellyn, I make known to you my mate, Lidaya," Farryn said. "Lidaya, I make known to you"—he hesitated, glancing at Jael—"my firstborn daughter, Jaellyn."

Lidaya's eyes narrowed, and her mouth drew into a tight line.

"I greet you, daughter of my mate," she said shortly, but before Jael could reply, she turned away and ducked through the door flap.

Jael sighed. It wasn't the first time she'd managed to offend someone without saying a word or doing a thing. It seemed that here, as well as in Allanmere, she was an inconvenient person to have around.

Farryn gazed after Lidaya for a moment, then shook his head and sighed.

"Pay her no mind," he said. "We've been mates for almost

three hands of years. It's hard for her to learn only now that another woman had a place in my heart, for however short a time, and that that woman and not she bore my firstborn."

Despite the awkward situation, Jael could understand Lidaya's discomfort. The discovery of Jael's mixed blood had given her mother a good shock, too, and Jael suspected that despite his easy and unconditional love for her, Argent had been a little shaken by the realization that his firstborn daughter had actually been sired by another man.

"She spoke my language," Jael realized. "Just as you do. How did you manage that?"

Farryn smiled.

"When I met your mother, I was given a wonderful magical device that let me speak to her and her companions. I brought this device away with me when I returned to my people, and I have it still. When we received word from the plains folk that you were arriving, and who you were, I took the device to our Enlightened Ones. They drank the magic from the device and so learned your language, then used their magic to teach that language to myself, Lidaya, and our children. It was only honorable, to assure you could speak with your own kinfolk."

Jael shook her head wonderingly and looked around her. The stone building they'd just come from was as dome-shaped on the outside as it was inside, although the outside was bare of the deep carvings Jael had seen within. The building appeared to grow up out of the stone of the mountain itself, as did numerous similar structures clustered about with surprisingly little distance between them. The paths between the buildings were stone, too, worn smooth by long usage. Because of the thick cluster of buildings, Jael could see nothing but gray stone and sky, and she shivered with more than the chill of the air.

Farryn noticed her shivering and removed the fur cloak he was wearing, draping it around her shoulders.

"Forgive me," he said a little stiffly. "I forget that you are used to warmer lands."

"It's not bad," Jael said, although the thick cloak felt deliciously warm. She turned back to Farryn. "You never answered my question. Why was the pendant taken from me? And our weapons?"

Farryn glanced around quickly, as if afraid of being overheard, and laid his hand on Jael's shoulder, drawing her down one of the paths.

"Your weapons were taken because of your disease," he said. "The Unformed Ones know how to use weapons, and none of us wanted you armed until we were certain that the Enlightened Ones had cured you completely. With one entirely of our blood, it would never have been in doubt, but—" He glanced at Jael uncomfortably and shrugged. "Your weapons will be returned now that you are well. There were many questions asked when the Enlightened Ones saw you bearing a sword and dagger made by our folk. Among our clans you'd not be permitted to carry them until you'd proven yourself in battle. I recognized the blades, though, as the sword your mother had wielded so bravely and the dagger I gave to the strange and courageous Shadow so many years ago. I told the Enlightened Ones you'd never have been given the blades, nor yet managed to reach us, if you were unworthy."

Jael said nothing, but another coal of anger fanned into flame in her heart. Unworthy! She'd traveled across half the world, dealt with highwaymen, shifters, dragons, mages, and enchanted forests, and they dared to think she might be *unworthy* to carry one of their precious blades? Grimly she forced her anger down. The Kresh knew nothing of what she'd gone through to find them. Getting angry at Farryn wouldn't do any good, anyway.

Farryn had fallen silent, and Jael turned to see him gazing at her rather sadly.

"You've said nothing of your mother," he said at last. "How has Donya fared?"

"My grandfather, Sharl, died while she was in the swamp," Jael said. "Mother became High Lady as soon as she returned, and married Argent almost immediately."

"Argent—" Farryn frowned. "Ah, the tall elf who collected the plants." He sighed. "Is she happy?"

Jael raised her eyebrows.

"With Argent? Yes. As High Lady of Allanmere, she's miserable, of course."

"Of course." Farryn smiled a little. "I can hardly imagine her in robes instead of armor."

"They have two other children," Jael continued, glancing sideways at Farryn. "Twins. Markus and Mera are thirteen years old now."

"Two at one birth," Farryn marveled. "How wonderful."

"When a human marries an elf, that's usually how it works," Jael told him. "But you *still* haven't answered my—"

Farryn held up his hand, sighing again.

"The soul keeper," he said, touching the pendant that hung around his own neck. "Tell me how you came to have it, and why."

Farryn listened sympathetically while Jael told him about the soul sickness she'd endured all her life, the many remedies they'd tried, and finally the elvan passage ritual that had revealed Jael's mixed blood and incomplete soul. He nodded thoughtfully when Jael recounted her adventures in the dragon's nest and her discovery of the pendant.

"And wearing the soul keeper healed that lack within you," Farryn agreed. "Tell me, didn't you find yourself changed when you wore the soul keeper?"

"Of course I felt changed," Jael said impatiently. "I could mold stone, I could control my beast-speaking—"

"No," Farryn said gently. "Changed in other ways, as if finding yourself a different person than the Jaellyn you knew."

Jael started to retort sharply; then she remembered her inexplicable impatience with Tanis, her shocking inclination to attack him in the dragons' hill, her uncharacteristic recklessness while fighting the hatchling, even her unexpectedly aggressive seduction—if it could indeed be called that—of Tanis. She felt herself flushing at the thought.

"Well, wouldn't suddenly having a whole soul change anybody a little?" Jael protested.

"Jaellyn, these amulets are called 'soul keepers' because they indeed hold a soul within them," Farryn said gently. "And the one you wore healed you because it indeed held a soul within it—but that soul was not yours. It belonged to a warrior killed by the dragons, and that warrior has earned the peace of Adraon's realm. You can't heal yourself with a stolen soul. If you had been one of us, and entirely lacking a soul of your own, the soul of the slain warrior might have possessed you utterly."

Jael shivered. It had never occurred to her that she might well be hosting someone else's soul in her body. And she'd tumbled Tanis, too, while—Jael gulped. The idea was rather disgusting, now that she thought about it.

"I didn't know it was somebody else's soul," Jael said at last.

"I don't think I'd have dared touch the thing if I'd known. What will you do with it?"

"The Enlightened Ones will conduct ceremonies to appease the soul for the indignities it has suffered, then destroy the soul keeper to free the imprisoned one," Farryn told her.

Indignities? Jael had the uncomfortable notion that Farryn wasn't referring to years spent in a dragon's nest.

"But what about me?" Jael asked. "I don't want somebody else's soul, I just want my own. All of it."

"I have spoken to the Enlightened Ones on your behalf," Farryn said slowly. "They are deliberating on the problem. The matter is complicated."

"What's complicated?" Jael asked indignantly. "I need a whole soul, and your people are the only ones who can give me one. What's there to deliberate about? Is it because I'm a half-blood?"

"The purity of your blood is not a concern," Farryn said, guiding her down another of the narrow alleys between buildings. "There have never before been half-bloods among us, but if Donya could bear my daughter, a daughter who carries the gift of stone, you are near enough to our blood. But you must understand that our children are schooled from birth in the conduct of a Kresh warrior under our laws of honor and are not given their souls until they have proven themselves under that code. The bestowing of a soul is not a light matter, and some of the Englightened Ones feel that you have not been properly prepared, being raised among strangers."

"Strangers?" Jael flushed again, this time with anger. "Those *strangers* were good enough to help you when you came to them, weren't they? And Mother wasn't too much of a *stranger* for a night's tumble, was she?"

"Enough." Farryn guided Jael through another small alley, and suddenly they were standing at the edge of a cliff.

Jael gasped in wonder at the sight. She'd expected more of the gray stone of the mountain, solid but bleak. Instead, she stood on the edge of one of two cliffs that formed a sort of gateway to a vast green and fertile valley, with a crystal-blue river running between the cliffs and bisecting the lush growth at the valley floor. Jael could see figures moving against the grass of the valley floor, and to her surprise there seemed to be more conventional dwellings there, hutlike structures built of wood instead of stone.

Jael turned around and looked behind her. The dome-shaped stone structures she'd seen literally covered the mountainside, clinging to the stone like the barnacles she'd seen encrusting the hulls of ships who came up the Brightwater to Allanmere from the coast. A few steep, narrow paths wound down the mountainside to the valley floor, and farther along the cliff was an odd arrangement of baskets and boulders hung on thick metal chains, apparently to transport people or goods up and down the mountainside. At the base of the mountain was a larger stone structure projecting slightly from the mountainside, the entire outer surface heavily covered with the carvings Jael had hitherto seen only on the inside of the shelter she'd been in.

"The entrance to our temple," Farryn said, following Jael's gaze to the larger structure. "Our Enlightened Ones dwell there."

"Who lives in the valley?" Jael asked. "I can see people down there."

"I do," Farryn told her. "And my mate and my children. Many of the Wind Dancing Clan live there, and all of the Silent Singers as well. The Stone Brothers, what few there are, prefer the mountainside, and I and my family spend our summers here, as it is much like the place where we lived far to the east. But we all go back and forth between the clans as we please. Only the Enlightened Ones live between and apart. I spoke to them on your behalf and acknowledged you of my blood. They examined you, healed you, and returned to the temple without giving an answer to my request." He sat down on the stone of the cliff's edge, gesturing to Jael to sit beside him.

Reluctantly Jael sat down.

"The Enlightened Ones, they're your priests, aren't they, or mages?" Jael asked. "But why won't they help me? It's not my fault I was born in another place with nobody to train me the way they want me trained. It's not my fault I'm a half-blood, either, or that I was born missing part of my soul."

"It's not a matter of fault," Farryn said gently. "No one knows if what you ask is even possible. Give the Enlightened Ones time. Likely they returned to the temple to commune with Adraon and seek an answer."

Or they'd simply avoided the uncomfortable issue by making a quick escape, in which case Jael could be sitting on a cliff waiting for a good long time.

"Well, what are Tanis and I supposed to do while we're wait-

ing?" Jael asked. She grimaced. "It's pretty plain your mate
doesn't want us around, and I'm sure she's not the only one."

"There are empty houses aplenty on the mountain, such as the
one you were inside," Farryn told her, indicating the thick cluster
of dome-shaped structures clinging to the hillside. "We haven't
been a populous folk since before our peoples divided, and those
of us who traveled east dwindled severely. I'll see that you're
made comfortable. No one will treat you unkindly. You and
Tanis can hunt with us. I'll welcome the chance to know you
and to hear how you and the lady Donya—High Lady Donya—
have fared in the years since I met her."

Jael grimaced but said nothing. What was there to say or, for
that matter, to do? She and Tanis had journeyed to the other side
of the world to find these people, the only ones who could give
her a whole soul, and she'd found them. She'd asked for help.
What more could she do?

Farryn took her hand, and Jael could feel the iron strength in
his fingers. She gazed at their joined hands, so like and yet unlike, his six-fingered hand and her more slender five-fingered
one, both with the same dark tanned skin and wiry muscles. The
solidity of stone beneath her was a comforting presence, sweetly
familiar, but in her mind echoed the ponies' discontent with their
hard stone shelter, and some part of her longed for green leaves
and the scent of moonflowers and moss on the wind. She'd bal-
anced miserably on the dagger's edge between elf and human for
years; how much longer could she teeter precariously on the dagger's point between the world she'd known and a very part of
herself she could almost, but not quite, touch? Gods, how much
better it would have been if she'd never tasted Bluebright or
found the amulet in the dragon's nest, never felt that wonderful,
heady wholeness.

Still, she was closer to her goal than she had ever come in her
life—well, other than when she'd worn the soul keeper she'd
found in the dragon's nest. And she'd waited over twenty years;
what harm could a few more days do? And what choice did she
have, in any event?

"I'll wait," Jael said reluctantly. "But not for long."

"If the Enlightened Ones don't answer soon, I will approach
them again," Farryn promised. "Come, you'll wish to eat
and"—he sniffed slightly, then grinned apologetically—"bathe.
It's as well for my people that you do not go about smelling of

the plains folk. I'll see that your belongings are returned to you as well. No warrior should be without her weapons."

He guided her back through the lanes between the buildings, and Jael marveled again that they met no one for some time. Farryn had spoken, though, of the numbers of dwellings that sat empty; likely the Kresh grouped together in one section of the cluster and whole areas went uninhabited. This time it seemed to Jael, although she couldn't be sure, that Farryn took her on a different route through the dwellings. This time, too, Jael saw a few Kresh here and there, standing in front of dwellings or going about their business through the alleys. Each one stopped to stare at her, and although Jael saw no hostility on any of the faces, neither could she read welcome or friendliness there.

Though the structures appeared identical but for their size, Farryn led her unerringly to one particular dwelling. A few skins hung drying on frames outside the door flap, and two children, a tall boy a few years younger than Jael and a slender, long-boned girl of about Mera's age, sat outside, too, both painstakingly carving designs into polished bones. They stood when Farryn stepped into view, saying nothing, but staring intently at Jael all the while.

"Jaellyn, I make known to you my son Lainan and my daughter Savela," Farryn said. "Lainan, Savela, I make known to you my daughter Jaellyn."

"I greet you, my sister," Savela said almost eagerly, her eyes flickering back and forth from Jael's pointed ears to her narrow hands. Like Lidaya, Savela did not extend her hand; Jael forced her own hand back down to her side. It didn't seem to be a Kresh custom.

"I greet you, my sister," Lainan said, but his voice was cold and hard as stone.

A little stung by Lainan's hostility—what harm had she ever done him?—Jael stood a little straighter. She turned to Savela first, and, much to the younger girl's surprise, embraced her.

"I'm proud to meet you, my sister," Jael said, although technically, by matrilineal elvan standards, her sire's children by another woman were only considered cousins. Savela stiffened for just a moment, then awkwardly returned the embrace.

Jael stifled a grin as she turned to Lainan. Pride forced him to endure her embrace, although he did not return it, nor did he acknowledge Jael's greeting. As soon as Jael released him, Lainan stepped back, holding aside the tent flap and waiting mutely for Jael and Farryn to enter. Savela followed Jael and Farryn inside, but Lainan only dropped the door flap closed behind them, remaining outside.

Farryn's dwelling was half again as large as the structure Jael had awakened in, and brightly lit by fat lamps set into niches in the round walls. The stone floor of the dwelling was warmly strewn with furs, and a large rock in the firepit radiated both light and heat so that the dwelling was cozily warm. Besides the ornate carvings on the interior of the stone dome, there were other decorations: small statuettes of carved stone, bone, and horn; a dragon's skull, carefully polished; clay bowls filled with sparkling stones, possibly gems. Storage baskets almost encircled the dwelling at the base of the walls. There were several sleeping pits instead of one, and in one of them, an infant of indeterminate sex was cuddled companionably with a wolf pup.

Tanis was there, curled up in one of the sleeping pits and apparently asleep. Lidaya was adding what looked like a handful of herbs to the pot hanging from a tripod over the glowing stone; she looked up only briefly as Jael and Farryn entered, but when Jael sat down she silently handed her a bowl of what turned out to be a thick, spicy stew. Savela sat down beside Jael, although she had apparently already eaten, as she shook her head when Lidaya gestured at the pot of stew.

"My youngest son, Dellan," Farryn said proudly, picking up both the baby and the wolf cub. Farryn sat down beside Jael, miraculously managing both the infant and cub plus the bowl of stew he accepted from the still-silent Lidaya.

"Let me take him for you," Jael offered, surprised when Farryn handed her the baby, much to Lidaya's silent but nonetheless obvious disapproval. Dellan roused, gazed up at the stranger holding him, screwed up his tiny face as if unsure whether to make a fuss or not, then sighed and nestled comfortably into Jael's lap, gazing at her curiously.

*My brother,* Jael thought. Dellan was an amiable baby, allowing Jael to examine his tiny six-fingered hands and six-toed feet without protest, only squirming a little when she traced the smooth, round tops of his ears. Jael, however, found him fascinating. She'd seldom seen babies; her friends at the Guild of Thieves, of course, never brought their children to the Guildhouse, and among the elves barrenness was common, and births rare.

Before she realized what she was doing, Jael took a well-chewed piece of meat from her mouth and fed it to the baby, who gurgled delightedly. Jael glanced up at Lidaya guiltily but was surprised to see the woman's expression soften, a faint smile pulling at the corners of her lips. Lidaya met Jael's eyes and gave her the briefest of nods, then returned to stirring the stew.

"Tell us about the land you come from," Savela begged. "Father says it's all green like the valley, full of trees and land where the earth is so full of water that you sink into it."

Jael was no born storyteller like Shadow, but she could describe Allanmere and the land around it—the Dim Reaches, filled with foul-smelling mud and old magic rotting in the soil, where strange creatures lived and where Farryn's ancestors had once made their home; the wide, rich plains dappled with farms; and of course the Heartwood, where the trees grew so thick that the sky could only be seen in clearings and where the sunlight trickled down like golden syrup between the leaves, where elves rode on the great spiral-horned deer and wove their homes in trees, and where some elves could speak to the beasts and fly through the wood in the minds of the birds.

Tanis woke partway through her stories and joined the circle around the glowing firepit, adding his tales of other lands, larger cities. It wasn't long before a strange Kresh male peered in at the door flap, and Lidaya beckoned him to join them; by evening there were at least ten others crowded into the dwelling, listening raptly to Tanis's stories and waiting patiently for Farryn to translate when Jael spoke. Sometimes the listeners looked so plainly disbelieving that Jael was half-inclined to tell them to go elsewhere to listen if they thought she was a liar; Farryn, however, remembered enough from his journey to Allanmere to substantiate some of what Jael told them, and Tanis staunchly supported Jael's accounts of the elves and the Heartwood.

By the time Jael and Tanis had talked their voices into a hoarse rasp, it was far into the night and they were reeling with exhaustion. As if at some signal, although Jael had seen none, the Kresh visitors rose as one and left as silently as they had come. When Jael and Tanis returned to their own shelter, guided by Farryn, they were surprised to find that someone—who?—had brought their packs to the shelter, strewn warm furs over the floor, and filled the sleeping pit with more furs and fur covers. Jael and Tanis were far too tired, however, to wonder at the unexpected generosity.

Jael took time, however, to squat down beside the firepit and examine her leg and Tanis's side. Apparently the Kresh's Enlightened Ones were healers of formidable skill; there was not even a scar left on her leg, and although Tanis had a jagged furrow in his side to mark his far more serious wound, the scar was as white and firm as on a wound years healed. There was no sign of the grayish discoloration on her skin or Tanis's.

Tanis took the precaution of removing the bracelet from his wrist and storing it in his pack before he joined Jael in the sleeping pit. In this unfamiliar place, where even her kinfolk found her an inconvenience, it was good to have a friend to keep her warm at night. She almost jumped in surprise, however, when Tanis slid his hand over her bare hip in a manner that indicated anything but weariness.

"Oh, please," Jael groaned. "I'm exhausted."

Tanis sighed and wrapped his arm around Jael's waist, pulling her close.

"It's not just being tired, is it?" he asked gently.

Jael sighed, too.

"Since they took away that soul keeper I found," she said miserably, "it feels like I'm right back where I started. The ponies have been griping at me all day, and then my bracelet—it's like we came so far for nothing."

"Not for nothing," Tanis corrected. "You're here with the people who can help you. And there's no reason why they shouldn't want to help you."

"There may be," Jael sighed. She told Tanis what Farryn had told her about the preparation of Kresh children to receive their souls. "They may have decided I'm not worth helping."

"Then we'll just have to change their minds," Tanis said firmly. "The next time we tell them stories, I think it's time they heard something of Lady Jaellyn's great adventures. Demons and dragons and shifters should impress just about anybody. Now go to sleep and try not to worry. Anyway, it's been more fun than sword practice with the High Lady every day, hasn't it?"

Jael smiled and turned over to pillow her head on Tanis's shoulder.

"I can't argue with that," she admitted. "Dragons, shifters, and all."

In the morning, Jael and Tanis were pleasantly surprised when Lidaya, bringing Dellan with her, led them to a large structure that contained several hot-spring baths like those in Allanmere. Jael learned they had been constructed similarly, the Stone Brothers creating channels for the hot subterranean water to reach the surface much as Allanmere's mages had magically drilled their shafts. Jael had always disliked the sulfurous smell of Allanmere's water, but now she found the odor comforting in its familiarity.

Apparently the Kresh, like the elves, had no objection to nudity and considered bathing something of a social occasion, for Jael and Tanis found several of the pools occupied by groups of Kresh sipping cold water and talking comfortably. There were a few abruptly terminated conversations and more than a few curious glances when Jael and Tanis followed Lidaya in, but as soon as Jael and Tanis had stripped and entered the water, the conversations recommenced and the watchers turned back to their companions. Jael realized with a tinge of amusement that most of them had probably been waiting for Jael and Tanis to take off their clothes, to see just how different the strangers were!

The rest of the day, however, proved to be less pleasant. Tanis joined a hunting party at Farryn's invitation; Jael, however, decided that since they'd be gone all day, she'd best stay in the village where the Enlightened Ones could find her if they wished. Besides, she again had no control over her beast-speaking, and hunting would, for her, likely only prove humiliating.

Savela and Lainan disappeared early in the day; Lidaya explained that Lainan would face his trials of adulthood in only a few months, and both children therefore spent their days learning from a number of different teachers. Lidaya herself was taking Dellan to the valley where she planned to visit some kinfolk; although the Kresh woman had thawed to Jael somewhat, she did not invite Jael to join her. With no one to translate for her or guide her through the confusing maze of dwellings, Jael was effectively confined to Farryn and Lidaya's house for the day; she wasn't even certain she could find her way back to the house where she and Tanis slept.

By midday, however, Jael could bear it no longer. She grabbed a warm fur from the sleeping pit and wrapped it around her, wishing she'd thought to bring her warm fur outer clothing to the bathhouse with her that morning, and set out to look around. By following the slope of the mountain downward, she could probably have located the cliff where she'd talked with Farryn the day before, but there was no point in going there; besides, that was in the uninhabited part of the village and there would be no one to help her find her way back in any event. She headed up the mountain instead; the bathing house was uphill, and with any luck, one of these Enlightened Ones might have come up for a bath.

Within a hundred paces she was completely lost in the bewildering maze of seemingly identical stone houses and narrow alleys between them. Jael fought down the utterly elvan impulse to scramble up to the top of one of the houses to get her bearings; but then, since all the houses looked alike, what would that tell her?

The cold mountain air did not bother Jael as much as it troubled Tanis, but after an hour of wandering in the cold with nothing but a sleeping fur, Jael was shivering and numb-fingered. She saw several Kresh, and discomfort finally won over pride; as soon as she encountered someone whose expression showed no overt hostility, she did her best to convey with gestures that she was looking for the house where she and Tanis had slept. The elderly male finally nodded his understanding and guided her back downhill, abandoning her at the door flap of a structure that seemed too large; when Jael raised the door flap, the warm, moist rush of air told her that she had been led to the bathhouse instead.

Well, at least it was warm, and it was a place where Farryn would think to look for her when he returned. Jael ducked inside and stripped off her clothes as quickly as her numb fingers would allow. She might not need a second bath, but the bubbling hot water would thaw her admirably.

In fact, Jael spent a warm, if boring, afternoon in the bathhouse before Farryn finally came to fetch her. Some of the Kresh who came to the bathhouse addressed her, but none knew her language and she couldn't seem to convey by gestures the need for someone to take her back to Farryn's dwelling or her own.

When Farryn arrived, he only raised an eyebrow puzzledly.

"We've been looking for you," he said. "A friend said she saw you here, but that was near midafternoon. Do you miss the hot springs of your home so badly?"

"No, I miss being able to tell people I can't find my way back home," Jael retorted. "And I miss being *able* to find my way around. I don't suppose those Enlightened Ones have been looking for me?"

Farryn shook his head apologetically.

"They would have found you easily," he said. "But perhaps you will settle for some supper."

Jael hadn't eaten since breakfast, and at the thought of supper, her stomach rumbled so loudly that it could be heard clearly even over the bubbling of the water.

"I see supper will suffice admirably," Farryn said, smiling. He gave Jael his own coat and guided her back to his home. There Jael found Tanis almost strutting around the firepit, where an unusually shaped piece of meat was roasting. This time both Lainan and Savela were there, eyes on the meat.

"I killed a drake," Tanis said without any preliminary greeting. "They're like dragons, but smaller, and they don't fly or breathe fire, but they hunt in packs instead of solitary. We killed three, and I got this one."

"I know what drakes are," Jael said a little irritably. Unaccountably, Tanis's bubbling satisfaction annoyed her. "Lots of folk in and around Allanmere have guard-drakes."

"It was a fine kill," Farryn said, "although few of us hunt with our swords. Drakes especially are risky to fight at such close range. But Tanis acquitted himself well. I will have the skull and the hide cleaned and prepared for him as a trophy."

It took some time for the large haunch to cook, and Tanis could talk of nothing but the hunt and his kill. The drake was good, but Jael was restless and discouraged by her boring and profitless day, and as soon as she'd finished eating she excused herself. The thought of another evening of telling stories somehow held no appeal.

"There's no need to come back until you're ready," Jael told Tanis, who had risen to join her. "I'm sure you have a few more stories to tell. I'm just tired."

Tanis was so late returning to the shelter that Jael was long asleep. He woke her the next morning, asking if she wouldn't like to join another hunt today, but Jael again declined, urging him to go without her. Tanis's company might have been pleasant to help pass the time, but truth to tell, Jael was in such a foul mood that she'd as soon be left alone. Wisely, Tanis understood and left her to go back to sleep. Jael slept until she could sleep no more, then passed another boring day in her own shelter, not daring to go exploring again. Tanis came to bring her to supper, but again she excused herself after she ate.

To Jael's surprise, Lainan offered to guide her back. Jael hesitated, but Farryn gave her an approving nod, and Jael accepted, thanking Lainan. Lainan walked in silence, however, until they reached their destination. When Jael started through the door flap, he stayed where he was, so Jael was all but forced to invite him in. Lainan followed her inside and sat down cross-legged by the firepit, watching her silently.

"I keep meaning to ask," Jael said, "about these rocks. What makes them give off light and heat like a fire, but never go out?"

"Most Stone Brothers can do it," Lainan shrugged. "They say there's a memory of fire in each stone that they call forth. But why do you ask? I thought you were a Stone Brother."

"I suppose I am." Jael sighed. "But I never tried to do anything like that. And I can't do much of anything at all with part of my soul missing."

Lainan was silent, staring at Jael narrowly over the glowing stone.

"Lainan, you've been looking daggers and spears at me ever since I came here," Jael said impatiently at last. "Whatever you came here tonight to say, I wish you'd say it."

"When did you learn that our father was your father?" Lainan asked almost idly, but the intensity in his eyes belied his calm voice.

"More than a year ago," Jael said. "But I promised my mother I wouldn't leave until certain things were settled at home, and until my swordsmanship improved so I could protect myself. And of course it took some time getting here, too."

"My father has sung songs of your mother, Donya, who slew a great lizard the size of a house, and her friend Shadow, who stole Adraon's healing secrets," Lainan said.

"Shadow stole—" Jael chuckled. "Aunt Shadow never told me that, but I can well believe it. The giant lizard part's true, or so I'm told."

"Then you've been raised by a mighty warrior." Lainan's eyes narrowed further. "What do you want of my father?"

"Nothing." Jael gazed back directly into his eyes. "I never meant to—embarrass—Farryn. All I want is the rest of my soul so I can live my own life. I certainly wouldn't have come all the way here if there'd been another way. When I found the soul keeper in the dragon's nest, I thought my problem was solved, and we'd have gone straight home if it hadn't been for the Singing Forest and the skinshifters. I didn't know I was doing anything wrong by wearing the amulet." She shivered.

"Tanis spoke last night of your great deeds," Lainan said wryly. "He made you sound a great warrior yourself."

"I'm not such a great warrior," Jael said with a shrug. "Anybody fights hard to stay alive."

"They will never grant what you ask," Lainan said suddenly. "The Enlightened Ones. They have no reason to do it. You're not one of us by blood, not entirely, nor by life among us. The tales of your deeds are only that, only words. You can wait in this house until the winter snows come again, and they'll still not summon you to the temple. You may as well go home to your own kind."

Lainan's words were the last blow to her already fraying temper. Jael jumped to her feet.

"By the gods, it seems like since I was born I've never been quite good enough for anybody," Jael exploded. "And I'm damned sick of it." She pointed to Lainan's sword. "Is there a guard on that thing?"

Lainan rose to his feet also, his eyes narrowing.

"There is, yes, for practice," he said. "Do you challenge me?"

Jael strode to her packs and drew out her own sword, carefully fitting the guard over the sharp blade.

"I don't want to kill you," she said, "and I hope you don't want to kill me, but by the gods, I can't take another moment of being stupid, clumsy Jaellyn who isn't worthy of being someone's sister or even of a soul of her own! So let's settle this right now. If you can defeat me, Tanis and I will start home at first light tomorrow. But if I win, tomorrow at first light you get me into that temple. If those Enlightened Ones aren't going to help me, they can by the gods tell me so in person."

"Gladly," Lainan said, drawing his own sword. To Jael's relief, he fitted it with a metal guard very similar to hers. The sword, too, was much like Jael's, although it seemed newer.

Jael kicked aside the furs scattered over the floor to make

room; they certainly couldn't fight outside in the narrow alleys between the buildings. She half-expected Lainan to demand some overly elaborate challenge ritual, but to her relief he took a ready stance without further ado, only waiting for Jael to raise her own sword before he launched his attack.

Jael had had no sword practice for weeks, and she'd never practiced against the style Lainan was using; his first swift stroke almost went through her guard, and she realized miserably that she'd slowed down in the weeks since she'd practiced against an armed opponent. She missed, too, the swift, sure balance she'd had when she found the soul keeper in the dragon's nest; fortunately, having never had a chance to use her new surefootedness in sword practice, she hadn't come to depend upon it.

Lainan's stroke was almost blinding in its speed, and again Jael barely turned it aside. He'd rapidly forced her into a defensive stand, too busy parrying his strokes to press an attack of her own. Gods, her mother's style was too slow for this kind of swordplay, the elvan style too subtle, and she'd had little success developing her own instinctive style when no one else seemed to use it, unlike Lainan, who'd been training probably for years—

*Stop thinking,* Jael reminded herself sternly, and she drew a deep breath, relaxing her muscles and flowing with the rhythm of Lainan's attack, waiting for an opening to press her own offensive. At last Lainan overextended ever so slightly and Jael was able to pull him off balance, breaking his pattern; by the time he had recovered, Jael had found her own rhythm. She had his measure now, and though he was well trained in a style similar to the one Jael tried to use—and much better at it than Jael, too—he'd never been exposed to the several different styles that Jael had worked with.

Now she exploited that knowledge, using moves and strategies he couldn't possibly know to break his patterns. Now Jael had the advantage; unlike Lainan, she was well accustomed to fighting against a style entirely different from her own, accustomed to altering her own patterns to adapt.

As Lainan tried again and again to create a pattern to beat down Jael's guard, to slip past her defenses, and was repeatedly confounded, he grew angrier and more frustrated. They were both becoming tired now, but Jael, worn down by long travel, unaccustomed to lengthy swordplay, and strained by the effort to incorporate moves never meant for her sword and style, could feel her strength failing quickly. She was utterly relieved when Lainan made the wrong parry, enabling her with an elvan maneuver to twist his sword out of his hand and send it skittering across the stone floor.

Lainan looked so furious that for a moment Jael thought he'd attack her, armed or not, but at last he raised his empty hands, fingers splayed, then lowered them to his side, breathing hard.

"You have bested me," he growled.

Jael was gasping for breath herself, but she picked up his sword and handed it back to him.

"Only just," she panted. "You're faster than me, and stronger, too. If I hadn't known moves you couldn't possibly have learned, you'd have had me in a moment or two. That trick wouldn't work on you a second time, I'll wager."

Lainan's scowl faded slowly. Abruptly he extended one hand; remembering the plains hunters, Jael clasped forearms with him and smiled.

"You fought well and honorably," Lainan said grudgingly. "Will you teach me what you know?"

"If you'll teach me, too," Jael grinned. "I have a lot to learn from you, too. As long as I'm here, that is."

This time Lainan almost smiled.

"A fair bargain," he said. "And tomorrow I'll take you to the temple, as I promised."

"And me," Tanis said. Jael turned to see him standing by the door flap, leaning comfortably against the stone. "I'm going, too."

Jael wiped sweat out of her eyes and laid her sword down.

"How long have you been standing there?"

"Long enough to realize I don't want to practice with either of you," Tanis said good-naturedly, "or no self-respecting dragon would want what's left of me. You've been in such a bad mood the last couple of days, I thought you might want some company."

"I think I've worked off my bad mood," Jael panted, grinning at Lainan. "I hope you have, too."

Lainan gave Jael the briefest of nods, sheathed his sword, and slipped through the doorway without a word. Tanis took off his fur jacket and laid it aside, pouring a cup of cold water for Jael.

"So you're tired of waiting for the Enlightened Ones to make a move?" Tanis asked. "What'll you do if they say no, they won't help you?"

"I'll just have to make sure they don't say no," Jael sighed. "There's nothing else I can do, is there? Look, let's not talk about it or I'll never sleep tonight."

"After that bout, you'll sleep," Tanis said, grinning. He pulled a few furs back over the floor. "Lie down and I'll rub your muscles."

Tanis's touch was gentler than her mother's, firm and slow and soothing, and Jael felt her taut muscles relax. She was near the firepit, and the glow of the heat against her bare skin was delightful. Despite the hard stone floor under the furs, she was starting to drowse when Tanis stopped.

"Just lie still a moment," Tanis murmured, and Jael could hear his footsteps across the floor. When he returned, he sat down on the floor beside her, the bottle of Bluebright in his hand.

"One last drink?" he suggested. "Soon you won't need it."

Jael started to decline—it was late and she was tired—but then she thought, *I'll just lie there and think about tomorrow.* It occurred to her, too, although she said nothing, that the last few times she'd lain with Tanis, the woman he'd been tumbling hadn't really been her, not entirely. Somehow she couldn't quite bring herself to tell him that, and for that reason perhaps she owed him, and herself, this one night.

Jael floated in the warm euphoria of the Bluebright, wonderfully aware and rejoicing in the sweet sensations of stone surrounding her, the tender insistence of Tanis's touch, the softness of the furs against her skin, but most of all being *Jaellyn* who could enjoy these things. When she drowsed in Tanis's arms, she held on to waking as long as she could, knowing that when she woke she'd no longer be all Jaellyn as she was this night, that the morrow might indeed mean the end of all hope that she'd ever be completely whole, permanently *herself*. That thought, the sensation of teetering on the dagger's point of her destiny, made each moment, each touch so much the sweeter.

She never remembered falling asleep that night, but she woke abruptly in the dim light of the dwelling to find Lainan standing over them, apparently unembarrassed.

"If you're still determined to go to the Enlightened Ones," he said, "let us go before my father learns of it. It's against all custom for those who have not proven themselves and gained a soul to enter the temple unless summoned there."

Jael and Tanis quickly donned their warm clothes, and, a little defiantly, Jael belted on her sword and dagger. They followed Lainan in the dim predawn light through the maze of alleys as quietly as they could, emerging at the cliff.

"We'll take a basket down," Lainan told them. "The path would be quieter, but it takes almost an hour to descend that way."

Jael eyed the strange basket contraption dubiously. One woven basket was large enough to hold the three of them comfortably, and the basket itself seemed sturdy enough, but the odd arrangement of levers, chains, and pulleys confused her.

"The basket is counterweighted," Lainan said helpfully. "There are several boulders attached to the chains. By pulling the levers, I choose how many boulders to release in accordance with the amount of weight in the basket."

Jael and Tanis exchanged puzzled looks, but as Lainan seemed to have faith in the device, they could do nothing but step into the basket with him and hope that he knew how to operate it. Lainan pulled three levers, and to Jael's great relief, the basket descended slowly but smoothly. Tanis, Jael noticed, clutched the rim of the basket with white-knuckled hands all the way down, although Jael was fascinated by the view of the valley floor approaching. Was this how a beast-speaker saw the ground, flying in the mind of a hawk? She almost regretted it when the basket thumped gently onto the ground at the base of the cliff.

It was only a short walk from the base of the cliff to the temple opening. Unlike the openings to the houses, this large arch was richly ornamented with the same sort of intricate carvings Jael had seen on the inside of the houses. Also unlike the houses, there was no leather door flap; this archway contained a door of solid stone, with no means of opening it that Jael could ascertain.

Lainan hesitated in front of the stone slab.

"Are you certain?" he said, gazing soberly into Jael's eyes. "The Enlightened Ones will not be pleased by this intrusion."

"I'm certain," Jael said firmly. "But if you're afraid to go in, we'll go by ourselves." She glanced at the door. "If we can figure out how."

"I will take you to them," Lainan said, although there was a tinge of uncertainty in his voice. "I gave you my word."

He turned back to the stone door, and for the first time Jael noticed in the center of it an indentation in the shape of a six-fingered hand. Lainan fitted his own hand into the space, and the door soundlessly pivoted inward. Jael gasped as the edge of the door came into view; it was thicker than the length of her arm. Beyond the door was a stone hallway leading apparently into the mountainside, lit by torches in wall sconces.

Lainan stepped inside, beckoning to them to follow. Jael took Tanis's hand and stepped through the door, too, shivering. The door swung slowly closed behind them.

Almost immediately Jael felt the tingling of magic surrounding her, and she shivered again. This was probably a very, very bad idea—

One of the torches flickered and went out, then another. Lainan looked up at the torches in consternation.

"Maybe we should leave," Tanis suggested, looking at the torches as well.

"No," Jael said, firming her resolve. "They can either help me or put up with the consequences of *not* helping me. Lainan, just show us where to go."

"We'll continue inward," Lainan said, glancing up again as another torch went out. "We'll be met. Undoubtedly the Enlightened Ones already know of our presence."

"A scrying spell?" Jael asked, stifling a grin.

"Many of the Enlightened Ones were born to the Silent Singers Clan," Lainan said. "They likely heard our thoughts as we approached."

Jael winced. She knew that the Stone Brothers were those who shaped stone as she did, she had guessed that all the Wind Dancers could run like the wind, as Donya had said Farryn could, and she knew that the Enlightened Ones were the Kresh's mages, but she hadn't had much opportunity to wonder how the Silent Singers Clan had earned their name. Some beast-speakers, she knew, were sensitive enough that they were bombarded with the thoughts of men and women, too. Jael had always thanked the Mother Forest that *she'd* not been burdened with that particular problem, especially in the city. She'd have to guard her thoughts well while she was here.

Two more torches flickered out. Lainan scowled uncomprehendingly.

"If this keeps up," Tanis said worriedly, "we're going to be in the dark. Can you see in total darkness, Jael?"

"Uh-uh." Jael stepped up next to Lainan as yet another torch went out. "Lainan, maybe we'd better hurry."

Lainan turned to face her.

"Do you know why the—"

"Welcome, young ones." A gray-robed woman stepped out of the shadows, and Jael started violently; the greeting had been in her own language. "You are expected. The inner circle will meet with you. Come with me."

Lainan did not hesitate, but fell into step behind the woman. Jael and Tanis exchanged glances and shrugged, following also. The hall was so silent that the sound of their footsteps, even their breath, seemed thunderingly loud. Jael winced a little to herself each time a torch extinguished as she passed by. She fancied that the gray-robed woman walked a little faster each time one of the lights died.

The hallway went straight into the mountainside for an amazing distance, and Jael continued to wonder at the engravings thick on the walls and ceiling. Surely the deep tunnels and intricate reliefs represented centuries of work. At last the hallway forked in different directions, and Jael could see other figures, almost all women, moving down the side passages, a few of whom gazed at the group curiously as they passed by. Their guide, however, continued down the main passageway, which eventually ended in another stone door. The door opened silently at the woman's touch, the Enlightened One standing aside and motioning to Lainan, Jael, and Tanis to enter.

Jael gasped involuntarily at the size of the dome-shaped room into which they stepped. It was as large as the main dining hall of the palace in Allanmere, and brightly lit by torches, candles, and fat lamps. Stone benches, apparently spun up from the stuff of the floor itself, formed rows facing a large, low platform at the far end of the room. Behind the platform was an archway similar to the door by which they'd entered the mountain, but this one appeared to be one piece of rock solid with the mountain. At one end of the platform was a large stone altar; at the other was a stone table surrounded by chairs fashioned from what appeared to be large bones—dragon, perhaps. Two gray-robed women and one man occupied the chairs now, all gazing impassively at Jael.

"Welcome, Jaellyn, daughter of Farryn, to the Temple of Adraon," one of the women said, inclining her head. "I am Seana, First One of the inner circle of the temple. My companions are Cadeta and Ronan." She fell silent, as if waiting for something.

Jael stepped resolutely forward, Tanis and Lainan following a little behind her.

"You know who I am," Jael said. "This is Tanis, my friend, and Lainan, Farryn's son. And I don't doubt you know why I came here."

"You have come to ask that we grant you that part of your soul that springs from our people," Seana said calmly.

*Don't go to the Kresh and beg for what you need,* Shadow had said. *Walk straight up to them and demand what should be yours.*

Jael squared her shoulders.

"No," she said. "I haven't come to ask that you give me that part of my soul. I've come to claim it. And if you won't help me, I'll come back here day after day and see how many of your spells I can ruin. That'll give you some idea of what it's been like for me for my whole life."

Lainan gasped and even Tanis looked startled, but Jael forced her voice to steadiness as she continued.

"I know I haven't been raised as one of your people," she said. "I know I haven't been trained as your children are. But my mother's the finest warrior in Allanmere—in the world, likely, if you ask me—and her husband, the man who's raised and loved me as if he were my father, is an elf with centuries of wisdom to share with his children. What I've needed to learn, I've learned from them, and I don't believe there's anyone on this mountain who could have taught me better."

The three at the table had listened calmly while Jael spoke.

"You speak to us as one claiming a right," Ronan said impassively. "But by what right do you make a claim of us? You have not earned this right among us."

"You've acknowledged me Farryn's daughter," Jael said hotly. "I'm one of you by blood. Isn't that enough?"

"It is not enough," Seana told her sternly. "For our own children full of our blood it isn't enough. A warrior's soul is earned through proof of honor and courage, not a right of birth."

"I will testify to both," Lainan said unexpectedly, stepping up to Jael's side. "Last night she challenged me to honorable combat, sword to sword, and bested me fairly and most skillfully."

"She's fought dragons and skinshifters with nothing but a sword," Tanis agreed, also stepping to Jael's side. "We have treasure from the dragon's nest and battle scars enough to prove we fought those battles, and we wouldn't be here alive if we hadn't won, would we?"

"Stolen treasure and scars?" Cadeta said scornfully. "These are the proofs of honor and courage you would take before Adraon to ask that He grant you a soul?"

Lainan nudged Jael gently.

"Ask for Adraon's judgment," he whispered in her ear. "All of our people are entitled to that."

"Fine, you think I'm unworthy," Jael growled to Cadeta. "To be truthful, I'm rather used to that. But if your god's the one who has to grant me a soul, then I don't much care what you think. Let your god judge me, if that's what it takes. But don't sit there and talk to me about honor while you, who don't know a grain of sand's worth about me, call me unworthy."

Cadeta looked inclined to retort, but Seana held up her hand.

"You ask for a judgment," she said. "If you ask again, I must grant it. Any of our people may go before Adraon; that is the law. If you are found worthy, Adraon may grant you what you ask. But be warned that if you are found wanting, Adraon's judgments are . . . final."

"Wait a minute," Tanis protested. "Maybe we'd better think about—"

"No," Jael said steadily. "I've had twenty-two years to think about it, and thinking is all I've been *able* to do until now." Then, louder, "I'm asking for that judgment. Just tell me what to do."

"Then we must grant you the judgment you request." Seana stood and beckoned. "Come forward, Jaellyn."

This time Lainan made no effort to step forward with her. When Tanis stepped up, however, Ronan raised a hand.

"You may not approach," he said kindly to Tanis. "These mysteries are for our folk alone."

Tanis took Jael's hands, gazing into her eyes.

"Don't do this," he said. "We don't even know what this involves, and if I can't help you—"

"I know." Jael forced a smile. "But you can't win the game

without risking your coin." She released Tanis's hands and stepped up to the platform. "All right. Let's go."

Seana led Jael to the back of the platform, to the large arch Jael had noticed earlier.

"Beyond lies Adraon's domain," she said. "There you may seek what you require. If Adraon finds you worthy, you'll find it. What trials may be required of you, I don't know." She smiled. "But I wish you success."

Jael hesitated. The stone certainly looked solid to her. She reached out one hand, gasping when her fingers seemed to pass directly through the stone. A furious tingling spread up her arm, and she quickly snatched her hand back.

"It's magic," she said unsteadily. "What if my just touching it—"

"You've requested a judgment," Seana said adamantly. "This is the way."

Jael swallowed. What would happen to her if she fouled a Gate midway through it? Would she be trapped on the other side, or halfway, or—

*Twenty-two years of thinking,* Jael thought. *No more what-ifs.*

Resolutely, Jael stepped forward.

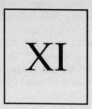

# XI

● For a moment Jael seemed to hover in a place that was no place; then she was standing on solid stone again. Before she could look around her, however, something struck her violently in the back, sending her sprawling forward to the floor.

For a moment, Jael was too stunned to react; as soon as she recovered her senses, she rolled, drawing her dagger as she did so. She scrambled to her knees and whirled—

—to face Tanis, sprawled and shaking his head dizzily.

"By the gods, I could have killed you!" Jael exploded. "What are you doing here?"

"When you disappeared, I ran after you," Tanis said sheepishly. "I almost pushed that woman—Seana—in with me, too, when she tried to stop me. But where is this?"

"I don't know." Jael stood slowly and looked around her.

To all appearances they stood in a small corridor, made of stone but otherwise quite ordinary. Behind them was a blank wall; ahead was an ordinary wooden door, such as Jael saw every day at the palace.

"Hadn't you better go back?" Jael asked worriedly. "I don't know what to expect, and if this god only deals with the Kresh, who knows what might happen to you?"

Tanis shook his head, taking Jael's hand.

"I'm not leaving you," he said quietly. "We've come this far together."

A sudden lump formed in Jael's throat, and she squeezed Tanis's hand.

"All right," she said. "Together, then."

She started forward, but Tanis pulled her to a stop.

"Wait," he said. "Hadn't you better take that with you?" He was pointing to the floor where Jael had fallen.

Jael looked down. At her feet was a wooden box lined with velvet, very much like the one in which she'd placed the piece of dragon's eggshell. The lid was open and the box was empty.

"I certainly didn't have that before," Jael said, shrugging. She picked up the box. When she closed the lid, she saw that the stylized eye depicted on the Kresh soul keepers was carved on the lid. "All right, we'll take it."

They stopped at the door, looking from the latch to each other.

"So, you've been a priest, or at least an acolyte," Jael said hesitantly. "What do you say to a god?"

"You're asking me?" Tanis asked incredulously. "The last time I ever tried to see my god in person, remember what happened? It turned out to be a Greater Darkling in disguise."

Jael sighed and shrugged, then raised her hand and knocked firmly on the door. There was no response. She knocked again, louder, and again waited in vain.

"All right," she said. "We go straight in, then."

The door opened easily. Whatever Jael might have expected—a sort of throne room, perhaps, or a gigantic chamber hung with gold and with rich tapestries—it was not what she saw: a long hallway, no wider than the one in which they stood, lined with shelves from floor to ceiling on both sides. The hallway was dimly lit from some unseen source, and Jael could see no end.

They stepped inside cautiously, Tanis still holding Jael's hand. Looking at the shelves, Jael realized they were far from empty—every shelf was heavily laden with knickknacks, bits of pottery, small carved statues, and other less definable items. There seemed to be no logic to the mess; dirty and draggled bits of cloth and leather mingled with skillful elvan wood carvings; seemingly random twigs and plain pebbles cluttered around an exquisite silver pendant set with red-purple gems.

Seeing the pendant, however, Jael scowled. She picked it up. Why, it looked very much like—

"This looks just like the pendant Urien gave me," Jael said suspiciously. "I've never seen anything like this silverwork before or since." Her eyes scanned the shelves, then widened. "And these carvings, they're just like the ones Mist used to do for— and look at this!" She snatched up a pair of gold earrings set with green stones and waved them in front of Tanis's startled eyes. "Solly's earrings, the ones I gave to Vedara!"

Tanis released her hand and walked slowly down the hallway, perusing the contents of the shelves.

"I think it's all yours," he said. "Here's the silver combs I bought you in Zaravelle. Here's a snare, too, tied the way you make them."

Now that Jael realized what she was looking at, she recognized much of the shelves' contents. Here was the small stone puzzle Aunt Shadow had brought her; here were the beaded leather boots Mist had given her on her sixth birthday.

"Most of this stuff I recognize," Jael said slowly. "But some of it—what, by the gods, is this?" She held up a tiny spoon that seemed to be formed from wood, but covered with leather.

Tanis laughed.

"It's a spoon for feeding babies," he said. "Metal cuts their gums when they try to suck on it. I'll wager it was yours, back when you were too young to remember." He picked up a swatch of cloth, sniffed it, and made a face. "I think this is one of your baby rags, too."

"But why's it all here?" Jael asked slowly. "Is it some kind of test?"

"Well, you've got an empty box, and you've got all this," Tanis said, waving to indicate the full shelves. "You came here looking for your soul, or part of it, anyway, so—"

"So it must be in here somewhere," Jael said, nodding. "Hidden among all this junk."

"Hidden among it, or just among it," Tanis agreed. "Maybe one of these things *is* your soul. Maybe that's the test, to see if you can find it."

That made sense, but Jael scowled as she looked down the long, seemingly endless shelves of mementos.

"But how will I ever find it in all this?" Jael asked disgustedly. "It could take days just to look at everything. Weeks."

"Well, you take that side, and I'll take this one," Tanis said resignedly. "And whenever you find something special, or something you don't recognize, maybe that'll be it."

Jael could propose nothing better. She sifted through the jumble of mementos, hoping against hope that she would feel something special, perhaps the special tingle of magic, to indicate her choice. Some items she recognized immediately, some seemed only vaguely familiar, and some seemed completely unknown to her, but she examined each one. Tanis worked more slowly, having to pause often to ask Jael to identify this item or that one, or to let her touch something he thought seemed unusual.

Did time pass in this strange place? Jael quickly grew discouraged and bored with the seemingly endless task, but she did not grow tired, nor did hunger or thirst trouble her. Had they been in the hallway for hours or days? Looking back, Jael was dismayed to see what a short distance they'd traveled down the hall. The door they'd come through had disappeared not long after they'd passed through it; now there was nothing in its place but blank stone wall, quite solid to Tanis's and Jael's touch.

"Jael, look at this," Tanis called. Jael had to walk a short distance back up the hall to see what he was holding. Her heart leaped as she saw a soul keeper in his hand.

"That's it!" Jael said excitedly, seizing the amulet. "You've found it!"

"Wait," Tanis said, grabbing her hand as she prepared to drop the soul keeper into the box. "Are you sure that's it?"

"Of course it is," Jael said impatiently. "I knew I had to have one of these, and here it is."

"No. I mean—" Tanis hesitated. "I mean, look at all this stuff. Isn't it kind of obvious to make it a soul keeper, exactly what you were looking for?"

Jael clenched her hand around the amulet, but Tanis's words had planted a tiny seed of doubt in her mind.

"What do you mean, obvious?" she demanded. "We've been looking for hours or more. It was hardly hanging there right in front of my face, was it?"

Tanis gently pried her fingers open and examined the medallion.

"I don't know," he said doubtfully. "It seems a little old and battered, doesn't it? Wouldn't yours be new?"

Jael looked more closely at the soul keeper, and her heart

sank. The seemingly invulnerable white metal was smooth and perfect, but the inlaid symbol on the front was stained, a few of the gem chips missing. The links of the chain were stained, too, and crusted in places with what might be dirt or dried blood.

"The dragon's nest," Jael said dully. "It's the soul keeper I found in the dragon's nest." A tear trickled unnoticed down her cheek.

Tanis gently wiped the tear away and pulled Jael into his arms, holding her warmly.

"It's all right," he said. "We'll find your soul if it takes a hundred years. Anyway," he added more jovially, "it's a good thing we haven't needed a privy, because I haven't found one of *those* yet."

Jael chuckled even through her tears.

"You haven't looked far enough, then," she said. "I found my old chamber pot halfway back there. At least it'd been emptied. I guess I should've become a priestess, entered one of those ascetic orders where personal possessions aren't allowed. Then there wouldn't be so much clutter to look through."

"Then the hall would be full of a thousand books and scrolls we'd have to look through instead," Tanis said good-naturedly. "Anyway, Jaellyn, it could be a lot worse. Think what we'd have here if you *had* become a thief. We'd likely have a thousand purses to empty instead."

Jael had to laugh at that, and she wiped her eyes.

"All right, all right," she chuckled. "But shuffling through all this stuff makes me wish I'd lived a simpler life."

"No firstborn daughter of a High Lord and Lady lives a simple life," Tanis agreed. "But it makes me wonder how much farther this can go on. After all, it's not as if you're centuries old like an elf. You're only two decades and a bit. Want to see if there's an end?"

"All right," Jael said eagerly. Then she hesitated. "But what if the hallway disappears behind us like the door did? We might pass up my soul and never be able to get back to find it."

"Well, we'll walk down the hall slowly and watch the shelves," Tanis said after a moment's thought. "If the beginning of the shelves starts to disappear, we'll know we mustn't go any farther. You examined all the stuff at the beginning pretty closely, anyway."

"That sounds good," Jael agreed after considering the suggestion. "Let's go, then."

They walked slowly down the hall, Tanis facing ahead and Jael watching the beginning of the hall. To her relief, the hall remained the same behind them.

"How much farther can this go?" Jael wondered after they'd walked for several moments. "I mean, as you said, I *am* only a little over two decades."

"Not much farther," Tanis said. "I can see something across the hall just a little ahead. It's awfully dark there, though."

Jael turned to look. Her keener vision saw movement ahead of her, and instantly her sword was in her hand; a moment later, however, she sheathed her sword and sighed irritably. She'd seen nothing more harmful than her own reflection in a mirror, and she told Tanis as much.

"There's more than one," Tanis said wonderingly. "Look, there's one across the end, but I can see light glancing off mirrors on the sides, too."

As they approached, Jael could see that there were, in fact, four mirrors, two on one wall, one across the hall, and one on the opposite wall.

"But why mirrors?" Jael asked slowly, stopping just a little before she reached them. Her reflection gazed back just as puzzledly.

"I don't—" Tanis fell silent, reaching out to touch the glass of the mirror at the end of the hall. "Jael, look at your reflection. Don't you think there's anything strange about it?"

Jael stared at the mirror. She could see nothing strange there. She waved one hand; the reflection waved back.

"No, it looks—" Jael stopped, gasping. Tanis stood between her and the mirror, a little to one side, but there was no sign of his reflection in the glass. Tanis stepped completely in front of her, and Jael shivered; leaning to glance around his shoulder, she could see her own unobstructed reflection standing alone in the mirror, eyes wide and wondering.

"Come here," Tanis said, beckoning. "Let's see what happens with the other mirrors. I can't see my reflection in any of them, either."

A little fearfully, Jael stepped forward to join Tanis in front of the mirrors. This time he echoed her gasp, and she reached for his hand, clutching it hard in her excitement and fear.

Jael's reflection was there in the mirror facing her, but it was no reflection of Jael as she had ever seen herself. Her reflection stood tall, taller than Tanis, her limbs strongly muscled instead of wiry and too thin and knobby at the joints. Straight black hair hung over her shoulders instead of her bronze curls, and her skin was the plain brown of her mother's skin after a warm summer with plenty of sword practice in the yard. Gone were the up-swept pointed tips of Jael's ears, and her eyes, no longer exotically tilted, were a simple warm brown. The bones of her face were stronger, like Donya's.

Silently, Jael raised one hand. The reflection echoed her move-ment. Jael numbly reached for the mirror, then snatched her hand back instinctively. Frankly, the thing frightened her.

"If you were all human, you'd look like that, I suppose," Tanis said quietly. "But look at this one."

Jael glanced into the adjacent mirror. In this reflection Jael was not taller; indeed, she was slightly shorter, more delicately built, her skin slightly paler. Her pointed ears remained, as did her delicate features, but her eyes were the brilliant green of new leaves, and her hair had faded to a pale cascade almost as light as Argent's silver-white locks.

"Look behind you," Tanis whispered, and slowly, fearfully, Jael turned, staring at the image that faced her.

For a moment Jael thought this mirror was simply like the one at the end of the hall, a plain mirror reflecting her as she was, for she seemed outwardly unchanged. When she raised her hand, however, she gasped as the reflection's hand waved six fingers, not five, back at her. As she studied the reflection further, she re-alized that the points of her ears had once again vanished, and there was a subtle change in the cast of her face that made her seem alien. Quickly she turned away, almost dizzied by the rev-elation. It was comforting to look into the end mirror and see herself once again as she was.

"What are these?" Jael wondered uncomfortably.

"Faces of yourself," Tanis guessed. "You're elf, human, and Kresh by blood. Maybe they represent the parts of your soul."

"Then this must be it," Jael said, shivering as she turned again to her Kresh reflection. "The missing part of my soul must be this mirror. I already have the elvan and human parts. But how can I fit all that in this box?"

"Jaellyn—" Tanis's voice was uncertain. "*Look* at it. Are you certain? It just doesn't seem like—like you, somehow."

Jael stepped close to the mirror, staring at her reflection. The strange set of her face seemed wrong, making Jael a stranger to herself. The hands, too, seemed too wide, awkwardly bristling with their extra fingers.

*Of course it does,* Jael thought impatiently. *I've grown up looking at elves and humans. I've never seen anyone who looked like that until I met Farryn and the others here. Of course that looks strange to me. And isn't that part of my soul a stranger to me, too?*

But was it? When she'd taken the dreaming potion at her elvan passage ceremony, she hadn't found a stranger within herself. When she'd drunk the Bluebright, it had made her whole, and she'd been relieved that it *hadn't* changed her, that she'd felt more herself than ever. How could her own soul seem strange and unfamiliar to her?

"No," she said slowly. "You're right. This isn't my soul. These are—choices, I think. Aunt Shadow and I used to joke about my sore feet, trying to balance on the dagger's edge between elf and human. It always seemed like it would be more comfortable to be just one thing or the other, to really know who and what I am. That's what these mirrors are, the three sides of myself, if I could choose to be just one thing."

"But why do you want that?" Tanis asked her gently, laying his hands on her shoulders. "You have the beast-speaking gift of your elvan blood, the stone molding of the Kresh, and from your human blood—" He hesitated, raising his eyebrows.

"The mage-gift," Jael said slowly. "Grandma Celene once told me I had magery in me. That's why I bend magic the way I do. And that's been a gift, too, sometimes, hasn't it?"

"Don't ask me," Tanis said softly. "I've always thought you were just about right, just as you are."

Jael turned to face him.

"Really?" she asked wryly. "Even when I trip over my own feet and shatter light globes and don't want to tumble with you?"

"Even when you melt holes in cave walls and sense dragons coming and dissolve hinder-spells," Tanis said firmly. "Besides, those globes you shattered in Zaravelle gave me the best haul of purses I've ever taken." He turned Jael gently around so she faced the mirror at the end of the hall. "Why take only one part when you've got them all?"

"You're right," Jael said, her heart suddenly light. "You're right." She raised her voice, almost shouting. "By the gods, I want it all, and I won't be tricked into settling for less!" She smiled at her reflection in the mirror, reaching out to touch the glass.

For the briefest of moments, Jael thought she touched not cold glass, but warm flesh; then the mirror shattered into a thousand pieces, brilliant shards cascading to the floor. Where the mirror had been was a plain wooden door, very slightly ajar.

Jael grinned, bending to pick up a bright shard of the mirror. She laid it gently inside the box in her hand, closing the lid firmly, and turned to Tanis.

"Ready to go home?" she asked.

Tanis took her hand, grinning back.

"Very, very ready," he said. He glanced back at the long hallway behind them. "But are you sure you don't want a souvenir?"

Jael groaned in mock agony, and, clutching Tanis's hand and the box tightly, stepped through the door.

Jael blinked, momentarily dazzled by the bright light around her. She stood in the large room in the temple, still clutching Tanis's hand so tightly that her fingers ached. Seana, Cadeta, and Ronan were exactly where she'd left them, but now Lainan stood at the edge of the platform, and Farryn was there, too, his face drawn in a scowl.

"When I found you gone from your house, I knew where you'd be," he said, shaking his head. "I ran all the way down the path. Jaellyn, how could you take such a risk?"

Jael glanced down. The box had vanished from her hand, but in its place was a soul keeper, sparkling and new. Jael turned and smiled at Tanis, hanging the chain over her head. Tanis smiled back, winking at her.

"How could we not?" Tanis answered for her, releasing Jael's hand and laying his arm around her shoulders.

Seana stepped in front of them, facing Tanis.

"What you did is forbidden," she said severely. "If Adraon had punished you for your impertinence, you'd have earned it."

Tanis grinned and half-bowed.

"Lady, any man who's spent as many hours as I have sorting

pebbles and smelling old baby rags has been punished enough," he chuckled. "I think Jaellyn and I both got exactly what we deserved. And if your god's angry with me, all the more reason to start home." He raised an eyebrow at Jael.

Seana frowned.

"You should stay here among us now," she said to Jael. "You've missed many years of learning already."

Jael exchanged another look with Tanis, then shook her head.

"I'll stay for a while," she said. "I'd like to get to know my kin here, and Lainan and I owe each other a few sword lessons. I'd especially like to learn that trick with the rocks in the firepits. But then I think it's time to go home. I've got another set of lessons ahead of me, from Grandma Celene, maybe. And I've got a book to deliver, too." She grimaced. "And likely a good long lecture from my mother about sneaking away in the middle of the night."

"I remember the lands to the east, when we traveled west from the great mountains," Ronan said. "We could fashion a Gate to take you near to your own land so that you need not pass the Singing Forest and the other dangers again."

Dragons, mages, skinshifters, rivers, highwaymen—

Jael glanced down at the dragon bracelet encircling her arm. She looked soberly at Tanis and saw him touch his side where the scars from the shifter attack were. Tanis met her eyes, and his own eyes twinkled.

"It's a kindly offer," Tanis said at last. "But, do you know, I believe when the time comes we'll take the long way home."

They walked from the temple, following Lainan and Farryn, and Tanis sighed happily.

"I suppose this means," he said, "that I won't have a single tunic left whole by the time we reach home."

Jael blushed, grinning.

"Then take if off faster," she said, "or learn to sew."

The huge door opened soundlessly at Farryn's touch, and this time Jael echoed her father's sigh. It had been sweet to feel herself surrounded by stone, safe and secure, but it was good to breathe the fresh air and see the sun, and to smell the green growing things in the valley. She'd missed that smell in the mountains. No doubt of it; Farryn would just have to find them a hut in the valley as long as they were here.

"So that's it, then?" Tanis asked her, smiling. "One whole soul of your very own?"

Jael bent and picked up a pebble. In her cupped hands it melted into a perfect sphere, then a cube. She handed it to Farryn.

"One whole soul," she said. "Of my very own."

"No more sore feet, then," Tanis chuckled, taking her hand again.

Jael shrugged.

"Who knows?" she said. "I'm still me, elf and human and Kresh. Maybe I'll teeter on the dagger's edge all my life. Gods, maybe we all do."

She smiled.

"But do you know, Tanis, I think my balance is up to it."